Bargaining

Bargaining

SASHA LACE

Montlake

Text copyright © 2026 by Sasha Lace
All rights reserved.

Published by Montlake, Seattle

www.apub.com

Amazon, the Amazon logo, and Montlake are trademarks of Amazon.com, Inc., or its affiliates.

EU Product Safety Contact:
Amazon Media EU S.à r.l.
38, avenue John F. Kennedy, L-1855 Luxembourg
amazonpublishing-gpsr@amazon.com

ISBN: 9781662532665
eISBN: 9781662532672

Cover design by The Brewster Project
Cover photography by Michelle Lancaster PTY LTD
Cover image: © Alfin Khoyr / Shutterstock

Printed in the United States of America

CONTENT WARNING

The loss of a parent who has been living with dementia (off page)

References to childhood verbal and physical abuse (off page; no graphic descriptions)

Explicit sex

Profanity

Chapter 1

CHARLOTTE

TWELVE YEARS PREVIOUS

Cole perched on the edge of my bed, straight-backed, with an uneasy grimace. "What do you need me to do?"

"I need you to look less weird." Sitting cross-legged, I propped the pillows behind me at the other end of the bed and adjusted the sketch pad on my lap.

"You told me to keep still," he hissed through stiff lips.

"But not like I'm holding you at gunpoint. Relax your shoulders."

He rolled his head on his neck. His biceps flexed under his Radiohead T-shirt as he stretched his arms over his head. "You don't want me for this. Anyone else would be better."

"Who? Dad wouldn't be able to pose for a portrait without giving me an art history lecture, and Tiff can't keep her mouth shut for more than five minutes. You're exactly what I need, and you have a very interesting face."

I held the pencil vertically in front of me. Squeezing one eye shut, I slid my thumb up and down, gauging the distances between his features. Not that I needed to. I already knew every detail: the intelligence shining in his light eyes, the sensual curve of his generous lips, the way his dark hair curled so deliciously at his nape.

He lifted an eyebrow. "*Interesting?* Is that a good thing?"

"Of course."

Freckles dusted the bridge of his nose—remnants of his summer spent island-hopping around Greece on the family yacht. A faint purple bruise marred his right cheek.

"Is something wrong?"

I coughed to cover my embarrassment at gawking at him. "I've just got to get this right. If I mess up the coursework, I'll fail art, and then I'll never get into art college, and then I'll never leave Ecclesdale, and I'll never do anything with my life or go anywhere—"

"There is no timeline where you fail anything. Do you want me to move?" He tipped his chin and flashed me a glance. "Shall I turn my face this way?"

"No. Your face is perfect."

His eyebrow lifted a fraction. "Interesting *and* perfect. This is the nicest you've ever been to me."

Warmth crept up my neck. "I meant to say, it's perfectly positioned. You just need to look less stiff and formal. More like a normal eighteen-year-old." I dropped my gaze to the sketch pad, daring to commit the first strokes. "When are you going to tell me how you got that bruise on your cheek?"

He smoothed a hand over my duvet. "When do you want me to take my clothes off?"

My heart stuttered. "I'm sorry?"

"I assumed when you asked me to model for you, it would be nude," he said, deadpan.

"Hilarious." I pulled a face but my mouth felt suddenly dry. "You can't distract me with talk of stripping. Dad can't help you if you won't give him a name."

His expression held perfectly level. "There is no name. I walked into a door. Now you can drop it."

Bullshit. It had to be another student at Dad's fancy boarding school. Cole didn't talk about it much, but I knew he hated the dorms. Otherwise, why would he spend so much time at his history teacher's house? No sane person would volunteer for more Latin than was necessary, unless they were trying to get away from something.

"You need to report them. Dad's school takes bullying seriously."

His tone filled with bland innocence. "You want me to report the door I walked into?"

"Yes. How else is it going to learn not to punch you in the face?"

He held the challenge in my eyes for a moment before he turned his face away. "Your dad's got a bee in his bonnet again tonight about the Dark Ages being unfairly represented. I don't mind. If I don't do this extra study, I'll fail history, and then I'll never get into Oxford, and I'll never do anything with my life." He gave me a wry smile as he repeated my worry spiral back to me.

I rolled my eyes. "Your family is obscenely rich. You can afford to fail everything, and it doesn't matter."

He wrinkled his nose. "It matters to me. I want to make my own way in the world."

Fine. I'd try again later to get it out of him. Cole was stubborn as hell. If he didn't want to talk about a bruise or his family or whatever was going on in his life, he wouldn't.

He craned his neck, trying to look at the drawing. "Can you make my nose look normal?"

I shielded my sketch pad from his view. "There's nothing wrong with your nose. Once I've marked out the sides of your face, I'll leave plenty of room for it."

He snorted and settled back into stillness. "Thanks."

"I didn't mean it like that. All portraits need plenty of 'nose room'."

"It's too late now. You've flat out told me you think I have a huge fucking nose."

Laughing, I threw the nearest teddy at him. "Your words, not mine. I happen to like your very average nose."

He caught the stuffed hedgehog smoothly and peered at it. It was the one he'd won on the tombola at the village fete a couple of years back. If it was anyone else, I would have felt embarrassed about still having soft toys all over the place. Cole was the only boy I ever had in my bedroom, so at least I didn't have to go crazy hiding all my books with half-naked men on the covers or stashing away my pencil collection. He didn't even seem to mind me burning my incense, which always had Tiff coughing and whining.

"Your nose can't be too much of an issue for you, anyway. Tiff said she saw you at a party last weekend, and every girl was falling over themselves to talk to you. It must be flattering. Is there anyone you have your eye on?"

Music from the TV downstairs rumbled softly into the silence.

"Not really." He kept his face still, but his gaze slid to mine. "What about you? Do you have your eye on anyone?"

"Me? No. You should see how immature and annoying the boys are at my school. It's nothing like Ashcombe."

"I thought the Ashcombe boys were a bunch of *private school poshos*?" His voice took on a sarcastic edge.

Guilt prickled my skin. Cole had overheard Tiff and me talking about the boys at the school where Dad taught, and now he'd never let me live it down. "I said I was sorry about that."

"I know." He shot me a sardonic smile. "I just enjoy watching you squirm."

"Dating is drama. I'm focused on getting out of here. I don't want to be tied down. All I want is to travel the world and paint. When I'm an old spinster, like thirty or something, I'll have lots of dogs to keep me company, and hope they don't gang up as a pack and eat me."

I looked up to see him watching me with a frown. "You don't think you'll do the 'marriage and kids' thing one day?"

I shrugged. "I can't see it."

His frown deepened. "Why not? You're too young to be this cynical."

Not cynical, but realistic. Hard to see anyone signing up to spend the rest of their life with me when I couldn't even find someone to kiss me on the mouth. Better not to think about it. Unlike me, Cole had kissed plenty of people. He'd probably been hooking up with girls all over Europe this summer. It shouldn't have mattered. He could kiss whoever he wanted.

"It's Friday night, and everyone is probably out, and I'm here doing this. I don't know if I'll ever find anyone willing to marry me," I said.

"It's your choice to stay in. You could be out having fun."

It was always the same old faces. Everyone knew everyone in Ecclesdale. Everyone was up in everyone's business. It was suffocating. Thank God I'd be out of this village soon.

"This is my kind of fun, and you're a fine one to talk. Studying history with my dad on a Friday night? You could be out having fun, too."

He looked me squarely in the eye. "This is my kind of fun."

Silence thickened between us. I added the contours of his sharp cheekbones and jawline to the sketch. His eyes traveled over the vision board I'd taped above my dressing table. Tiff and I had made them together. Mine was full of exotic places I'd cut from travel magazines, galleries I wanted to visit, and brightly colored Post-its with inspirational quotes that felt cringe now that Cole was studying the board so intensely.

A bride and groom sat haphazardly at the center of the collage. The bride wore a huge white dress covered in lace and crystals, fit for a royal wedding. My own bloody vision board had sold me out. Now I couldn't deny that the squishy romantic in me wanted to be swept off my feet one day.

"I tell you what, if you get to thirty and you're not married, then I'll marry you," Cole said quietly.

My shoulders tensed. "I don't need your pity proposal. That vision board was Tiff's idea. I did it to humor her."

"It's not pity. You'll be doing me a favor. I don't want to get eaten by a pack of dogs, either. Poor bastards might choke on my huge fucking nose."

"There is nothing wrong with your nose. Don't get a complex. I highly doubt you'll be short of options."

He moved across the bed and sat next to me. "I highly doubt you'll be short of options, either, but we should make a pact just in case. Don't leave me on the shelf. You're not that cruel. If neither of us is married by the time we're thirty, we marry each other. Deal?"

Chuckling, I shooed him away. "You'll survive on the shelf. Go back to your spot. I'm not done."

He offered me his hand. "We need to shake on it. I'm trying to ease your worry. You can travel the world and paint, and I'll be at home with all the dogs, making sure they don't turn against you and eat us."

"Whatever. This is a lackluster proposal from you, Cole. No ring. You think I'm wearing that dress like a walking marshmallow for someone who can't be bothered to get on one knee?"

He slipped off the bed and kneeled in front of me. His eyes shone with an unusual earnestness. "I mean it. I'll be your backup. That way, you never need to settle for less than you deserve. You've got a husband in the bag. You just travel and enjoy your life, knowing you'll never end up alone if you don't want to be."

Butterflies fluttered in my stomach. Tough to decide whether to whack him with my pillow and start the pillow fight to end all pillow fights or drag him to me and kiss him until I couldn't breathe. This whole thing with Cole had become so confusing. Once, we'd been kids, riding bikes together and playing video games, and now my body responded to him in all these intense and unfamiliar ways I couldn't control.

Cole kneeling so close was making my palms clammy. It was such a stupid conversation. Cole would leave Yorkshire as soon as he graduated and meet some upper-crust aristocrat at Oxford. Someone unfathomably posh and wealthy like him, who he could take home to his family without embarrassment. People like me and Cole didn't end up together.

I shook his hand. How else would we ever get this portrait finished? "OK. Fine. We'll both have each other in the bag."

His skin was warm and smooth against mine. My body tingled with a curious mixture of nerves and excitement. His delicious Gucci Guilty cologne invaded my nose—spice and cedarwood. Heat spread through me. My eyes had become so accustomed to free rein, I had to force my gaze away.

Eventually I flipped my sketch pad closed on the bed next to me. "I'd better let you get back to Dad before he moans at me again for hogging his one-man dead poets' society."

"Are you going to let me see the masterpiece?"

Whenever I showed people my art, it was like letting them see under my skin. "Do I have to? Honestly, I was hoping I could just make art and never have to show anyone."

"You have too much talent to keep it to yourself. Come on. You can be brave. It's only me."

I'd have to get used to it if I was going to pursue this seriously. At least Cole was a safe person. He wouldn't judge me. I found the page in the sketch pad and turned it in my lap to present to him. "Don't laugh and please be kind. Constructive criticism only."

He took the pad and examined it with an inscrutable expression.

My stomach dropped. "You don't like it?"

He raked a hand through his dark hair. "No. It's . . . You made me look . . . I don't know . . . nice."

Nice? Oh God. That is bad. Art was supposed to be beautiful or shocking or thought-provoking. It was supposed to make you feel something. Nice was a million times worse than *I hate it.* I took a sharp breath. "What's wrong with it?"

He rubbed a hand over his neck and dropped next to me on the bed, so close his thigh brushed mine. He was difficult to read at the best of times, but the look in his eyes and his closeness made my heart thunder.

He spoke as though he was choosing his words carefully. "Whenever we hang out, I feel like . . . I'm this version of myself that is the best me. The way I am with you, the way you see me, is the way I want to be." He frowned and scrubbed a hand over his face. "I don't know if I'm explaining this right, but that's what I see when I look at this. I wish I could be the person in this drawing all the time."

I opened my mouth and closed it, lost for words. Cole rarely opened up or shared anything about his feelings. He moved closer, his face inches from mine.

His throat bobbed as he swallowed. "I don't have any friends up here apart from you and your family."

"I don't have many friends either," I said too quickly.

His gaze kept drifting from my eyes to my lips. Gently, he brushed my hair back from my face. My whole body buzzed with anticipation. His knee bumped mine. I held perfectly still, despite my sudden breathlessness. The heat of his body and his scent made my mind spin. He leaned in, his breath warm against my cheek.

His voice dropped to a whisper. "Charlotte. I . . ."

I'd known this boy forever, but he was looking at me in a way I'd never seen before. My pulse pounded in my ears, and I was alive to the moment in a completely new way, raw and sparking, like an exposed wire. My heart hammered so hard, he could probably hear it. A knock sounded on the bedroom door. Cole leaped off the bed as if his backside was on fire and stood. Dad burst into the room, looking crumpled in the way he did when he'd been poring over his journals for too long.

"I found it." Dad flapped a book in his hand. "The *Anglo-Saxon Chronicles*. You can borrow it, but I absolutely need it back. This has my margin notes."

Cole's voice was calm and clipped. "Thank you. I can't wait to get stuck in." Cole put his arm around my dad's shoulder and guided him to the door. "I want to talk more about the château restoration project in Burgundy you were telling me about. I've been wondering about what stone they used. It wasn't a royal castle, so they couldn't have afforded ashlar blocks in the thirteenth century?"

Dad's eyes lit up. "That's very astute, Cole. No, the team were originally giving the stones too good a finish—"

"Why don't you tell me about it downstairs? I want to take notes." Cole threw me a casual look. "OK to pick it up another time?"

My heart still pounded in my throat. For one breathless moment, I thought he was going to close the gap between us. Was he? Had I imagined it? Was that it? My one and only chance blown by my father's impeccably bad timing.

I forced a breezy smile despite my thundering heart. "Yes, get out of here. No history talk. You both know I'm allergic to the Middle Ages."

Chapter 2

COLE

PRESENT DAY, COLE'S THIRTIETH BIRTHDAY

A smartly dressed woman was waiting for me in reception. "Welcome back, Mr. Thorner. Your brother has requested your company in the conference room."

"Which brother?"

The woman jogged to keep up with me, her clicking heels echoing around the gleaming foyer. "Lucas."

Bloody Lucas. It was always the same thing, and I had no time for morose shit about how I was a terrible uncle who didn't visit enough.

"I'm busy."

"Mr. Thorner . . . the other Mr. Thorner . . . told me you'd say that. He told me not to accept no for an answer."

I cut a sharp glance at the woman. Honey-blonde waves framed a pleasant face. A smart suit wrapped around her slim frame. Lucas had to be fucking her if he'd convinced her to bug me like this before I'd even got back to my office. How did he find the time? I hadn't taken a woman out for ages.

"You work here?"

She flashed an aggressively cheerful smile. "I'm Olive. One of your PA's assistants. We spoke on the phone an hour ago."

I'd never seen this woman before in my life. "Are you sure?"

"Yes. I'm sure, Mr. Thorner. You asked me to set up a meeting with Gabe Rivers."

"And have you done it yet?"

She dropped her gaze. "No. It's . . . He declined. He said no to a meeting."

"What reason?"

She cleared her throat. "His exact words were, 'I have no interest in ever doing business with Cole Thorner.'"

My jaw ticked. *What the fuck?* I'd had a handful of interactions with Gabe Rivers at corporate functions, and they'd always been unremarkable. I stormed up the stairs.

"Mr. Thorner, wait. Please. Lucas said I needed to bring you to the conference room the minute you got back to the office."

I turned on the stairs and gave her an unflinching glare. The kind my father was famous for. He always teamed it with a tilt of the head and a downward tip of the chin. Despicable as he was, I'd always admired his ability to say "Go fuck yourself" with no actual words. It was an art form I'd been perfecting over the years.

The woman shrank under my gaze. Pink spots dotted her cheeks. She looked like she was about to burst into tears. The one thing she should have been doing was leaving me alone. Instead, she took a couple of steps up toward me.

"Please, Mr. Thorner. It's important."

I let out a sigh. Obviously, my *go fuck yourself* glare still needed work. I glanced at my watch. Just after 6 p.m. It would have been nice to get out of here before midnight, but if I had to do another night in this office, then so be it. I needed to find out what the fuck kind of problem Gabe Rivers had with me.

I headed back down the stairs. The woman who claimed to work here slumped with visible relief. I marched past her through gleaming open-plan offices. She paused outside the dark conference room. No Lucas. No lights on.

She shot me an anxious glance. "I'm sorry. Please don't blame me for this. I lost the coin toss."

Blame her for what? A chill went up my spine. *Oh no. No fucking way. They better not be pulling some shi—*

The fishbowl space flooded with fluorescent light.

"Surprise!" A melodic chorus of shouts rang out in unison.

People in stupid little hats stuffed every inch of the room. Party poppers exploded. A sudden blast of Stevie Wonder erupted from somewhere. My teeth gritted. Lucas held his arms open.

"Happy birthday, you old bastard." His lips curved in a begrudging smile. "Thirty is a big one. You can ignore all the others, but you have to mark thirty."

My heart pounded. A surprise party. My life was about minimizing surprises. It was about scrupulous control and discipline. That was the only way we'd achieved everything we had. A room full of expectant eyes trained on me.

I took a deep breath and blew it out slowly. I'd done a stress management course once. An hour out of my calendar to breathe. Breathing was free. I couldn't keep a roof on this building for free or pay wages for free. There were cheeses, glistening olives stuffed with little chilies, and fancy charcuterie. Fruit was piled high on silver platters. Champagne tumbled in a mini fountain. I wanted to get that tray of olives and ram the entire lot down Lucas's throat. What was he thinking?

"Turn it off," I muttered.

Lucas leaned in closer. "What?"

"Turn this racket off," I shouted over the music.

Stevie Wonder halted abruptly, and a brittle quiet swept in. Smiles dimmed to anxious whispers. You could govern either by fear or love. I hadn't dragged myself onto the *Sunday Times* Rich List by a desire to be loved.

My voice sounded low and dangerous. "Is this what I pay you for?"

Lucas's hands landed on my shoulders and gave me a gentle shake. "It's your birthday. Have a drink before you disappear again."

I shrugged him off. This wasn't good enough. Nobody here was trying. Only me. I never fucking stopped. *Fuck turning thirty. Fuck Gabe Rivers not answering my calls. Fuck stuffed olives.*

"Enjoy your champagne." I addressed the crowd of bewildered faces. "You're all fired."

Chapter 3

Cole

"You can't fire your entire company." Lucas fell into step alongside me.

"Not the entire company. Just everyone at that party."

"The people who stayed late for *your* party, you mean? To celebrate *your* birthday?"

"No one gives a fuck about my birthday. Everyone is there for the free booze."

Lucas paused at the elevator. I strode past him to the stairs.

"Can't we take the elevator like normal people?"

I took the stairs two at a time. "We live in an obesogenic environment. An elevator is a shortcut to cardiovascular disease. What were you thinking? A surprise party is the most misjudged thing that's happened around here since you grew that beard."

Lucas jogged to catch up with me. His hand flew defensively to his chin. "There's nothing wrong with a beard."

"In general, no, but teamed with that hair, you look like you're about to sell me an overpriced wood-fired pizza or tell me you do burgers differently."

Lucas chased me up the stairs, half a step behind. "You're salty because Gabe Rivers doesn't want to talk to you."

He knew about that? My shoulders stiffened. I paused in the stairwell. "Are you spying on me? You're worse than Dad. I don't even know Gabe Rivers. There's no reason for him not to take my calls."

"Why are you so desperate to talk to him?"

"Mind your own business."

Lucas rested a hand on the banister, catching his breath. "You're trying to get him to sell you that hotel in Rome again? The one Mum liked?"

Fuck you. I kept my voice level despite my irritation with his prying. "Which part of 'mind your own business' don't you understand?"

"You won't get anywhere with Gabe Rivers. I heard he thinks you're an arsehole. Don't worry about it. Everyone does. It's even on your Wikipedia page. *One of England's richest men and most notorious arseholes.*"

I stormed up the stairs, my brogues echoing through the silence. "Why do you know what's on my Wikipedia? There isn't a single citation on that page."

"Consider this conversation your verification. People with integrity don't want to do deals with verified arseholes."

I turned, just enough to meet his eyes. "Gabe Rivers doesn't have integrity. He's been all over the tabloids for years."

"Everyone says he's changed. He's settled down. Got himself a wife and kids." Lucas pushed his glasses up his nose. "Listen, Gabe Rivers is the least of your problems. The shareholders aren't happy. There has been talk of *leadership more aligned with the brand.*"

"What's that supposed to mean?"

"Your flagship is a chain of family-friendly resorts where kids go to splash in waterparks and make their parents question their life choices. The brand is treehouses and toasted marshmallows. Wholesome. Authentic. Not *arsehole-ish*."

"*Arsehole-ish* isn't a word."

"I got it from your Wikipedia page."

We hit the landing. London stretched out in the floor-to-ceiling glass. "The shareholders can go fuck themselves."

Lucas pressed his lips together. "Right, or they could club together and fuck *you*. You need to tread carefully."

"Isn't this what I pay you for? You're the Head of Social Impact. You're supposed to make us look good. Can't you plant more trees or write another sustainability manifesto?"

He chuffed out a humorless laugh. "You can't just outsource your conscience. The shareholders are still looking at their CEO."

"What would you have me do? Magic up a wife and kids from somewhere? Toast some fucking marshmallows?"

His brow flickered with amusement. "It wouldn't hurt. You just need to tone it down. Be more reflective of the brand. Remember the names of your staff. Ask if people have plans for the weekends. Bring in donuts. You're not . . . nice."

This was my company. I didn't need to explain myself. And not nice? I could take that, but not authentic? That was unfair. I authentically didn't give a fuck about people's names or what they did at the weekend. I was the most authentic person in this building. Lucas should have backed off, but he followed and stood next to me at my office window.

I cut him my *go fuck yourself* glare. "Why are you still here? I'm staring broodingly out of the window. It loses impact with company."

"The kids keep asking after you. They want to see their favorite uncle."

Here we go. How I'd made it into the favorite-uncle spot was anybody's guess. Although with Theo as the other option, the bar wasn't high. It was probably because I'd brought them back that VR game console from Tokyo. My nephews were more mercenary than any cutthroat business mogul I'd ever had to deal with.

"You know how it's been," I said.

"Yeah, I know how it's been." Lucas rocked back on his trainers. Trainers in the office, and I was the one the shareholders were moaning about. "Thirty. How does it feel to be old?"

"You tell me. I take it that midlife-crisis beard is what I have to look forward to?"

Amusement shadowed his expression. "Time is flying."

"Mr. Thorner?"

I turned to see the back-stabbing assistant who'd dragged me off to the party. "Didn't I just sack you?"

Lucas rolled his eyes and gave me a pointed look. "Ignore him. You're not sacked. Sacking your entire office is too much paperwork."

The assistant darted a nervous glance at me. "You've had a call. It was . . ."

Jesus. Did people think I had nothing to do all day? "Spit it out."

"It was from your old school. One of the teachers has passed away. Mr. Ackroyd. They're informing the alumni about the funeral." She swallowed. "I'm sorry."

The high-pitched whine of a vacuum invaded the silence, jarring me. My mind filled with memories. *Rolling green fields. Endless summer days. Charlotte Ackroyd's scrunch-nosed smile. Her laugh.*

I stared past my reflection to the sea of soaring, faceless towers, and I had the strangest sensation that I was falling from the tallest skyscraper. Flailing through the night outside, bitter air rushing to meet me, sucking the breath from my lungs. Lucas and the assistant who should have been packing up her desk for dragging me to that surprise party bullshit were both staring at me. My chest hurt, like I'd taken a punch in the ribs.

"I should pay my respects."

Confusion crossed Lucas's face. The words hung in the air, strange and unbidden. They puzzled me as much as my brother. I had no time for trips up north. No time for funerals of teachers I hadn't seen in over a decade. No desire to revisit enough dirty, rotten childhood trauma to fill a truck.

Lucas raised a sardonic eyebrow. "Well, look at you. You should tell the shareholders you're taking time out to go to the funeral of a teacher you haven't seen since you were a teenager."

Not a bad idea. "Do you think it would work?" I pulled out my phone. "I'll ring Beatrice and mention it."

Lucas snorted and rubbed his beard. Charlotte invaded my thoughts again. *The scent of her soft hair. The taste of her lips.* She'd be devastated. She'd adored her father. Irritation prickled my shoulder blades. Why was everyone just standing around in my office? The room was closing in. Alone. I just needed a minute. Anything that wasn't this terrible news.

"Go back to work. Both of you." I sat at my desk. "Or fuck off. Either is fine."

Lucas's muttered words hung in the air after he left. "Verified arsehole."

Chapter 4

CHARLOTTE

Sympathetic eyes followed me as I moved through a host of familiar faces at the wake. Every inch of this pub was full of Dad. It was as bad as the house. I swiped clammy hands down the black shift dress my sister had lent me. It fell a little short above the knee and pulled too tight up top for a funeral. I didn't own any decent dresses. No point. Caring for Dad hadn't left room for wearing frocks.

Tiff held out her arms when she saw me approach. "You doing OK?"

I nodded and dived straight into it before I could chicken out again. "We need to talk about the house."

She glanced around at the sea of mourners. "Jesus, Lottie? Now? Really?"

"I'd do anything to keep it, Tiff. Anything."

She stiffened. The words soured my mouth. Now wasn't the time, but she'd already contacted the estate agent and things were snowballing. We'd had this conversation a million times. Even before Dad had died. When his health had gone downhill, we'd had to have these conversations. This had been coming for a long time. It wasn't a shock. It wasn't fair to bring it up now of all days, but I couldn't do what was being asked of me. I couldn't just pack up Dad's house and move on.

She sighed. "Come on, Lottie. Don't. Not today. You know we have to do it."

I *did* know. I couldn't afford to buy Tiff out, and the money from Dad's house was our inheritance. We had to sell and split everything. Tiff had kids. She needed the cash. It was a family home. Dad had wanted it to be a family home. There was no point holding on to a house we couldn't afford to keep up. I could barely cover the bills, let alone pay to do all the work it needed. Then there was the small issue that I didn't have anywhere else to live.

She eyed the glass of wine in my hand and frowned. "Now's not the time."

It never is. "Just give me some time. We don't have to put it up for sale straight away. Let me figure something out—"

"Not now, Lottie." Her lips thinned and she smoothed the sleeves of her black jacket. "I can't do this with you now."

My stomach sank. It wasn't worth begging, her eyes had already drifted. She blew out a breath and peered across the busy pub lounge.

"Have you seen who's here? Cole Thorner."

Impossible. Heat flashed through me. The room tilted. Somehow, I managed a word. "Where?"

She inclined her head to the side, trying to be discreet and failing miserably. I let my gaze travel over the tall man in a well-fitted suit engaged in somber conversation at the bar. *Oh. My. God. It's him.*

Tiff watched Cole with a thoughtful expression, as though it was completely normal to see him here. "I always thought he walked that line between beautiful and terrifying. It's those eyes. Such a weird shade of blue." She swung back to me. "Weren't you obsessed with him?"

Yes. Hopelessly, embarrassingly besotted. I scoffed. "Obsessed? Nope."

Tiff kept her voice to a whisper. "I heard he's some big shot down south now. He made a fortune in property or hedge funds or whatever rich people do in London."

That wasn't news to me. I'd googled him plenty of times over the years. Of course he'd done well in life. He'd come from unfathomable wealth. All the boys at Dad's school had. Dad had adored Cole. They'd spent hours in the box room Dad called a study making each other laugh with painfully geeky Latin puns that went over everyone else's head.

"What is he doing here? I didn't see him at the service," I said.

Tiff watched me with a frown as I swigged my wine. "The school contacted alumni. A lot of Dad's old pupils were invited to the wake."

Right. Of course. Cole's gaze caught mine and held. A shock of adrenaline went through me. *Don't stare. Look away.* But I couldn't tear my face away because Tiff was wrong about Cole's eyes. They weren't weird. They were intelligent eyes that looked straight through you and gave nothing away, mesmerizing and sultry. Impossible to escape from. I should know. I'd spent enough time gazing into them.

The memory hit me, sudden and intense. *Firm lips moving against mine. The taste of spearmint gum and heat. Persuasive hands groping under my T-shirt and cupping me through my bra. The first time I'd ever felt the pulse of desire between my thighs.*

Cole had been my first kiss. He'd promised me the world after an epic make-out session and it had all been lies. He'd awoken sensations I'd never experienced before and never truly felt since. Then the bastard had moved to live with his dad in the US and ghosted me. And now he was here. At my father's funeral.

I forced my gaze away from Cole and threw back my drink. The wine was helping, even if it made me feel like a gaming console with a diagnostic running in the background. My connection to the world was patchy. A couple of buttons on the controller didn't work. Everything was laggy. I couldn't even remember how I'd got from the crematorium to the pub for the wake, but I'd stood and greeted people. I'd made small talk.

My eyes drifted back to Cole, to find him still looking at me. "I need more alcohol."

Tiff's frown deepened. "Don't you think you've had enough?"

"Nowhere near."

I had to get out of here. My lungs heaved for air that wouldn't come. I weaved through somber mourners and stumbled over a barstool to get to the exit.

A hand on my arm steadied me. "Are you planning on ignoring me all evening?"

The deep masculine voice made my heart pound an erratic rhythm. He didn't speak like anyone in this pub. He'd always sounded clipped and posh, even when he'd lived here. He took a step closer. His cologne enveloped me, spicy and masculine. Cole used to smell like a teenager—of grass and cigarette smoke—but now he smelled dangerous, like money and power.

His expression pinned me to the spot. His lips, his cheeks, his nose, everything coming back to me in a rush, like an old, beloved song on the radio. I still knew the lyrics, but the melody was off-key. This was my Cole, but not really. An aloof edge lay under the commanding presence. He had a polished veneer and a cold, hard look that was new and unsettling. Maybe I was off-key to him, too, after all these years. Shadows under the eyes. Jaded. A vaguely familiar stranger. Heat stole through me. Too much wine on an empty stomach. The room was spinning.

"I'm not ignoring anyone." The words were polite and automatic. "Thank you for coming. Excuse me. I need some air."

I plowed through the back door of the pub. A chilly wind blasted me and made me brutally aware of how tipsy I was. The wine had gone straight to my head. Birds trilled too loudly in the hedgerows. The door swung open and Cole joined me outside. The Fox and Hounds was a small mock-Tudor building with a white facade and oak beams. On Friday nights, most of the village turned out to drink beer and watch their kids playing in the pub garden. This pub had been Dad's preferred spot for tutoring the older boys. He'd only ever invited his favorite student to the house. Cole was the son that Dad had always wanted. We'd always joked he loved Cole more than us.

"I'm sorry for your loss."

If you were that sorry, you would have known. You would have been here with us. "It was expected. He was ill for a long time."

Cole stared out at the tree line. The fading sun cast its rays over the grass in streaks and turned the sky mauve. Silence fell. An unbearable awkwardness. The old me would have filled this quiet with conversation, but I couldn't. A strange pressure had been building behind my eyes that made my head ache. It was unreasonable to be expected to make polite conversation, and too weird to be back with Cole, here of all places.

I would have quizzed him on his life, but I had nothing inside. I couldn't talk to anyone, least of all a ghost from my past. Also, I didn't care about Cole Thorner. He'd never replied to my messages. He'd left this village without looking back. I'd cried over him for months. He hadn't given me any closure. I'd had to find my own way to move on.

Time to find Tiff and sober up.

"Thank you for coming. Dad would have been touched to see so many of his old pupils here." I turned to go back inside.

"Everything looks the same around here."

His words stopped me at the door. We'd spent our summers riding bikes around the woods together, playing tennis, and wrestling. Ecclesdale was probably still charming and twee to him. Cole had moved on. Everyone had. Apart from me. I hadn't even made it through a term at art school before Dad got sick. Still, no regrets. I might have been bitter at the world right now, but never at Dad. If I had to live my life a thousand times over, I'd always make the choice to be at Dad's side when he needed me. Nothing mattered more.

Easy for Cole to waltz back in and look down his nose at us. "A lot has changed, actually. The post office has become an off-license. We've got a retail park with a Starbucks. They sell chicory in the Londis now. Big things are happening around here. I always wondered what happened to you. I considered alien abduction the most likely possibility, but then I hear you're some fancy CEO in London?"

He adjusted his cuff links. The gold glinted in the dying sun. "I'm doing OK. No aliens."

No apologies for not keeping in touch. For ghosting me because he'd moved on to bigger and better things. I'd loved him in that intense, all-encompassing teenage way, and I'd been so easy for him to leave behind. Now that I was older, I had more of an understanding. We'd been young. We were from different worlds. He'd got what he wanted from me and apparently it was enough. I hadn't mattered enough to him. It had cut deep. I'd been discarded since by other crappy men, but Cole had set the precedent for abandonment.

"According to Wikipedia, you're filthy rich now."

A smirk played on his full lips. "According to Wikipedia, I'm also an arsehole."

Sounds about right. "What's it like being a filthy-rich arsehole?"

"It has its perks."

He squinted at the trees in the distance. A frown creased his brow. "If neither of us is married by the time we're thirty, then we marry each other."

"I'm sorry?"

"That's what we agreed. Do you remember?"

I remembered the pact. I'd spent months practicing his surname in my diary. To my absolute annoyance, I felt my cheeks get hot. "I don't know what you're talking about."

"I turned thirty last week. My brother tried to throw me a party." He said it as though it was a terrible thing.

"You don't like parties anymore?"

He lifted his cuff and glanced at his expensive-looking watch. "You're not married."

"How do you know I'm not married?"

His inscrutable eyes traveled over my face. "Maybe I looked at your Wikipedia page."

"No. You didn't. Nothing I've ever done would warrant more than a sentence on Wikipedia, let alone a page. Charlotte Ackroyd was born. She wanted to do something with her life, but she never left Ecclesdale. At least she got to try chicory. The end."

The words sounded bitter, even to me. I wasn't myself. The wine had made me too candid. I hadn't been myself for a while. But if I couldn't feel like that today, when could I?

Cole's expression was cold and distant. "That was four sentences."

Yep. Definite arsehole-ish vibes. "Why do you care if I'm married, anyway? Are you going to hold me to the pact?"

He kept his gaze fixed ahead on the trees. "A deal is a deal. We shook on it, as I recall."

It had to be a joke, but it was hard to tell. Teenage Cole had always had me cracking up with his dry-witted charm. But his voice was brusque and businesslike. No smile. A hard face. Nothing left of the teenager I'd known behind that polish and killer suit. Is this how he conducted his business? No wonder he'd climbed to the top. That kind of world was probably full of sociopaths. He didn't intimidate me. Nothing else could touch me today. I was already too numb.

"A verbal agreement when we were kids won't hold much weight in court."

"You'd be surprised. I've got excellent lawyers. One perk of being a filthy-rich arsehole."

I scoffed. "You'll have to wait before you whisk me down the aisle. I've still got three months. I'm betting on countless marriage proposals before then."

He pierced me with his gaze. "Well, if no one comes forward to claim you, I'll see you at church."

Hilarious. I don't need anyone to claim me. I'm not lost baggage. Even if that's how I feel. Today wasn't a time for banter . . . or whatever this was. "Excuse me. I should . . ." *Drink more wine. Try not to weep. Collapse in a corner.* A shiver ran through me.

Cole took off his jacket and moved to slip it over my shoulders.

I dodged away. "No. Thank you."

"You're cold."

"I don't want your jacket. When you disappear and ignore my messages again, I don't want to be worrying about how to return it. That suit looks like it cost more than this pub. I don't want that responsibility."

His mouth opened and closed again. He slipped his jacket back on. I fought to keep my eyes firmly away from where his impressive biceps bulged in his crisp dress shirt. A wake was no time for checking out Cole's gun show, no matter how much wine I'd quaffed.

"Come inside," he said.

Not yet. I can't face it yet. "I'm fine."

"If you won't take my jacket, then you're coming inside."

His clipped voice left no room for dissent, but I was beyond taking orders. I'd freeze my tits off before I let a man boss me around.

"I said I'm fine." My voice came out sharper than I'd intended.

He folded his arms. The picture of nonchalance, if it wasn't for the tension in his jaw. My head pounded. My hangover was kicking in. I'd never felt more wretched. The lump in my throat was as sharp as an arrow.

"Thank you for coming all this way. Dad would have appreciated it. I'll see you around."

A small smirk pulled at his lips.

"Something funny?"

He shook his head. He'd probably never been dismissed before. It looked like it had amused him. This Cole Thorner probably had his employees sniveling and quaking in his wake. Maybe I should have apologized, but I just wanted this conversation to be done. He cleared his throat. The weight of some unspoken words flickered in his eyes before he gave me a curt nod and disappeared. It shouldn't have surprised me. Disappearing was Cole Thorner's specialty.

Chapter 5

Cole

Twelve years previous

"You didn't have to do all this."

Charlotte dug into the hamper and laid out more and more food on the picnic blanket. "It's nothing."

I grabbed a chunk of crumbly homemade shortbread and sat back to admire the view of the stone houses in the valley below. The moor stretched around us, stark and beautiful. The gentle bleats of sheep drifted on air crisp with the tang of cut grass.

I'd miss nothing about school, but I'd miss all of this. Ecclesdale was so far removed from everything, it was another planet. I'd been distraught when Dad had sent me up here, but it was a different life. A kind of peace that was impossible to find anywhere else.

Charlotte passed me a soft drink from the cooler. "Your parents are going to take you to The Ritz or somewhere fancy to celebrate tomorrow and I'm here feeding you Scotch eggs and pickled onions."

The shortbread got caught in my throat and made me cough. Yes, my dad would take me somewhere expensive, but it wouldn't be celebration on his mind. Ever since his assistant had rung to tell me Dad was flying in from New York to discuss "something important", I hadn't slept. My heart wouldn't stop pounding at the thought of whatever he was about to drop on me. God only knew what punishment he'd concocted for whatever perceived slight. With Sir Philip Thorner, it could be anything.

The many colorful bracelets on Charlotte's wrist jangled as she held up her can of lemonade. "A toast. To you and your big clever brain for acing all of your exams. This is it for you now. You're going to be a history professor, dressed in tweed, in some oak-paneled office."

"Sounds perfect. Although I'm never going to be able to pull off tweed the way Roy does." I clinked my can against hers. "And here's to you on your way to the big city. I can't wait for my invite to your first big exhibition."

She gave me a weak smile and sipped her drink.

"What's the matter? You're supposed to look happy."

She pulled her knees up to her chest and retied the lace on her sparkly purple Doc Marten. "Nothing. I'm just freaking out. It's a lot to process. I feel . . ." She chewed her lip and shrugged one shoulder.

I turned to give her my full attention. Surely she wasn't having second thoughts about art school? "What?"

She blew out a long sigh. "Honestly? Guilty. Tiff hardly ever comes home. I don't want to leave him on his own. It feels selfish."

"Roy? He'll be fine. I've never met anyone happier in their own company. He'll spend his time reading and pottering around and when he finally looks up from his books, you'll be home for Christmas."

She picked a daisy and began plucking off the petals. "I know, he's just been . . . off lately. He doesn't seem himself. I don't know what it is. Have you noticed him acting . . . weird?"

Roy had always been an eccentric. He could give a blow-by-blow account of the Battle of Trafalgar, but he couldn't make toast without burning it if left unsupervised in the kitchen. "Not really. He's just Roy."

"It's not just Dad." She swallowed and darted a glance at me. "We won't see each other much anymore."

"Oxford is an hour away from London. I told you, you'll never be able to get rid of me."

She kept her gaze fixed on the village in the valley below. "It won't be the same."

"No, it's going to be even better. I can't wait to show you London. You're going to adore it, and Roy's already said I can come back and spend Christmas here. It's not that long." I poked her in the ribs. "You're getting out of here. It's what you've always wanted. Life is about to start. You're allowed to be excited about it, you know."

She flicked her thick dark-chestnut hair over her shoulder and peered at me. Her voice was soft. "The truth is, I'm going to miss you, that's all."

Some scratchy feeling made my chest tight. "I'll miss you, too." *More than you'll ever know.*

I'd been coming over to study for years so I could spend time in Charlotte's orbit. Getting away from that grim school was just a bonus. Things had been different between us the past couple of months. So much of our time together felt charged, like maybe Charlotte was finally looking at me the way I'd always dreamed she would. I hadn't dared jeopardize what we had. There was too much at stake. If I couldn't come over to the Ackroyd house, then there was nothing for me in Ecclesdale.

Sheep bleating grew loud, piercing the stretching silence. Things were different now. We were both leaving. This was the right time to tell her how I felt. There was still too much to lose, but everything to gain. This could be the start of a new chapter. I opened my mouth to try and articulate it, but she spoke before I could.

"I'd love to meet your family. It should be easier when I'm in London."

Coldness spread through me. "They're not in London much."

She turned to face me. "But sometimes they must be?"

"Maybe. I'm sure we can figure something out."

She swallowed, and her voice took on a brittle edge. "Are you embarrassed by me?"

Are you kidding me? "Of course not."

She nodded, but she didn't look convinced.

"I have a present for you, anyway." She dug into the hamper, pulled out a picture in a frame and handed it to me. It was a watercolor of the view in front of us—Ecclesdale with its little stone houses and rolling green fields beneath wispy clouds.

"You did this?"

She nodded and shot me a shy glance. "I thought you could take a piece of Yorkshire with you."

A pang pulled at my heart. "It's beautiful. Thank you."

"You're welcome."

I grabbed her hand. "Listen, you could never embarrass me. My family is just . . . it's not like yours. When I came up here, I wanted to leave it all behind." My skin prickled with shame. There was so much I wanted to tell her, but the words would never come. "My family aren't close. It's difficult sometimes, but you'll meet them one day, I'm sure. It's not you. Never think that."

She looked down where our hands joined. The wind lifted her hair and blew it off her face. Her cheeks and nose were pink with the cold. She'd never looked more beautiful.

"You survived Ashcombe. You must be relieved you don't have to go back," she said.

"I hate that school, but I wouldn't change anything, because it brought me to your family . . . to you."

She hadn't let go of my hand. I twisted it in mine and studied her violet nail varnish.

"You don't ever have to worry about anything in your future. Your life is about to begin, Charlotte."

"I don't want to lose you."

"You won't."

She bit her lip and peered at me. There was something so fascinating about the movement, I couldn't help but fixate on her mouth.

Her voice was a murmur. "You're staring at me."

I tore my gaze away. "I'm sorry. Sometimes I wonder if . . ." I took a breath, searching for the right words, but my heart was racing too much to find anything eloquent. "I want to kiss you."

Her eyebrows lifted in surprise. "What?"

Shock went through me. I'd actually said it. I'd started now. Too late to back down. My breath came in sharp snatches. "Actually, I've wanted to kiss you for years."

"Then why haven't you?"

The wind whipped a strand of hair across her face, and I brushed it away from her cold cheek. Any excuse to touch her. "Because I didn't want to fuck things up between us."

A small smile ghosted her lips. "But you don't mind fucking it up now?"

"You can tell me no, and it doesn't have to be weird. I'll never mention it again."

Everything inside me was wound so tight. Nothing in the world mattered apart from her next words. All traces of humor vanished from her visage. Her eyes darted over my face, reading my expression. Her voice barely broke a whisper.

"It won't fuck things up."

Oh, thank God. My shoulders dropped with sudden relief. *Is this a good idea? What if it ruins everything? But how could it when it feels like this? Fuck it.* I lifted her chin, tilting her face toward me. "I hope I can live up to all those books you read."

I covered my mouth with hers, then I was drowning in sensation. The soft press of her lips. Her tongue exploring the recesses of my mouth, insistent and probing. Her lemonade taste. Feverish warmth all over my body. *Finally. Finally.* I was kissing her. Charlotte was kissing me. I'd waited for this for so many years.

I pulled her tight against me and she whimpered. *Closer.* I wanted to get lost in her. No one knew me like this woman. She was the only person I could be myself around. It was so hard to open up to anyone, but I wanted to give her a map to all the places inside of me that I kept hidden from everyone else. With Charlotte, I was funnier, and cleverer, and . . . just better than I had any right to be. I couldn't imagine my life without her.

Her hand came to rest lightly on my neck. It sent sparks of electricity all over my body. My insides were heavy and light at the same time, like I could float away, only I wouldn't because Charlotte Ackroyd would always tether me. I felt her smile against my lips before she broke away.

Pink tinged her cheeks. Her grin was the widest and most unguarded I'd ever seen. So beautiful. So funny and wise. So under my skin that she'd peeled it back. I traced the smooth line of her jaw with my thumb. "You don't know how long I've waited to do that."

Chapter 6

Cole

Present Day

Moonlight illuminated the crumbling stretch of uninspiring pebble-dash houses. I should have instructed my driver to return me to London, but Charlotte looked sadder than I'd ever seen her, and I had to fix that. The world was full of pricks who deserved whatever shit they got, but not her. Charlotte only deserved good things.

The pact rang in my head. *If neither of us is married by the time we're thirty, we marry each other.* It was a silly promise made between teenagers, but I'd meant it. I'd always seen my future with Charlotte. My father had ripped me away from here. I'd never wanted to leave Ecclesdale without this woman. Maybe it wasn't so silly. Maybe it was the answer to my prayers.

It was an audacious notion, but nothing good in business came without risk. What if I married Charlotte Ackroyd? It was an arrangement that would work for both of us. She was everything Lucas told me the shareholders wanted. Sweet. Wholesome. Authentic. Charlotte Ackroyd was toasting marshmallows around a campfire in human form.

Leadership more aligned with the brand? Charlotte looked like an angel with her guileless hazel eyes and hair the perfect shade of chestnut. I could knock these shareholders out with a wife who was the very embodiment of the fucking brand. If notorious family man Gabe Rivers saw me with my lovely, wholesome wife, then who was he to think me an arsehole? He'd been a playboy once and somehow he'd convinced everyone that now he had integrity, so why couldn't I?

With Charlotte on my arm, everyone would think I was an outstanding human being. A man who looked past the glittering socialites and heiresses and married his down-to-earth childhood sweetheart. A man of the people. All Charlotte had to do was show her face at a few corporate events, and then she could go back to whatever she wanted to do, like an employee. A wife/employee. I'd help get her out of here and give her enough money to live a fabulous life.

One thing was certain, I couldn't leave her alone in this village. Not with all that sorrow around her pretty eyes. She'd been the happiest person I'd ever known, and now she was so pale and fragile-looking. It wouldn't do.

"I'm going inside. I don't know how long I'll be."

My driver inclined his head. "Right you are, Mr. Thorner."

I got out of the car. Rain pelted my Armani suit as I strode up the drive to number fourteen. Moss bloomed in the window frames of the beat-up teal Mini Cooper parked outside. The car had a flat tire, and duct tape securing the windscreen. Charlotte's car? Probably. From all accounts, Roy had been housebound for the past couple of years.

I knocked again. Seconds turned into an eternity as I waited. I'd stood in front of this door so many times as a kid. This house had seen better days. A crack marred the small window in the entryway. The flowers in pots on the step were brown and wilted.

A swell of nerves washed over me. Was this crazy? It felt crazy. Normally, there would be a plan. Meetings. Spreadsheets. Contingencies. I didn't act on an idea until I'd figured out the next ten steps. I smoothed my tie with clammy hands. I never got clammy hands. No. This was fine. It made perfect sense. I had to make sure Charlotte could see how it made perfect sense. If she wanted to put more adventures on her Wikipedia page, I could take her out of this village and show her the world.

Finally, Charlotte swung the door open. Red rimmed her glassy eyes. She still wore the tight black shift dress she'd had on earlier, but her dark-chestnut hair was piled on her head in a messy bun. My heart hammered. I'd mixed with some of the most desirable women on the planet. Women didn't make me nervous. But Charlotte always had.

Her eyebrows lifted in surprise. "Cole?"

Her tongue swiped out to lick her full lips. It was a nervous habit. I'd done my best to train myself out of all those tells and unconscious tics that gave away your true feelings. I supposed Charlotte hadn't had cause to do the same. Memories of the time I'd kissed her battered me. Not my first kiss, but a kiss that had altered my brain chemistry. I'd never had a kiss anything like it since. I'd never even fucked a woman and felt anything close to that rush in my chest. She was so beautiful. *God.* I'd missed her voice, her hair, her gentleness, her mouth.

She frowned and swiped at her damp cheeks. "I don't know why you're here, but honestly it's not a good time."

This is reckless. This is what reckless people do. "I know. But I have a proposal."

She tapped her foot impatiently. "What proposal?"

Focus, Cole. Not reckless. This is business. Good business. "A literal proposal. I want you to marry me."

Her brow drew downward into a frown. She stared at me like I was a door-to-door salesman she was humoring but wouldn't consider buying from in a million years. "Not now. I'm not in the mood for bullshit."

Then she shut the door in my face.

I had to knock three times before Charlotte returned to open the door.

"What is it?" Her tone rang with weary impatience.

I peered past her into the dark house. "I was hoping you'd invite me in."

"Why? Are you a vampire? Do you need an explicit invitation before you cross a threshold?" She looked me up and down and her lips curled slightly. "You'd make a good vampire, actually."

"It must be that air of mystery I've spent years cultivating."

She raised a sarcastic brow. "I meant the fact you disappear without a trace more than a decade ago and then pop up again looking like you haven't aged a day."

She thought I hadn't aged? Her delivery hadn't been complimentary. In fact, it had been downright sneering, but I'd still take it. "I need to talk to you. It's important."

She rolled her eyes as though she could never imagine a word of importance ever emerging from my lips and drifted back into the house. *Fine.* That was invitation enough for a human. I followed her inside and sat next to her on the sofa. We'd both instinctively avoided the armchair. Roy had always sat there next to the bookcase. It looked empty and forlorn without him.

The Ackroyd house had been a second home to me once. I'd been here most nights after school, revising my Latin verb conjugations. Latin had been a nightmare. I'd only been here to catch a glimpse of Charlotte, hoping she'd invite me to watch some trashy show with her or play *Mario Kart*. It had been the best kind of escape from the grim dorms at boarding school.

Charlotte was eyeing me with half suspicion, half disdain. I'd often imagined what I'd say if I ever saw her again. It had never sounded right.

She glanced impatiently at the watch on her wrist. "Do you want a cup of tea or do you only drink directly from the vein?"

I leaned back in the chair. "What do you think about my proposal?"

She pinched the bridge of her nose and closed her eyes. "Honestly, I was trying to be polite and ignore it in case you were having some kind of seizure."

"I meant it. I want you to be my wife. We made a pact."

She opened her mouth and closed it again. Charlotte had rendered me speechless twice today with a glance, so it was only fair I returned the favor.

Confusion shadowed her features. "It's been a really long day. I'm not sure what kind of game you're playing, but I'm starting to wonder if you're out of your mind—"

"It's not a game. I want to alter people's perceptions of me."

"Because everyone thinks you're an arsehole?"

My jaw ticked. "Right."

"I fail to see what I have to do with it."

I'd missed her accent. That soft Yorkshire brogue was so soothing. Charlotte pronounced her words with a *t* that was so subtle it was barely there. The shareholders were going to love it. No one could fail to be charmed by this woman.

"You're the ideal candidate. I came home for a funeral and reconnected with an old flame. We remembered the pact we'd made. I realized I couldn't live without you, and I whisked you back to London. It's a romantic story, don't you think?"

She blinked. "We haven't seen each other for twelve years. You don't love me."

"Love is beside the point. I'm talking about a business arrangement."

"So you want me to be what? A pretend wife to convince people you're not an arsehole?"

"That's the gist."

She wrinkled her nose. "That sounds like the kind of thing an arsehole would suggest. Wouldn't it just be easier to edit your Wikipedia page?"

"This is bigger than Wikipedia. People also think I'm an arsehole IRL."

She snorted, moved to the window, and twitched the net curtain to one side. "Is that guy waiting out there for you?"

I joined her at the window. "Yes."

"Does he want to come in? Shall I take him a cup of tea?"

"It's his job. He'll be fine."

"It's his job to wait in the car for you while you propose to a woman you haven't seen in twelve years on the day she buries her father?"

"It's his job to do whatever I tell him to do."

She looked up at me from beneath her thick lashes. Moonlight fell through the fraying net curtain, painting her face in intricate patterns. There wasn't a woman I'd come across who could compare. All these years, and I'd never been able to get her out of my head.

I followed her gaze out of the window to the rusting, battered Mini. "Is that your car?"

"Honestly, Cole, I think it's time you left—"

"It looks like a wreck. Is it still running?"

"I need to take it to the garage. It wasn't exactly high on my list of priorities."

My phone buzzed loudly in my pocket. I swiped Lucas's irritating face away. "This is a good deal for both of us. Marry me, and I'll give you whatever you want in return."

She pressed her fingers against her temples, rubbing in circles as though soothing a headache. "Let me get this straight. You want to pay me to be your fake wife?"

"Correct."

She braced her hands on the window ledge. A bitter smile thinned her lips. "It's been twelve years. No messages. No phone calls. No emails. Nothing. Not a peep from you. Then you turn up at my father's funeral with all this nonsense?"

"I had my reasons for leaving."

She folded her arms tight across her chest. "And did you have your reasons for ignoring my emails? For never returning my calls?"

Yes. A sour taste rose in my mouth. Roy had begged me to cut off contact. He'd also begged me not to tell her. Now wasn't the time. Maybe there would never be a time to betray a promise made to a dead man. It didn't mean I still couldn't convince her to marry me. Any good negotiation relied on both parties recognizing the merits of the deal. This deal had value whether she hated me or not.

Her disparaging gaze roved over me. "You moved on and forgot about me. You didn't want to do long distance, and you didn't have the balls to tell me and put me out of my misery. I'm a big girl now, Cole. All grown up. I can take it. Just tell the truth."

"Let me lay out the terms. This isn't just about me. Be my wife and I can give you anything."

She picked up a framed photo of Roy posing with a tennis racket in his hand and stared at it blankly. "No. Not anything."

OK, anything besides resurrection. Money couldn't fix grief, but it was still easier to be sad in a hammock in the Maldives. She let out a long sigh. Why was she here alone? Her sister should have been with her, or anyone, for that matter.

"Have you eaten this evening?"

Her absent gaze fixed on the chipped window frame. She wasn't listening. I moved out of the living room to the dim kitchen. A clean detergent smell hit my nose, but the room was in as much disarray as the living room. Books piled high in teetering piles. Pots and pans spilled out of boxes everywhere. The laminated cards with instructions taped to the cupboards and appliances stopped me in my tracks. *Shut the fridge. Turn the kettle off. Switch off the oven.*

Someone at the wake had told me that Roy had suffered with dementia. I hadn't really processed that at the time. Now, it hit me square in the face. Charlotte had been in this house looking after him. Hard to imagine what that had been like. I weaved through the clutter and surveyed the sparse contents of the fridge and cupboards. There was enough to make a sandwich, but not much else.

"What are you doing?" Charlotte's voice drifted from the doorway.

I took off my jacket, hung it on the back of a chair, and rolled up my shirtsleeves. "Making you something to eat."

Her eyebrows rose with alarm. "You don't have to do that."

I flicked on the kettle. "What about sleep? Have you been getting any sleep?"

"I'm fine. You don't have to worry about me. This is none of your concern."

I found a tin of tuna and a handful of wilted lettuce for the sandwich. The salad was pathetic without cucumber, but Charlotte had always hated it anyway. She wrapped her arms around herself and watched me butter the bread.

"Come back with me to London. I have staff. People who can take care of you."

Her eyes widened. "Take care of me? I don't need that."

I found a plate and presented her with the food. Then I made us each a cup of tea and planted a steaming mug in front of her. It wasn't much, but it would get her through tonight.

"I can get you out of this village."

She stared at the sandwich as though it was an unidentifiable object recovered from an alien spaceship. Maybe it was bad. I had a chef. I hadn't made a sandwich in years.

"Did you hear me?" I repeated gently. "I can get you out of here."

Her red-rimmed eyes darted to mine. "Who said I want to leave Ecclesdale?"

"You did. You said you had nothing to go on your Wikipedia page. I've got hotels everywhere. Paris. Tokyo. Dubai. A private jet. I can give you the world, if that's what you want."

She chewed the skin around her thumbnail. That meant she was processing. Good. I'd let her. A little space and then a well-timed nudge. That's how I'd get this deal over the line.

"I don't belong in London. I belong here." She pressed her palms to her eyes. "I can't deal with this today. This is madness."

Her eyes met mine, and they glimmered with tears. My heart contracted. I had this strange compulsion that if I could just pull her into my arms, I could kiss her hard enough to take the pain away. It wasn't possible. Life fucked us all in a multitude of ways, over and over. I couldn't take away the pain in Charlotte's eyes, but I could ease her burden.

"I'm offering you a lifeline."

Charlotte smoothed a hand over her face. "And do you think we'd be happy in our fake marriage? Are we going to have fake sex? And fake children? Send them to fake school?"

"We can iron out the details."

A bitter laugh escaped her. "Why can't you find a wife the normal way? Look at you. You're a big shot in your suit and tie. I'm sure you're not short of offers."

Because a real wife would tie me down. Because the business of destroying my father was a full-time job. But even I could see it was time to have a woman on my arm. I needed one on my terms, who I could pick up as and when I wanted for corporate events and put back down again without fuss. No mindless dates. No gold diggers. No drama. Charlotte needed a way out of this village and the opportunity to live a good life once she'd risen from the fog of grief. What better way forward for both of us?

I pushed the mug toward her. "Drink your tea and eat your sandwich. I can order food in if you don't want it."

"I'm not hungry." She shook her head and pointed to the door. "I've heard enough. Please, it's time for you to go."

"Come back to London with me."

"No." She shook her head vehemently. "No way. Please. I have a splitting headache. You need to leave. I mean it. I want you out."

I pulled out my phone. "I'm ordering pizza."

She scrubbed both hands over her face. Her voice was a slow and lethal whisper. "You're not listening to me. I don't want to eat. I don't want to talk. I don't want to look at you for another minute. You're not welcome here. Please just leave me alone. Why are you not getting this?"

I never walked away from a deal, but she looked ready to punch me in the face or collapse and weep. Maybe both. As much as it pained me to walk out of here, we'd have to pick this up another time. I pulled out a business card and put it on the kitchen table. "Call me when you're ready to talk. Anytime. Day or night. You still have six months. The offer remains open until April 14th."

Her eyes flickered with surprise and darted to mine. "You remember my birthday?"

Yes. Once, I'd known everything there was to know about Charlotte Ackroyd. I took a step closer, close enough to see the tears glistening on her cheek. She'd been my first love. My fucking obsession.

My fingers itched to swipe the stray tear from her freckled cheek, but I held myself in check. "We were friends, weren't we?"

She opened the front door. Cold night air blasted us. Her face was pale. She probably wouldn't eat that bloody sandwich. I'd order the pizza when I got back in the car. She didn't have to eat it if she didn't want to. Better to have the option.

"You must eat. Keep your energy up." I stepped outside. "Take your time to think about the proposal. Call me whenever."

She stared past the wrecked car on the drive at nothing. Memories of my mother flooded my brain. When she'd been in the grip of depression, she'd been like this. Far away. Wounded. Absent.

"It will get easier. Just take one day at a time." Platitudes, but she wasn't interested in anything else I could offer. "Call me if you want. Any time."

"Call you?" She eyed me with a mix of confusion and despair, as though waking from a bad dream to something worse. "You think you can ghost me for twelve years and then turn up here like nothing happened?"

No. I'm under no illusions about that. "I'm here now. I can be here if you want to talk or if you need anything. Anything at all. I want to help you, Charlotte."

She chuffed out a faint humorless laugh. "You can help me by leaving me alone. Goodbye, Cole. Have a pleasant life."

Chapter 7

Charlotte

Six months later

"Tall ceilings," the woman remarked.

She hadn't taken her shoes off. Nor had her husband. It made my teeth itch. Dad had hated shoes in the living room.

"Yes. Tall," I said, because I didn't know what else to say, and I wasn't sure if I was supposed to be giving a sales pitch. Tiff had coached me on some choice lines, but considering I wanted these people out of my house as quickly as possible, it was probably better to keep my mouth shut.

The man wandered to the French doors and peered through the smudges in the glass at the back garden. Once upon a time, Dad had sat out there on sunny days with the radio on and his book of crossword puzzles. The man's bored eyes glided over Dad's antique roses, the bird table, and the shed. He appeared to be counting the cracks in the paving flags.

The pond had been home to Dad's koi carp, sparkling with flashes of gold as one swam near the surface. Now, algae and leaf debris floated on the dirt. It was another job for my list.

"We'll have to dredge that pond." The woman wrinkled her nose as though this small body of water had personally offended her.

I hadn't asked their names, and I didn't care enough to ask now.

"And get it paved out front to fit both cars on the drive," the man said.

My stomach dropped. Dad had worked so hard on his beautiful hydrangeas. I'd done my best to keep them going. I made to protest, but they disappeared into the kitchen as though they already owned the place.

The woman's eyes roamed over the breakfast bar with disinterest. She hammered a fist on the wall that partitioned the kitchen from the dining room. "We can knock through and make it open plan. It will be a great space for entertaining."

Ridiculous idea. That was a structural wall. They'd knock it through and the entire house would fall down. With any luck, they'd still be inside at the time of collapse.

The man sighed and glanced at the battered kitchen island. "I still think we'd be better with a newbuild."

The woman shook her head. "I want character. This place actually feels like a home."

Because it is a home. My family's home. Every scratch and dent in this place told a story. These strangers wouldn't appreciate that. Who did they think they were? Walking in here with their dirty shoes, rubbing their greedy hands together, thinking about lowballing us on an offer. I wouldn't be accepting a pound below the asking price, that was for sure. Tiff had definitely let the estate agent underprice us.

I turned my face to the kitchen window so the intruders in Dad's house wouldn't catch my irritation. There was no reason to dislike these people so intensely, other than that they didn't deserve this house. The sooner we got this over with, the better.

Squeezing around the kitchen island past them, I ushered them back through the hallway. "You probably want to see the bedrooms."

They ambled up the stairs. The woman glanced at Dad's stair lift. "Will you be getting rid of that or is that our responsibility to remove it?"

It was on my list of the million jobs I had to do to get the house ready. "The company will come and collect it."

"Will you leave any of the furniture?"

"Maybe. I don't know." I'd have to, otherwise I'd be trying to ram it all into the one-bedroom flat I'd found to rent. But it was hard to even know where to start. Most of it was so old-fashioned, it wouldn't get a good price second-hand, but I couldn't bear to throw it away.

I hung back on the landing while the couple surveyed the bedrooms and the bathroom. The woman nodded enthusiastically when she saw the maroon bathroom units.

"I saw something like this on Instagram the other day. The retro aesthetic is a vibe."

They probably thought I was out of earshot, but I caught the man's sarcastic reply. "Sure. I wouldn't change a thing."

Resolve hardened my heart. It was bad enough that we had to sell. At least we could sell it to the right people. Dad would have wanted decent people moving in here, not people who didn't appreciate his rose bushes or took the piss out of his bathroom. And absolutely not the kind of psychopaths who didn't take their outdoor shoes off in the living room.

The woman twisted in a circle, surveying Dad's bedroom. Nobody came up here. A stale smell hung in the air, even when I opened the windows. Dad had slept downstairs. I'd spent most of my nights next to him on a camp bed. It was easier when he needed to use the commode.

A saccharine smile formed on the woman's face. "I like it, actually. It's cozy. I always felt like, when it was the right house, I'd know. It's like falling in love, isn't it? When it's right, you just know."

No. You don't know. Go and fall in love with someone else's house. I gave her a polite nod when really I wanted to roll my eyes so far back I'd see my own brain. It didn't matter what my heart was saying. I had to dig deep and get this done. This wasn't just about me. It was about Tiff. Tiff had kids and loans. She needed the money.

I smacked my hands too loudly on my thighs. "Shall we wrap it up? Thank you for coming."

The couple chattered happily as they followed me to the front door.

"Oh." The woman clapped her hands suddenly. "I forgot to ask the obvious. Why are you selling?"

Because Dad is gone. Because my sister is forcing me. "I'm not."

The words hung in the air between us. My heart pounded.

The woman's eyebrows rose in surprise. "You've had another offer? Already? The estate agent said we'd be the first to view."

"Right. I'm sorry. We made a mistake. It's not for sale anymore."

Stop. What are you doing? Panic gripped me. My mouth was spewing words that my brain hadn't approved. If this woman phoned the estate agent to tell them the house wasn't for sale anymore, then Tiff would know I'd messed this up.

Maybe it would be different if it was someone nice. Someone who had complimented Dad's roses and didn't want to bulldoze a structural wall. No. Who was I kidding? Even if the world's best person walked in here, I'd struggle with it. Malala could show up carrying her Nobel Peace Prize and declare she wanted to set up a school for girls, and I'd still be annoyed she needed to knock a wall through to fit in the desks.

"Sorry about the inconvenience." I folded my arms. "Thanks for coming."

"Are you sure?" She exchanged a glance with the man that was so soppy it made me wish I hadn't thrown the sick bucket away. "We kind of love this house."

Tough luck. I loved it first and much harder. "Yes. Sure. Big mistake. Not for sale. Goodbye."

I closed the door before I had to face any more excruciating awkwardness. Tiff was going to kill me. We'd been having the same conversation for six months. I sank down against the hallway wall to sit on the faded carpet. The constant ache in my chest was like a knife buried so deep, I'd never be able to remove it. We had to sell. It was the only way.

Framed photos cluttered the opposite wall. They were all group shots of boys standing shoulder to shoulder in bottle-green uniforms. The hairstyles changed over the years: mullets, buzz cuts, curtains, even a mohawk. What had happened to all these kids from Dad's school? They probably had dazzling careers and partners and kids of their own. They'd probably traveled. They'd probably done exciting things.

My gaze landed on Cole in the back row of one of the photos. A strange heat buzzed through me. I stood and traced a finger over the sullen-looking teenager who had once been the most important person in my life. Cole Thorner could afford this house. It was such madness. He'd shown up here like a genie offering to grant my wishes, and all I had to do was marry him. The problem was, he hadn't made it clear whether the deal would also involve rubbing his magic lamp. Marrying a man who had treated me the way Cole had was preposterous. No one in their right mind would ever consider it. But I *had* been considering it. How could I not? The offer had drifted to mind constantly over the past six months. My head was such a mess after losing Dad, I couldn't give it the proper attention. One of my old paintings on the wall caught my eye—a carpet of bluebells among tall trees. I'd spent every spring in the woods painting. I'd been obsessed with the way such beautiful flowers could bloom in the coolest, shadiest parts of the forest. Back then, my future as an artist had glittered brightly in front of me.

I pulled out my phone and texted the number I'd saved. My thumb hovered over the keypad. Six months had passed since the wake. It was so surreal that maybe I'd imagined the whole thing. I took a deep breath and messaged. *Is the offer still open?*

I added another line in case he was regularly proposing to women from his past. *It's Lottie, by the way.*

I chewed my fingernails, feeling increasingly nervous. Maybe he'd propositioned someone else and already had another fake wife. Cole wasn't the type to wait around for things. He was impatient. If he wanted something, he'd always gone after it. I added another line. *It's fine if it's not open anymore. I just wanted to check.*

Blue ticks appeared next to the messages, but no reply. Perhaps I was going crazy. Grief could send you mad, couldn't it? Maybe that entire conversation with him was some epic multilayered hallucination. Dots danced on the screen as he replied. *Hello, Charlotte. The offer is still open.*

A jolt of adrenaline went through me. No. It was ridiculous. My head was a mess. This was too much to process. I tapped out a reply. *Actually, forget it. Sorry. I changed my mind. I can't.*

I shoved my phone deep into my pocket. *No more of that.* Cole Thorner was a genie best kept firmly in the bottle.

Chapter 8

I couldn't begin to guess how long I'd been standing in the hallway, staring into space. Instead, I drifted from room to room like a ghost, taking paintings off the wall and putting them back up again. Those people were mad, wanting the house in this state. There was so much wrong with it, I didn't even know where to start. Paint had chipped off the internal doors and skirting boards. The wallpaper was yellowed and peeling. It was like being caught in quicksand. I'd step into the spare room and catch sight of the gray mold blooming in patches, or the garage and see the pile of rusted bicycles and tools, and I was sinking. Easier to shut the door and retreat.

It was my fault the house had fallen into such a mess. Looking after Dad took up so much of my time, and I'd tried to fit in shifts at the local pub to keep us afloat. Now, I just didn't have the energy. It needed to be emptied and cleaned. Tiff had suggested a clearance company, but that was no good. There was too much that needed to be hand sorted. They'd just throw everything away.

A key twisted in the front door and I went back to the hallway. Tiff stormed inside, stopping to tug off her boots and hang up her leather jacket in the closet stuffed with Dad's old coats and umbrellas.

She planted her hands on her hips. "The estate agent called me. What were you thinking? You can't just tell people the house isn't for sale."

Hello, lovely to see you, too. I'm fine. Thank you for asking.

She moved past me into the living room and flung open the curtains. Daylight dazzled me. Blue skies. Bright sun. Somehow, it had slipped my mind that it was daytime. I was still wearing pajamas.

She thrust a large manila envelope at me. "This was in the porch."

I tossed it on a side table and flopped into a frayed armchair. "You didn't see these people. They were talking about knocking a wall out. What kind of people walk all over someone's carpets in outdoor shoes? Psychopaths, that's who. Antisocial behavior like that is an indicator of more serious criminality."

Tiff let out a deep sigh and cradled her face in her hands, like I was exhausting her. I probably was. It wasn't my intention. Tiff approached her grief by attacking it with a sledgehammer. She wanted the house cleared and sold. Done and dusted. When she'd cleared all the Dad admin from her inbox, maybe then she'd drop to the floor and howl, but not a moment before.

If I could have physically wrapped my arms around this house and carried it away to somewhere safe where no one would bother us, I would have. Every book, every ornament, every teaspoon destined for the charity shop was a little shard of glass twisting in my heart.

"It's true, Tiff. I watched a documentary about it once. You know these people who graffiti bus-stops or park in disabled parking spaces when they don't have a permit? Nine times out of ten they turn out to be murderers. Anti-social behavior, you see. I'm sure it's the same with not taking off your shoes."

Tiff held her head in her hands and sighed. "I know this is awful. It's all terrible and painful, and I don't want to do any of this either, but these are cash buyers. Do you know how rare cash buyers are? We have to get this done."

I let out my own deep, dramatic sigh, because Tiff needed to know that she was exhausting me, too. "I'm sorry that I'm not willing to sell our childhood home to psychopaths. We don't have to rush into this. Can we at least discuss renting again?"

"Cash-buyer psychopaths." Tiff stood at one of Dad's over-stuffed bookcases, pulling out dusty tomes and leafing through them absently. "This is what we agreed. We're not renting. It's delaying the inevitable. Who wants to be a landlord? You'll get no peace. The place is falling apart. We'd need a new boiler. Rewiring. Everything . . ." Her eyes shifted to the envelope I'd put down and she wrinkled her nose. "Aren't you going to open that? It looks important."

Nope. It's never important. I drifted away to make tea. Tiff started a tale of woe about being left out of the school mums' group chat, but I let her voice fade to a drone. In the kitchen, the dark linoleum had been trodden to gray. The floral curtains hung faded and threadbare. Somebody else would come in here. They'd rip this floor up and tear these curtains down. My stomach started to hurt again.

When I returned to the living room with the tea tray, Tiff was stacking an empty cardboard box full of Dad's books.

"What are you doing?"

"Life can only be understood backward; but it must be lived forward," she said.

"Pardon?"

"Kierkegaard." She snapped the book in her hand shut and dropped it unceremoniously into a box. I resisted the urge to dive and snatch it back.

Tiff's expression was deadpan. "I always found philosophy so depressing. This Kierkegaard dude sounds like another barrel of laughs."

"I heard he got left out of the school mums' group chat and that's when his melancholy took root."

"Fuck off." She rolled her eyes, but a faint glimmer of humor flashed on her face. "I was the first one to discover that the head teacher was having an affair, and I always volunteer for the bottle tombola. I'm an asset to any mums' group chat. Who wouldn't want me in their clique?"

"I don't know. Your meme game is so strong, too."

She nodded her head in firm agreement. "I know, right? At least someone appreciates my memes." She scooped the envelope off the table and thrust it at me. "Open it. You can't just let letters pile up in the porch."

Fine. I opened it to humor her, with my best "this is a pointless exercise, but you're insanely irritating so I'm doing it to shut you up" expression, so she'd get fed up and go home. I slid out a wad of neatly printed paper, and the bold "Marital Contract" header jumped out at me. A bright yellow Post-it clung to the front page, with a handwritten "To Charlotte. For your urgent review. Cole."

I flipped through, scanning the document. It was all bullet points and inscrutable legal jargon. *For goodness' sake.* He'd actually drawn up a contract? What was he thinking?

"Cole?" Tiff's eyebrows shot up. "You've kept in touch? Didn't he dump you and do a runner after you kissed him?"

I had no energy to get into it all, but it was preferable to being lectured about the house.

"He kissed me. And yes, we . . . parted ways, and now he wants to marry me because he can't be bothered to find a real wife. He's such an arsehole these days that he needs a stooge to come to his events with him, like some weird employee/wife to convince people he's not that much of an arsehole."

Tiff's incredulous laugh came out in a burst. "You're joking?"

"I wish I was."

Another slim envelope slipped out of the paperwork onto the floor. Bending down to retrieve it, I read the handwritten note on the front: "You've been carrying too much for too long. You need to rest. I have a resort in the Maldives. Silk sheets and a private chef on call. Stay as long as you like. You won't have to lift a finger."

I eased the envelope open and scanned the details of how to organize a flight on his private jet. My heart pounded. He couldn't be serious? Who could accept something like that?

"What's that?" Tiff demanded.

"Nothing." I hastily stuffed everything back into the larger envelope. "No one should even be a billionaire. The rich get richer and the poor get poorer. They could solve world hunger, but they just swing their dicks around instead."

Curiosity lit her eyes, and she grabbed the envelope from my hand. She pulled the contract out and scanned it. Her eyes darted over the printed pages. "Right, all those Ashcombe boys were entitled manbabies, but I've dated plenty of entitled manbabies that I've had to support financially. At least you'll get a Birkin out of it."

Tiff fell silent as she scanned the contract. While she was distracted, I returned Dad's books to their rightful place on the shelf. Tiff gasped. The contract dropped heavily onto the coffee table. She covered her mouth with a trembling hand.

"What is it? What's wrong?"

She spun to face me with wild eyes. "You need to sit down and read this."

"No. Thanks."

She thrust the paperwork toward me and spoke slowly, with quiet emphasis. "You *need* to sit down and read this."

I made no move to retrieve the stupid thing from her. "I'm not interested."

She flipped through the pages frantically, her voice rising with every word. "You just have to go to a few parties and travel around with him. It's hardly a chore."

"I don't even like him. He ghosted me. You know how long it took me to get over him." I sounded whiny, but my sister always had a way of bringing out the petulant kid inside of me.

"Good. This is your chance to get even. Spend his money. Make him pay for what he did. Take him to the fucking cleaners." She rapped her knuckles on the table for emphasis.

"I'm not a prostitute. I don't care if that's how some people choose to make their money, but my body is not for sale."

"Calm down, Julia Roberts. This isn't *Pretty Woman*. No sexual contact. He takes great pains to mention it in several bullet points. Cole wants your sparkling personality. He's not offering you billionaire dick. Imagine the places you could see. A man like that isn't staying in a Motel 6. You only have to do a year. That's all. One year. You can endure anything with an ending."

"Who wants to *endure* a year of their life? I want to figure out what comes next. I'm about to turn thirty and I have nothing to show for it."

Tiff stroked the contract worshipfully, like it was some previously undiscovered edition of *Pride and Prejudice* with an extended Mr. Darcy epilogue. "This comes next. Let it be this. You deserve this. Let this obscenely rich man spoil you and take you to all these fancy events. It's a dream come true. You can put up with it." She grabbed me by the shoulders and turned me around to face her. Her excitement spilled over into a grin. "You're doing it. No debate."

"You want me to marry an arsehole?"

"Give him a year, and he'll give you five million pounds." Her hands fluttered everywhere, and she laughed wildly. "Five. Million. Pounds. Either you bloody marry him, or I will. Cole Thorner isn't just any old arsehole. He's a cash-buyer arsehole."

Chapter 9

Cole

A dozen executives, ranging from useless to abysmal, sat around a long table under gleaming office lights. Geoff, my chief financial officer, clicked through another disappointing slide in his shoddy undergraduate-level presentation. It looked like he'd thrown it together last night. He deserved to be sacked on that basis alone, but I couldn't stomach another one of Lucas's "you can't sack everyone" lectures.

"As you see, this is the first year the shareholders won't be receiving a profit," Geoff said.

I leaned back in my chair and tried not to yawn. I could have done without a meeting with my board of directors today. A decent night's sleep had evaded me ever since I'd heard the news about Roy. Impossible to get the image of Charlotte looking so forlorn on her doorstep out of my head. I was so tired lately, my eyes felt like piss-holes in the snow. The air-conditioner hum grew loud in the silence.

Lucas raised an unimpressed eyebrow. "You could at least pretend you care."

I'd employed Lucas because it was good to have people around who weren't too scared to be honest with me, and occasionally he came up with a useful suggestion. Today wasn't one of those days. Today, he was just annoying the fuck out of me.

"The shareholders have been profiting off my hard work for years. They can suck it up for now. Loss is part of business. I'm not worried about it."

Lucas squeezed his stress ball in his hands. "They won't be happy."

So? Plenty of people aren't happy. I'm not happy right now, listening to this bullshit. I'm not happy with Ryan's coffee breath and the way Malcolm's ties are bright enough to trigger a migraine. I'm not happy that Gabe Rivers still won't return my calls, or that I went to great lengths to put the perfect contract together for Charlotte and she hasn't replied.

It had taken six months for her to even text. Now she hadn't responded to my follow-up on the contract.

"The shareholders' feelings don't interest me. I'm interested in how we get back on track," I said.

"The shareholders should interest you."

"Why? A couple of voices of dissent aren't an issue."

Lucas held my death glare without flinching. "People say that Beatrice might flip."

This fucking brother of mine never lets anything drop. "Beatrice has always been loyal to me."

"You've pissed her off, like you manage to piss everyone off. Apparently, you were rude at last week's annual conference, and she's annoyed. She's not the only one. A couple of others are getting braver and calling for new leadership. If enough of them flip, they'll have the majority vote, and then you're out."

My blood turned to ice. They could get fucked. This was my company. I wouldn't be dictated to by people who got high off the smell of their own farts. I wouldn't even be having this conversation if Charlotte had agreed to the deal. Nothing would have shut the shareholders up faster at that annual conference than pulling my wholesome childhood sweetheart wife out of the bag.

Lucas sat back in his chair with a smug look. "Just a suggestion, but maybe if you held the shareholders in a little less open contempt, it would help your cause."

"I hold most people in open contempt. I don't know why they're taking it so personally."

The door opened, and my PA stepped in hesitantly. I snapped my gaze to her. "The building better be going up in flames. I can't imagine any other reason you'd interrupt us in a board meeting."

She hurried to me and leaned down to whisper in my ear. "I'm sorry to disturb you, Mr. Thorner. You asked me to inform you immediately if I had a call from a Miss Charlotte Ackroyd."

Heat climbed the back of my neck. I angled my body away from the table. Everyone was still looking at me, but I dropped my voice to a whisper. "Charlotte called? What did she say?"

"She's in reception."

Fuck. She's here now? In the building? My tie felt suddenly too tight. I stuck a finger under my collar to loosen it.

"You're fully booked for the next three weeks. Shall I make her an appointment and send her away?"

I caught my reflection in the floor-to-ceiling window and smoothed my hand over my hair. "No. Escort her to my office." I stood and addressed the room. "Let's pick this up another time."

Muttering broke out among the gathered board.

"We still have another half hour of this meeting. We haven't even covered the essentials," Lucas said, glancing at the clock.

Charlotte had come all this way. How? Train? Why hadn't she called me to let me know? I would have picked her up in the chopper. "We'll reschedule. Talk among yourselves if you like."

Lucas blew out an impatient breath. "Talk among ourselves? These are crisis talks, Cole. Who's going to run the meeting?"

"I trust you can figure it out."

"You can't just walk out of here. This is too important."

I was out of the door before I had to listen to anyone telling me what I could or couldn't do.

From my office on the mezzanine, I watched my PA escort Charlotte through the rows of desks in the open-plan area below. A turquoise dress hugged her curves and thick thighs, and a cherry-red handbag shaped like an old-fashioned telephone bounced at her hip.

People usually approached my office with slumped shoulders and fear in their eyes. But Charlotte glided on her worn Converse, lost in her own world. Her lips moved slightly as though she was rehearsing what she wanted to say. She looked like a rainbow cutting her path through a sea of monochrome. Heads turned subtly to watch her progress. She didn't appear to notice.

The air caught in my throat. Did this mean what I hadn't dared hope? She wanted to discuss the contract? *Don't get too excited.* She'd backed out once over text. Maybe she was coming here to tell me never to contact her again. But couldn't she do that over the phone?

I took my position behind my desk and shuffled a stack of paper, pretending to look busy as she walked past the glass at the front. No sense in her thinking I had nothing better to do than cancel all my meetings and stand around waiting for her. Her knock sounded.

"Come in."

She stepped inside and hovered by the door.

"Charlotte, what a surprise. You should have let me know you were coming. I would have arranged transport." I smoothed my tie and gestured to the chair opposite. "Please. Take a seat."

Her unimpressed gaze slid over endless sparkling chrome and glass. "Nice office." She took in the expansive London skyline behind me with a skeptical brow. "I never imagined you working somewhere like this."

"Somewhere like what?"

A wry smile played on her lips. "It's very . . . corporate." She raised a hand to her ear, miming a telephone. "Buy low. Sell high."

I drank her in from behind my massive mahogany desk. Shadows danced under her eyes, but she looked in better health than when I'd last seen her. Charlotte had been pretty as a teenager, but as a grown woman she was breathtaking. Even as she mocked me, heat thrummed under my skin. Her little smirk made it impossible to think of much else besides bending her over my desk and making her mine.

I cleared my throat. "What can I do for you?"

"Tiff thinks I should marry you."

"And what do you think?"

She perched on the chair opposite my desk with her deranged telephone-shaped handbag in her lap. "It's a lot of money. I suppose I'd be mad not to take you up on it." She chewed the edge of her orange-painted thumbnail. "So if the offer is still open, I'm considering it, but we need to iron out some details."

The offer was more open than ever, since the shareholders had decided now was the perfect time to gun for me. "I'm all ears."

"First off, you're asking me to lie." She pulled the contract out of her bag, flicked through the pages, and presented it to me on the desk. "Tiff knows what's going on, but you expect me not to tell anyone else the truth?"

I glanced at the section she'd highlighted neatly in neon yellow. "That's generally how a confidentiality clause works."

"I don't like to lie."

"You should try it. You might enjoy it. The arrangement has to stay confidential. That's nonnegotiable."

Her eyes narrowed with a flicker of resentment as she assessed me. I held the challenge in her gaze. *Go on. Argue for it. Let's have some fun.*

Her shoulders lowered and she gave a small, resigned shrug. "Fine."

"Fine? That's it?"

"You said it was nonnegotiable."

"So, you just give up?"

Her eyes searched my face and darted away. "It's not worth the fight." She flicked back a few pages and tapped at the contract. "This states you expect my loyalty and fidelity. What does that mean? Do you expect me not to date outside of our . . . arrangement?"

Yes. Ideally. Did Charlotte date much? I'd checked in on her over the years. Nothing creepy. Just the occasional calls to old contacts in the area. Whenever I'd asked after her, she'd always been single.

"There might be some flexibility down the line if you want to take a lover—discreetly, of course."

Her expression flickered with a brief wry spark. "Take a lover? I didn't realize we'd stepped into the Regency period."

That teasing smirk again. Yes, I wanted her pressed beneath me over this desk, but first I needed her sitting on my face, moaning for me while I tasted her. "Next objection?"

She shrugged. "No one should make big life decisions after a bereavement."

"There's no better time. Death shows us how short and precious life is. There is no guarantee of tomorrow."

She rolled her eyes, but her voice was indulgent. "That one sounded rehearsed. You've got all the answers, haven't you?"

"I try."

Her eyes slipped away. "I made that marriage pact because I was a stupid kid and I was infatuated with you. I won't put my heart at your mercy again. This is strictly a business arrangement. I can't forgive you for ghosting me."

Infatuated with you. She made it sound like a crush. Something short-lived and silly. It had been more than that. Charlotte had been everything to me. A knot tightened in my chest. "You're right. This is strictly business. We keep our hearts out of it. I don't have one anyway. You were right about me being a vampire."

A shadow darkened her face. "You did have one. Before."

Everything was different before. "What else have you got?"

Pink tinged her cheeks, and she fidgeted with the clasp on her handbag. "Sex."

"What about it?"

"It's off the table."

I held her gaze and lowered my voice. "No problem. It doesn't need to be on a table. We can do it anywhere."

She tried for a confident tilt of her head, but her flush deepened. Her voice was chiding. "You know that's not what I meant. No sex anywhere. No physical contact whatsoever. We need to be clear on that."

"There has to be some physical contact. This needs to look real. We're supposed to be a couple in love."

She frowned. "How much physical contact?"

"I'm open to negotiation. What are you comfortable with?"

"With you?" She let out a humorless laugh. "None."

My jaw ticked. "Let me rephrase: What are you willing to *tolerate* to make this look convincing? A normal couple would touch in public. If you want to specify where I can touch you, we'll put it in the contract, and I'll stick to those areas. Your hands, for instance? Would it be acceptable to hold your hand?"

The expression of barely concealed disdain on Charlotte's face made it clear she wouldn't choose to hold my hand even if her life depended on it. I'd dismantled family businesses and had a warmer reception.

She folded her arms tightly across her chest. "If you must."

"Are you comfortable with hugs?"

She shifted in her seat and pulled her dress down over her thighs. "I'm not opposed to it, if it's necessary."

"Are there any parts of your body you don't consent for me to touch in public?"

She wrinkled her nose and let out a chuff of laughter. "Oh, for God's sake, Cole. Stop making it so weird. You're overthinking it. Just act like a normal respectful human in a relationship in public and keep your hands to yourself in private. It's not that deep."

"I'm trying to make this comfortable for you. The contract is in both our interests. Better to just hash it all out now. What's your stance on kissing?"

Silence crackled between us. I let it breathe. Any good negotiation needed silence. Whoever controlled the pace controlled the outcome.

Her eyes traveled everywhere except to me. "You can kiss me on the cheek if you must. Not on the mouth."

"We'll have to kiss on the mouth at the wedding."

She sighed. "Fine. One mouth kiss at the wedding. No tongue."

"No tongue. Agreed."

She bit her lip and shot me a glance. "And what about you? What are you comfortable with?"

"I encourage you to touch me whenever you want in public. The more convincing it looks between us, the better."

She stared at me with slight goading in her eyes. "You encourage me to touch you? And do you have any limits you'd like to formalize in the contract, or are you giving me free rein to grope you?"

I raked a hand through my hair, just for something to do with it. This negotiation was more awkward than my unsuccessful attempts at flirting with her as a teenager. Still, I kept my voice calm and measured. "Do whatever feels natural for you in the moment . . . within reason."

She raised an amused eyebrow. "Within reason. Got it. I'll try and resist sticking my hand down your pants during the wedding speeches."

Charlotte had always made jokes when she was uncomfortable, but I needed her to take this seriously. If we didn't get this part right, the arrangement would never work. "I'm not playing here, Charlotte. I need to know that you're in with me on this."

"I know, I'm sorry." She blew out a breath. "This is just a conversation I never expected to have. But I can do what you're asking. You don't have to worry."

"Good."

Her eyes slipped away. "Good."

I asked the question that had been bugging me, just to move us on to something more palatable. "What made you change your mind about accepting the offer?"

"I can't afford to buy Tiff out of Dad's house." Her gaze dropped to her Converse. "But I can't bring myself to sell it."

So I'd get what I wanted because she felt cornered. That wouldn't do. Her quiet capitulations and careful eyes felt all wrong. This had to be an informed decision, not an act of desperation.

"I'll give you the money for the house. You don't have to marry me. No strings. It's a birthday gift. You can take it and walk out of here."

Her eyebrows flew up. "What? It's too much. I can't accept that."

"It's nothing." I opened my drawer and pulled out my checkbook. "You can have it now."

"Why?"

"Because coercion and consent are different things. I don't want you to agree to this because you're being backed into a corner. And I don't want you to marry me because Tiff thinks it's a good idea. You need to sign this contract because it's the best thing for you."

She fell silent as she fiddled with the gold hoop in her ear. Enough. I wouldn't force her into something that made her uncomfortable, no matter how much I wanted it. I grabbed a pen and lowered my hand to the check.

"Wait." Her hand slid across the desk. "This isn't just about what Tiff wants. Five million is a lot of money. This is what I want."

I lowered the pen. "You're sure."

She gave a resolute nod. "Yes."

Five million *was* a lot of money, but nothing compared to how much I'd lose if my shareholders had beef with me. I couldn't fight a war on two fronts. If I was going to take down my father, then first I needed to get my own house in order. I'd never be able to ruin him without my company backing me. Sir Philip Thorner needed to pay for what he'd done to my mother. This was perfect timing. A lovely young wife would shut the shareholders up so I could get on with it.

She gave me a speculative glance. "You know you could ask anybody."

"I don't trust anybody. Not a single soul on this planet."

She frowned. "But you trust me?"

"Yes."

It had been so long since I'd seen her, but I knew this woman. There were so few good people in this world, but she was one of the best. She was also one of the few people in my life that my father hadn't sunk his claws into yet.

She rubbed the back of her neck. "I can't even imagine what Dad would have made of all this."

Roy had been a good man. He'd been the father I always longed for, but he'd put his own child first, and I respected that. I'd asked him for help, and he'd turned me away. He'd acted in Charlotte's best interests, to protect her future. I'd wanted to protect her, too. But Charlotte could never know. She idolized Roy. I wanted to help her, not piss on her father's grave.

"I think Roy would have been happy to see you taken care of."

She glanced at me, but her eyes wouldn't meet mine.

"You can leave all the arrangements to me. Let me take care of everything. You won't even have to buy a wedding dress."

She fixed her gaze over my shoulder at the view of the city skyline. The soft clicks of keyboards and polite telephone conversations drifted in from outside.

She cleared her throat. "Fine."

"Fine?"

"I'll sign the contract."

I tried to keep the eagerness out of my voice. "You'll marry me?"

She tucked a loose strand of hair behind her ear, and flashed a weak smile. "May as well. Not like I've had any better offers."

Chapter 10

CHARLOTTE

White marble and bronze inlay gleamed on every surface of the huge checkerboard-tiled entrance hall. Dramatic crystal chandeliers glinted overhead. Light from the vast bay window fell in dazzling strips over a grand piano. The effect was the most Instagrammable space in existence. A room so bright I wished I'd worn sunglasses.

Cole took my suitcase from his driver and lifted it inside. "Mayfair is a very exclusive area."

No shit. I scanned the luxurious space. "It's not too shabby."

He beckoned me to the window. "See the view of Green Park? Buckingham Palace is just behind that. I bought this from a duke."

"Rubbing shoulders with aristocracy, huh? Did he know you'd be shacking up with Yorkshire riffraff in here?"

He cocked an amused brow. "Let me show you the rest. Four floors. Five bedrooms. Five bathrooms. It's poky, but there's a pool and gym in the basement."

Poky? He guided me forward with a hand on my lower back. It was the briefest of touches. He probably hadn't realized he'd done it, but it sent a shock of heat through me. A huge corridor with a gleaming parquet floor divided the first floor in two. There was enough artwork on the walls to fill the National Gallery. The reception rooms and kitchen were more of the same, a mix of old-world charm and stark minimalism.

I poked my head into a study brimming with books. Everything was neat and orderly. Not a thing out of place. The books that stuffed the many bookcases all looked heavy going: history, philosophy, and politics. Just like Dad's library. Probably a load of melancholic philosophers and depressing poets. Tiff would not approve.

"You should have a look through Dad's books. See if there's anything you like. I can't throw them away, but I can't read them either."

He moved closer. His spicy cologne invaded my nostrils. "Why can't you read them?"

Because Dad had spent a lifetime poring over those books, talking in raptures about the Anglo-Saxons and obscure medieval kings, and one by one each historical figure had evaporated from his mind, until one day he'd forgotten more than most people ever learned. I swallowed past the lump in my throat. "Because most of them are medieval history."

"What's wrong with that?"

"It's my least favorite time period. It's always about men in codpieces and chain mail getting hard-ons about slaughtering each other."

His lip twitched. "I hope they aren't getting too many hard-ons. That's probably quite uncomfortable in a codpiece."

"Do you remember when Dad took us to the battlefield at Stamford Bridge and it was just a plaque on a housing estate? Other kids were smoking behind the bike sheds and we were being lectured about the end of the Viking era in a car park."

Cole raised an eyebrow. "Technically, Stamford Bridge wasn't the end of the Viking era. Even after Harald Hardrada was slain, there were a few further Viking attacks."

My burst of laughter took me by surprise. "It doesn't matter how well you scrub up in that suit, you're still a history nerd."

He raised an affronted eyebrow. "I'm not a nerd."

"Of course you are. You just used the word 'slain' in a sentence. Embrace it. You're still gaga for Edward the Confessor. No wonder you were Dad's star pupil."

"Edward the Confessor was a very underrated king." His dark brows slanted. "And I wasn't a star pupil. I wouldn't go that far."

"You were. I can't imagine any of his other students spending their weekends translating Latin texts. That is a commitment to history."

His expression was inscrutable. "That's me. Committed to history."

"Do you remember how Tiff got all worked up because the bakery was shut? An army defeated and my sister was crying over a sausage roll."

Another small laugh bubbled up, but I stifled it. It felt wrong, like I shouldn't have been doing it yet. Dad's loss was still so raw. I hadn't had many opportunities to laugh over the past couple of years.

I looked up to find Cole studying me intently. "You're allowed to laugh. Even when you're grieving."

His closeness was so bracing, so masculine and powerful. Cole wasn't a loud person. He was often quiet and still, like a predator, but his presence commanded attention. Butterflies flitted in the pit of my stomach. I smoothed my expression into something approaching neutral, despite my pounding pulse. "Shall we carry on the tour?"

His eyes skimmed my face again before he gave a small nod. I followed him in silence upstairs. In the largest bedroom, an enormous bed with a wall-to-wall headboard dominated the space. This sparse, orderly room was the opposite of the home I'd left. With so few lived-in touches, it was more like a show home.

The cream chaise by the window still had plastic covering on it. Easy to wipe clean from the multitude of sex sessions this man was probably having in here. It screamed playboy bachelor pad. He'd probably had sex in every room in this place. How many women had seen the inside of his bedroom? I didn't dare imagine. I shouldn't have even been thinking about it.

Cole was scrutinizing my face again. "You don't like it?"

"It's incredible. I just worry I'm going to be invading your space."

"You won't. My work means I'm hardly here, anyway."

He stepped out of the bedroom. I followed him back downstairs, glad to be away from his bed.

"I have other properties. This is my smallest but my most convenient. I don't spend much time here. I'm always at the office or traveling." He turned to face me. "I'm sure you'll be spending more time in the house than I will. You need to love it. We'll have a look at my other places. You might be more comfortable in the countryside, or in Paris. I have a lovely place in Kyoto."

"Japan?"

"Yes, or we can choose somewhere you like and you can have that if you don't like it here."

How could this actually be happening? It was so surreal to see Cole again, let alone touring the house I'd be living in with him. I roamed the gigantic, gleaming kitchen and opened the fridge. Tupperware boxes full of food lined the shelves. We hadn't even talked about the wedding. How quickly did he want to do it? How many people? I could only imagine the sort of people Cole would invite. Would they all be looking down their noses at me because I only knew the names of the streets around here from playing Monopoly?

"Marco stocks the fridge every morning, but you can tell him if there's anything in particular you like."

I shut the fridge. "Marco?"

"My chef. The housekeeper will be here later. If you have any problems, phone my PA. She knows you're here and I've told her to look after you." He pulled out his wallet and passed me a black credit card. "If you need anything, don't hesitate."

"I can't spend on your card. I feel weird spending money I haven't earned."

"You're earning it. This is part of the deal. Go shopping. Eat out. Have fun. Spend as much as you want, then visit some museums. Most are free in London so it all evens out."

I managed a faint smile. "That's not how money works."

"I've organized a spa day for you tomorrow."

"A spa day? Why?"

"It will do you good." He grabbed his overcoat from a peg in the entrance hall. "My driver will take you anywhere you want to go. It might be late when I get back. Don't wait up. Make yourself at home. We can talk about the wedding tomorrow."

He headed out of the door without looking back. *Sure. The wedding. The part where we stand up in front of friends and families and lie about being madly in love. No biggie.*

Chapter 11

COLE

I'd assumed Reuben would know his way around a golf course, but his hot-pink polo shirt, lemon-patterned shorts, and green argyle socks suggested otherwise. He glanced uneasily at the driver offered by his young caddy and lowered his voice. "Is that the right one?"

The caddy nodded. "Yes, sir."

All the gear, no idea. Reuben had dragged me away from Charlotte to Scotland, and he didn't have a fucking clue.

"What's new with you?" I put just enough energy into my voice to look like I gave a shit. I didn't. But always better to keep your enemies close. Reuben was a talker. He often let slip useful snippets about Thorner Enterprises.

He pulled off his neon-orange baseball cap and mussed his hair, making it flop all over. Someone had to be paying him to wear that outfit. We'd already had to pause twice so he could upload content for his poor, delusional followers.

His smile was sheepish. "Oh, you know. A bad couple of races. We'll do better in Abu Dhabi. I'm sure of it."

Formula One bored the life out of me. I wouldn't be asking follow-up questions. I took my time lining up my shot. If my father had sent Reuben here to spy on me—which was always a distinct possibility—then I'd better demolish him on this course.

With a solid stroke and a satisfying ping, I fired the ball down the emerald fairway. I shielded my eyes from the sun to watch it sail off and land in the rough. Dad's voice played in my head. *Pathetic. Can't swing a club for love nor money.*

Reuben gave me a good-natured pat on the back. "I finally got the big boss-man out of the office. Thought it was about time I hung out with my bro."

Bro? Nope. We shared DNA. It may as well have been from a sperm donor. I hadn't known about this man growing up. Reuben's mother had been my father's secretary. Philip Thorner left us for them. Traded one family for another. This guy was supposedly the upgrade.

Just because Reuben had the same blue eyes and dark hair as the rest of us, it didn't make us brothers. That suspiciously straight nose was definitely not a Thorner nose. It had to have come from his mother or the hands of a skilled surgeon. And that was definitely his mother's cheesy grin. Smiling so widely and unashamedly wasn't in the Thorner DNA.

Reuben held his tongue between his teeth as he lined up his shot. With a flourish, he launched his ball. It landed near mine in the rough. Surprising that he'd actually made contact.

I walked casually past Reuben. "How's things with Philip?"

"Dad?" He fell in step next to me. "Oh, you know. Evil schemes. World-domination plans. Probably working on a piranha tank to torture his rivals."

This was rich coming from the son my father had chosen. Philip Thorner had destroyed my mother. He'd made my life a living hell. This kid didn't know how good he'd had it. I located my ball within the long grass. *You'll never make it, boy. You're good for nothing.* I lined up the shot and launched the ball. It bounced nicely onto the green and rolled gently toward the pin.

Planting his feet, Reuben swung his club. The shot was clean enough to make the ball leap back onto the green. A smile of pride lit his face. This was my chance to probe him while his guard was down.

"Anything new with the business?"

"Dad doesn't talk to me about business stuff." He adjusted his ridiculous baseball cap. "But this is great, isn't it? Me and you hanging out. This is what I've always wanted. A chance for us to get to know each other. Maybe we could get Lucas and Theo to come next time? The four of us brothers hanging out?"

Lucas maybe, but Theo? Not a chance. Theo was as sociable as a rottweiler after a tooth extraction. On the green, I tapped the ball lightly with my putter. It landed just short of the hole. Irritation tightened my hands around the club. *You need to toughen up, boy. Your mother made you soft.*

Reuben tilted his chin and surveyed the grounds. "It's beautiful up here, isn't it?"

It was, but I was itching to get back to London. Time out of the office always made me angsty, and now I had an engagement ring to shop for, a wedding to plan, and Charlotte to get back to. She'd looked a little lost at the London house. It probably wasn't the right place. I had to find somewhere for her to stay where she'd be comfortable.

Reuben slapped his cap back on his head backward. "Oh, there was one thing. You'll never guess who Dad had over to dinner the other night. Gabe Rivers."

I kept my voice level. "Gabe Rivers, huh?"

Reuben readjusted his position and drew his club back. He fired his ball just short of the pin. "They're in talks about a hotel in Rome."

You better be fucking kidding. "La Dolce Vita?"

Reuben shrugged. "Sounds right."

I brought my club down too sharply and missed the ball. No way. Absolutely no fucking way was he getting his hands on that hotel. Why did he even want it? La Dolce Vita had been Mum's favorite vacation spot. It was fucked up that my father wanted it after what he'd done, like a serial killer removing their victim's finger as a trophy. All the times I'd try to talk to Gabe about it and he'd sell to my father? Over my dead body.

"How far has he got with it?"

"Not far. He hasn't made a formal offer yet. But you know what he's like. He won't give up."

No, he wouldn't do that. A stubborn streak was as much a part of the Thorner genome as this fucking nose. My father must have caught wind of my plans. It wouldn't be the first time. Now, he was out to sabotage me. If Reuben had nothing more to tell me, then I needed to jump on this immediately.

Reuben putted his ball. He flashed a shit-eating grin and shrugged. "Beginner's luck."

Smug fucker. I should have done better on that first swing. This was a waste of time. I'd had enough. Enough of Reuben's grinning selfies and his vertigo-inducing outfit. It wound me up just look-ing at him.

I pulled out my phone and sent my PA a message to ready the jet. "Work emergency. We'll have to cut this short."

Reuben's face dropped. "Already? We've only just started."

"You know how it is. Work comes first."

His laugh was all white teeth. "You've got it twisted, Bro. Work to live, not live to work."

My father had wanted an heir, and instead he had a work-shy kid who spent his time racing fast cars and lazing around on yachts. Reuben hadn't worked a day in his life. Hurtling around a racetrack like a madman didn't count. Dad had played the worst game of poker when he'd left us for a new family. He'd twisted when he should have stuck.

He held up his phone on his selfie stick and flashed a hopeful smile. "One with my bro for the grid?"

Nope. "Goodbye, Reuben."

"Another time? I'll ask Lucas and Theo to come." His imploring voice chased me across the fairway.

Good luck with that.

◆ ◆ ◆

I phoned Theo from the office. He answered on the fourth ring. *Sloppy.*

"I'm in the middle of something." His voice was a derisive growl.

And people called me the arsehole brother. Theo's charm knew no bounds. "I need your help. Philip's not going to be happy with me in the coming days."

"What have you done now?"

"He wants a new hotel. I'm going to make sure he doesn't get what he wants. But it's only fun if it blindsides him. He mustn't know what I'm planning until I'm ready."

My father always knew what I was up to. Anyone else would have called me paranoid, but not Theo. Theo knew what Philip Thorner was capable of. I'd long suspected my father had spies in my company. Rooting them out wasn't easy.

Strange noises filtered down the phone: clanking metal, thuds, grunting. It sounded like he was at the gym or some kind of orgy. Theo was such a dark horse it could have been either, or both. An orgy in a gym was probably a perfect Sunday morning for Theo. He never took a call with video. Only ever voice.

"You haven't wound him up enough already? People heal, Cole. They try to move on."

I'll heal in hell. It was easy for him to say. He'd moved out as soon as he could. "Philip hasn't moved on. He won't leave me alone."

"He would. If only you'd stop poking him. He's like a wasp at a picnic. Just keep still and don't flap your hands so much and he'll buzz off."

Yes, he was a wasp, and he'd spread too much venom. He'd ruined my picnic. He'd ruined my fucking life. "Are you going to help me or not?"

A deep sigh. "I know a counterespionage specialist. We'll set up surveillance. Scan for bugs. Standard cybersecurity measures."

An ache blazed between my shoulder blades. I'd been up all night working, and my spine wasn't happy. "I need thorough security countermeasures and monitoring of threats."

I could hear his condescending smile in his gravelly voice. "I know what you need. I'm on it."

"What do you know about Gabe Rivers?"

"The football club boss? Not much. He was on the party circuit when he was younger. Bit wild. Seems to have settled down."

"I need a meeting with him, but he won't take my calls."

Theo snorted. "Sensible man."

Idly, I lifted a silver ball on the Newton's cradle on my desk, watching the metal spheres tap lightly against each other. "If you hear anything about his whereabouts, let me know. I'm not averse to accidentally bumping into him somewhere."

"Stalking him, you mean?"

He sounded nonplussed by the prospect. Theo's security firm had an impeccable reputation. On the surface, everything was above board. My brother was a war hero with a medal for bravery, but he'd come back from Helmand different in a way I couldn't put my finger on. It wasn't just the physical scars. It was something rippling beneath the surface. A darkness that I didn't like to think about too much.

"Just some light stalking," I said.

A pause. "I know he's hosting a big fundraising shindig next week. Lots of high-profile people. I've got my team running security on a few attendees."

"Perfect. I need a ticket."

"Then get one."

The line went dead. Prickly fucker was always hanging up on me. I swiveled in my chair to take in the jagged London skyline through the expanse of floor-to-ceiling windows: the shining ribbon of the Thames, Big Ben, the Houses of Parliament. Clouds drifted in a clear blue sky. A warm feeling spread through me. What a beautiful day to fuck with my father. It always gave me a smile.

I put a call through to my PA. "I need a ticket for Gabe Rivers's charity fundraiser next week."

"Just one?"

Actually, no. This was the ideal time to debut my charming new fiancée. "Make it two."

Chapter 12

CHARLOTTE

Harrods. I'd seen it on the TV. How surreal to be walking inside a building so iconic. Enticing smells drifted from the fragrance counter. We passed by busy high-end boutiques and displays of sparkly handbags and shoe heaven full of brands that I'd only ever dreamed of owning: Gucci, Prada, Valentino.

Cole glided over the marble floor with so much authority, I almost had to jog to keep up with his long strides. He looked like a million dollars in his elegant suit and polished brogues. I glimpsed my fuzzy yellow jumper, denim skirt, and rainbow tights in a shop window. I could hardly argue when he'd said we needed to go shopping. Most of my clothes were from vintage and charity shops, and I didn't want to stick out at his fancy events.

We passed through a home goods store and my heart pounded. Everything looked crazy expensive and fragile. It would be so easy to swing my handbag and accidentally smash a priceless vase. I stopped to look at a tiny bejeweled ornamental dog.

Cole watched me. "You want it?"

"It's an ornamental sausage dog that costs two thousand pounds. What would I do with it?"

"Put it on the mantelpiece and look at it?"

"I'd rather put two grand on my mantelpiece and look at that."
I moved to admire a cabinet of glossy plates and bowls.

"You like this stuff?"

"I loved throwing pots at art school." *It was about the only thing I had loved there.*

He raised a dark brow. "Why exactly were you throwing the pots?"

"It's what they call it when you shape clay on a wheel. Throwing."

"But you stopped? You couldn't *throw pots* at home?"

"I didn't have time or space. You need a wheel, a kiln, and a glazing area. It's not a cheap hobby."

He pressed his lips together thoughtfully, but said nothing further. I dragged myself away from the delicate porcelain. Cole wasn't hurrying me, but he had to have better things to do than this. We carried on up the grand central escalator until racks of glittering dresses caught my eye.

"I can handle this alone, you know. I don't want to drag you around dress shopping like one of those beleaguered boyfriends you see sitting outside the women's changing rooms on a Saturday morning."

"I don't feel beleaguered. I had my PA clear my diary."

I raised a skeptical eyebrow. He was probably here because he wanted to make sure I chose the right thing for his image. Cole knew far more than me about fashion. He always looked impeccable. I followed him toward racks brimming with stunning sparkly frocks. A beautiful long midnight-blue Vivienne Westwood gown hung at the front of one rack. I couldn't resist feeling the luxurious fabric between my fingers.

"Try it on," he said.

"It's seven thousand pounds."

His crisp voice took on a commanding edge. "I didn't ask the price."

This was a dress for a long, elegant, willowy woman. Not me. A song drifted to my ears above the low, ambient chatter and bustle. "Cheek to Cheek" by Fred Astaire. A number from one of Dad's favorite old musicals. The song hurtled me back to the house. It was just the two of us in the living room. *The scent of shaving cream. The rasp of whiskers against my face when I kissed him on the cheek.* Sometimes, music had been the only way to reach him. When he'd been confused and upset, I'd put this song on to soothe him.

A lump wedged in my throat. The lights overhead dazzled. Everything in this place was too sparkly and bright and showy. This wasn't me. I didn't own any designer dresses. It was weird to even contemplate trying on a seven-thousand-pound dress.

"This was a mistake," I said.

"What?"

All of it. I shouldn't be here. "Sorry, it's this song."

He raised a questioning eyebrow.

"It was one of Dad's favorites."

His eyes, which were usually cold, glittered with unexpected compassion. "Let's get you back. I'll go alone tonight. It's too soon."

No. This was why I was here. To help Cole. This is what I'd signed up for. I sucked in a deep breath. "It's fine. I'll be fine. Sometimes I'm OK. Sometimes I'm not. Grief is complicated, I guess. Dad was ill for so long. We knew it was coming, but it doesn't make it easier . . ."

He searched my face. "I understand. You want to give this party a miss, just say the word. I don't mind."

"No. I want to find a dress, and I want to come with you to the party. Dad would have wanted us to carry on." I pasted on a trembling smile.

He studied my face carefully, then signaled to a shop assistant hovering nearby. "Excuse me. Can you help my . . ." He paused and a small line formed between his brows. He cleared his throat. "Can you help my *fiancée* find something special for a ball tonight? She'd like to try this on."

Fiancée. I waited for the assistant to laugh at the audacity of someone like me being engaged to this flawless man and wanting to try on this seven-thousand-pound dress, or some other sign that we'd been rumbled, but she flashed a broad smile. "Of course. Right this way, please."

I stepped out of the dressing room. The dress clung to my body, pulling tight over my chest and hips to give my curves a sleeker silhouette than I was used to. It was like glimpsing a stranger in the mirror. This woman looked like a movie star on the red carpet. The only problem was my cleavage. I'd barely squeezed one boob into this dress, let alone two.

"Well? Will I do?"

Cole's eyes traveled over me like he was trying not to look too hard but couldn't help himself. I did a funny curtsy with a flourish because I couldn't meet his eyes. Everything about this was odd. I'd had to adjust to the idea that I'd never see this man again. Now, we were here, doing this. We didn't feel like friends, but not like strangers either. It was some weird gray area full of awkwardness, misplaced familiarity, and tension.

"You look . . ." His eyes widened slightly before he smoothed his expression. A tell in his usual cold poise. "It's a beautiful dress."

I twirled in the mirror and the cool fabric rippled deliciously against my skin. "The problem is that it's strapless."

"Why is that a problem?"

"I've got too much up top for strapless."

"I wouldn't say it's a problem," he murmured.

The heated look in his eyes made a warm shiver run up my spine. I tried to keep my expression nonchalant despite my racing heart. This was out of my comfort zone. I hadn't worn a fancy dress in so long, and never anything like this. It mattered that I looked the part. Cole was investing in me. It mattered that I could pull this off. Otherwise, I'd embarrass him in front of people he was trying to impress. I didn't want to embarrass myself either.

His approving gaze lingered so long on my body, it made my skin prickle with goosebumps. It was like being teenagers again. When we'd kissed, it was the first time a man had touched me. I could almost feel his thumb circling my nipple. My body flooded with heat.

"Cole?"

His eyes snapped to mine. "Hmm-mm?"

"Do I look OK?"

"Turn around."

I did a slow spin and his icy eyes held mine in the mirror.

He rocked back on his polished brogues. "You need to wear something that makes you feel good. Do you feel good?"

Everything sat just right. Classy and sexy. "I think it's incredible, but you don't think it's too much? Too . . . revealing?"

I adjusted the fabric over my cleavage, and his eyes tracked the movement. The way he was looking at me made my nipples firm into hard marbles. Now it looked even more indecent. His gaze dropped to my chest again and darted away. I had to stifle a laugh. It's like this man had never seen a pair of boobs before.

"You have seen boobs before, right?"

"Pardon?"

"Boobs? Like, for real in the flesh? You've touched other boobs besides mine, I hope."

The teasing words were out before I could stop them. It was the kind of thing I would have wound him up with when I'd caught him sneaking peeks at me when we were young.

A smirk pulled at his lips. Cole didn't flirt. He wasn't the type to play games. He just went after what he wanted. The tension eased from my shoulders when he swiftly changed the subject. "Shall we find some shoes to go with this?"

I let out a long sigh. Who was I kidding? I couldn't pull off a dress this flashy. "I'd better try something else."

"Please don't." His voice was rough and edged with authority. "I want you at my side tonight in this dress. Let's get you something sparkly to go with it. I want to see you dripping in diamonds."

God. He was flawless. So handsome and polished. So used to getting everything he wanted. The way he'd been looking at me made my skin hot and tight, but I couldn't lose my head. No emotions. No sex. Cole had shown a complete disregard for my heart in the past.

He was dangerous and I couldn't make any clear-headed decisions after the past couple of years I'd had. Better not to tease him or get sucked in. It wasn't my fault I had great boobs. He could look all he wanted, but only a fool would let him touch. I'd been a fool when I was younger. Not now.

I did another twirl in the mirror. My heart was still as heavy as a stone, but a glimmer of something light gripped me. If I had to go to some fancy event, then at least I'd look the part. As I turned back to the dressing room, I thought I heard him mutter under his breath.

"Best seven thousand pounds I've ever spent."

Chapter 13

Cole

The limousine glided through the city. Charlotte hadn't taken her eyes from the window. Blue was definitely her color, and I didn't give a fuck about straps or whatever she was worried about, because her perfect voluptuous tits had made it hard to form a coherent sentence. I couldn't stop myself from another glance to drink her in. She kept her face turned away. Her fingers fidgeted in her lap.

"Nervous?"

She turned to meet my eyes. Her hair fell in lush dark waves, and crimson glossed her lips. A dazzling diamond choker sparkled at her throat. "Aren't you? This could go spectacularly wrong."

"In what way?"

She glanced at the partition between us and the driver and lowered her voice to a whisper. "In the way that I don't want to mess it up. What if someone figures out what's going on?"

"Why would they?"

She dropped her voice even lower. "Because people might ask questions, and I don't want to embarrass myself. What if we get quizzed? We hardly know each other anymore."

"We know the important things. It will be fine. Everyone at these events is fake. No one asks questions because they care about the answers. Just follow my lead. This is the perfect dry run. Nobody that matters is here."

Her hand fluttered to her diamond earring. "It's going to be full of fancy people. This isn't the kind of place I fit in."

"Look at me, Charlotte."

She snapped her gaze to mine.

"You fit in anywhere you want to fit in. You look incredible. Just be yourself. If anyone makes you feel uncomfortable, then you tell me."

A small smile pulled at her lips. "And if anyone asks about the wedding? We haven't discussed it yet."

Fine. Now was as good a time as any. "I don't care how we do it. A wedding is just an admin task in front of an audience."

"Admin with an audience?" She shook her head and let out the smallest chuff of laughter. "Pass the smelling salts, please. I might swoon."

I tried not to stare at her mouth. I wanted to make her laugh again. "Am I wrong?"

"I don't think that's how most people approach it."

"It's how we're approaching it. I just have to make sure it's the right audience. I'm thinking something low-key so it's less pressure to perform. Close family and friends for the service, then afterward we'll have a reception with the people I need to schmooze. How does that sound?"

Her jaw clenched, and she turned her face back to the dark city rushing by outside. "How soon?"

"As soon as possible."

"Can we do it back home?"

"Ecclesdale?"

It wasn't a bad idea. It would sell it nicely to the shareholders. A twee little venue in Yorkshire. It's not what any of them would expect from me. They could take all that charm and authenticity and shove it up their arses. "Yes. If you like."

"I always imagined Dad walking me down the aisle." She kept her face turned to the window. "But anywhere will do. It's not real, anyway."

My fingers itched to wrap around her hand and give her some reassurance, but we had boundaries in the contract for a reason. It was bad enough that the sight of her in that dress was giving me a hard-on. *Get it together.* This wasn't a party. I was here with one purpose: pin Gabe Rivers down to a meeting. A charming fiancée on my arm would be my secret weapon.

Shit. How could I forget the most important part? Reaching into the pocket of my tux, I pulled out the ring box.

"Here." I put the box into Charlotte's hands. "For you."

"What is it?"

Hesitantly, she flipped the lid. The enormous diamond glinted in the cool blue limo lights.

"It's emerald cut. Internally flawless."

It had cost six million, but that might be an overwhelming piece of information to absorb. She peered down at the ring in my hands and brushed her finger over the glittering diamond.

"This is too much. I don't know how my finger is going to stand the weight of it." Her eyes drifted over me and they held a hint of wonder. "So this is our official engagement?" Her expression turned wry. "I take it you're not going to get on one knee?"

"I'm afraid I don't kneel for anyone anymore, Charlotte."

She gave me a long, probing look, as though she was trying to peel back the years and uncover the person she'd once known. The Cole she was looking for was long gone. No hope of finding him. No wonder she looked faintly disappointed. The engine's hum filled the tense hush between us. Warmth climbed the back of my neck and I turned my face away to take in the bright city lights blinking past outside.

The journey passed in silence until we pulled up at the entrance to the Natural History Museum. Charlotte sucked in a sharp breath. I turned to face her and took in the engagement ring newly glittering on her finger. *Mine.*

I gave her a nod. "Remember, just be yourself. Don't oversell it. Let me do the talking."

Her shoulders were tense, but she fixed on a sardonic smile. "Fine. No overselling. Let's just go and pretend to be madly in love."

Chapter 14

CHARLOTTE

Dramatic lighting illuminated the grand entrance of the museum. Candlelight glinted from sweeping stone staircases and Romanesque arches.

"What a place for a party." I stared awestruck at the spectacular blue whale skeleton suspended from the ceiling.

Elegant guests in their finery gathered in small groups, or danced. The low, resonant melody from a string quartet bounced from the Victorian architecture and tall ceilings. Nothing in Ecclesdale could ever have prepared me for this. It was like stepping onto the set of a fancy BBC period drama. Cole had lied. This wasn't just any old party. It was a grand ball.

Cole plucked a champagne flute from a passing server and handed it to me. I'd have to resist the urge to get plastered, and pace myself. The place was full of famous people. I'd already spotted one of the Rolling Stones. Cole was scanning the sea of tuxedos and sparkling gowns on the dance floor with casual disinterest. His eyes landed on something at the back of the room and recognition flared in his expression.

"There's someone I need to talk to."

He smoothed his black tie. Not that it needed any adjustment. He was impeccably tailored, as usual. The sharp lines of his suit hugged his broad shoulders and his crisp white shirt was perfectly pressed.

He held out his arm. "Shall we?"

I slipped my arm through his. The solid contact at my side made heat course through me. His cologne hit my senses like a drug. He smelled delicious, spicy and sinful. I clung to his arm as he weaved across the crowded dance floor.

My stomach twisted with anticipation when I realized who we were making a beeline toward. Gabe Rivers. This was the chairman of Calverdale United. Dad had been a huge Calverdale fan. A couple of years ago, Gabe had been daily headline news fodder. He hadn't been in the tabloids as much of late, or maybe I just hadn't been paying as much attention to the world outside.

The sicker Dad got, the more insular life had become, until it felt like we were just living the same day on repeat. I never could have imagined I'd have a day like today. Being out somewhere so magical and full of life was a shock to the system.

"Oh my God. I know exactly who that is. He's even more handsome in the flesh," I muttered under my breath.

Cole shot me a look laced with amusement. Annoying that I hadn't had the restraint to keep my inner monologue internal.

"Try not to drool."

"I'm only human."

"I know, but don't forget you're supposed to be enamored with your new fiancé."

The dazzling smile slipped off Gabe's face and was replaced by wariness as we approached. Not surprising. Cole had been nothing but nice to me, but I couldn't help but notice most people seemed to be on guard around him. It was the aura he gave off, cold and controlled, like a coiled snake waiting to strike.

"Cole. It's been a while."

The two men shook hands and exchanged pleasantries.

"It's a pleasure to see you again. I'd love you to meet my fiancée, Charlotte."

Cole rested a possessive hand at the base of my spine. Warmth radiated through the fabric of my dress, and his thumb moved lightly back and forward, stroking. The light strokes reached much further, as though they'd found their way between my thighs. Tingles raced across my skin, and my cheeks flushed.

Gabe quirked a brow. "Fiancée? Congratulations."

We shook hands, but Cole's palm still rested at the small of my back and the contact was short-circuiting my brain. His little finger traced the bumps of my spine. My body stiffened in shock. It had been so long since a man had touched me. We probably should have rehearsed touching like this to at least give my poor ovaries a chance of acting normal after such a long dry spell.

"We were childhood sweethearts." Cole shot me a charming, indulgent look as he answered a question that no one had asked. "I went back home and all those feelings came rushing back. It was like we'd never been apart. I knew there was no way I could leave her behind. Isn't that right, darling?"

Darling. The rough tenor to the word sent a shiver through my body. I was too startled to do much else than nod. He sounded so convincing, even when he was talking utter bullshit. Cole had apparently found it very easy to leave me behind.

Gabe's tight expression relaxed a fraction. "When are you tying the knot?"

Cole slipped his hand around my waist and pulled me close. "As soon as possible. I can't wait to make this woman my wife."

Gabe nodded his approval. "Good for you. Married life is a treat. My wife is around here somewhere. We've got most of the team here tonight, celebrating. I'll have to introduce you."

Cole's thumb traced smooth circles at the base of my spine, and to my annoyance my body responded desperately. Heat curled through me and pooled in my lower belly. How embarrassing. It was hardly my fault. I hadn't had sex for at least a year. Maybe longer, and then it had just been some crap hookup. The giant whale carcass hanging from the ceiling watching this all unfold had probably seen more action than me.

I had a man who looked this hot and smelled this good touching me and gazing at me as though I was the only person in the room worth looking at. *Nope. I can't do this. This is inhumane. This situation requires more alcohol.*

I took a gulp of champagne, struggling to keep my composure. "My family has always supported Calverdale United."

Gabe smiled and lifted his glass. "Glad to hear it. You should come and watch the game next week."

Cole traced his thumb up my spine again. My nipples hardened painfully. It was probably some classical conditioning psychology from my teenage years, like a dog trained to salivate when a bell rings. Cole had been my first kiss, and now his touch was a bell clanging in my ear, even though my brain knew how dangerous he was. *Enough.* This man was terrorizing me with his sexiness.

"Excuse me," I whispered in Cole's ear. "I need to go to the ladies' room."

He frowned. "Everything OK?"

No. You're touching me and I like it too much.

"Fine." I knocked back the rest of my champagne. "Won't be long."

◆ ◆ ◆

Get it together. You can do this.

I stepped out of the bathroom. I'd been in there an unreasonably long time, but I'd had to wait until my breathing settled down. This was too much. This whole thing was a terrible idea. It wasn't as though it was going to get easier, either. This was a bunch of people that Cole had said he didn't even care about impressing. What about when we did this in front of people who knew him? At some point, we'd stand up in front of an audience and have to kiss.

My nose bumped into something solid. I stepped back, and a hand reached out to steady me. I'd crashed into a handsome man. But of course. It was impossible to step a foot in this place without being in the orbit of another indecently attractive posh person in formal wear.

"Excuse me. Are you OK?" The man spoke with an American accent that I hadn't been expecting.

I smoothed my hair. "Fine. Sorry. My fault."

He stuck out his hand. "Reuben Thorner. It's a pleasure to meet you."

"Thorner?"

He flashed a wide grin. "Yes. Did I see you arrive with Cole? I'm his brother."

A brother with an American accent? Really? Cole had rarely spoken about his family, but I knew he had two brothers: Lucas and Theo. I allowed my curious gaze to pass over the handsome stranger. There was some family resemblance, but not a lot. He had the Thorner height and dark hair, but he had an amiable smile and a playful glint in his eye. Not even a hint of brooding. Very un-Thorner-like.

"I'm actually a half-brother. I grew up in New York. I don't see Dad's side of the family as much as I'd like." Reuben followed my gaze to Cole. "Typical. My brother arrives with a beautiful woman on his arm and still spends the evening talking business." A strand of hair flopped casually over Reuben's forehead. He brushed it back with a flirtatious smile. "Cole is all work. He never switches off." He presented his arm. "Luckily, you bumped into the fun brother. Shall we dance?"

I couldn't help my laugh. "And you bumped into the fiancée."

His eyes widened with incredulity. "I'm sorry?"

I flashed him the ring so huge it looked like a candy ring sported by a toddler. "Cole and I are engaged."

His eyes widened further, as though it was preposterous. Perhaps it was. Cole probably turned up to these parties with a different woman every time. All of them no doubt more refined and elegant than me.

I waited for Reuben to burst out laughing and call me out for lying, but he chuckled genially and reached for my hand. "Well, in that case we're definitely dancing. I need to get to know my new sister-in-law."

Chapter 15

Cole

"You're not an easy man to get an audience with," I said.

Gabe's smile was noncommittal as he scanned the party. "The football club takes a lot of my time."

"I'm sure it does. I heard you're thinking of selling La Dolce Vita."

He raised an eyebrow. "Word travels fast."

"I didn't think you'd ever sell."

"Property was my father's interest. I'm not attached to the hotels. I'd rather invest in my team."

I lowered my voice. "Whatever my father offers, I will better it. Shall we get a meeting in the diary?"

Gabe's shrewd gaze roved over me. "This is a party. It's no time to talk shop."

"Fine, I'll have my people talk to yours. This week?"

He wrinkled his nose. "I don't think so. I'm not one to get in the middle of family drama."

"No drama. I just want to throw my hat in the ring if you're selling. You'll find me an easier person to do business with than my father."

He frowned. "I've heard a lot about you and your father, Cole. I get it. My dad could be a difficult man at times. Family grievances are never worth it. Life is too short, believe me."

"This is business. It's not personal. I'll make you the best offer."

"Not everything is about money." He flashed a charming smile, but his voice was firm. "My wife is waiting for me. Excuse me."

Gabe headed off into the soirée. *Fuck!* I eased my tie around my collar. It didn't matter. You only fail when you stop trying. Failure wasn't a viable option. I'd find a way in. My jaw ached with tension. I scanned the room full of fake-ass people having shallow conversations. I had to find my fiancée. She'd been so long she must have fallen down the toilet. I'd brought her here to make me look good, and she'd ditched me at the earliest available opportunity.

Among the sea of bodies, I spotted Charlotte in the arms of another man. Surprise froze me to the spot, but it morphed quickly to anger. *Fucking Reuben!* The sniveling little weasel had his hands all over her. I should have been the only one touching my fiancée, even a pretend one.

My fists clenched by my sides. Reuben was holding her too close, as if he had any right. Rage blistered through me. I wanted to plant my fist squarely in this bastard's face. I weaved toward them, but a firm hand on my shoulder stopped me.

"You never grow up, do you, boy?"

The bitter words sent a shudder through me. My blood ran cold. He wasn't supposed to be here. Theo had given me the guest list. This man wasn't on it. I steeled myself to turn around and face my father.

Sir Philip Thorner's cold eyes scanned me. "I saw you talking to Gabe Rivers."

He hadn't aged a day since I'd last had the misfortune of being in his orbit. His salt-and-pepper hair was perfectly coifed. His tux was immaculate. If Charlotte thought I looked like a vampire, then this was my sire. He'd taught me how to drain people dry in corporate boardrooms. How to toy with your prey before you sank your fangs into the jugular. Philip Thorner was a mean, soulless man. By the time he was done shaping me in his image, I wasn't much better.

His thin lips took on an amused twist. "Don't these little games get boring for you?"

When he spoke to me in that tone, I was a powerless kid again. Scared. Obedient. He'd bullied me. Made me feel out of control. *Never again.* "I don't know what you're talking about."

The strings of the violin screamed in my ear. His voice dropped to a vicious whisper.

"You're pathetic. Vindictive. Spiteful. Just like your mother. You won't go far like this."

He wanted an outburst from me. He'd never seen me as a person. Just as someone to criticize and belittle. I'd best him by not giving him what he wanted. I kept my tone level and composed. "Never speak about my mother again. You don't have the right. We've all moved on, Philip. I've changed. I'm not the man I was in New York."

"Changed? Don't kid yourself. You're a Thorner. Men like us don't change." He leaned in closer, forcing me to inhale his sour old-man cologne. "That hotel is mine. Stay out of it."

"Why do you even want it? What does it matter to you?"

"It's the best hotel in Rome. Why wouldn't I want it?"

The truth flickered in his eyes. He wanted it because he knew what it would do to me. He wanted it because my mother had loved it. And I'd loved her. *I need to get Charlotte the fuck out of here. I can't ever let him near her.* A wave of stark panic went through me. I'd made her vulnerable. I'd got cocky and selfish. What had I been thinking, bringing her into my world? My father destroyed everything I cared about. What if I couldn't protect her? I'd kept away from Ecclesdale for all these years. It should have stayed that way. I'd been weak.

I twisted and strode with purpose through twirling guests to where Reuben, the snake, had his hands on Charlotte.

"We're leaving."

Charlotte's eyes widened. "Already?"

Reuben frowned and swished Charlotte away, giving me his back. "Shame on you, Cole. This is terrible etiquette. Interrupting in the middle of a dance."

Rage exploded inside me at his stupid grin. Nothing made me sicker than coming face-to-face with my father when I was unprepared for battle. Reuben extended his hand so that Charlotte could do a twirl. She spun with a smile on her face, and he pulled her back to him. His approving eyes roved over her body, landing where her beautiful breasts curved above the bodice of her tight gown. Jealousy coursed through my blood, hot and sour like poison. He had no fucking right to look at her like that. How could she let him hold her? How could she be so at ease with the golden boy, of all people?

I fought to keep my voice low and level. "That's enough. Put your eyes back in their sockets and take your hands off my fiancée."

"You'll get her back, don't worry." Teasing sparkled in his eyes. He was always so carefree and fun. He'd lived such a charmed existence. That floppy hair and endlessly sunny disposition made me sick. Everything was always such a big fucking joke for him.

"You didn't warn me Philip would be here."

"And you didn't tell me you were engaged!" Reuben shook his head in surprise. "He changed his mind last minute. Apologies. I didn't know I needed to warn you."

My fingers burned to grab Reuben by the collar and shake that easy smile off his face. But causing a scene wouldn't serve my purpose here. Word would get back to Gabe, and I'd look like the problem. Philip Thorner would win.

"Take your hands off my fiancée."

Reuben laughed. "Someone is jealous. I told you, I'll give her back to you."

This bastard. My breath burned my lungs. The music was too loud. There were too many people. I had the strangest sensation, like I was in motion, driving a fast car with no brakes. My words exploded, raw and loud. "Remove your hands from my fiancée before I remove them from your fucking wrists."

Reuben frowned and held still. A couple of nearby dancers turned to look. Charlotte's lips parted in shock. Heat climbed the back of my neck. Fighting to keep any scrap of civility, I reached for Charlotte's hand.

"We're leaving. Now." My words came out as a rough command despite the guilty sensation creeping over me.

She snapped her hand away from me, surprise and hurt glittering in her eyes. This wasn't me. Not with her. I didn't give a fuck if the world thought I was an arsehole, but not Charlotte. I didn't want to lose my temper in front of her.

Her eyes searched my face. "What's the matter?"

"Nothing. Just do as I say."

Her expression filled with belligerence, and she folded her arms. "Do as you say?"

I glanced over my shoulder, scanning for my father. He'd still be lurking around here somewhere. My pulse pounded a sickening rhythm in my throat. *I need to get out of here.* "I brought you here, and now it's time to go."

She clamped her jaw tight and stared. Her breasts curved above her folded arms and I fought not to let my gaze wander down. She looked magnificent. No wonder Reuben had headed straight for her and put his filthy hands all over what was mine.

"I was dancing with Reuben since he's the only one here who asked me to dance," she said.

I took a deep breath. Regaining my composure was all that mattered. That's what I'd learned in New York. The world could be falling apart and, as long as you didn't let it show, everything would be fine. Philip Thorner didn't get to make me feel like this anymore. I'd have him dancing to my tune soon enough. No one got to make me feel out of control.

"I'm not messing around here, Charlotte. It's time to go."

We stared at each other, each assessing the other's annoyance. Her frown deepened before she unfolded her arms. She gave Reuben a nod. "It was nice to meet you, Reuben. Thank you for the dance."

She gave me an unimpressed look before she sauntered ahead of me through the crowd.

Chapter 16

"I'm paying you for your loyalty. If you plaster yourself all over another man in public again, the deal is off."

Cole hadn't spoken a word to me on the limo ride back to his place. He'd just sat there seething and communicating in increments of increasing jaw torsion. Then he chose this as his opening gambit? *Plastering myself?*

"People are right about you. You're an arsehole online and IRL." I dropped my clutch bag on the side table and ripped off the Saint Laurent heels my poor feet had been stuffed into. "What is your problem? A man asked me to dance. So what?"

His lips thinned in displeasure. "None of that was about you."

I hopped around on the cold marble, alternately rubbing each aching foot. "No, because heaven forbid a man might want to dance with me!"

Cole held perfectly still in the large marble foyer. He measured me with a calculating stare. Despite his inscrutable expression and polished veneer, something dangerous rolled beneath his cold poise. This wasn't the Cole I knew. Years had passed between us, but I'd never seen him this upset. He'd always been so reserved and self-possessed. Cole was like if "unbothered" had a next level. He didn't lose his temper or lash out. Something was rattling him. Something really big. *What has this life done to you to get you so twisted up like this?*

"You could have danced with anyone there but him."

"He's your brother. What do you think is going to happen?"

"That man is not my brother. He was doing it on purpose to make me jealous, and you walked right into it."

This thing between us was supposed to be civil and emotionless. I'd been trying to blend in. I'd been doing what he'd asked me to do. Anger surged through me, but I didn't even try to be a good girl and suppress it. It felt good. Wild and powerful.

He came close, looking down at me intently with his glacial glare. "Do you like him?"

"What?"

"Do you find Reuben attractive?"

I threw my arms wide, exasperated. "So what if I do? These things don't happen to me. I never have handsome men asking me to dance at fancy balls."

"Handsome? That clown? Did he offer you something? To spy for him?"

"Of course not. Do you realize how paranoid you sound?"

"What did you talk about?"

You. All we talked about was you. I wouldn't give him the satisfaction of knowing. His head was already too big. "It's none of your business. I could have fucked him in an alley around the back of the building and it would still be none of your business."

His eyebrows hitched, and he stepped back as though I'd slapped him. Had I shocked him? The good girl he'd left behind in Ecclesdale had rarely sworn. But then, she'd never had to deal with the things I had over the past couple of years. I'd watched my father's slow decline and been powerless to stop it. A grown man having a tantrum because of petty jealousy wasn't about to faze me.

His voice was composed but it held a lethal edge. "Don't mistake my generosity for weakness, Charlotte. I'm paying you an inordinate amount for a service. Please take some time to review the contract. I expect your loyalty in public, at least."

Generosity? Like I wasn't doing him a favor too, signing up for this farce. This marriage was his idea, not mine. I could still walk away. "That's right. You're paying for a service. You don't own me. The contract doesn't control my thoughts or my desires. Maybe I just wanted to feel something different for a change."

Something light and exciting. "Maybe I wanted him to take me home tonight. I'm not the sweet, innocent girl you left behind. I'm not a nun, Cole. Yes, I found him attractive. Most would. He's objectively handsome. So what?"

Everybody around me had spent their twenties screwing around and making mistakes. I hadn't. He couldn't blame me for getting swept up in a moment.

His voice was low and calm, but somehow more chilling than when he'd snapped. "That's what you were looking for? A chance to feel something different?"

Yes. No. Maybe. "Tonight was a lot for me. You didn't warn me you were going to touch me like that or look at me like that."

He watched me with a somber expression. "Like what?"

"You know like what."

He gave an irritable tug of his sleeve. "I made you uncomfortable?"

Yes. But not in the way he was worrying about. "It's something I'll have to adjust to. It's been a long time since a man touched me, if you must know."

"How long?"

Long enough that my hymen had probably regrown. Looking after Dad hadn't left much scope for meeting men. "It doesn't matter."

He searched my face, his eyes questioning. "You're not . . . ? There have been other men?"

I batted my eyelashes with faux innocence. "No, Cole. I've been saving myself for you. All these years, I've waited."

His brow arched in concern. "You have?"

I couldn't help my laugh at the surprise in his eyes. "I'm joking. It's just been a while, that's all. I'm not used to . . . physical stuff."

His eyes narrowed. "How many men?"

"You don't get to ask me that."

He pierced me with his brooding gaze. I saw it then—a flicker in the inscrutable depths of those beautiful eyes. He wasn't just angry, he was struggling. He looked like a drowning man fighting an undercurrent. Something was very wrong. *What is going on inside that head of yours?* An ache speared my chest. Some stupid urge made me want to reach out and touch his face, to comfort him, to throw him a lifeline. But I didn't dare.

"You'll need to get used to the physical stuff. It would be a mistake to kiss for the first time again in the church with everyone watching. We should rehearse it so it doesn't freak you out or look too staged. We need to get it out of the way beforehand," he said.

I'd told him the touching made me feel weird and his take-home message was to do more? How had we gone from arguing to talking about kissing? My heart thumped. Cole had run away from me once before and broken me. He'd do the same again given half a chance. I had to stick to the contract and keep this a business arrangement. If I played this right, I'd walk out of here with a life-changing amount of money. I could do anything with five million. This man didn't get to have any sway over my emotions. I had to let him kiss me and have it mean nothing.

"Fine. Kiss me, if that's what you want." I rolled my shoulders back in defiance.

He stepped closer, his eyes blazing. "Is it what you want?"

My breathing came too sharp and erratic. "It makes sense."

"I agree."

He ripped off his jacket and threw it over the grand piano. Angrily, he removed his cuff links, tossed them next to his jacket, and rolled his crisp white shirtsleeves to the elbows. Dark hair dusted his defined forearms. This man had never done a day's hard graft in his life, but he had the muscular arms of a laborer. How was it even possible?

His jaw clenched, and his breath was shallow. "Well? How do you want to start?"

I dragged my eyes away from his forearms. *Now?* Anger made my heart pound, but I couldn't deny the pull to give in to the tension that bound us so tightly. To give up the fight and melt into him.

"It's a wedding kiss. That means tasteful and respectful. Just imagine we've tied the knot." I tilted my chin up and adopted a low, solemn voice. "You may now kiss the bride."

A brief flicker of amusement pulled at his full lips. "Who's that supposed to be?"

"I don't know. The celebrant."

He swept a loose strand of hair from my cheek and propped it behind my ear. "Oh."

My pulse pounded in my throat. I lifted my chin higher. Every fiber of my being screamed for me to close the gap between us. "Are you going to get on with it, then?"

His eyes dropped to my lips. "I don't like to be rushed."

No. I knew that, but there was something new flickering in his eyes—anticipation? Desire? He lifted his hand to my face and smoothed his thumb over my cheekbone. Electricity crackled between us, raw and volatile.

"I like to take my time," he said.

"It's not about taking your time. It's about practice—"

His soft lips pressed against mine, warm and tentative, stealing my words. A rush of nerves made my body hot and heavy. His other hand rested on my throat, and his mouth caressed mine in a kiss that was so gentle it was barely touching, yet persuasive enough to send my stomach into wild swirls. He tasted sweet, like the orange juice he'd been drinking at the party.

Cole had kissed me once before, many years ago, and now my body had some strange sense that those intervening years were nothing and we were picking up where we'd left things that day. As though he hadn't broken my heart. As though the past years hadn't broken my spirit.

Cole's warm mouth and his thumb resting gently at the pulsing hollow of my throat made everything evaporate. It was just me and him. A deep sense of peace dissolved the nerves in my chest. *Me and Cole.* And for one reckless moment, my heart wanted to pretend that the years in between the last meeting of our lips were melting away. That time meant nothing. That not a day had passed. We were just kids in love. I'd always been his, and he'd always been mine. Our lips were always meant to be doing this.

His tongue glided into my mouth and against mine. There shouldn't have been tongue. This was supposed to be a wedding kiss in front of an audience. Chaste and sweet. Not whatever was going on here. This was escalating wildly into groping and grinding against each other. His probing tongue explored every inch of my mouth. His cock pressed against me, and it felt thick and hard. Flames crept over my skin. My fingers curled into his soft hair. *I should stop this. God, I don't want it to stop.*

He cupped my breast through my dress and moaned against my neck. Heat pooled between my thighs, along with an unbearable ache. I'd never have taken this measured control-freak man for a moaner. My back hit the wall. With a hand either side of my head, he boxed me in. His lips traveled along my jaw and down my throat. I should have pulled away, but I was too high on him to protest. High on his scent, the relentlessness of his lips, the feel of his hard chest pressed to mine. We were practically dry-humping each other. This was dirty and unexpected, but so fucking hot and intoxicating. My body was still responding to him like a horny teenager, whether I wanted it or not—racing heart, weak knees, fluttering stomach.

"I need to touch you." His voice was thick and unsteady in my ear.

"Do whatever you want." I sounded needy and desperate, but I was too turned on to be embarrassed.

One hand wrapped around my ass, squeezing, and the other slipped up my inner thigh. With a deft hand, he pulled my underwear down and drew a finger through my folds, parting me. There was no resistance. The wetness at my core slicked my thighs. A groan escaped him, and it was the most erotic sound I'd ever heard. His knee nudged between my legs, and his finger came to rest lightly on my swollen clit. My body set alight. My breath came in shuddery gasps.

"You're my fiancée. I brought you here for me. No one else. Do you understand?" He whispered the words hotly against my collarbone, like a prayer. He rubbed my clit in a smooth, light motion that made my toes curl.

"If you want a man to touch you, then you ask me. If you want to feel something different, I'm willing to oblige."

Somehow, I found words to speak. "This isn't in the contract."

"We can amend the contract."

"I'm sure we can when it suits you."

He slipped a long finger inside me, silencing me. His words were rough against my ear. "That's right, sweetheart. My contract. My rules."

A moan left my lips. I wanted to surrender. I needed to fall apart and let him put me back together again. I shouldn't have wanted it, but the ache was unbearable. He worked my clit in firm circles. It usually took me a long time to orgasm, but pleasure sparked at the base of my spine and rolled behind my hips. I could barely breathe from the need to come. My legs began to shake. The sensation was so intense, a whimper left my mouth. He watched every play of emotion on my face as he worked me with his expert fingers. Another shuddering whimper escaped me.

A slight smirk curved his lips. His crisp voice was icy and aloof. "I know, baby. It feels good, doesn't it? Your pussy feels so good for me, too. Are you dripping like this for me or for him?"

He couldn't even help being a condescending prick when he was doling out more pleasure than should have been humanly possible.

I sucked in a few desperate gasps of air. "You're jealous? Is that what this is?"

"I took you to that party to be with me, not him. You're never going to let him touch you again."

He curled his finger, hitting a spot that made my pussy clench. My breath left me with a strange hissing sound. I couldn't stop myself from grinding shamelessly against his hand.

"Say it." He slipped in another finger and held perfectly still.

"Say what?"

He withdrew his fingers sharply.

"Fuck!" I clamped my thighs together to soothe the desperate need.

He interlaced his fingers with mine and pinned my hands high above my head against the wall. "Tell me what I want to hear. You'll never let him touch you again."

I was so close to the edge, I would have said anything to make him carry on. "Please. Don't stop."

"As much as I enjoy hearing you beg, I need you to tell me you'll never let Reuben touch you again."

Of course I wouldn't. What did I care about Cole's brother when I had Cole touching me like this? Reuben was lovely. He was gorgeous and charming in a bumbling, sincere way, but golden retriever men weren't my type. My type had always been Cole. Only Cole. I looked him squarely in the eyes. "Reuben who?"

"Good girl." He drove two fingers back inside of me, filling me, curling upward. His thumb played with my clit in unyielding, deliberate strokes.

"Stay away from him. Stay away from my father."

"I didn't even know your father was there."

"Good."

He tugged down the zip at the back of my dress and freed my breasts. He groaned as he pulled my bra cups aside and buried his face in my cleavage. The indecent slippery sound of his fingers pumping into me as he sucked on my nipples made my face hot.

"Dripping all over my hand. You needed this, didn't you, Charlotte?"

Yes. I needed it. But it's too much. Not enough. It had been so long. Too long since I'd felt any pleasure in my body. His lips found mine again, and he kissed me deeply, smothering my moans. I'd forgotten this kind of unbearable, raw aliveness. The sparking heat of skin against skin. He latched onto my nipple with his mouth and sucked hard. Release ripped through me, sudden and overwhelming, like a river bursting its dam. I was coming. Coming harder than I ever had in my life. A stream of indecipherable sounds left my lips. I cried out and buried my face into his shoulder. His masculine scent filled my nose, and I breathed him in.

"Eyes on me," he commanded. "See who makes you feel this good."

I gripped his shoulder tightly and lifted my face to meet his gaze. His inscrutable eyes held mine as I shook with release. He didn't stop soothing my clit until every tremor left my body and I collapsed limp against him, still quivering and panting.

The contract had been ridiculous, but it was important. We both knew where we stood. This shouldn't have happened. He stepped away, still watching me intently. I yanked my dress down from around my hips and smoothed it. Orgasms complicated matters that could have been straightforward. I really shouldn't have let that happen.

What had just come to pass wasn't funny, but a dark humor gripped me, and I couldn't help myself. It was ridiculous. My life had become ridiculous. I had to find the humor in it or I'd fall to the floor and weep. A laugh bubbled up and burst out of me. It echoed around the still entrance hall.

He raised a dark brow. "Something amusing?"

"I was just thinking that was a good effort, but we might need to tone it down for the big day."

"Agreed." He arched a dark brow and smoothed his shirt. "It's going to need some work."

Chapter 17

COLE

Music has always soothed me, and after what had just transpired, I needed to calm the fuck down. At the piano, my fingers moved over the keys. Schubert's "Ave Maria" began to take shape—a favorite of my mother's. I surrendered to the tender melody as though it was something organic that could reach inside of me and untangle the anguished knot that had tightened since laying eyes on my father.

I'd lost control with Charlotte. The look on her face when I'd had her writhing on my fingers would be emblazoned in my mind forever. I'd never forget the feel of her slickness. The smell of her. I'd just made myself come so hard in the shower, but it wasn't enough. My body was fevered. It wouldn't be enough until I could sink into her and feel her bucking and clenching around my cock.

I felt her presence in the doorway before she'd said a word. My body always had a sense of her in a room. My eyes were always searching for her.

I stopped playing. "How long have you been standing there?"

"Not long." She drifted closer. "You play so beautifully." Her hand hovered over my shoulder before she withdrew it quickly. "Don't stop on my account. Please. I'd love to hear more."

I twisted on the piano stool to drink her in. A lilac silk gown wrapped around her curves, and her dark hair fell damp from the shower in a cascade down her back. I never played for an audience, but I couldn't deny her anything. It wasn't a particularly difficult piece, not the kind I'd play to impress someone, but I carried on with it regardless.

I let my fingers caress the keys. The music wound around me in invisible threads. Every note so intense in the stillness. Memories of a time when life was simple rushed over me. *Charlotte and me riding our bikes in the woods. Sun dappling through trees. Charlotte's laughter ringing in my ears. Pure freedom.*

The song reached its gentle climax, a break in the tension, before I finished the piece. Silence swept around us. Charlotte's head bowed low. She looked as sad as the day of her father's funeral. I'd brought her here to soothe her sorrow, but tonight I'd made it worse. A heavy weight compressed my chest.

"I overreacted earlier. I apologize. Reuben pushes my buttons." I patted the seat next to me on the piano stool.

She sat. Her shoulder brushed mine, and her floral fragrance hit my nose. She kept her gaze fixed on the keys. "He seems harmless enough."

"He's in my father's pocket. I don't trust him."

She shot me a tentative look. "You don't talk about your father. You went to work for him, but you don't anymore?"

"That's right."

She nodded, encouraging me to continue. The words wedged somewhere between my heart and my throat and I pushed them back down. No point in trying to explain my fucked-up family. It would only make me look weak. "About what just happened between us—"

"Forget it. We can pretend it didn't."

"Is that what you want?"

"It's better if we stick to the contract."

I spread my fingers over the keys. "We could amend the contract."

"Orgasms but not feelings, right? You already told me you don't have a heart."

"Sex and feelings are two different things. You have physical needs that I'm happy to satisfy. We can keep them separate. It doesn't have to be deep."

She shook her head and her mouth curved in a sarcastic smile. "Not deep. Of course."

Her silk gown had a Japanese pattern, cherry blossoms and temples. My fingers itched to slide her robe down, sweep her hair to the side, and plant kisses along the bare skin of her shoulders. To trace the curve of her neck with my lips.

"I've been clear about what I can give to this. I don't have time for or interest in a relationship. It's not me. It's not what I want. But it's clear we have chemistry. I can make you feel good if you'll let me. Look at it as a pleasant distraction."

"I get it, Cole. You want casual. I've met men like you before. Emotionally unavailable. It's tiresome. You want a woman at your beck and call, but if she dares to want more from you, she's needy and demanding. You get twitchy if she leaves a toothbrush at your place."

I opened my mouth to protest, but there was some truth in her words, and maybe I'd got tired of it all. My friends were settled down. I couldn't deny that the past couple of years had felt lonely. I didn't have time for the emotional investment in a relationship. My energy had to be channeled elsewhere. If I was going to make my father pay for what he'd done to my mother, I had to stay focused. Emotions were something I couldn't afford, but low-effort hookups felt meaningless lately. I hardly bothered. That's why this was the ideal scenario. A wife on my own terms with orgasms thrown in to keep us both happy.

"Sex is just sex. It's a physical release. Whatever it is, our bodies respond to each other," I said.

"Yes, we have chemistry, but we also have history." She let out a deep sigh. "I can see this heading down a road I'm not going to like. It's better in the long term if we stick to the contract. You hurt me once before. I'd be an idiot to go there with you again. It's better to stop now."

She was making a good decision, but disappointment ground in my gut. "But you still want to marry me?"

She gave me a small smile. "I may as well. I'm here now, aren't I?"

As much as I longed for this woman in my bed, this would have to do. A marriage on paper. I could keep her close and take care of her. The craving would pass. I let my eyes linger on her one last time before I rose from the piano stool. It didn't feel right to bring her here. Charlotte didn't seem happy in the city. London wasn't good for the soul. I'd get her out of here. Take her to the countryside. Build her an art studio. Whatever it took to put a smile on her face.

"I have a place in the Cotswolds. I'm busy with work this week, but I'll take you to see it next week. Would you like that?"

She kept her face turned away. Her voice sounded a million miles away. "Sure. Whatever you want."

Chapter 18

We drove down one narrow, winding country lane after another, past acres of neatly trimmed hedgerows and quaint villages. The rolling fields dotted with sheep reminded me of home, except the Cotswolds were too polished. They lacked the rugged wildness of the Yorkshire countryside. Everything was neat and uniform. Pristine panoramas suited Cole, but they weren't for me. I missed the bitter wind and starkness of the moors.

After an endless trundle along a gravel driveway, Cole's driver drew to a halt. I looked out of the window and my mouth fell open. Ancient ivy-covered stone rose upward and outward at the heart of a sprawling estate. There were too many windows to count. This wasn't a house, it was a stately home.

Cole opened the car door for me and held out his hand. "We've got a tennis court, croquet lawn, gym, cinema, Estonian igloo sauna. Two pools, indoor and outdoor."

I stepped out into warm sunshine. "Estonian igloo sauna?"

"Yes."

"And why did you bring me here, exactly?"

"So you can have a look. You might prefer it out here. It's cozier than London."

Cozy? Maybe for a Saudi prince. I peered up at the turrets on the roof. "It's enormous."

He shrugged. "Space is good."

I spun, taking in the perfect expanse of immaculate countryside. It had been at least half an hour since we'd passed through a small village. This was even more remote than Ecclesdale.

"But you'll still be in London for work?"

"Yes. I'll come back when I can, to keep up appearances."

I'd probably never see him again. Was that the plan? Drop me off here in the middle of nowhere and pick me up again when he next needed me? It shouldn't have bothered me. This was what I'd agreed to.

I folded my arms. "If your plan is to leave me here, then I'd rather go back home. I'll be happier at Dad's place."

"I need you in one of my properties, or people will talk. If you don't like it here, then I have places abroad. Maybe you want something completely different. I have a little French château, or there's my lodge in Zakopane if you like to ski?"

Of course I didn't ski. Posh people skied. "What does it matter where I am? No one will know."

"Because you are my fiancée. People will notice, and then they will talk. I can't take the risk. It will look odd if you go back to Ecclesdale alone."

"What am I supposed to do out here all day?"

His face brightened, and he beckoned me to follow. "Excellent question. Come with me."

I followed Cole past tinkling fountains and manicured lawns to a beautiful cottage garden dotted with wildflowers. A sheep bleated somewhere in the distance, and another replied. The aroma of freshly cut grass scented the air. Nestled in the greenery was a rustic outhouse with glass doors and lilac-painted timber frames.

"I know it's a little out of the way, but I thought you'd appreciate hearing the birds while you work."

"Work?"

He opened the double doors. "I've had it all decked out with the latest equipment, but if I've missed anything, then let me know."

A potter's wheel on a sturdy base dominated the bright space. Plants and tools lined the worktops and shelves. Artsy-looking books were piled high by the huge ceramic sink. A cozy armchair loaded with cushions and patchwork blankets sat in the corner.

"It has electricity and water. The kiln is the largest allowed in a residential space, but we had to put it in the shed next door so it's properly ventilated."

I drifted toward the huge easel. An intimidating blank canvas stared back at me. "What is this?"

"It's your art studio. Do you like it?"

I ran a hand over a smooth worktop. I'd made an offhand comment about pottery and he'd made this for me?

My chest felt suddenly tight. "I don't really do this kind of thing anymore. When did you do all this?"

"It didn't take long."

I opened my mouth and closed it again, speechless. What was not to like? It was perfect. A little creative oasis just for me. I'd be able to sit out here with all this beautiful natural light spilling in and work on ceramics. It was a dream I'd never even dared to have, except I didn't do this anymore. I hadn't even picked up a brush since I dropped out of art school. This was the old me. The girl I'd been before.

I turned on a tap and held a finger under the warm splash of water. "I don't even know if I remember how. I'm not good enough for my own studio."

"You don't need to be good. It's a way to have fun. We'll hire a tutor to start you off, if you like. You'll soon remember."

Gold glinted by the window and I wandered over and picked up the ornamental jeweled sausage dog that I'd seen in Harrods. A couple of neat stacks of bank notes were piled next to it.

I looked up to find Cole watching me with a solid, brooding look. "Two grand. You can look at both of them."

"Pardon?"

"You said you'd rather look at two grand than the ornament. Why not have both?"

I hardly remembered what I'd said. My brain was foggy lately. I was probably spewing all kinds of nonsense, although I did recall saying this dog was ridiculous, and I had no use for it. "I can't take this from you. Any of this. It's too much."

"This is your home now. Whatever you need, you can have."

A fancy-looking coffee machine sat near the sink. There were little boxes of tea bags and snacks. I picked up a packet of Wagon Wheels. These had been my go-to treat as a kid. I'd been addicted to them. Had Cole remembered? Now I had my own swimming pool and tennis court and Estonian igloo sauna and art studio? This was too much. A rush of emotion overwhelmed me and I threw my arms around his neck.

"Thank you."

He stiffened and held perfectly still. "You're welcome. I hope you'll be happy here."

Awkwardly, I disengaged from him. His aloof expression made a twinge pull at my chest. He'd made no attempt to return the hug.

He pulled his sleeve up and checked his fancy watch. "I have to get back to the office. Work is intense at the moment. Call my PA if you need anything. The house is fully staffed. You don't have to lift a finger if you don't want to. Remember, you can spend anything you want on the card. It's yours." He pressed a cold metal key into my hand. "Goodbye, Charlotte."

"When am I going to see you next?"

A line formed between his brows briefly before it disappeared. "When I've made the wedding arrangements. Forget about me. There is nothing for you to do here other than relax and enjoy yourself. This was the deal. You marry me, I make your life better."

Chapter 19

CHARLOTTE

The blank canvas stared me down. My fingers hovered over the pot of fresh brushes, but I didn't dare pluck one out. I hadn't had space for art in my life for a long time. Looking after Dad had been demanding, but I couldn't use it as an excuse. I just hadn't felt the urge to draw or paint. Not since the shambles that had been art school.

I perched on the stool at the pottery wheel. Birdsong drifted in through the window in the stillness. What was I supposed to do here? My life had changed overnight. Without Dad, I had this space in my heart where he'd been, and an empty expanse of time to fill. I drifted to the enormous tub of clay by the sink. The canvas was too intimidating, but I could at least try to throw a pot. Cole had gone to all this trouble. I had to give something a go.

I lifted the lid and grabbed a mound of wet clay. It would need to be wedged first to get the air out. That's about as much as I could remember. On the table, I pressed and folded it with my hands, smoothing it. Then, I put the mound on the wheel and began spinning it with my foot on the pedal. The clay slid wet and cold between my palms. Wet earth filled my nose, and I expected it to trigger all those bad memories of art school—the criticism, the tears, that feeling of never being *good enough*. But my mind fell into a calm, focused fixation.

The repetitive whir of the wheel soothed me. A small cylinder took shape between my fingers. A pencil pot, maybe, or a small plant container – something, anyway. Something I'd created myself from scratch. I stopped the wheel and examined my finished product. Not great, but not terrible either. An achievement, after all these years. A small smile lifted my lips. It was a start.

◆　◆　◆

Spring turned into summer, and I passed a host of sunny days perfecting my technique on the wheel. I settled into a routine, working all day, and stopping only to eat one of Elain's delicious salads. Lunch was taken alone on the shady steps of the pottery studio, watching the sparrows splashing on the bird table. Late afternoons, I sometimes took a dip in the outdoor pool, followed by dinner in the cozy snug at the back of the house. Most nights, I fell asleep on the couch in front of *Dating in the Wild*.

At the sink in the studio, I carefully measured out the components needed for a glaze. I'd been experimenting for weeks, trying to find a shade the specific color of Dad's eyes. The trouble was, it always looked different when fired. The closest I'd got was a muted ocean blue, but I needed something lighter.

I wiped dirty handprints down my apron. Things got messy in the studio. By the end of the day, I always had specks of clay caked into my hair. Cole would have hated it. He was so neat and well groomed. No wonder he'd had to put so many miles between us. He probably couldn't stand the chaos.

Cole had sent me the odd message to check in since he'd dropped me here, but otherwise I'd heard nothing from him. On impulse, I pulled out my phone and sent him a text.

Do you want to see a dirty picture?

The reply was instantaneous. *You have my attention.*
I snapped a photo of the studio interior and the glaze-splattered sink and pressed send.

Not what I was expecting.

I tapped the phone against my chin, wondering whether to write more, but my phone buzzed before I could reply.

You're enjoying the studio, then?

I love it.

Good.

I waited, but there was no further reply. *Good? Is that it?* It should have been enough, but I couldn't help myself.

You don't need me for anything? No fancy parties where I can flirt with rich, handsome men?

Nothing on the immediate horizon. I'll let you know.

When are we saying I do?

Soon.

A movement outside the studio caught my eye. Someone was outside, but it wasn't time for Elain to bring lunch yet. I moved to the window. My sister plowed over the lawn toward me with my nieces at her side. Tiff was making hard work of dragging an enormous suitcase along the grass behind her. I stepped outside to greet them. Both little girls broke into a run and threw themselves at me when they saw me. I dropped to my knees to hug them so hard they almost floored me.

Tiff set her case down. Her face was pale and pinched. Dark shadows lurked under her eyes. My heart sank.

"What's wrong?"

Her mouth opened in dismay. "I've left Paul again. I need somewhere to stay."

◆　◆　◆

"I went back to Dad's house, but it was too depressing. There's mold in the back room." Tiff stretched her legs on the lounger and watched Clara and Imogen dive-bombing each other loudly in the pool. "I have a friend at work looking for a new place. They've got a toddler and a baby on the way. The house would be ideal."

"Which house?"

"Dad's."

No way. "It's not for sale."

"It's just sitting there empty, Lottie. It's damp and falling into disrepair."

"It's not for sale."

"But it's not healthy to hold on to it like this."

A sudden crick in my neck made me wince. These loungers were too hard. I adjusted the pillow behind my head. "I'm moving back in. When Cole doesn't need me anymore, I'm going back."

"It's not a house for a single woman. It's a family home."

My nieces were play-fighting in the pool, splashing water in each other's faces. I tried to take a calming breath. A strong chlorine odor burned the back of my throat. "It's my house now. Not your problem."

Tiff wrinkled her nose. "It's my problem if squatters move in and turn it into a crack den."

I gave her a dubious look. "In Ecclesdale?"

"Where better? No one would ever guess. Crack dens happen everywhere."

This is why the school mums had booted Tiff out of the group chat. Because she was annoying and never let anything go.

"Why are you so insistent about selling? You've been paid off. What does it matter to you?"

"Because I think it's healthy for you to let go. I don't like the idea of you sitting in that house alone, drowning in memories." She turned her face away. "Clinging on to it won't bring him back, Lottie. He's not there anymore."

A surge of anger made my blood hot. *So fucking righteous and patronizing.* She opened her mouth to keep nagging me, but I cut her off.

"Do you think you can work things out with Paul?"

Her face hardened. She shook her head and pain flickered in her eyes. "No."

I sighed. Tiff broke up with Paul all the time, but this time she looked genuinely distraught. It was probably why she was giving me grief about the house again. "You can stay here as long as you need. I don't see the girls enough. Stay for a vacation."

"You don't need to check with Cole?"

Yes. Probably. He wasn't particularly easygoing about change. But that wasn't Tiff's problem. I waved a dismissive hand. "He doesn't care what I'm doing out here as long as I'm not bothering him."

She peered around the pool and slathered her shoulders with sun cream. "I can't bloody believe this place." She watched Clive pottering around, trimming the hedges. "You have staff."

"I know," I whispered.

"You're like some sickeningly rich person now. I don't know you anymore."

"I'm engaged to a sickeningly rich person. There's a difference."

"In less than a year, you'll be five million pounds richer. Then *you'll* be the sickeningly rich person. Good for you. You've really landed on your feet." She dropped her voice low. "Where is Billionaire Dick, anyway?"

I snorted. "Keep your voice down. He's in London. He does his own thing, and he doesn't bother me."

"Separate lives." She nodded sagely. "Like a real marriage, then."

I chuckled. "If you say so."

She lowered her sunglasses and nodded her approval. "So you get this place to yourself and you don't even have to suck anyone off? Talk about living the dream."

"Stop. There is none of that. You saw the contract."

Just one noncontractual orgasm that we never needed to talk about. I let my eyes drift shut. The sound of splashing and my nieces' cheerful voices filtered to my ears. At least they'd stopped trying to drown each other. Footsteps sounded, and I opened my eyes. A dark figure blotted out the sun. My heart jumped, but my excitement was short-lived. This man looked a little like Cole, but it wasn't him. Reuben was dressed in clothes that looked casual but must have cost a fortune—dark-patterned tailored shorts and a lilac Balenciaga hoodie with what looked like a small coffee stain on the chest.

"Hey there!" He flashed a beaming smile.

An uneasy feeling settled over me. Cole had flipped his lid when I'd danced with his brother. He wouldn't be happy about this.

It was weird, because this man was all cheerful affability and good grace. Difficult not to like. But that was Cole's choice. Now I had to sit here feeling awkward about it.

I straightened on the lounger. "What a lovely surprise."

He held out the biggest bottle of champagne I'd ever seen. "No problem. I was passing. I thought I'd stop by and say hello."

"Cole isn't here, I'm afraid."

Reuben's smile widened. "That's a shame."

Tiff lurched over me and snatched the champagne bottle. "Thanks. I'll take that."

"Reuben, this is my sister, Tiff. Tiff, this is Cole's brother, Reuben."

Reuben almost tripped over his expensive-looking loafers in his effort to thrust out his palm to Tiff. Pink tinged his cheekbones as he shook her hand enthusiastically. I'd have to get rid of him. It was perfectly innocent, but Cole wouldn't like it. Cole had been good to me with the house and the studio. I wouldn't piss him off for no reason.

Tiff lifted her sunglasses and surveyed Reuben. "Hi." A curious smile lifted her lips. "The famous Reuben Thorner. I watched Monaco on the TV last week."

He brushed a hand through his floppy hair and laughed. "Oh God. The less said about that the better."

I twisted to look at Tiff. "Famous?"

"You didn't know your brother-in-law-to-be is famous?"

He flashed a self-effacing grin. "I'm not *that* famous. I just drive cars."

Tiff's impressed gaze drifted over him. "Not just any old cars. You're definitely famous."

Reuben frowned and scratched his unruly mop of hair. "You know, I can never seem to get hold of Cole. His PA is like a guard dog. What's he up to these days?"

Miriam was perfectly nice. She'd probably just been told to screen Reuben's calls.

I shrugged. "The usual. He works hard."

"He definitely does that." His eyebrows rose in amazement. "I have no idea how he sits in an office all day. I can't think of anything worse."

Tiff swung her legs over the lounger and sat upright. She held up the champagne and studied it. "This looks fancy."

Reuben pulled up a deck chair and sat with us. "I swiped it from Dad's cellar. He only has the best."

Tiff grinned. "Better crack it open then. I want to know everything about the season so far. Do not spare me a single detail."

Reuben's lips curved upward. "You like Formula One?"

"Not really." Tiff smiled sweetly. "But I like the drivers."

Chapter 20

COLE

I left the helicopter and headed for the back of the house. Voices and the distinctive soft thwack of croquet mallets drifted on the breeze. A little girl with dirt on her nose and dark hair in a messy ponytail appeared from nowhere. She scanned me up and down and wrinkled her nose.

"Are you Dick?"

"I'm sorry?"

"Mum keeps talking about Billionaire Dick. This is his house." She pulled a crumbling chocolate chip cookie from her skirt pocket and shoved it into her mouth. "Mum's left Paul because she says she can't put up with his shit anymore, and now we've come to live with Auntie Lottie."

Tiffany was here? Elain hadn't mentioned it. My housekeeper gave me regular updates on how Charlotte was doing.

"Where is your aunt?"

"Everyone is playing croquet with Reuben."

What the fuck? Elain raced around the corner, red-faced and panting. She took the little girl by the hand. "There you are. Your mum told me not to let you wander off."

Elain's eyes met mine. "Cole? We didn't know you were coming."

Rancor sharpened my voice. "Why didn't you tell me Reuben was here?"

"I'm sorry. I didn't get round to it. It caught me off guard. Everyone arrived today." Remorse glinted in her eyes and she wrung her hands in front of her. "I was about to message."

She looked genuinely contrite. Enough to make me feel guilty. Elain was the only person in my employ who could do that to me. Perhaps because she reminded me so much of my mother. "I know you would have. I apologize for my tone."

She smiled warmly. "You should join in the game. Everyone is having fun."

They wouldn't be having fun when I got hold of Reuben. At least I was here now. He needed reminding that Charlotte was mine. I pasted a smile on my face. "Maybe. Thanks."

I marched away to find the adults at the back of the house. It had been an impulsive decision to visit Charlotte. I needed to brief her on the wedding arrangements. It wasn't something that needed to be done face-to-face, but her text this morning had been out of the blue. Elain had mentioned that Charlotte wasn't eating as well as usual. I'd needed to see for myself that she was doing OK.

Fucking Reuben! What was he doing here? Had he come to make a move on Charlotte, or was he here to spy? Probably both. I should have been keeping better track of his movements. My heart pounded in anticipation of seeing Charlotte. It was like being a teenager again, desperate to catch a glimpse after one of Roy's revision sessions. Charlotte had been on my mind constantly. She was the first thing I thought about when I woke up and the last thing when I went to bed. I could hardly concentrate or get any work done. The highlight of my day was Elain's report and the photos she sent me of Charlotte's progress in the pottery studio.

I rounded the corner of the house, and a scene of chaos greeted me on the lawn. Tiffany guffawed as she swung her croquet mallet awkwardly at a ball and completely missed. She thrust the mallet at Charlotte, grabbed a champagne bottle from Reuben, and took a big swig.

Charlotte took her turn. Reuben and Tiffany cheered loudly when she finally hit the ball after several abysmal attempts. A smile lit her lips. A genuine smile that made her nose scrunch in the way I'd always loved. Warmth filled me, but then she high-fived Reuben, and any warmth I felt was swiftly replaced with fury.

Charlotte froze when she saw me approaching. The mallet dropped heavily from her hand and thudded on the grass. "Cole?"

She looked well. Freckles dotted her cheeks, and her hair fell in a glossy ponytail down her back. Her patterned blue sleeveless sundress had a low, sweeping neckline. It cinched at the waist, high-lighting her beautiful curves. It was a dress made for frolicking in meadows, weaving daisy chains, and making love in soft grass. She looked divine, but it was her eyes that made my heart jolt. They were animated and full of life.

I smoothed my expression. "Having fun?"

Her cheeks were red. "I didn't know you were coming."

I let my disparaging gaze rove over the balls scattered all over the grass. "Clearly."

Reuben lurched toward me with a daft grin and his hand out-stretched. "Cole. So good to see you. I was just in the area—"

"Not now." I turned my back on him and walked toward the house. "Come with me, please, Charlotte."

◆　◆　◆

I hovered in the doorway of the pottery studio. The place was sheer chaos. An assortment of pots lined the shelf and clay splattered the worktops and floor. The mess made my skin prickle. Charlotte grabbed a filthy apron from a hook by the door and threw it over her head.

"I didn't know they were coming. Tiff just turned up here this morning. Then Reuben. I didn't know how to get rid of him."

"And you decided champagne and croquet might do the trick?"

"No, you're right. It was a mistake." Humor edged her voice. "That's like posh people catnip. He'll be here forever."

"Reuben is a snake. He can't be trusted."

"Give me a break, Cole. You don't trust anyone. You're paranoid. I think you've got him all wrong, anyway. He's harmless."

Poor little Reuben. We'd walked away from him giving one of Charlotte's feral nieces a piggyback ride. It was all part of his lovable idiot act. "Don't be fooled. He wants to use you to manipulate me."

Charlotte took a lump of clay from a big tub and dropped it onto a work surface. She worked it with flat palms, pressing down on alternate sides. "Not everyone is out to manipulate you."

"No. Not everyone." *Just mostly everyone.*

I braved the chaos to drift a little closer. "And your sister? How long is she staying for?"

She lifted the clay, folded it in half, and pressed it down again with her palms. "I don't know."

"You didn't think to tell me? Any changes to your living situation need to go through me. I'm not running a guesthouse."

Her hands froze in midair, and she turned to face me. Her eyes blazed. "People go mad, you know. If you leave them in isolation for too long. I'm not a hermit. It's not unreasonable for me to spend time with my family and friends. Tiff needs me. We're supposed to be a happy couple. Normal couples have their family and friends over and it's not a big deal. Why are you here, anyway? I didn't know you were coming. How long are you staying for?"

"I came to talk to you about the wedding. It's booked. Next week."

Her eyes grew large. "Next week?"

"Is that a problem?"

"You don't think you could have given me more warning? I haven't even got a dress."

"Everything is taken care of. You just need to show up on time."

"You've done everything? What if the dress doesn't suit me?"

It would. I remembered the kind she liked from all those years ago. Besides, she'd look good in a bin bag. What did it matter? "It will."

She stepped close enough that her earthy smell engulfed me. A speck of clay sat on the bridge of her nose. I longed to wipe it away. Any excuse to touch her. Heat coiled in my belly.

She folded her arms, annoyed. "You should have let me choose my own dress."

"If you don't like the one I chose, get another one."

Her voice hardened. "You have to be in control of everything, don't you?"

A wave of unwelcome excitement went through me to have her so close. My eyes dropped to her lips. So fucking plump and luscious. "No. I like to make your life simpler. I thought you'd be happier if I just got on with the arrangements."

I wanted to kiss her. To lift her onto that work surface and fuck her, regardless of the mess in here. Bad idea. Really fucking bad idea. What was wrong with me that it turned me on so much when she was pissed off with me? Maybe because it was better than seeing her sad. At least if she was angry, she was plugged into the world. It was the numbness that hurt me. It reminded me too much of my mother.

She swiped two beige handprints down her apron. "Fine. You're the one trying to impress people. I don't care what the dress looks like."

She picked the clay up again, kneading and flattening it. "I'll see you at the church. I won't keep you any longer."

The sound of children's laughter drifted from the garden. Did she expect me to walk away and leave her here with Reuben? No fucking way. He didn't get to share air with her. The minute I left here, he'd move in on her.

I stepped close again. "You need to tell Reuben to leave. He's not welcome in my home. If he shows up again, you don't entertain him."

Electricity crackled between us in the small space. She peered up at me.

"I'm not responsible for your brother's behavior. It's not my fault if he visits *your* home."

"He's not my brother."

Her pretty eyes narrowed. "What is it with this jealousy? Why? How is it going to look if I ban your own brother from setting foot on the property? That's not what a secure marriage looks like. Can't you see you're putting me in a difficult position?"

"He's *not* my brother."

She chuffed out a humorless laugh. "You're impossible sometimes. You know that? You put me out to pasture here all alone, as far away from you as possible. Why are you so worried about Reuben? What does it matter to you who I spend an afternoon with, as long as it's discreet?"

"Your little drunken game of croquet is hardly discreet, and you're not out to pasture. There are plenty of people to keep you company: Elain. Clive. Lauren."

"They're paid to do jobs here. They don't have time to play croquet or sit around for a chat."

"I can pay someone to play croquet with you."

"That's the answer to everything for you, isn't it? Something's bugging you, throw money at it."

She was mad with me, and drunk, from the look of her shiny eyes and the way she was going at that clay like she had a personal vendetta against it. You could never get sense from drunk people. A memory forced its way into my consciousness.

My mother sprawled on the bathroom floor of her New York penthouse, with an empty vodka bottle and a tub of pills spilled across the tiles. I hauled her up in my arms and over the toilet bowl.

"Mum? Can you hear me?"

Her voice slurred. "You're the only one . . . he doesn't care about me."

Panic threatened to undo me, but I had to stay calm. This had happened so many times before. It would be fine. I just had to act quickly. "What did you take?"

"You're too good to me."

"You're not going to think that in a minute." I forced my fingers down her throat.

Charlotte's sigh brought me back to the studio. "If we're done here?"

"We're not done. I've booked Rome for the honeymoon."

"Rome?"

The shock in her voice held me at the door. I couldn't tell if it was good shock or bad shock. "Yes. Is that acceptable?"

She shook her head in disbelief. "Is that acceptable? Are you kidding me?" Her eyes softened. "I can't believe you remembered."

I'd booked Rome because Theo had informed me that Gabe Rivers was known to spend time training with his team in the football offseason. Since I couldn't pin this bastard down to a meeting, I'd have to "accidentally" bump into him at his hotel.

She gazed at me with a more tender expression than I deserved. "Dad studied in Rome when he was a postgraduate. He talked about it all the time. This is a dream. I can't believe it."

A sliver of guilt ran through me, but if she was happy, then this worked well. "I'm pleased you're happy."

That part was true, anyway. Charlotte's nose always scrunched when it was a genuine smile, and I couldn't get enough of that.

She beamed and wrapped her arms around her middle, hugging herself. "I have so many things I want to see. Oh my God. I'm going to get to see the Sistine Chapel. I've always wanted to visit the Vatican." She gave a little squeal of delight, bounced on her heels, and clapped her hands in delight. "It's going to be so special. Thank you, Cole. I mean it. Thank you so much." She ripped off her apron and darted past me out of the door. "I have to tell Tiff."

My chest filled with warmth. If I'd have known it would make her happy, I would have taken her to Rome on day one.

"Wait." She spun on her heel. "Is it OK if Tiff and the girls stay here for a while? You're right. This isn't a guesthouse. I should have asked. And you're just going to have to put up with Reuben popping by if we're going to pull this off. I'm not frog-marching your relatives off the property. It looks suspicious. You have nothing to be jealous about. He's not my type, anyway." Her eyes darted to me and she looked away.

"You said he was handsome."

"That just means I have eyes. It doesn't mean I'm going to do anything about it. You're going to have to trust me if we have any hope of making this arrangement look convincing."

I'd always prided myself on my unyielding approach to negotiations. I never gave ground. Things always went my way in the boardroom, except none of that seemed to apply with Charlotte. There wasn't anything I wouldn't give this woman, and all she'd have to do was ask.

I nodded. "Fine. I trust you. You don't have to turn Reuben away, but he better not make a habit of stopping by. Your family can stay as long as they need. Let me know if you need anything else."

Chapter 21

Much to my irritation, Cole had chosen the perfect dress. A long, layered Valentino number that gave me a dopamine hit every time I swished the elegant train. I gazed at my reflection in the bedroom mirror while Elain fussed with the delicate veil. My hands felt clammy in the long white-lace gloves. All eyes would be on me walking down the aisle in this next week. Would they buy it? We needed people to see a bride, when all I saw was a fraud.

Elain sighed softly. "Look at you." Her smile was a little teary. "What a gorgeous pair you make. I'm so happy for you both. Marcia would have loved you. She'd be so thrilled about Cole settling down."

"Marcia?"

Elain hummed lightly as she smoothed out a crease in the train. "Cole's mother."

"Cole doesn't talk much about his family."

"Strange." She fanned the veil back from my face. "They were very close. Marcia lived here." A sudden smile crossed her lips. "Here. Come with me."

I followed her out of the bedroom, down a hallway, and into a wood-paneled office. A large walnut desk dominated the room, and bookcases lined the walls. I hung back by the door. "Are we supposed to be in here?"

She beckoned me with her hand. "Cole won't mind. You know how laid-back he is."

I spluttered out a laugh. That was one word that would never be associated with Cole in my vocabulary. "Laid-back? Are we talking about the same Cole?"

She chuckled but gave me a curious smile. "He's very good to us."

"Seriously?"

"Maybe he's different in the office. The staff here have no complaints. He treats us all very well."

Elain pointed to a picture on the wall. A woman who looked to be in her mid-twenties reclined on a sun lounger next to a sparkling swimming pool. A chic white trouser suit wrapped around her tanned, slender frame. But it was the framed watercolor of rolling green hills next to the photo I couldn't take my eyes from. *I did that.*

The memory hit me in a rush. *Wispy clouds in a bright blue sky. Cole's lips touching mine for the first time. I'd been high on life that day. High with that naive feeling you have when you're young that anything is possible. That the world is just waiting for you with open arms.* I'd given that picture to Cole the day before he left. He'd kept it all this time?

"Beautiful, wasn't she?"

Elain's voice dragged my gaze back to the photo of Cole's mother. Cat-eye sunglasses perched on her loose golden hair and her glossy lips were parted in a radiant smile. There were three children in the picture. An older boy and girl who must have been around nine and a young boy with dark hair and a sullen expression. It was unmistakably a young Cole.

"Yes. Very beautiful."

Elain gave a wistful sigh. "Marcia was a lovely woman. Very kind and soft. Always generous. If she saw a problem or if someone was in trouble, she would do anything to fix it. That's where Cole gets it from."

I couldn't help my incredulous laugh. "Cole? I'm not sure about that."

She raised an affronted eyebrow. "Yes. We're so grateful for him. My grandson, Marco, was a handful growing up, but Cole told us he needed something to focus on. We could never have afforded culinary school without Cole's help. Now he works for Cole as his personal chef. I don't know what we would have done without him. He's changed that boy's life. And he gives so much to charity."

"He does?"

She glanced at me in surprise. "He funds all kinds of causes: addiction charities, homeless shelters, and education projects. Most of these places wouldn't be able to stay open without him. He's a great philanthropist."

"Cole? Cole Thorner?" Were we even talking about the same man? Was he paying this woman to say these things?

She looked perplexed. "Yes. Why do you seem so surprised?"

"Because I had no idea. Why doesn't he tell anyone?"

"I suppose he doesn't feel the need."

I returned my attention to the photo, to the two happy children and the glum-looking Cole. "Who is this little girl?"

Elain's smile was wistful. "Penelope."

"Who?"

A shadow crossed Elain's face, and she moved to the door. "It's not really my place to say. Maybe you could ask him."

"He doesn't talk about himself much."

"You're about to be his wife. You should ask him. He should trust you more than anyone."

Fake wife. Although, he did seem to trust me. He'd told me as much. Lifting my train off the ground, I followed Elain to the door. A worn spiral-bound pad on the bookcase caught my eye. It looked out of place among the neat rows of vintage leather-bound books.

I plucked out the pad and flipped through the pages. Pencil sketches and glued-in postcodes of exotic locations filled the pages. There were pages and pages of hands. I'd been obsessed back then with trying to recreate the hand shapes in Michelangelo's *The Creation of Adam.* The entire Sistine Chapel was a work of genius, but the central part of it had always thrilled me. There was so much drama and tension in those almost touching fingertips.

My heart skipped a beat. The book hurtled me back to Ecclesdale and the days I'd spent in the woods sketching and painting. God. I'd been a pretentious kid. I'd really fancied myself an artist. It hadn't taken me long to realize I wasn't good enough. Art school had knocked the wind out of my sails.

"These are my drawings," I said, clutching the book to my chest.

Elain raised an eyebrow. "They are?"

"It's one of my scrapbooks. I had dozens. I used to take one everywhere with me. Why would Cole have this?"

She shrugged. "You were friends, weren't you? Maybe he picked it up sometime by accident?"

It was a possibility. Cole had spent so much of his time in Dad's study, and he was always borrowing books. It would have been easy to pick it up by accident.

She eyed me with a wistful expression and held out her hand. "Come on. Let's get you out of that dress before it gets creased."

I returned the book to the shelf, even though it was mine. Elain might have found him laid-back, but I didn't like to think how he'd react to the idea of us snooping around in his study.

She beamed at me. "You're going to knock him out when he sees you in this. I can't wait to see his face."

Maybe, but more likely he would be indifferent. It seemed Elain and I had spent time with entirely different men.

Chapter 22

CHARLOTTE

The solemn notes of the organ drifted out of the church, and I braced myself to walk up the stone steps alone. Tiff helped me with my makeup this morning. She'd offered to walk me down the aisle, but I'd said no. We'd both know that it should have been Dad. It would have been too much unspoken. Better to do it alone so I'd have some chance of holding myself together.

I took a breath, but before I could open the door, Cole emerged from the church. A smart tuxedo jacket wrapped around his broad shoulders. A small spray of lilacs poked from his buttonhole. I'd never seen a man more handsome in my life. A rush of nerves gripped me. What was he doing out here? He didn't want to go through with it anymore?

"What are you doing?"

He stared at me as though lost in thought. "You look . . ." He swallowed and cleared his throat. "You like the dress?"

"I like it. You did well." I toed his shiny brogue with my ivory satin slipper. "You don't look too bad yourself."

It was the understatement of the century. He looked like he'd stepped off the cover of *GQ*.

"Thanks." His face remained impassive as he offered his arm. "Shall we?"

My puzzlement must have shown on my face because he spoke in a low, soothing voice. "I saw Tiffany sitting in there. I didn't want you to have to walk in on your own."

Really? That was more thoughtful than I would have expected from him. *Dad should be doing it.* Tears pressed at my eyes. *Oh God. Think of the mascara.*

"You're supposed to meet me at the altar. This has to be bad luck."

Cole raised a sarcastic eyebrow and whispered low. "I'd hate to start off our fake marriage with bad luck." He motioned with his arm. "Come on, Miss Ackroyd. Let's make an honest woman out of you."

This was it. The point of no return. It had been a mistake not to do this in a registry office. The solemnity of the church made my knees tremble. We were about to lie to an entire room full of people.

"Everyone is going to be pissed off if they find out we're lying," I whispered.

"I have no intention of lying when I say those vows."

"What? This is just admin for you. You said it yourself."

"So? That's what a marriage is. Admin. We make promises and we work to fulfill our contractual obligations. I won't let you down, Charlotte. I'm signing up to be your husband. This is a marriage of convenience, but it's still a marriage. I'm a man of my word. You're doing me a favor. I won't forget that."

Cole slipped his arm through mine and guided me gently toward the stone steps. Panic spiraled through me. This shouldn't have been like this. It should have been real. It should have been Dad walking me down the aisle to stand before a man who loved me deeply. The last time I'd been in church, it had been to say goodbye.

The weight of my grief pinned me to the spot. "I can't do this without him."

Tiff's voice played in my head. *Think of the money.*

My voice came out a desperate whisper. "I don't want to cry. My mascara will run. Please tell me something funny. Please don't let me cry. Not now. Please."

Cole watched me with a serious expression. "When Theo was little, I found him eating a couple of the cat's biscuits. I managed to convince him he was going to turn into a cat."

"What?"

"He believed it hook, line, and sinker. Lucas pretended to call an ambulance. Theo burst into tears when Lucas told the imaginary doctor on the other end of the phone that we could see whiskers coming through."

A small laugh bubbled up. "That's really cruel."

"This is the family you're joining. Prepare yourself. I'm an arse-hole, and I'm still the best of the bunch."

"Thanks for the heads-up. If we're doing this, then I should probably warn you that I'm a terrible cook, like really bad. Once I made a pad Thai that I had to throw in the bin because it was so bad, but it still smelt so terrible we had to put the bin outside. Tiff told me she'd never emotionally recover from how awful it tasted. Also, I have a weird phobia about automated car washes. I don't know why. It's the noise and the huge, soapy rollers."

"Noted. Good job we have a chef." He lifted a wry eyebrow. "Also, this really explains a lot about the state of your car."

Birdsong filtered around us. A hysterical wave went through me. Marriage? My breath came in shallow gasps. Being trapped in a car wash would have been preferable to this feeling.

He gripped my hands. "Breathe. Just breathe."

"I'm breathing."

He raised a sardonic brow. "As a vampire, I don't need to breathe, so I'm fine. Of course, there is a chance I could combust when I step inside the church."

He held the heavy, arched wooden door open. Cool air and the scent of lilies engulfed me. Candles on tall plinths flickered light against stained glass and painted stone in a wash of vibrant watery colors. It looked beautiful. A sea of faces turned to look at me. These had to be all the people Cole was trying to impress. I focused on my side of the church. On Tiff and my nieces. I didn't have many people I could invite. My social life had died a death a long time ago, but I had a scattering of aunts and cousins and extended family I hadn't seen since Dad's funeral.

"Now we walk. One foot in front of the other. Focus on me. I've got you. Let's take this day one step at a time." Cole's low voice in my ear reassured me. "OK?"

A wave of gratitude passed over me. He hadn't let me cry. My grief wedged in my chest as something bittersweet but manageable. I could get through it. *At least for the next step. And then the next.*

"I'm going to have to keep checking in case smoke starts pouring from under your collar." I sniffed the air. "I think I can smell burning."

He smirked as we glided up the aisle together. His low whisper against my earlobe sent a warm shiver through me. "I haven't combusted yet. Maybe you're my redemption, Charlotte."

Chapter 23

Cole

Light from the stained-glass windows made Charlotte's chestnut hair gleam like she was wearing a halo. I held her hands and felt her fingers tremble. I'd never expected to marry. *Love is a weakness to be exploited, boy.* Today wasn't about love. It was about putting things right by Mum and making sure my father didn't win.

The minister was talking, but I couldn't stop my mind from drifting. Being back in Ecclesdale again was affecting me. The memories still held too much sway over me. My father's voice in my head was louder than ever.

I heard about your exam results. Apparently, you got the brains in the family. Unfortunately, Reuben takes after Janice. Your brother is not the brightest spark. I need you in New York.

A life? In this place? It's time to get serious. The Thorner name means something. Play your cards right and you're on the cusp of taking over an empire.

Charlotte's tremulous voice reverberated around the church as she echoed the minister's words. "I, Charlotte Ackroyd, take you, Cole Thorner, to be my husband, to have and to hold from this day forward."

Charlotte's beautiful eyes locked with mine. "For better, for worse, for richer, for poorer, in sickness and in health."

I took a breath, trying to focus, but Dad's goading in my mind clamored too loud.

I'm bankrolling your cozy life here. I'm paying for your mother in that expensive rehab. I could pull the plug at any minute. You'd all be penniless without me. You do as I say, or you all feel the consequences.

Charlotte squeezed my hands, bringing me back to the present. "To love and to cherish, till death us do part, according to God's holy law. In the presence of God I make this vow."

Silence swept around us. I couldn't take my eyes from this beautiful woman pledging herself to me. We both knew it was false, but there was a lifetime where this could have been true. In some other timeline there was a Cole and Charlotte making these vows and meaning every word. A stark sadness gripped me. That boy was gone. My father had destroyed him. Now, there was just a heartless creature in his place.

I'd done things at my father's command that I'd never imagined myself capable of. I'd dismantled family businesses. Bankrupted people. Taken them for every penny. I'd made grown men weep in boardrooms all over the world. Philip Thorner had shaped me in his image—ruthless and calculating—and perhaps in some moments I'd surpassed even his cruel acts. He'd created a monster. By the time I'd escaped, the damage had been done. Now, I was too stained to repent. I should have been burning in this church for my sins. I should have been set aflame the minute I'd set foot inside.

The minister inclined her head to me. "Ready, Cole?"

I nodded. The minister took a step back. I'd written my own vows. If I was going to stand up here and do this, then I'd tell the truth.

"I, Cole Thorner, take you, Charlotte Ackroyd, to be my wife, to have and to hold from this day forward."

The eyes of the audience were trained on me, and I should have cared about them because this was the whole point, but in this moment, all that mattered was this woman in front of me. This serenely beautiful woman who had agreed to a crazy scheme to help me out.

"We made a pledge to each other years ago. I was a boy then, but I saw my future with you, Charlotte. There is no one else in the world I would stand up here and make these promises to.

"I cared about your father, and I know it is so devastating to be here without him, but I vow I will do the best by him and take care of his beloved daughter. You will be mine to protect and to look after. I promise to give you a life that most people could only ever dream of. You will never want for anything. I will meet every need you have of me.

"We are entering this marriage as adults and equal partners with our eyes wide open. You will always have honesty from me. I will never do anything intentionally to hurt you. You are giving me a chance to be a better man, and I'm grateful. I will always take you just as you are."

Even if Charlotte was only making me a better man in the eyes of others, it mattered. Charlotte gazed at me, tears glimmering in her eyes.

"To love and to cherish, till death us do part, according to God's holy law. In the presence of God I make this vow."

We exchanged rings. My hands trembled a little in the dreadful moment I thought the wedding band wouldn't fit before it eased onto her finger.

"I now pronounce you husband and wife. You may kiss the bride."

Our first kiss invaded my mind. All those years ago on a picnic blanket overlooking this beautiful village where I'd felt like I had a home for the first time. Our future together had held so much promise, and the next day I'd left her behind. I'd broken her heart, and hardened mine into something unrecognizable.

I cupped her cheek and kissed her in a chaste, restrained way. A fake kiss to end a fake wedding. Except my heart pounded against my ribs and my chest filled with a kind of lightness I'd never known. This was a business deal. Admin in front of an audience. A kiss should have felt the same as signing on the dotted line. I'd got the deal done, but none of this felt fake, and I'd meant every word of those vows. And at long last, after all these years, Charlotte was mine.

Applause rang out in the church, and Charlotte's grin was so broad it made her nose scrunch in the way I loved. *Loved. Love. Still love.* It hit me like a proclamation from on high, as though it was written on a stone tablet and handed to me as a revelation. I'd always loved her. I'd never stopped. She was so funny and beautiful, creative and kind. She was a heavenly creature. Too good for the likes of me.

And now she was my wife.

My fucking *wife* who was only marrying me for the money and seemed to hate me, and there wasn't much I could do about it without besmirching the memory of her dead father who she had on a pedestal, and even then it might not be enough because it didn't negate the fact that I was a prick. But worst of all, I'd made her vulnerable. I'd put her on my father's radar. It was the epitome of selfishness.

Love! For fuck's sake. I had no time for love. Loving my wife was a huge fucking spanner in the works.

She kept her smile fixed on the pews as she whispered low in my ear. "Pretty swell piece of admin. I think we pulled that off. Whoever wrote those vows for you deserves a pay rise."

Chapter 24

Cole

I'd always despised other people's wedding receptions, but never one as much as my own. This was the opportunity to show off my beautiful wife and mingle with the shareholders, but I didn't have the stomach for it. Not yet. My suit hugged too tight and my jaw ached with the tension of pretending. Not a drop of alcohol had passed my lips, but I felt tipsy, and not in a good way. Love? *I am in love with my wife.* A really fucking bold statement for my brain to make, and yet it wouldn't stop. I loved her. Everything about her.

For someone else it would have been a good thing, but this was a disruption I hadn't anticipated and definitely didn't want. Feelings didn't come with a receipt. It was really fucking difficult to get rid of them, but I had to figure out a way to make them stop.

Charlotte sipped from a champagne glass and laughed with Tiffany. I had to stop staring at her, but my eyes always found her in every crowd. This had been a mistake. I'd had a contract drawn up specifically to keep feelings out of this. I had no time for an actual wife or a genuine marriage. There were only two options: I could try to make this marriage work, in which case I had less than a year to win Charlotte over and do this for real, or I could resist.

We could live our separate lives and these feelings would pass. The first option was unacceptable. It would derail everything in my life. I had a job to do and a focus, and a wife needed time and attention. I was already thinking too much about her when I should have been schmoozing and convincing all these bastards here that I was a top-notch bloke brimming with integrity.

The easier option was to get over it. If I got Charlotte out of my sight, then I hardly had to see her. Everything would go back to how it was before. Feelings were just ephemeral states. I made decisions with my head, not my dick, and definitely not my heart. Love was an inconvenience at best and dangerous at worst. Love was a distraction I couldn't afford. I owed it to my mother to focus my energy on bringing down Philip. I'd committed to spending every day making him pay. Anything else would be a betrayal. The problem was I'd never been able to get Charlotte out of my head. For all these years, no other woman had compared. It would be easier if she was someone else. If she wasn't everything I'd ever wanted. There was only one choice: I would have to live with it.

"I never thought I'd see this day." Lucas held out his hand and shook mine. "My brother is a married man."

My other brother, Theo, glowered at Lucas's side. One side of his face shone with a mesh of scars from the explosion that had nearly finished him off. Not that he'd ever speak about it. It was hard to get a word from this man about anything, let alone something that mattered. He'd been a miserable bastard before he traveled the world driving tanks and blowing things up, and now he was ten times worse. Captain Gloom had left us the minute he was old enough to enroll in the army.

"Congratulations," Theo growled, raising his glass in the most lackluster salutation imaginable.

"I didn't expect you to come."

"Didn't believe it when I got the invite. Had to see it with my own eyes." He took a sip of orange juice and scanned the party. "Where's Reuben?"

"Posing on a yacht somewhere, I imagine."

"You didn't invite him?" Lucas narrowed his eyes. His voice was chiding, which it had no right to be, considering I was the only one that had suffered through a round of golf with him.

"He's a pain, and I don't trust him."

Lucas scoffed. "He's harmless. He's a little puppy who wants to make friends."

A puppy who was trying to hump my wife's leg. No thanks. "I don't buy it. I can't trust anyone who laughs like that."

Lucas raised an eyebrow. "Like what?"

"I don't know. He laughs at jokes that are barely amusing. He acts like he's being graded for enthusiasm, and he's so weirdly clumsy."

"You make him nervous. He's trying to impress you," Lucas said.

"He's trying too hard."

"He wouldn't have to try so hard if you didn't have such a chip on your shoulder." Lucas rolled his eyes and followed my gaze to Charlotte. "Your new wife is very sweet. How did you get a woman so nice to agree to this?"

I kept my voice low and level. "I'm paying her."

Lucas laughed darkly and patted me on the back. "Good one. You'd need to. She's way out of your league."

Don't I know it. Theo watched me over the rim of his glass. Nothing got past him. He liked to stand around with his massive muscles, eyeing everyone with watchful mockery, like a Bond villain's evil bodyguard.

Lucas smiled and raised his glass to Beatrice and a couple of the other shareholders gathered by the buffet table across the room. "I've heard people talking about how this is you turning over a new leaf. This marriage is making you look good, Cole. You couldn't have timed this better."

Beatrice gave me a wave. I pasted a smile onto my face and waved back. *That's right. Drink my champagne. Stuff your face with my fucking vol-au-vents while you plot my downfall.*

Beatrice had shed a few tears during the ceremony. The shareholders seemed appeased for the moment. Now I had to hope that my new status as a respectable family man was enough to convince Gabe Rivers to pick up the fucking phone.

Theo gave me a knowing look and raised his glass. "How convenient. You found a wife just when you need one."

"What can I say? Sometimes things fall into place. I'm lucky like that."

Charlotte appeared next to me, pink-cheeked and grinning. She'd never looked more beautiful. A rush of heat went through me.

She threaded her arm through mine. "Do you mind if I steal my husband? It's time for the first dance."

Lucas pushed his glasses up his nose and smiled genially. "Please. Take him away. We won't miss him."

No. Not a good idea to be holding her close and swaying. I had to make these feelings go away, not nourish them with lovey-dovey music and closeness. I shrugged out of her grip.

"I don't dance."

She plastered on an overbright smile. "But that's what people do. It's a normal thing to dance at a wedding. People are waiting to see this. It will be weird if we don't."

Lucas raised a "what are you playing at?" eyebrow. Theo watched the exchange with a too-interested expression. My gaze flicked back to the shareholders. Fine. I'd have to. With her hand wrapped around mine, Charlotte dragged me to the middle of the dance floor.

"Everyone is looking at us," I said through gritted teeth.

She slipped her arm around my waist and rested a hand gently on my shoulder. "Because we look good in formal wear."

I couldn't argue on that score. There couldn't be a more beautiful bride than my wife. It gave me great pleasure to see that Charlotte had worn the dress I'd chosen. The moment I'd seen it, I'd known she'd look incredible in it. All I wanted was to strip away all those pretty layers of white lace and bury myself in her. Music poured from the speaker. "Can't Help Falling in Love" by Elvis Presley. The irony of the song choice wasn't lost on me.

"Thank you for today," she whispered, peering up at me. "For making this easier for me." She stood on tiptoes and whispered in my ear. "I don't know why everyone says you're an arsehole. Sometimes, you're not actually *that* much of an arsehole."

"Such high praise. You'll make me blush, Mrs. Thorner."

She froze in my arms. "We haven't had a conversation about changing my name."

"There isn't a conversation. You're Thorner now."

Her eyes narrowed. "No."

"No? People will expect you to take the Thorner name."

Panic flashed in her eyes. "I'm keeping my surname."

"It has to be done. It's in the contract, if you bothered to read it."

She frowned and pulled away.

"Keep dancing," I whispered into her hair, catching a hint of citrus. "People are watching."

"I take it back," she muttered. "You *are* that much of an arsehole."

I pulled her back into my arms. Her hair tickled my chin where she rested her head against me.

She blew out an irritated breath. "I just hope you don't snore and ruin my sleep tonight. I'm exhausted."

We were flying to Rome in an hour. I had no time for a honeymoon, but we had to keep up the pretense. This honeymoon had to look real in case there were paparazzi sniffing around, but now I had the unhappy prospect of a fortnight sharing a suite with my wife. I needed to spend as little time as possible with Charlotte from this point on, not cozy up to her in the dark.

She watched me with a discontented look. It should have been a turnoff, but she was so sexy when she was pissed off with me. At least it was a spark of life.

"I'm not changing my name. You'll have to amend the contract," she hissed.

"You already signed it."

She let out an angry huff and her fingers clutched my shoulder so tightly they burned. "Then set your lawyers on me. I'm not doing it."

"If you want your money at the end of all this, you're doing it."

There was no way out of the sleeping situation, but it was only two weeks. I'd send her off with a guide to do tourist things in the day, and at night I'd keep myself busy. The penthouse was big enough to keep a distance, and Rome was a big and exciting city. Charlotte would have plenty to do alone.

When we got home, I'd send her off back to the Cotswolds. She was content there, and I had Elain, one of the few people I trusted, to keep an eye on her. Problem solved. The song ended and couples filtered onto the dance floor. If I put as much distance between us as possible, it would allow these feelings to pass. Everything would be fine. If I wasn't anywhere near her, then I couldn't be tempted by her. Out of sight, out of mind. This was manageable, but for now, people were watching us, and it would defeat the entire purpose of this farcical event if I didn't hold her close.

"We'll be leaving soon." I pulled her flush against me. Her soft breasts rested against my chest and made my heart pound. "Another dance until then, Mrs. Thorner?"

Chapter 25

There is no pain like a migraine. Sometimes I could feel one coming on, and sometimes an attack came from nowhere. This one had taken me by stealth. It was probably the stress of lying through my teeth all day and then the pressure changes inside the private jet. I let my head rest against the leather car seat. Rome flashed by in a blur of ancient ruins, cobbled streets, and picturesque moonlit piazzas, and I had no energy to look.

"You OK?" Cole spoke without looking up from the laptop balanced on his knees.

A pulse thundered behind my right eye, and pain radiated down the side of my head. The dress weighed heavy on my shoulders and the fabric pinched. Enough. Only sleep would fix this. Cool sheets. Darkness. Tomorrow would be a new day. "Fine."

The car stopped, and the driver opened the door. I stepped out onto a narrow walkway lit by vintage lamps. I'd expected a characterless luxury resort, but the tall, crooked building ahead looked charming with an unassuming stuccoed facade, shuttered windows, and ornate balconies.

Cole joined me. "La Dolce Vita. It's one of the best hotels in the world. The penthouse suite has the most amazing view of the city."

La Dolce Vita? A shock ran through me. "Dad talked about this place."

"He stayed here?"

No. He'd never have been able to afford that. Dad had lived in university dorms while he studied for his thesis. "He visited. He was interested in the crypts underneath."

"Crypts?"

"This hotel is famous. There's an entire network of ancient tunnels under here."

"You know more about it than me." He raised a wry eyebrow, but there was a hint of unease in his voice. "I'm more interested in the Michelin-star restaurant."

Most married couples probably have the hottest sex of their life after their wedding. Cole and I were not most married couples. This was bad even for a fake wedding night. We were in Rome, in an unfathomably luxurious hotel, and I barely had the will to look out of the window. Instead, I had mind-bending agony and an uninterested groom who'd immediately disappeared to the balcony with his laptop.

Cole flicked the light switch, and blinding light flooded the enormous bedroom. Gold glinted on every surface, dazzling me. The suite was the epitome of Italian elegance, all marble and clean lines, but in its fully shining glory it was about to melt my brain.

"Have you seen my laptop charger?"

Pain blazed at my temple. "Turn it off!"

"What are you doing in the dark?"

Tears filled my eyes. My voice came out an anguished cry. "Please. Just turn off the light. I'm begging you."

He flicked the switch again. A strip of light from the bathroom highlighted his silhouette in the doorway. He watched me as I rifled around inside my suitcase on the bed. Even this simple movement felt impossible.

"What are you looking for?"

Please go. "Nothing. Your charger is on the dining table."

I let out a moan of frustration as I threw aside toiletries and T-shirts.

"It doesn't look like nothing," he said quietly.

"I have a migraine. I need my drugs."

I found my triptan nasal spray in a zipped pocket. Finally! I wedged the cool plastic into my nostril and pressed the trigger on the canister. A disgusting taste hit the back of my throat. I sank down on the bed with my head cradled in my hands, trying not to cry because it would only make the pain worse. My tight dress dug into my ribs with each labored breath.

Cole moved closer. "What do you need?"

"I have to wait for this to kick in. That's if I got it early enough for it to work."

A small sob escaped me. I hoped so. Sometimes these things lasted for days, and we were in this place I'd always dreamed of visiting. I stumbled to stand in front of the mirror and fiddled with the back of my dress. Tiff had laced me into it this morning. It was a beautiful dress, but I'd been wearing it for hours in two different time zones, and if someone set fire to it, I wouldn't miss it.

Cole stood behind me, his tense, hard body radiating heat. "Let me help you."

"I'm fine."

Gently, he caught my hands and held them still. "Stop fussing. I've got it."

His hands worked carefully to unfasten the delicate buttons and untie the tight laces at my back. With each gentle tug, he created space for me to breathe a little easier. I watched his focused expression in the mirror. Despite the overwhelming pain, his warm breath on the back of my neck kicked my body into alert. My nerves thrummed with an unwelcome thrill. He looked more captivating than ever as a groom. I hadn't been able to take my eyes off him all day.

He caught my gaze in the mirror. "How often do you get these migraines?"

I'd been staring at him too boldly, but I didn't have the energy to feel guilty. "Once a month. Twice if I'm unlucky."

"For how long?"

"Years."

"Have you seen a specialist?"

It took too much effort to talk. "On the NHS? I'll die of old age before I get halfway up the waiting list. Nothing helps anyway. It's just something I have to deal with."

A wave of nausea gripped me. I groaned and squeezed my eyes tight.

"That's it. I'm calling a doctor."

"No. I just need to lie in the dark and give the medicine a chance to work."

He pressed his lips. "I'm booking you in with my doctor as soon as we get home. I'm not having you suffering like this."

He loosened the last ribbon, and the dress gaped open at the back. I took a deep breath. The pulse in my head was dimming a little. "Thank you."

He pulled back the heavy comforter on the enormous bed. "Let's get you in here."

"I can manage."

"You don't have to manage. I'm helping."

Every movement triggered another pulse of pain. His commanding voice left no room for dissent, and I didn't have it in me to protest. It hurt too much to talk.

"What causes migraines?"

"No one knows. Probably all that suppressed feminine rage. Please shut up. We need to stop talking to each other. It hurts."

He raised a dark brow. "Understood."

Gently, he helped me out of the heavy dress, peeling it off until I stood in my underwear. The bridal lingerie Cole—or, more likely, a put-upon assistant—had picked out was sinfully sexy. My boobs nestled in a structured balconette bra, and a white lace suspender belt held up sheer thigh-high stockings. At least the dim light hid my embarrassment.

I fiddled with the suspender belt clips, trying to free my stockings. They were so bloody fiddly and everything was too difficult.

"Stop." Cole caught my fingers and held them still.

Silently, he reached down and unfastened each clip. His deft fingers brushing my thighs made heat pool in my lower belly. Without a word, he dropped to his knees and slid the first stocking down. Cold air caressed my skin as he worked the silky fabric gently over my calf.

"Lift your foot," he commanded.

I rested a hand on his shoulder and lifted my foot so he could pull the stocking over my ankle. Repeating the motion, he peeled my other stocking down slowly. His unwavering gaze held mine as his fingers traced the skin at the back of my knee, leaving goosebumps in their wake. Shivers raced through my body. I couldn't lie. I'd played out the scenario of Cole on his knees for me many times before. His cool, unhurried words from when he'd made me come rang in my ears. *You needed this. Didn't you, Charlotte?*

Cole was so skilled with his fingers, I couldn't help but wonder about his tongue. I'd never had a man go down on me before. It wasn't something I'd ever imagined I'd enjoy. It made me feel too awkward, but with Cole I just knew it would be different. He never made me feel awkward. It was always so natural between us.

"You said you never kneel for anyone." My voice came out a husky whisper.

He tipped his head up and his dark eyes glimmered earnestly. "You must be my exception."

◆ ◆ ◆

Cole pressed a wet flannel on my head, and the cold relief made me moan. A gentle click sounded on the bedside table. "Water here."

"Thanks."

The mattress depressed as he lay down in the darkness next to me.

"Are you sure there's nothing I can do?"

He'd already helped me into my pajamas and guided me between cool sheets. I'd been able to slip my bra off discreetly through the arm of my pajama shirt.

"Nothing. You don't have to stay."

"I'm not leaving you alone like this." He rested his head on the pillow. "I'll stay just in case you think of something."

I had no strength to argue, and I didn't want to. His calm presence soothed me. Nobody took my migraines seriously. Tiff dismissed them as headaches, even though she was a drama queen if she caught even a sniffle. I closed my eyes, praying for the fog that clouded my brain to lift. The medicine had taken the edge off the pain, but a dull pulse still thrummed behind my eye.

"I don't want to miss out on Rome. I've always wanted to be here."

"If you're not better in the morning, I'll get you a doctor first thing."

"What are we doing tomorrow?"

He shifted his position on the bed. "I've organized a private tour for you. The guide will take you to the sights."

"What about you?"

"I have work to catch up on."

I rubbed the tight tendons at the back of my neck. He was planning to spend the honeymoon working? It's not like I had legitimate grounds for company, since it wasn't a real honeymoon, but I'd at least hoped for a companion to explore with. Disappointment ground in my gut, but I kept it from my voice.

"Are you going to take any time out to explore?"

"I've got a lot on."

"But this is Rome. History-nerd heaven. You can't just stay in the hotel."

"I'll survive," he said quietly.

"You're not even coming to the Sistine Chapel?"

"No."

A pang pulled at my heart. I could convince myself it didn't matter, but it would be a lie. All of these sights would be better in Cole's company. Was he really going to send me off alone with a guide? This was a sham marriage, but it didn't mean we couldn't negotiate it in a companionable way. I'd expected too much of this man, and given his track record, I should have known better.

In the dark silence, the conversation we'd had earlier drifted to mind and rankled me anew. "I meant what I said before. I'm not changing my name."

"We need to share a name. It's about how it looks. Let's not talk about it now. You need to rest."

Another wave of sickness passed over me. Pain and frustration sharpened my voice. "This isn't me just trying to be awkward. Plenty of people don't take their spouse's name. It's not unusual."

"Not now," he said quietly.

Resolve hardened my heart. I had no energy, but I'd have to fight him on it. It was too important to back down. "Give me this one thing, Cole. I don't care about the rest of it. You can bring me on honeymoon and pawn me off with a guide because you can't be bothered to spend time with me. Work yourself into the ground in the most beautiful city in the world if that's what you want. I'll take it without complaint, but please give me this. I'm an Ackroyd." My voice broke. "I can't lose another piece of my dad."

Silence. Cold water from the compress on my head dripped uncomfortably down my neck. Cole would never capitulate. "What about Ackroyd-Thorner?"

"It sounds ridiculous. Too long," he said.

"How are we going to get through this year if you're never willing to compromise?"

Silence wrapped around us again.

"You're right." His low, clipped voice shocked me. He'd been quiet for so long I thought he'd fallen asleep.

"I am?"

"A marriage is about compromise; a fake one, even more so. This is a partnership. We'll both be Ackroyds."

My heart pounded. "You're not serious?"

"As long as we're a united front, it doesn't matter which name." He turned onto his side, his face inches from mine. "If you need anything tonight, let me know."

My eyes filled with sudden tears. If only Dad were here. He'd be touched by Cole as an Ackroyd. I couldn't think about Dad too much. He'd been at the forefront of everything today, walking beside me every step.

I kept my gratitude simple so as not to burst into tears. "Thank you. I think Dad would have loved that."

His low voice came out rough. "Good. I've never liked being a Thorner anyway."

"I really missed him today." A hard lump made my throat ache.

I couldn't stop the tears I'd been bottling inside all day springing to the surface. Then I was crying. My whole purpose had been taking care of Dad, and now I had no purpose. It wasn't fair. None of it. How could anyone suffer the way Dad had? How could someone be gone forever? It was senseless.

Without a word, Cole pulled me into his arms and held me while I cried. My throat was raw, but it was impossible to stop. I'd been so stoic all day, but I couldn't be anymore.

"I miss him. I miss him. I miss him."

He stroked my hair. "I know. It will get easier."

"I'm on my own now."

"You have your sister and your nieces," he said, more softly than I'd ever heard.

"They have their own lives."

The tears kept coming. Cole held me tight, but I clung to him even tighter. This man who'd known my father, too. This man who my father had loved once. Who I'd loved. I cried until my body was exhausted. My eyes burned, and my body was weak from the effort. I thought I heard Cole's soft murmur before sleep claimed me.

"You're not on your own. You'll always have me."

Chapter 26

Cole

La Dolce Vita came with its own ancient ruins underneath. *How fucking marvelous.* It would hugely inflate the price. What's more, the place seemed to have been restored with a limitless budget. There were polished marble staircases, frescoes, original period features, and Roman busts in the lobby. It was part museum, part hotel. If the shareholders were pissed off with me now, then they were going to be furious when I put an offer in on this place. It wasn't at all in keeping with the brand. I'd be lucky to get any backing for this. I'd be lucky not to fucking bankrupt us.

"Just think. This dates back to antiquity. These tunnels are over two thousand years old." Charlotte's smile was charmed as she peered around the dimly lit winding cavern.

Antiquity was going to cost me a fucking fortune. This was a bad investment. Gabe probably wanted to get rid of it because it was costing too much to maintain. My father would probably stick a casino or something in these crypts. Not like he gave a fuck about culture and history. He'd do what he always did. Sack everyone. Strip the place and run it at half the cost.

Charlotte's sandals echoed on stone as she moved further into the tunnels. My head ached with exhaustion. It had been impossible to sleep last night. My mind hadn't stopped racing. It was terrible to see Charlotte in pain and not be able to do anything to fix it. Awful to feel so helpless. I ran a finger over the scarred stone walls. Had my mother been down here? She'd never had much interest in history. She would have been here for the luxury spa and the perfect Aperol spritz in the terrace bar.

Charlotte beamed. "This place is another level. I love all of the period features. Did you see the frescoes in the reception?"

Right, the bloody frescoes. More added to the price.

She pulled out her phone and scrolled with an animated expression. "Nobles and royals visiting Rome used to meet at this hotel. There's so much history here. No wonder Dad liked it."

My phone buzzed with a call from the office. I itched to get back upstairs to the room to work. I'd already taken too long off.

"My driver is going to take you to meet the tour guide."

Charlotte's face dropped. "You sure you don't want to come?"

"I can't."

She blew out a breath. "OK, well. I'm going to have fun in the Eternal City." She smiled. "Enjoy your spreadsheets and your . . . whatever else it is you do. See you for dinner?"

"I'll grab something quick in the room."

Her eyebrows rose. "Nope. You said you were interested in the restaurant. There's a world-famous chef and a view over the city to die for. We need to eat together. It will look weird if I eat alone." She gave me a playful boop on the nose. "See you later, Mr. Ackroyd."

My skin tingled with the warmth of her touch. Our eyes locked for a moment. I tried to keep my expression calm, but my pounding heart betrayed me. Her hand hovered a fraction too long before she swooped it away and pressed her arm to her side.

Her cheeks reddened and her gaze darted away. "I'm sorry, I have no idea why I just did—"

"It's fine." I resisted the urge to brush my nose and feel where her fingertips had been. "Enjoy your tour. I'll see you for dinner."

I worked in the hotel bar. The air conditioning was distracting in the bedroom and the balcony was too hot. This was just right. Nice to have a bit of a buzz, but still quiet enough to concentrate. I took another sip of perfect coffee. Whoever had made this was an expert. When I sealed the deal on this hotel, I'd have to make sure we held on to the barista. My father usually sacked everyone when he made a new acquisition. It wasn't a nice way to do business, but it was often easier. Fresh staff were usually more amenable to a new vision and change in operation.

I called Lucas. His face appeared on the screen. "What's wrong?"

"I need to talk to you about the offer on the hotel."

His brow knitted. "God. I thought it had to be an emergency. Why are you calling me on your honeymoon?"

"Because the world doesn't stop just because I'm in Rome."

"No. But work should. Go back to your wife."

"What does it matter to you?"

He scraped his embarrassing beard and smirked. "Fine. It doesn't. Carry on. What about the offer?"

"We won't be able to beat him on price. I'm thinking of a different angle for the negotiation. It's a high-end boutique hotel. Gabe Rivers might appreciate if we make promises about preserving what his father has built here."

Lucas sighed. "That may be, but I think you should drop it."

"Why?"

"Because you've only just won the shareholders back on side and now you want to piss them off again?"

"Who's going to be pissed off?"

"All of them."

Fuck.

Lucas pushed his glasses up the bridge of his nose. "You know why the Roman Empire collapsed, don't you?"

"Let me guess. The emperor had a bunch of wankers with too much power on his board?"

"The emperor stretched himself too thin. He bit off more than he could chew. Probably an egotistical bastard. You run affordable family resorts. Stay within the brand remit. This is personal, not business. You know you have to drop it."

Lucas only cared about the business when he had his begging cap in hand, asking me to fund another hospital wing or a multi-million-pound research project. His background was science. He didn't know the first thing about business. "If I want business advice from you, I'll ask for it."

I was about to hang up when I remembered something. "What do the boys want me to bring them back from Rome?"

"I'll ask them," he said, scratching his head.

"Don't forget." No way was I giving up my favorite-uncle spot to Theo.

Chapter 27

Cole

The waiter escorted us to a table in a quiet corner of the hotel restaurant. I held out Charlotte's chair, but she was too busy gazing at the enormous crystal chandeliers to notice.

"How was your first day exploring?"

Freckles dusted her nose. Her eyes were full of awe as she sat. "We went to the Colosseum, the Pantheon, and the Spanish Steps. Dad always used to talk about the Roman Forum, but it's even more amazing than I'd imagined." She patted her stomach in contentment. "And I've decided I need to eat gelato with every meal."

"And your head feels better?"

"Yes, thank you."

"I still think you should have rested today. You took plenty of breaks?"

"Renata wouldn't let me walk ten paces without stopping to drink water. It's just as well. My feet are going to end up as hooves with all these cobbles." She wrinkled her nose. "Renata is very nice, but she fusses over me even more than Elain."

Good. Theo had found Renata for me. She was a professional bodyguard who just happened to know Rome like the back of her hand. If my wife was walking around this city all day, then I wanted her safe. Theo only had the best on his team, and I'd told Renata that if she wanted a big fat tip, then Charlotte didn't need to know that she was anything other than a tour guide. "Good. It's hot out there. It sounds like your guide is just being cautious."

"It's definitely hot. You should come with us tomorrow. Get some sunshine."

"I'm up against it with work."

She nodded sagely. "You keep telling me that. But I know the truth."

An uneasy feeling crept over me. Was I making it too obvious? If she accused me of having feelings for her, I'd have to deny it. It had almost killed me last night to see her in those stockings. Thank God for migraines, because otherwise I would have been on my knees begging her to let me spend the night worshipping her body.

I kept my face neutral, but braced myself. "What truth?"

She raised an amused eyebrow. "Vampires can't risk direct sunlight. It's too bright out there."

The tension in my jaw relaxed. "True enough. That's also why I ordered the risotto without garlic."

She lowered her gaze to the menu and shot me a furtive glance. "There are no prices on here."

"People who stay in places like this don't talk about money." I raised a sardonic eyebrow, so she'd know I didn't take any of this stuff seriously. "It screams nouveau."

"Also because it would give us plebs a nosebleed to see it in print. I'd have to sell a kidney to afford a crouton in here."

A smart waiter appeared. He hovered with a pen in his white-gloved hand. "Good evening. It's a pleasure to have you here again, Signor Thorner."

"Ackroyd. It's Signor Ackroyd now."

It felt strange to speak it out loud. What would Roy have made of me taking his name? He hadn't wanted me anywhere near Charlotte in the end. I could only hope I wasn't pissing off his ghost. Charlotte shot me a charmed look. Good that she was pleased. Even better when my dad heard I'd so easily ditched his legacy. *Fuck being a Thorner. Fuck him.*

The waiter inclined his head to Charlotte. "Signora, may I take your order?"

She scanned the menu again with an anxious look. "I might need a minute. My Italian is rusty." She fiddled with the silver hoops in her ears and muttered under her breath, "And when I say rusty, I mean nonexistent."

"Do you want me to order for both of us?"

Her shoulders relaxed a fraction. "If you don't mind."

I ordered way more than I would normally for two, but Charlotte deserved a treat. The waiter left, and I looked up to find her watching me.

She gave me a faint smile. "Italian, huh? You do it with the accent and everything."

"We have a few offices over here."

"Where else?"

"All over. Everywhere."

"No wonder you're always so busy. I'm flattered you tore your-self away from the screen for dinner."

Busy. Busy. That's me. At some point, I'd have to break my plans to the shareholders. Maybe I could send Lucas in to soften the blow. He could do these things in a genial way. People trusted Lucas. It was the glasses and the single-dad thing. Lucas would never have to pay a companion to make him look like a decent human being. Annoying.

I still had some things to finish up tonight, but I wanted to make sure Charlotte ate well after seeing her so ill yesterday. The change of scene looked like it was doing her good. We fell into companionable silence while the waiter poured the drinks, and I fought not to stare at the green flecks in Charlotte's eyes. The waiter offered me wine, but I declined.

Charlotte watched me over the rim of her wineglass. "I just realized something. I never see you drink alcohol."

"Because I don't."

"What? Never? Not even beer?"

Mum's decline had put me off alcohol for life. "Not even beer."

Her eyes darted over my face as though trying to solve a puzzle. She frowned and shook her head, joining the dots. "I don't have to drink if you're not. I'll get them to take it away."

"You carry on. I'm not in recovery, if that's what you're thinking, I just like to keep a clear head."

She nodded, but the uneasy wrinkle between her brows didn't diminish.

"Tell me about Rome. What have you enjoyed most?"

I listened to Charlotte talking with animation about the Colosseum until the waiter returned with a host of trays and deposited plate after steaming plate. The rich aroma wafted in the air. She ate a mouthful of risotto. Her face melted in pleasure, and a low moan escaped her lips. Chatter from the other part of the restaurant faded. I couldn't drag my eyes away from her mouth. I wanted to taste her. It wasn't enough to feel her come on my fingers. I wanted to feel my pretty wife come on my tongue. Heat spread through me.

"Is this what food actually tastes like? Why did no one tell me? I could get used to all this. Beautiful sights. Sunshine. Incredible food. The Italians are winning at life." She licked her lips and waved her fork over the rice. "What do they put in this stuff? Crack?"

"Truffles. Crack would be cheaper."

She chuckled. "You know, I forgot how funny you are."

I raised a brow. "I'm not funny."

"You are when you're relaxed. You used to always make me laugh." She swirled her wine in her glass and took a sip. "Can I ask you something that's been bugging me?"

I nodded.

She glanced over her shoulder and lowered her voice. "Why me? You could have hired a professional. An escort or an actress. I'm sure you're surrounded by women a hundred times more elegant and refined than me."

"I don't need elegant and refined."

She flinched. The words had been careless. I hadn't meant them to sound bad, but she had to know what I meant.

"I just mean to say that this is about weaving a narrative. You represent my life before I became the Cole Thorner that the world knows. You're a normal person from a normal place. Unfiltered and authentic. You have that accent. You open your mouth and, no matter what you say, it sounds homey and trustworthy. A good girl like you will impress the people I need to impress."

She swirled a finger around the rim of her wineglass. "A good girl? Is that how you see me?"

"I remember when you hyperventilated after I stole a pick-and-mix from the cinema. When all the other kids were sneaking out to get drunk in the park, you were doing watercolor sessions for the old people at the nursing home."

"So you married me because I'm just the right level of uncool? I see."

Her face dropped. That was the thing about Charlotte. She could never keep anything from her face. Every emotion played out so clearly. She'd be a terrible poker player. That was one of the first things Philip had taught me. *Never show your hand. Never let anyone know what you're thinking. Everyone is out to manipulate you. Don't let them.*

The chink of silverware drifted to us. "I didn't say that. It doesn't matter either way. I married you because you're exactly what I need."

"And how do you know I'm still a good girl? You haven't known me for years." Her eyes held a glint of goading.

Was she flirting with me? Too much wine.

"That's true. You'll have to tell me. Are you still a good girl, Charlotte?"

Her cheeks pinked, and her brow furrowed. I watched her throat bob as she swallowed. My cock stiffened, all too interested in a conversation it had no business being involved in. Her squirming only served to give me a raging hard-on. I couldn't get the image of her in that white lingerie out of my mind, or the way she'd trembled when I'd slipped her stockings down her tempting thighs.

There were a million ways I'd enjoy making Charlotte Ackroyd blush. I'd spent years rehearsing them in my head with a fist around my cock. *Get a grip.* This wasn't about flirting. There was no reason to be using a low voice. No reason to be leaning so close. I cleared my throat and sat upright in my chair.

She picked up the seafood fork. The silver glinted in the light as she studied it. "I'm not a saint."

"That makes two of us."

"I keep thinking about . . ." She bit her lip and whispered, "After the ball. What happened between us . . ."

Definitely tipsy. She thought about it too? Her orgasm face had blazed into my brain. "You said it couldn't happen again."

"I don't think it should, but that doesn't mean I have to stop thinking about it. So, no, I'm not a good girl. I signed up for a year of celibacy and now all I can think about is what we can't do together."

Her cheeks flushed a brighter red. She glanced over at the bar. "Anyway, maybe I'll get lucky and meet some handsome Italian stranger on this trip. No strings."

Drunk and horny. "Is that what you want?"

Her eyes met mine. "People have physical needs. It's not unreasonable. You said you wouldn't have a problem with it if I'm discreet."

My hand tightened around my fork. I'd changed my mind. I'd definitely have a fucking problem with it. Also, it was impossible to be discreet here. I wanted to buy this place. What if word got back that my wife was fucking the bellhop on the honeymoon?

"I told you, I'm happy to facilitate your physical needs."

Her face clouded with uneasiness. "I don't want you to. It's too messy between us."

"So you'd rather fuck a stranger?"

A tired look passed over her face. "It's easier."

It wouldn't do. This couldn't get too deep, but that didn't mean some prick got to put his hands all over my wife. She'd signed the contract. She couldn't seriously be thinking about hooking up with someone already? I kept my voice low and composed.

"I'm sure you can wait until we get home. Consider letting the ink dry on the marriage certificate before you spread your legs for some random."

Her swift recoil was as though I'd slapped her. She stood.

"Sit down," I said calmly. "People are looking."

"Tell them I've lost my appetite."

I couldn't take my eyes off her ass in that dress as she stormed away, because she was so fucking sexy even when she looked like she wanted to punch me.

Chapter 28

CHARLOTTE

Six scorching days passed, and I saw a lot of Rome and very little of Cole, which was fine by me. I spent my days exploring bustling piazzas and eating caramel gelato fast before it melted all over my hand. Renata did a good job of explaining the sights, even if I couldn't shake the feeling that she was babysitting me.

At the hotel bar, I sipped a perfectly zesty and sweet cold limoncello.

"May I join you?" Cole's clipped voice drifted to my ears.

If you must. I looked at him and shrugged. Cole had barely spoken to me for days. He could sit wherever he wanted, and I didn't have enough fucks left to give after the way he'd treated me on our honeymoon. He'd been kind to me the night of the migraine, but ever since he'd treated me like a sickness to be avoided. I hadn't expected him to act like a real husband, but neither had I expected to feel like a huge inconvenience.

Amazing that he'd dragged himself away from his phone. How could anyone come to the most beautiful city in the world and never leave the hotel room? The man was a pathological workaholic.

It was tragic, really. Some mornings, I was sick to my stomach with grief, but at least I was pushing myself to keep going and explore.

He sat and ordered himself mineral water and another limoncello for me. "It's late. Aren't you coming to bed? What are you doing down here alone?"

"I'm hiding from my husband."

He straightened a couple of coasters so that they were perfectly aligned before putting his glass on one. "I see."

I shouldn't have been so angry. He was right. I'd signed the contract. I should have known I'd be looking around this city alone. He drank his water quietly. Of course he would put the onus on me to make conversation.

"I suppose you're wondering why I'm hiding from my husband?"

He arched a dark brow. "Not especially."

Tough luck. You're going to hear it anyway. "Because he's an arsehole. He's such an arsehole it's literally on his Wikipedia page."

A wrinkle appeared between his eyebrows. "You know you can't trust these things. I'm sure it's not verified."

"No. I trust it. But I don't care about him, anyway." I drained the rest of my limoncello and put the glass down too heavily on the bar. "It doesn't matter that he's an arsehole. I only married him for his money. He's an excessively rich arsehole." *And excessively sexy, but he won't be hearing that from me. His head is already too big.*

He ran his elegant fingers up through the condensation on the side of his glass. "And why do you think he's an arsehole?"

"Everyone does."

"Right, but why do *you*?"

"I wouldn't even know where to start."

His gaze met mine. "Try."

Fine. If that's what he wanted. I wasn't in a good mood tonight. Rome was wonderful, but Cole's behavior this week and all the walking around in the heat had made me tired and irritable.

I pierced him with a sharp look. "For a start, he brings me here to this beautiful place and then he ignores me and makes me feel like I'm invisible. He hardly ever talks to me. He'd be happy with casual sex but looks physically ill at the idea of any kind of commitment."

I could have stopped there, but all this shit-talking while he watched me moodily was cathartic, so I sucked in a breath and plowed on.

"He's rude and patronizing. He acts jealous and possessive even though he couldn't care less about me. Years ago, he ghosted me and treated me like dirt. I thought I loved him once, but I was just a deluded kid. A long time ago. He's never cared about me."

He turned his face away. His clipped, unfeeling voice twisted like ice around my heart. "I'm surprised you married him if he's that bad."

"Like I said, he's very rich, and everything ends. Anything with an end can be endured."

His voice dripped with icy disdain. "Is that how you feel? Your husband is something to be *endured*?"

"Yes."

His disaffected gaze roved over me. "Pity you're stuck with him. I just hope he's paying you well." He pulled his phone from his jacket pocket. "I have to go back to work."

Of course you do. He turned his back on me and disappeared.

Chapter 29

COLE

"I've been here over a week. Where the fuck is Gabe Rivers?"

Theo's gravelly voice came down the line. "I had it on good authority he'd be there. He must have changed his—"

Crackling filled my ears. I stormed to the other side of the balcony to pick up better reception.

"I can't hear you. What was that last part?" I barked.

"His football team has had a big win. He's probably got caught up in the celebrations."

"Keep me posted on his movements. I need to know exactly when—" Crackling filled my ears again. "Theo? Are you still there?"

The line went dead. *For fuck's sake.* The sun beat down. I unfastened the top button of my shirt. It was too early to be this hot. I hadn't even had an espresso yet. Anger made my nerves raw. I was paying five grand a night for patchy Wi-Fi.

"Vatican City today." Charlotte popped her head around the balcony door.

Her hair hung damp from the shower and a towel wrapped tight around her chest, pushing up her full, shapely breasts. I fought to keep my gaze from drifting down to where the towel skimmed her delicious, thick thighs. She moved to the balcony and peered at the impressive panorama over Rome. This had to be the best view in the city. The Colosseum and Roman Forum dominated the mosaic of terracotta rooftops and winding cobbled streets.

Her eyes filled with wonder. "You could stay here forever and never get bored. How am I going to fit it all in?" Her voice was bright. "Sure you don't want to come today?"

"I have too much work to do." I paced to the other end of the balcony, holding my phone up to see if any magical little bars of reception would appear.

Charlotte rolled her eyes. "Leonardo. Raphael. Michelangelo. Donatello. We're talking about all the turtles in one place. Iconic Renaissance art and history at its finest. But why would anyone want to take time off work for that?"

"Because it's inhumanely hot and overcrowded with tourists."

"It's not that bad. You can't take a break?"

"I'm the head of the company."

"So? Don't you have minions?"

None that I could trust not to sell the company for magic beans.

"You're on honeymoon. People are going to think it's weird that you're working."

"I can't afford to take time off."

She threw her hands up. "We're in Rome. You can't afford not to. You can't put a price on beauty, Cole."

"Yes. You can. This suite costs five thousand euros a night. My work obligations come first. That's the first point in the contract. If you want to go on more trips like this, then you'd better let me do my job so I can bankroll it."

Hurt glimmered in her eyes. "Of course. Sorry I mentioned it. Do what you need to do."

She disappeared back into the suite. A guilty feeling swept over me. I'd been too harsh, but it was the adrenaline thrumming through my body. Why could I never take time off without my company falling to shit? I'd hardly slept last night thinking about her words in the hotel bar. Everyone thought I was an arsehole, and I didn't give a fuck, but it rattled me how much she despised me. These past few days in Rome had lifted her spirits. I didn't want my shitty attitude bringing her down.

I dialed Theo's number again. He answered on the fifth ring. *Sloppier than ever.*

"I'm in the middle of something," he growled.

"Any security updates?"

"Stop calling me. You're on honeymoon." I could hear his disapproving frown in his tone.

"Answer my question."

"For fuck's sake. You're going to make me lose the bet."

"What bet?"

"I gave the two of you a year. Lucas said six months. Stop thinking about work or you're not going to make it past a week. Lucas said your shareholders are grumbling. They won't like you offering on this hotel—"

"What is Philip offering Gabe? He's filled my company with moles. Maybe it's time I returned the favor. I want eyes and ears inside his office. I'm sick of him getting the jump on me."

Silence filled the line before his low growl. "I can't help you with that."

"Why not?"

"Because if we park the ethics to one side, you're asking me to commit corporate espionage. You want to get yourself locked up? You don't need to stoop to *his* level."

Then what? Let Philip win? Not going to happen. Sweat dripped down the back of my neck. I needed to get out of this heat, and I needed a fucking espresso. "You used to get paid to blow shit up and kill people in Helmand, and now when I ask you to do something for me, you've developed a conscience?"

"Fuck you." The line went dead.

Bastard. My heart pounded as I stepped back into the suite. Cool air and a hint of Charlotte's floral perfume offered welcome relief. She didn't turn around when I walked back in.

"Are you mad at me?"

"Nope." She gave me an overbright smile. "You're right. Work comes first. It's in the contract."

She propped a wide-brimmed white hat on her head and grabbed her sunglasses. She looked like a Roman goddess in that yellow sundress, like she'd been born from sea-foam and had temples built for her and cults worshipping at her feet. What would it be like to spend a day in Rome with her? Hot and overcrowded, probably, but wouldn't it be worth it to watch her face when she peered up at the Sistine Chapel ceiling for the first time? Maybe I could go with her. Would she even want that?

I opened my mouth, but the words wedged in my throat. My father's voice played in my head. *Speak up, you stuttering idiot.* Charlotte grabbed her handbag and slipped it onto her shoulder.

"Was there something else, Cole?"

Her expectant gaze made my heart pound. My phone buzzed in my pocket. Lucas again. What now? The office had probably burned down while he was photocopying his arse.

"No. I have to take this call." I turned my back on her. "Have a nice day."

In the suite, I video-called Lucas. "How many people are in this sweepstake speculating how long my marriage lasts?"

Lucas tapped his beard gently. "Ten or eleven?"

"You fuckers. Who?"

"I'm not a snitch. We can't help it. No one saw you as the marrying kind, and your wife is just so . . . nice. And you're . . ." He smothered a smile. "You know . . . you're *you*. Reuben gave you the best odds. He thinks you're going to go all the way. Till death do you part."

Fuck Reuben. He'd probably be the one sending me to my grave.

Lucas chuckled darkly. "Look, I'm sorry. We're just kidding around. Everyone can see how perfect you are for each other. We all see the way you look at each other. You two are the real deal. It's very sweet. Everyone is very impressed. The shareholders have piped down. This was the right move."

Fuck. Were we actually managing to pull this off? "We look sweet to you?"

"Yes. I wish my wife had looked at me the way yours does. You're lucky. We're all happy for you, honestly. Enjoy your honeymoon. Stop thinking about work and have fun." He waved a chiding finger. "And under no circumstances buy any luxury hotels until we think of a way to soften up the shareholders. You've made them happy with your new image. Don't immediately fuck it up.

"The kids are asking after you. You should come over when you get home. Bring your wife." He smirked. "That's if she hasn't already divorced you before the flight home. But please don't let that happen, because then Olive wins the bet."

"Olive?"

"Your PA's assistant. You still haven't learned your assistants' names?"

Even my assistants were in on it. My teeth gritted with irritation. "You expect me to remember the names of the assistants to my assistant?"

"Yes."

"You all need to get a life," I said, hanging up the phone. *And I'll buy a fucking hotel if I want to.*

◆ ◆ ◆

I glanced up from my laptop to watch the sunset over the piazza outside. It was late, and Charlotte wasn't back yet. I couldn't get Lucas's words out of my head.

I wish my wife had looked at me the way yours does.

It gave me a tense feeling inside. How? How had Charlotte looked at me at the wedding? Whatever goodwill she'd had then had evaporated on this honeymoon. Now, I was something to be endured.

I fired off a text to Charlotte. *Where are you?*

It took at least five minutes before she replied. *The contract doesn't specify a need for me to share my minute-by-minute location with you.*

My jaw ticked. *Then I'll get it amended. Where are you?*

> *The bar. It's a vibe tonight. A lot of good-looking Italians down here.*

> *You're a married woman.*

> *I'm just looking. Is that OK, or shall we get the contract amended to forbid eyeballs?*

Jealousy coursed through me. She was taunting me. I had no one to blame but myself. This was my own fucking fault. I'd created this situation. I left the suite and found Charlotte sitting at the hotel bar. A red one-shouldered cocktail dress accentuated her beautiful curves. Her chestnut hair was straight and slicked off her face. She must have come back to the suite to get changed while I was working in the restaurant where they actually had some decent fucking Wi-Fi.

I made my way over. "Hiding from your husband again?"

"If you met him, you'd understand." She drained her glass and grabbed her handbag. "I was just leaving."

"Stay for a drink."

She sighed and traced her fingers absently up the stem of her empty wineglass. Her face was a mask of barely concealed contempt as I ordered more drinks. A grim silence stretched between us. Charlotte stared ahead at the bright bottles behind the bar. She'd been to the Vatican today, and she still looked miserable. This was my fault. I had to lighten the mood somehow and put this right.

"So you're still mad at this arsehole husband of yours?"

She shot me a glance. "Honestly, I'm over it. I couldn't care less about him."

"Cole Thorner, right? I was curious about him. I read his Wikipedia page. There are a lot of factual inaccuracies."

She rolled her eyes and twisted the corners of a coaster. "No doubt."

"For a start, it says his first company was Vexo Conglomerate, but I happen to know that's not true. I know about this guy. I used to work for him."

She threw me a dubious glance. "You worked for him? In what capacity?"

"I was his . . . handyman."

"Do you even know what a handyman does?"

"Of course. Handyman things. I hammered nails. Carried large planks of timber around on my shoulder. Sanded wood. You know the kind of thing."

"Sure. If you say so." Her gaze dropped over my Armani suit and she raised a sarcastic eyebrow. "You certainly look the part."

"It's true. Anyway, this Cole Thorner guy told me his first business was a car-washing gig. He used to go around the neighborhood with his business partner, washing cars."

She used the coaster to fan her face with casual disinterest. "I heard about that, too. It's probably not on his Wikipedia page because it was a terrible business venture. He spent so much on equipment he never made any profit."

"Oh no. He got plenty out of it. He told me it was the best investment of his life." I leaned in and lowered my voice. Her sweet perfume enveloped me. "Apparently, he had a lot of water fights with his business partner. He often got to see her in a wet T-shirt. You couldn't put a price on that."

Her cheeks pinked. *Good.* Embarrassing her was better than upsetting her.

"I take it you read the part about him being an arsehole?"

"I saw no credible sources. Anyone can edit these things."

"Probably because there are too many sources to list." She slipped down from the stool. "If you'll excuse me. I'm going to bed."

I grabbed her wrist lightly, holding her in place. "Have you ever wondered why he's such an arsehole? What made Cole Thorner the way he is?"

"I can't imagine." Every inch of her spoke of defiance, apart from her eyes. She couldn't hide the curiosity flickering in their depths. "Perhaps his handyman, who seems to have such an intimate knowledge, could enlighten me?"

I didn't do this. I didn't talk openly about the past. But Charlotte wasn't just anybody. *I wish my wife had looked at me the way yours does.* If I was ever going to trust anyone, then I could trust her, even if it was difficult. I had to try, because right now she was looking at me with the same contempt that everyone else showed. And this animosity was ruining the trip I'd wanted her to enjoy.

She studied my face. Her voice was strained and weary. "I didn't think so. You don't know anything about Cole Thorner. Honest communication isn't my husband's strength, and you must have been so busy . . . hammering all those nails."

I glanced over my shoulder at the restaurant. A few people chatted in the corner by the window, but we were more or less alone. "He told me a few things. But if I tell you, then you have to promise not to tell anyone. You ought to know your husband is a private man."

She lifted back onto the stool next to me. Her earnest eyes met mine. "If my husband knows anything about me, I hope it's that he can trust me."

I nodded. "He knows that."

The few memories I had of Penny filled my head. A *gap-toothed smile. Bright eyes. Sleeping-bag races down the stairs.* The Thorner dysfunction went back much further than my sister, but that's when everything had fallen apart.

"There is something that will never be on the Wikipedia page. Cole's older brother, Lucas, had a twin, Penelope. She was sick for most of her childhood, and sadly, she died young."

Charlotte stared at me in astonishment before her eyes filled with sympathy. "I'm so sorry. My husband never talks about his family."

I swallowed past the sudden lump of nerves in my throat. "I heard the family all coped in their own ways. Lucas went into himself. He locked himself in his room with his experiments until he could disappear to medical school and bury himself in trying to find a cure for the disease that had robbed him of his twin. Theo escaped to the military. The mother numbed herself any way possible, and the father left his broken family behind and replaced them with a shiny new one in New York."

She leaned into me, tilting her face toward mine. "And what about the other brother? What about Cole?"

Her eyes met mine, and they glimmered with kindness. Her empathy made my blood turn to ice. *Never show your hand, boy.* I couldn't risk anyone perceiving me as weak, but it felt good too, like putting down a boulder I'd been carrying on my shoulders.

"He was relieved when his father left. Philip Thorner was a cruel man, but he saved his worst ire for his most disappointing son. Cole wasn't like the other Thorner boys. He was . . ." A stab of some old, long-buried despair stole my words. *Speak up, idiot boy.* I kept my gaze fixed on the mirror behind the bar and the man reflected back at me. A grown man, not an idiot boy anymore. But not a man I cared to look at for too long.

Charlotte's hand covered mine. "He was what?"

The warmth of her touch radiated over my skin. "He was a serious, sullen creature who didn't utter a word until he was seven, and then said very little. He couldn't read or write. The letters were always mixed up in his head. He felt stupid and ashamed because the things that came easy for others didn't come easy for him.

"For a while, he had a stutter. It didn't matter how he heard the words in his head, he couldn't say them clearly. Philip Thorner thought him stupid and an embarrassment. The Thorner men had a long tradition of attending Eton, but the stuttering child was sent up north to a boarding school so remote no one would have to think about him again."

Charlotte squeezed my hand in hers. "His father was so wrong about him. Cole Thorner is the smartest man I've ever known. He's so clever it's frightening."

"I've heard it said that every kid just needs one adult who believes in them. Cole was lucky that he had a teacher who understood that this strange, quiet boy needed a little patience and encouragement. Cole felt he'd landed somewhere safe for the first time."

Charlotte looked at me uncertainly. "But he left. If he was happy, why did he leave?"

"Because the time came for Philip to groom an heir for his business, and the boy he'd once thought stupid had worked hard enough to become his best option. Philip threatened him. If he didn't fall in line, he'd ruin everything Cole cared about. He was definitely capable of it."

Charlotte's eyes widened. "That's blackmail."

"Yes. Cole bided his time until he could form his own company and make his own fortune. When Philip found out that his son was planning to betray him, he punished him. By the time Cole found out his mother had been kicked out of rehab, it was too late. She overdosed that night."

Charlotte's eyes shone with tears. Her hand moved to cover her mouth. "Oh my God. I didn't know. I'm so sorry."

The pain I never allowed myself to feel gripped my chest. When Mum had died, the shock had been a chisel strike to my heart. It had cracked me like a rock in one swift stroke to the equator. I'd wrestled with the guilt for years.

I rubbed the spot in my chest where it ached. "It hit him hard. Cole loved his mother."

Charlotte shook her head, processing. "Why didn't you tell me? Or Dad? Dad would have helped you."

I did. And no, he wouldn't. "Because it was something he had to handle himself. This is life. It's a lot of pain. A lot of mistakes and regrets. It's all history."

She peered at me intently, then laced her fingers with my hand on the bar. It was a gentle touch, but the heat sent a shock through my body. My stomach clenched tight. My pulse pounded. The chatter in the bar faded away, and I couldn't take my eyes from her beautiful eyelashes and the tiny freckle patch on her nose. I ached for this woman. I always had. All I wanted was to take her up to our room and show her that she was mine. That she'd always been mine. Charlotte had always seen the good in me. But she was the type to see the good in anyone. Too good to drag into my dysfunction.

Her voice was soft and tentative. "Dad used to say that history was the most important thing a child can learn. We are the product of everything that has come before. A book would never make sense if you ripped out the first act. It sets the scene for everything to come."

Disappointment ground in my gut. I knew that. There was no way around what had happened in the past.

She swallowed. "But sometimes I think it would be so nice to wipe the slate clean. To put it all down for a while and breathe. Do you ever feel like that?"

I looked down where our hands joined. "Put it down?"

"I don't know. It's all so heavy. You can't rip out the first act or the ending, but imagine if you could just put the book to one side? Or even just open it in the middle and find a blank page. No past. No future. Two strangers meeting in a bar in the most beautiful city in the world. Just for a moment in time."

"I don't understand."

She threw back the rest of her drink and drew a deep breath, as if gathering courage. "You said you're a handyman. What's your name?"

"My name?"

"Yes." Her eyes were full of vulnerability and hope. Full of pleading with me to play along. "Mine is . . . Natalia. I came here with my husband, but he doesn't pay me attention."

My heart pounded at what she seemed to be offering. A chance to put the book to one side? It had been so heavy, and I'd carried it for so long. There were no blank pages, but I longed for one so desperately. I'd never returned to Ecclesdale in order to keep the Ackroyds safe from my father and because I hadn't wanted to infect her with my bitterness and anger, but one night? How could I refuse?

I forced my tone not to betray my eagerness and frighten her away. "My name is Sean."

"That's a good, honest name for a handyman." Her voice held a hint of amusement.

"It's a pleasure to meet you, Natalia." I lifted her hand to my lips and kissed the back of it. Tingling lit my stomach. "Your husband is a fool for not paying attention to such a beautiful wife."

"He doesn't care about me at all. He works all the time. He went back to London and left me alone in his fancy suite for the night. I've been lonely for a while now." She chewed on her bottom lip and glanced at me. "And I think there's a problem with the walls in the suite."

The air crackled between us. "What kind of problem?"

"A problem for a handyman. Something fell off the wall and now it needs to be . . . nailed."

Her cheeks flushed bright red. The double meaning in her smile couldn't have been more obvious. My heart pounded, but amusement made my lips curve. I'd always fantasized about getting this woman into bed, but I'd never reckoned on the foreplay being the opening to a bad porno.

"Nailed? I suppose you're looking for a man with a large hammer?"

Her lips curved into a smile as she fought to suppress her laugh. "I do appreciate a man who is good with his hands."

We both needed to go into this with our eyes open. I needed to know that she was sure. She needed to know it wasn't too late to back out. "A blank page. For one night?"

Her gaze was tentative, and her voice barely above a whisper. "One night."

"You're sure?"

All traces of humor slipped from her face. She swallowed. "Yes."

Shit. A rush of nerves went through me. We were doing this.

"Then I'd better have a look at this wall." Gathering her in my arms, I guided her down from the stool. My lips found her ear to whisper low. "Sean is good with his hands, but even better with his tongue."

Chapter 30

Charlotte

"You didn't tell me your thoughts on the Sistine Chapel." Cole's rough whisper was hot against my cheek as he laid me down on the bed.

"I haven't seen it yet."

I pulled him down so that his hard body covered mine. We'd lost my dress and his trousers on the way to the bed. This was Rome's fault. The buzz and the heat and the limoncello and the sadness around Cole's eyes. I captured his mouth in a kiss, savoring the warmth and softness of his full lips. This man made me feral with lust. Shivers raced through my body, and I ached with the need to be full of him. His slow, teasing kisses shredded my patience. He was always so measured and unhurried. It had taken every ounce of self-restraint not to rip off his clothes when he was kissing me so slow and deep in the elevator.

Raising his mouth from mine, he peered into my eyes with a slight frown. "What? Why not? I thought you'd been to the Vatican?"

I frantically worked the buttons of his shirt. "I did, but I didn't get the chance to see it."

He spoke between hot open-mouthed kisses on my neck. "Why not? Isn't that the part you were looking forward to?"

I'd had the chance, but something had held me back. I didn't even know what. It was stupid. I'd built it into too big a thing. What if it didn't live up to my expectations? "I don't know. I just got too in my head about it. I can't explain."

He hesitated, watching me. "But you're planning to go? There's so much in there that you'll love. *The Last Judgement. The Creation of Adam . . .*"

Seriously? Now? I was more interested in the creation of bone-melting orgasms. Some reckless impulse had driven me in the bar downstairs. Cole had opened up in a way I'd never thought him capable of. There were still things I couldn't excuse, and his revelations hadn't suddenly made him a suitable prospect for a genuine relationship. But I couldn't help how my body craved him. If it was for one night, then I'd take one night.

I pulled off his shirt and took in his glorious, powerful presence in his tented boxers—the dark hair covering his defined pecs, his toned abs, the delicious V of his hips. This is what he'd been hiding beneath those sharp suits. A perfect marble sculpture made flesh and bone.

"I don't understand why you wouldn't go and see it if you had the chance?"

Can't we just drop it? "Are all handymen so interested in Renaissance art?"

He raised a dark brow. "I'm interested in *you*."

"No. That's not what this is." I ran my hands up the hard, taut planes of his back. "Sean doesn't care about my opinions on the Eternal City," I whispered into his ear. "Sean just wants to use me like he's getting everything he wants from me because he's never going to see me again."

Cole's throat bobbed as he swallowed. Perhaps he was expecting the inexperienced, blushing girl he'd left behind all those years ago. The tattoo hidden behind the dark hair on his chest, just above his heart, drew my gaze. It was Latin script, but I'd never have a chance of deciphering it. Best not to ask. It was probably a mood killer about crushing your enemies and drinking out of their skulls.

His hand slipped inside the cup of my bra and his fingers traced the outline of my nipple. Tingles raced from his touch, and thoughts of tattoos and anything else at all slipped out of my head. He unfastened my bra and threw it to one side.

His gaze fixed on my breasts, and he gave a tormented groan. "Fuck. Look at you."

I fought the urge to cover my breasts with my hands. My body wasn't perfect by any beauty standard, but I'd made my peace with it. If the pain of my father's slow deterioration had taught me anything, it was that aging is a gift. I was grateful for my soft stomach, round ass, and dimpled thighs. Grateful for a healthy body that worked. There was more right with me than wrong. Cole's hungry gaze roamed over me, his obvious approval searing my skin.

"So beautiful." He sucked a nipple into his mouth, and my body arched against him.

His voice was cool, but fire smoldered in his dark eyes. "Are you saying you want Sean to fuck you like he doesn't care about you?"

The pulse at my core wouldn't be relieved with soft and gentle. That's not what my body craved. "I'm saying I haven't done this for a long time, and I want to lose myself. That is, if Sean's into it . . ."

He circled my nipple lightly with his thumb and then pinched it just hard enough to sting. "Don't worry about that. He's into anything when it's with you."

He pushed my legs apart, kissed his way down my body, and positioned himself between my thighs. With a finger, he hooked my underwear to one side and then his mouth was on me. He spread me with one delicious flat-tongued lap between my lips and fixated on my swollen clit, teasing and probing. Pleasure shock-waved through me.

"Oh my God. That's better than I thought it would be."

His hot breath against my clit made my toes curl. "I don't know whether to take that as a compliment or not."

"I just mean because no one's ever done this to me."

"No one?" His tongue delved inside of me and my limbs melted like gelato. "They've missed out. This is the most delicious pussy I've ever had."

He slid off my underwear and devoured me as if he'd never come up for air. A gasp left my mouth. My hands found his soft hair, and I writhed and bucked against his face. He explored my breasts, playing with my taut nipples between his fingertips while he worked my clit with his tongue.

My fingers ached where they clawed the sheets. "You don't have to stay down there too long. I don't know if it's going to happen like this."

He pressed my thighs down with his palms, folding me in half for better access. "You taste so good. I'm staying down here until I get lockjaw."

He returned to his work, sliding a finger inside while he tongued and probed. Climax claimed me with a force so sharp and sudden it was painful. My thighs clamped around his head, but he spread me wide and gripped my ass, holding me against his face. Involuntary shudders made my body writhe across the bed, but his mouth was glued to my clit, and no matter how I jerked away from him, his hands always dragged me back.

Hot sparks crackled over my skin. Electricity sizzled from the arches of my feet to my crown. I was drowning in this cold, controlled man who I'd never imagined could be so raw and passionate. His tongue soothed my sensitive, pulsing flesh. I gripped his shoulders, marking his skin with my nails and chanting his name over and over like a benediction.

The world dissolved, and there was nothing but senseless ecstasy. No beginning. No end. No merciless, gnawing grief. Just a blank page in the middle of a book with limitless possibilities for a new story.

◆ ◆ ◆

Cole pulled off his boxers. I tried not to make my wince obvious. He had a beautiful cock, long and thick. If I could walk straight tomorrow, it would be a miracle.

"Sean wasn't lying about the size of the hammer."

With a smirk and a firm grip on my hips, he dragged me to the end of the bed.

His voice was low and serious. "You think your husband doesn't care about you, but I happen to know he does."

He maneuvered me onto all fours.

"He does?"

"He might not be good at showing that kind of thing, but he cares about you. And he respects you."

He smoothed his hands down the length of my back and placed a kiss at the base of my spine. Sincerity threaded through his voice. I cared about him too. It was complicated and weird and some days my heart was too sore to know much beyond grief, but I was glad he'd come back into my life, even if it was under such strange circumstances.

"Sean, on the other hand? I'm afraid good, honest, decent, hard-working Sean couldn't give a single shiny fuck about Natalia. He was in that bar tonight because he wanted to get laid. Anyone would do."

I adopted a scandalized tone. "Don't tell me Sean's a scoundrel?"

"He's an absolute bastard. Always cutting corners and ripping people off. He just wants you for your body. For this juicy ass."

He slapped my ass. The sound rang out loud in the bedroom. I couldn't help my laugh. "Juicy?"

"Yes. So fucking round and juicy. It drives him wild."

He slapped it again, harder. The laugh died on my lips and turned into a moan at the tingling mix of pleasure and pain. His hands cupped my breasts.

"He wants you for these beautiful, bouncy tits."

"Sean's a boob man?" I should have known from all the times I'd caught Cole sneaking glances at my chest when we were younger.

"Yes, and he's never seen better than these." He squeezed my breasts, feeling their heavy weight in his palms. "He can't believe his luck tonight."

"But Sean must have had a lot of women?"

"Not as many as you'd think. None that has ever mattered. He's always been too hung up on a woman from his past."

I had no time to process that because he started playing with my clit, circling and pinching. It was still too sensitive from my orgasm. "Fuck. It's too much. Please."

"What about Natalia? Has she had many boyfriends?"

"A couple. Nothing serious."

"Did she love any of them?"

"No. This isn't the time. Sean never stops talking. I thought he wanted to get laid?"

He grabbed a fistful of my hair and pulled my head back lightly, making my spine arch. With his hands under my chin, he forced my gaze up to meet his.

"He fixed your wall, didn't he? You should talk to him with more respect."

"You're right."

I turned around. He stood at the end of the bed, tall, naked, and confident. I'd imagined him like this many times, but no fantasy could do his sculpted masculinity justice.

I kneeled on the bed in front of him. "Sean deserves some gratitude for a job well done."

With one hand gripping the base of his shaft, I took him into my mouth as far back as I could and worked him. His fingers wound into my hair, pulling it away from my face. A moan escaped his lips. I popped him out of my mouth and flicked the salty head of his cock with my tongue.

"I love to hear you moan."

"Only for you." He cupped my face and traced my cheekbone with his thumb. "So fucking beautiful on your knees."

I worshipped him with my mouth and tongue, sucking and licking, tasting heat and salt. He reached around and circled my throbbing clit with his fingers. Pleasure shot straight to my core.

"Most of all, Sean wants to feel you like this, dripping and trembling." His voice dropped to a rough whisper and he slipped a finger inside me. "He's going to slide in right to the hilt and you're going to take every inch."

I popped him out of my mouth again. "Sean talks a good game."

A lethal glint of humor flashed across his face. "You think he's all talk?"

"I'm waiting to find out."

He grabbed a foil packet from his wallet on the bedside cabinet. His eyes glittered with lust as he sheathed himself with a condom. With a firm grip on my hips he dragged me back around, shifting me into position on all fours. He stood behind me. Nudging my legs wide, he dragged the blunt head of his cock through the slick heat between my thighs. Once. Twice. I shuffled my knees wider, weak and desperate. Every one of his movements was so unhurried.

"Your husband might care about you, but you've sassed Sean so much, he's going to fucking ruin you. Is that what you want?"

"Yes."

Standing behind me at the foot of the bed, he spread me with his thumbs and impaled me with his cock, bottoming out. The punishing stretch was so deep, I sucked in a harsh gasp. I could take the fullness, but only just. There was no time to adjust before his fingers dug into my hips and he was moving inside of me in swift, hard thrusts.

"Too much?"

This man had always been too much for me, but I still wanted him. I arched my back, pushing into him, craving more. "Keep going."

I lost myself in the fantasy. One night to be so completely free and fucked like nothing else mattered. The wet slap where our bodies joined sent a thrill through me. He slowed, pulling out completely and ramming back to the hilt in long, slow thrusts that made me want to weep with pleasure. I bucked against him, meeting his rhythm stroke for stroke.

"I always knew it would be like this between us." He smoothed a hand between my shoulder blades. His tone was low and reverential like a hushed whisper in the Vatican Museums. "It's like you were made for me. You feel so fucking good, you must have been."

I turned my head to look at him. His intense gaze met mine. This had started as a game, but this was Cole behind me. Cole filling me so brutally. My first kiss. My first love. My first heartbreak. The boy I'd been desperate to catch a glimpse of whenever he'd come over to study with Dad. I'd pressed my ear to the door and listened to him speaking Latin in that low, rumbling voice. God. How I'd wanted him. How I'd dreamed of knowing him and being like this with him. How he'd destroyed me when he left me.

He thrust into me in a slow, steady rhythm until my trembling knees gave way, and even then he didn't stop. He piled pillows under my stomach, letting them take my weight while he propped my ass in the air. A firm palm between my shoulder blades pressed me into the bed. Reaching underneath us, he rubbed my clit while he worked.

Everything dissolved into heat and sensation and Cole's glorious, relentless pounding. Another brutal, jerking orgasm seized me. I was still trembling when he pulled out, my body beginning to relax. He caressed my way-too-sensitive clit with his tongue. Sucking. Probing. Delving.

"I just came," I cried.

"Not done with you yet. You've got more for me."

Fuck. I could get off on the way he was looking at me alone, with so much focus and care. He worked me with his tongue and skillful fingers. I'd die if I came again. But he didn't stop. It was too much, like losing my footing and tumbling down a mountainside. Nothing to break my fall.

A sudden overwhelming rush of emotion gripped me. All these years. All these wasted years when it could have been like this. My body writhed and quaked. Hands gripping my ass, he drove into me, stretching me with hard, rapid strokes. I was clay, soft and malleable, and he had the power to shape me into anything he wanted. He'd always had that power over me. He'd shaped me into a woman who knew better than to ever trust a man like him. I came again, crying out and shattering around him.

His breath was hot against my ear. "That's a deep one, baby. I can feel you milking my cock. I've waited so long to feel you like this."

I clenched around him purposefully as his thrusts became erratic. His tormented groan filled my ears as he found his own release. We collapsed together in a sweaty tangle of limbs, skin on skin. A musk of sex and Cole's masculine scent hit my nose. I breathed him in like a drug I'd been denying myself and had no hope of quitting.

Breathless and panting, he gazed into my eyes. My body pulsed and quivered with aftershocks. Sex had never been like this. I hadn't even known my body was capable of such senseless pleasure. Maybe it wasn't unless it was him. Maybe that first time he'd kissed me all those years ago had conditioned me, like imprinting. He'd branded me and made me his. And from the look on his face, maybe it hadn't been like this for him either.

His fingers found my clit, but I couldn't take another orgasm. "Enough," I cried.

He withdrew his hands immediately and held them up in mock surrender. "One more?"

"I can't."

He raised an amused eyebrow. "You've got more for me."

"No. Please. You're torturing me. Enough."

"I'm addicted to watching you come." His smirk was the sexiest thing I'd ever seen. "You want another, just say the word."

Chapter 31

CHARLOTTE

"I need to shower." I disentangled myself from Cole's strong arms.

He wanted casual. A stranger in a bar. Another layer of make-believe. Fake marriage. Fantasy sex. It had to stay that way. It was the only way to protect my heart. I'd never recover from him leaving me a second time. I'd never give him the opportunity.

He clasped me back to his body and his mouth captured mine in a deep, long kiss full of lust and need. "Not done with you yet," he murmured against my lips.

His hands explored the hollows of my back, and it wasn't long before we were grinding against each other, his skin hot against mine. His hands and mouth were all over my body, exploring and savoring, like he couldn't leave a patch of my skin unmapped. I clung to him, breathing him in, needing him again. Alarm bells rang in my head despite the thrill running through me. This wasn't a casual kiss, and it needed to be.

Gently, I backed out of his arms. "I'm all sweaty, I really need to shower."

I also needed to pee. I'd already had a migraine in Rome, and I didn't need to add a UTI to the list of ailments.

His hand roamed over my hip, spreading tingles across my middle. "I'll shower with you. No point wasting water."

Despite his commanding tone, there was something vulnerable in his smile.

Resist. It has to be a one-time thing.

"I can't imagine you've ever had trouble paying your water bill."

He wrapped a strand of my damp hair around his finger and gazed at it. "It's not the money. It's the right thing to do for the environment. You should know I care deeply about the environment."

"Right. That's the first thing that comes to mind when I think about billionaires—just how much good they do for the planet."

His eyes sparkled, and his tone filled with bland innocence. "I fund plenty of conservation projects."

"Like what?"

He planted kisses along my collarbone. "Rhinos."

It was so random, I couldn't help my chuckle. "Rhinos? Why rhinos?"

"Why not rhinos? They're critically endangered. It would be a terrible loss if they went extinct."

"Of course. It makes perfect sense that you'd be the patron saint of rhinos. They're irritable and unpredictable. Solitary creatures. Thick-skinned. Quick to charge when they perceive a threat."

He raised a dark brow, but humor danced in his expression.

"Why don't you tell anyone about your charity work?"

"Why would I tell anyone? I don't need anyone to know."

"Philanthropy is good for your image. Being a do-gooder earns you more karma points than being married."

"I don't do it for karma points. And it's not part of the image I've built."

"So you're happy with the way people perceive you? It doesn't bother you? You want people to think you're an arsehole?"

"I don't care, as long as they know that I'm strong."

"Generosity isn't a weakness. In a world like this, it takes way more strength to be kind than it does to be a dick."

"My father views it as a weakness."

"So when you say you need people to think you're strong, by *people*, you mean your father?"

"OK, Carl Jung. Settle down." He kissed me again, deep and slow, his hand cupping my ass. "Why are we talking so much when we could be kissing?"

My body sang with his touch. I had to say no. Time to draw a line under it. This had been a skit. It wasn't real. But it felt so good to be light and fun. Something beyond the pockets of normality I chased with Tiff. Beyond anything I'd thought within my reach. This was a pocket of heaven.

His hand caressed my shoulder, making it difficult to focus on anything but the warm brush of his fingers. "You know what's more fun than a shower? Put those stockings on. And the heels. Nothing else."

"I can't take any more. I'm serious. Another orgasm and you'll finish me off." The words fell from my mouth unbidden. "But I don't want to be accused of not doing my bit for the environment." *And if I can't resist touching him again, then I can blame the rhinos.* "But please don't make me come again, I can't take it."

A smile twitched his lips. "Just a shower. I promise."

I couldn't trust his promises or that arrogant smirk. He'd proven that. But death by orgasm at this man's hands wasn't a bad way to go.

Chapter 32

COLE

Dull buzzing woke me. I answered my phone quickly before Charlotte stirred.

"Rumor is Gabe's going to be there sometime in the next few days. He's organized some away time for his team," Theo growled.

I blundered through the dark suite into the early morning sun on the balcony. What fucking time was it? It had been years since I'd slept in. "You're sure?"

"He hasn't accepted Philip's offer. Apparently, he wants assurances there won't be staff changes. He doesn't want people to lose their jobs. It seems Mr. Rivers is a rare beast in this world. A rich man with empathy."

Theo's unspoken words rang loud. *Unlike you.*

I took a moment to process. This gave me a good chance in negotiation. I couldn't give a fuck who worked here, as long as Philip didn't get what he wanted.

"Also, I know why he's selling. The hotel is hemorrhaging money. Those ancient tunnels cost a fortune to preserve. A lot of the art is on loan. Hotels were his father's passion. Gabe's selling everything up and plowing the money back into his football team. He likes this hotel the most. It's one of the last to go."

"Good to know. Thank you."

Theo grunted. "Don't ask me to do anything like this again."

The line went dead. I could still taste Charlotte Ackroyd on my tongue. Pigeons cooed and church bells rang somewhere. The sun was rising over Rome, bathing its ancient domes and charming terracotta rooftops in soft light. The view out here had never looked more stunning.

I leaned on the balcony, drinking it in. I'd worked for hours out here, but never really looked across to the ruins of the Roman Forum. Now I allowed my eyes to feast on the panorama. A city over two thousand years old. An empire risen and fallen. It was phenomenal. My heart, which was usually racing, thinking about some work bullshit, beat a steady drum. It was like waking up to a new city. Waking up a new man.

Charlotte Ackroyd. I'd imagined making love to her so many times, but I'd never imagined it would feel so right. Sinking into her had been like heaven. My beautiful, funny, kind Charlotte. I hadn't spent all that time with Roy because I'd cared about history. I'd learned a dead language just so I could sneak a glance at her. She felt so good and sweet, like toasted marshmallows and rolling green fields. Like riding my bike through the woods and meadows full of wildflowers. A different life entirely. One not shackled by pain and regret.

"Work already? You really don't stop, do you?"

Charlotte appeared in the doorway. She had on my shirt and nothing else. I couldn't stop my gaze from trailing up her irresistible bare legs.

"That shirt looks a lot better on you than it does on me." I pulled her to me by the lapels. "But it's going to look even better on the floor."

My mouth covered hers, and I kissed her, drinking in her goodness.

Confusion flickered across her face as she pulled back an inch, her hands still resting on my shoulders. "Last night was fun, but I thought it was a one-night thing."

"It doesn't have to be."

She raised an unimpressed eyebrow, but her tone was indulgent. "We've been through this. Orgasms are not in the contract."

"But they could be. We're two consenting adults having fun."

"I have plans this morning. I'm not traveling all the way to Rome and spending my time in the hotel room. Renata's taking me to the Trevi Fountain."

Slowly, I unbuttoned the shirt she wore, kissed a line down her body, and dropped to my knees. "Cancel your tour. Let me propose a new itinerary. It involves me licking you until your legs give way."

Amusement danced in her eyes as she peered down at me. "That's not what we agreed."

"No, but are you open to negotiation?"

Cupping her ass, I peppered kisses over her inner thighs. She wasn't wearing underwear, and it took everything I had not to zero in on her pussy. A little tease never went amiss.

She smoothed a hand through my hair. "But this is my chance to see Rome."

I pushed her back gently against the glass doors that divided the suite from the balcony and nuzzled between her thighs, inhaling her. "I understand. But I have a desperate need to eat your pussy this morning, so I'm going to do that, and then I'm going to spend the day making you come in every position imaginable."

She moaned and dug her fingers into my hair. "Renata is expecting me. We're going early to beat the crowds. I'm not missing out on a day in Rome just because the patron saint of rhinos has the horn. I might not get this chance again. You can't just change the rules of the game when it suits you."

"Sweetheart, no, you've got it all wrong. I made the game, so I control the rules." I pulled away, and she gave a growl of frustration.

"I thought you wanted me to stop?" I brushed her thigh with my thumb and a tremble ran through her.

"Let's at least go inside. This is indecent on the balcony," she muttered.

The sun beat down hot on the back of my neck, but fuck it. There was no way I'd stop when I had her like this. "It's fine. The Italians love to eat alfresco. When in Rome . . ."

I focused on her clit, probing and sucking. The smell and taste of her made my cock ache with the need to be inside of her.

She groaned and writhed against my face. "I don't want to miss my tour. You're going to make me late."

I pulled away a fraction, but kept my gaze on her glistening pussy. "I need to feel you come on my tongue, and I'll take you on a tour afterward."

"*You'll* take me on a tour?"

It wasn't my original plan, but I'd tour the moon if it meant she kept her legs open for me. "Yes."

"I thought you had work?"

Nope. Gabe Rivers wasn't here yet. I grabbed her thigh and hooked it over my shoulder, opening her wider. "I can take a break."

Her tormented moans filled my ears as I drove my tongue in and out of her. She arched her spine and spoke between breaths.

"A break? Are you physically capable of that?"

I dragged my fingers through the slick heat between her thighs and circled her clit.

Her knees trembled. "This isn't a fair negotiation while you're doing this to me."

"Life is unfair."

"This is arsehole-ish behavior. You know I'm going to agree to anything."

That's the idea. I stood and kissed her, delving my tongue into her mouth, exploring. My fingers still worked steady circles on her clit. She was close. I knew because, last night, I'd tuned into her responses. Her breathing got fast when she was about to climax. She seemed to appreciate it rough and dirty, which was fine with me, because I was going to spend this week ruining her for any other man.

I plunged a finger inside her. So tight and wet. All mine. My Charlotte.

"Why don't you be a good boy for once in your life and get back on your knees?" She gave me an unimpressed look and pushed my shoulders down. "As I recall, you vowed to make me come on your tongue, not your fingers. Although, honestly, I prefer both at the same time."

Gladly. I sank to my knees and stared at her above me. The Roman sun painted her chestnut hair in gold, and of all the magnificence in this city, she was the most divine. I lapped and sucked her clit until her legs quaked and I had to grip her ass to hold her upright.

The moment I thrust my fingers into her, her thighs clamped and she gasped. She came loudly, pulling my hair and clenching around my tongue. I worked her through every quiver and moan until she sagged against the balcony door.

She let out a soft sigh and peered down at me. "What are you doing to me?"

A trace of sadness invaded her voice. I felt it too. Among the thrill and the heat was a sense of remorse. In a different life, we should have been like this since forever. With a different start, maybe we could have spent the past decade like this. Nothing had ever felt more right.

I scooped her into my arms and carried her into the bedroom. "I could ask you the same question."

My cock was so hard it was uncomfortable to walk. I would have preferred to bend her over the balcony and feel her pulsing and twitching after her orgasm, but not without a condom. I'd never fucked anyone without protection, and although this woman made me lose my mind, I wasn't that reckless. I laid her down gently. "We need a condom."

"We don't." She sprang up and headed to the bathroom.

"Where are you going?"

She didn't turn around. "I need to shower and get ready for my tour."

"Get back in this bed."

She paused at the bathroom door. "Tour first. If you do a good job as my guide, you might get a reward later." She gave me a shrug and a sardonic smile. "Then again, you might not. Let's hope you've brushed up on your Roman history."

Chapter 33

Charlotte

"That's it. It's official." Cole stopped in the middle of a small piazza and peered at his phone. "We're lost."

No surprises. We'd always got lost when Dad took us to tour historical sights. I sipped a hot cappuccino from a takeout cup and perched on the low wall surrounding a tinkling marble fountain. I kept my tone teasing. "I thought you prided yourself on your expert sense of direction?"

"That's really not a helpful comment. What do you think?" He gestured to the crumbling stone steps that led up to a church. "Is this the same church from back there or different?"

A line of nuns streamed past him, like a black and white river around an island. The nuns headed to the church, which looked identical to at least a dozen we'd passed. "I have no idea."

The hum of distant mopeds filled the air. Cole brushed an imaginary speck of dirt from his tailored chinos. It was so rare to see him without a sharp suit on, but even hotshot CEOs had to bow to the heat in Rome. God. He looked sexy. Anyone could pick me out as a tourist with my sunburnt nose and backpack, but in his designer sunglasses and chic linen shirt rolled at the cuffs, Cole blended in like a stylish local.

"It doesn't matter." I held my arms out and tipped my head up to the sun. "Soak it in. I want the authentic Rome experience."

"But we could be missing the important stuff."

"Are you kidding me? This is the important stuff. Renata has had me marching around to all these different sights. I want a spontaneous day."

I set off walking again, and Cole fell in step alongside me. Church bells rang out somewhere. The warm breeze carried the sweet pastry smell of a bakery. We passed through one cobbled street after another until we found ourselves on a wider road, thrumming with small cars and mopeds.

Cole shot me a sidelong glance. "You know the Italians only drink cappuccino in the morning."

I laughed as I pitched my empty cup into a bin. "So what? I'm a tourist."

"I thought you wanted the authentic Rome experience?"

"I do, but I'll drink my hot frothy milk whenever I choose, thank you very much."

A small single-decker bus slowed as it rattled down the road next to us. The sign above the front window read *Villa Adriana.* It hissed to a halt at the stop.

A reckless impulse grabbed me. "Come on. We should get on that."

"A bus?" Cole's eyebrow quirked as though I'd suggested chartering the bus to the moon.

"Yes, quick."

He folded his arms and shook his head. "No. Absolutely no way."

I grabbed his hand and dragged him toward the bus stop. "Yes. Absolutely yes way."

He wrinkled his nose. "I have a driver on call."

"It will be fun to get out of the city. I read about this place in the guidebook. We're being spontaneous."

An older nun elbowed Cole out of the way. "Look how many people are getting on this." He pulled out his phone. "I'm calling the driver."

I poked him in the side. "Stop moaning. Normal people ride on the peasant wagon. Wait. Have you ever caught a bus before?"

He fiddled with the cuff of his pristine shirt. "Not that I recall."

"You can't go your whole life having never ridden a bus. That's just weird."

He smirked. "I'm sure I can live with it."

"Come on. I thought we'd have fun today?"

He raised a wry eyebrow. "Don't think I don't know what's going on here, Charlotte. You're wresting control of my tour. I'm supposed to be the guide."

I tilted my head and gave him a knowing smile. "I'm sorry. It must be difficult for you. I know how you love to be in control."

His brow furrowed. "To honor and obey. That's what you signed up for. I take it you have no plans to fall in line any time soon?"

I laughed. "Not a chance."

"I bet they don't even have air conditioning on this thing." He flattened his lips and scowled up at the bus.

"You're so adorable when you get all frowny," I said.

He rolled his eyes, but his lip twitched. "I'm not frowny."

"You're so frowny. Please. We have to be quick, or it's going to go without us. I really want this. Would it kill you to do one spontaneous thing in your life?" I put my hands together in prayer and gave him puppy-dog eyes. "Pretty please."

His steady gaze met mine and softened. "You don't have to beg me, Charlotte. I'm never going to say no to anything you ask of me. Haven't you learned that yet?"

I blinked. He hadn't spoken to me with such softness since he'd delivered his vows, and he'd only been doing that for the benefit of the audience. Maybe I'd misheard.

His eyes sparked with mischief. "But if I do this, then I have a request of you."

"Go on."

He leaned close, forcing me to inhale his delicious cologne. His voice was a seductive whisper. "Sean wants to fuck Natalia in the wedding dress."

Heat flushed through my body. Not a good idea. Last night was supposed to be a one-off. Except I'd let him go down on me this morning. That hadn't even been role-play. I'd been moaning his name. No one else's. It wasn't as though I didn't want it. Nothing felt as good as Cole's mouth between my thighs.

I stood on tiptoes and whispered back. "I don't think that dress is going to fit him."

His lip curved. "Hilarious. You're in the dress. And I want the whole package. The veil, the stockings, the heels . . ."

"You drive a hard bargain, Mr. Ackroyd. Some of us didn't go to fancy business school. I don't stand a chance in these negotiations."

"I wouldn't worry. No class could prepare me for you. The trouble is, one smile and you hold all the cards. I'm just a helpless idiot desperate to get what I want."

"What do you want?"

He leaned in close again, his voice rough and unsteady. "The same thing I've always wanted."

I raised a questioning eyebrow, but he didn't say a word. What was that supposed to mean? My heart pounded at his nearness, and for a moment the crowd jostling around us fell away and it was just him. Last night, there had been no boundaries between us. He'd stripped away all of my inhibitions. I'd let him see and touch me in ways no man had before. But that was a game. Now I had to be sensible. I took a step back to defuse the tension between us.

The last passenger stepped onto the bus. The doors hissed as they were about to close.

"Quick." Grabbing his hand, I pulled him up the steps. "Don't worry. I'll look after you. If you're a good boy, I might even let you have the window seat."

Chapter 34

There was something different about the quality of the light in Rome. Sunlight dazzled on ancient stones and smooth columns. We strolled the length of a sparkling green rectangular pool that held a mirrored reflection of the sky. Smooth marble gods lined the walkway.

A group of people stood at easels painting the surrounding cypress and olive trees beyond the ruins, and I could understand why. There had never been a brighter, bluer sky or a more tranquil setting. Beauty unfolded around every corner. Every inch begged to be committed to paper.

I perched in a shaded spot at the edge of the pool and listened to the audio tour I'd downloaded on my phone. Dad had toured us around so many old battlefields and ancient abbeys when we were teenagers. I'd taken having an expert tour guide for granted. Cole had always hung off my dad's every word while I'd been counting down the minutes until I could escape to the gift shop. I paused the app and pulled out an earbud to tell Cole what I'd learned.

"So, this was Emperor Hadrian's country getaway. It's an entire village with baths, libraries, and a theater. He collected all the things he liked from Greek and Egyptian culture. It's kind of like your Cotswold mansion, except he couldn't afford an Estonian igloo sauna."

"Cheapskate." Cole shot me a wry look and sat next to me.

"Here." I held out an earbud to him. "Want to listen?"

"Sure." He took the earbud and popped it in. We sat shoulder to shoulder, the white cord stretched between us. He leaned in closer, tilting his face to me, and it reminded me of all the times Cole had coaxed me to listen to some obscure indie band when we were kids.

He peered up at the crumbling stone pillars. "It'll look great when it's finished."

I laughed. "Please. That is such a Dad joke."

He nodded. "That was one of Roy's finest."

"I miss him," I said. "It's so weird, the two of us being here without him."

"I know," he said softly. "I was thinking the same thing. I miss him, too."

I pulled out my earbud and Cole did the same. I'd thought I was prepared for it. I'd lost my dad slowly, in pieces, over all those years. We'd had him back those last few days. His body was tired, but his whole soul had sparkled in his dark eyes. Alzheimer's had stolen our names from his mind, but he was still there in those hugs. I'd felt him. That was something to be grateful for, at least. I peered up at the clear blue sky and let the warm breeze caress my skin. He'd needed peace. I could only hope he had that now.

I cleared my throat. "Dad talked about you the past couple of years."

Cole propped his sunglasses on his head and darted a glance at me. "He did?"

"He'd always mistake male doctors or nurses for you and lecture them about the Byzantine Empire or something. We never corrected him. It made him happy to think you were there. He was in and out of hospital so many times in that last year. We knew it was coming. We kept him at home, which is what he wanted."

Heat pressed behind my eyes, but I held my tears in check. I didn't want to be sad today. Dad wouldn't have wanted me to come to a place like this and be sad. "It doesn't make it easier, but we did everything we could for him. I'm glad for you that you can remember him how he was when he was well. That's what he would have wanted."

Cole was silent for a long time. He stirred a pattern in the dirt with a stick. After a while, he spoke in a quiet voice. "You were a good daughter. You cared for him when he needed it."

A pang pulled at my heart. "I'm not a saint. Sometimes it was difficult and frustrating, even though I wanted to be there for him. Now I wake up and I'm thirty. My twenties have vanished."

"But now you can do anything you want. Paint in Florence. Study ceramics in Kyoto. The world is yours. You're going to have so much money, you'll never want for anything."

"When we're done, you mean. When you pay me off?"

His eyes slipped away. "Yes. When I pay you what you've earned."

We fell into deep silence. The breeze whispered through the trees at our backs. After a while, Cole shot me a sidelong glance.

"Hadrian must have been a busy man. He had time to build his wall and do all this."

"Nobody works harder than Hadrian. You missed the part earlier where it said he made beards fashionable."

"I'll have to tell Lucas. He'll be glad to know he was fashionable once. He's only two centuries too late."

I laughed, and a knot of tension unwound inside of me. My only defense in this life was humor. Better to laugh than to cry. Cole had always seemed to understand that about me. I'd always felt able to laugh easily around him.

"You don't get on well with your brothers? They seemed so nice at the wedding."

He gave a small nod. "They aren't that bad, but never tell them I said that."

I leaned back on my hands, my arms taking the weight and my fingers splayed on the warm ground. The pool looked so inviting. I took off my sandals and dipped my feet into the cool water. "I spoke to your nephews. They said you're their favorite uncle."

A smile ghosted his lips. "Did they now? They must be angling for something from me. I'll have to bring them a gift back from this trip."

My gaze drifted back to the group of artists working at easels.

Cole slanted his head to watch me. "You want to join them?"

I tipped my face to the sun and closed my eyes. "Me? No, I can't just tag on someone else's art class."

"We can arrange something for you? You could come back here tomorrow and paint?"

I swirled my feet in the pool, tracing circles with my toes. "I don't do that anymore."

"Paint? Why not?"

The trickling water from the fountain grew loud. Something hot rose in my chest. Panic, or maybe irritation. *Please don't press me about it.* "I just don't."

"Never? You used to love it."

"That was before."

He opened his mouth to ask a follow-up question, but some crazy impulse seized me and I splashed a little cold water from the fountain at him. The spray landed across his chest. *Oh God.* My stomach dropped. The air around us stilled. Bird trills from the surrounding trees grew deafening in the tense silence. Cole's inscrutable gaze dropped to the wet stain on his expensive-looking shirt and rose to lock with mine.

"I'm sorry." Heat blistered the back of my neck. "I don't know what I was thinking. I didn't mean to—"

A laugh erupted from him, cutting me off. It was a rare and genuine laugh, causing his eyes to crinkle at the corners. "What was that for?"

Relief flooded me. *Thank God.* He wasn't bothered. "I just . . . I didn't know how else to shut you up."

He shook his head in amusement. "So you splash me?"

"It worked, didn't it?"

The silence grew loud again, and I wondered if he might splash me back. The old Cole would have. The old Cole wouldn't have been able to resist retaliating. But he didn't. He stood and offered me his hand. "Come on. What do you want to see next?"

Heat spread through me when I took his hand and let him pull me to my feet. "The Maritime Theater? It's a little island with a drawbridge that Hadrian built so he could be alone when being so filthy rich and important got him down." I flashed a teasing grin. "I think you'll appreciate it."

We spent the day strolling the extensive picturesque grounds, and maybe it was the sunshine, or being somewhere so beautiful, or just doing something impulsive for once, but I had a new sense of lightness. I hadn't clowned around in forever, but it had always been fun on our teenage excursions, trying to crack Cole's serious visage and amuse him. Getting him to laugh so unselfconsciously was like finding a cheat code on a video game and unlocking a fun new level. I needed more of it.

As we walked around, I gave the statues silly names and imitated a few poses, pretending to be a goddess or a water nymph. It didn't take long for Cole to join in with the fun in his own way. He made up outlandish facts about the ruins and teased me for taking so many photos. Of course, I reminded him how rich it was for an obsessive workaholic to accuse *me* of *not living in the moment*. In a shady spot, we ate the takeout picnic the hotel had given us, and then walked back to sit at the edge of the pool.

"Am I safe sitting by water or are you going to splash me again?" he asked, turning his face up to the sun.

"It depends on how annoying you plan to be." I held my hands up in mock surrender. "I'll try to resist, but no promises."

A companionable silence fell between us, until he shot me a curious glance.

"What about sketching? Do you still sketch?"

Not this again. We'd been having a perfectly lovely day. I pulled my feet out of the water and held them out to dry in the breeze. "It's almost like you're begging me to splash you."

He smirked. "You wouldn't dare do it again. When was the last time you sketched?"

I sighed. "Shall we look at something else? This place is huge."

His eyes traveled over my face. "How did you like art school? You never talk about it."

"Seriously, let's move. We only have half an hour before the last bus back."

His compelling gaze bored into me. "I remember you always had a sketch pad tucked under your arm. You took it everywhere."

A flush rose in my cheeks. "Don't. I looked so pretentious. I'd spend so long in the woods painting the bluebells. Days and days. I don't know what I was thinking." I slipped on my sandals and stood. "Let's carry on."

He peered up at me with a hand over his eyes to shield his handsome face from the sun. "You could never be pretentious. That's not part of your nature. You have a gift. Something really special. Roy thought so, too."

My jaw tensed. I just wanted this conversation to be over, and I knew Cole too well. The more I tried to change the topic, the more he'd dig in.

"It's true. He told me often how proud he was. He had that sketch you did of your guinea pigs framed on the wall in his study."

I hid my face in my hands. "Oh God. The guinea pigs. Don't make me cringe. That's just what dads do. He was being nice."

Cole stood. His voice was firm and uncompromising. "Roy believed in you, Charlotte. Your father wanted you to pursue your talent all the way. You need to know that."

"I know that." *That was never the problem.*

I set off walking. Cole fell in step alongside me as we rounded a corner to another expanse of ancient ruins. He stopped me with a hand on my arm.

"Why did you drop out of art school? What happened?"

I froze. I'd never told him that. "How do you know I dropped out?"

"At the wedding, Tiffany told me she hasn't seen you pick up a paintbrush in years. You haven't touched the equipment in that art studio apart from the pottery wheel. I'm curious why you don't sketch anymore when you used to do it nonstop."

The sun bore down unbearably on the top of my head. Sweat pooled along my spine beneath my sundress. I set off to find another shady area. "I need to get out of this bloody sun."

Cole grabbed my arm again to stop me from stomping off. "Did something happen?"

"I just grew out of it, that's all." My ponytail clung to my neck, and I gave it an irritable flick out of the way. I pulled my arm free from his grip. "We've been having such a good day together. Can we not do this?"

His eyes narrowed. "Why does it make you so defensive?"

"Because you won't drop it. If you must know, I dropped out to look after Dad. Then I didn't have time for it anymore." *Not entirely true.* But Cole didn't need to know the truth. I set off again, marching toward shade. "What does it matter to you?"

"Because all you ever wanted was to go to art school. Tiffany said she'd offered to help with your dad's care, but you took it all on yourself."

My jaw clenched painfully. "Tiff shouldn't be talking about me to you."

"You didn't like art school?"

What was going on here? Why was he pushing it? I threw out my arms. "No, I didn't like it, if you must know. My father told me he had this awful disease, and my best friend had disappeared and wouldn't reply to my messages. I was heartbroken, Cole. It was a terrible time in my life. I came home, and I couldn't paint or draw. My art just . . . evaporated. Is that what you want to hear?"

He paled. "You lost your spark because of me?"

Spark? What a pressure-laden word. If I had a spark, then life had long since extinguished it. It's probably why I hadn't been able to set foot in the Sistine Chapel. It was too painful to see something wonderful that had always inspired me. Almost like I didn't deserve to be there anymore. Not this version of me.

I let out a humorless laugh. "Is that what you took from that? It wasn't about you. It was all of it. I was young and naive. I didn't fit in. My tutor had it in for me. He was constantly on my back, criticizing me. Nothing was ever right for him. He failed me on my portfolio. He told me I wasn't good enough to be there. I got so in my head about it that I lost my confidence."

He frowned and took a step back. "I need a name."

"A name?"

"The tutor." He pulled out his phone. "I need to know whose life I'm about to ruin."

"Don't be ridiculous. It was more than a decade ago. It's my fault anyway. I let it get under my skin, and then I couldn't get over it. It doesn't matter." I blew out a breath. "Can we drop it now? Please."

Cole ran a hand over the rough stones. "Your passion can't just . . . evaporate. It's still there. It's just buried."

A pulse pounded in my temples. I should have worn a sun hat today. It was too hot out in the open like this. Light bounced off every surface, making me squint.

"I just want you to be happy. That was the deal. You've spent a lot of time looking after everyone else. This is your time to decide what *you* want. To put yourself first. I assumed you'd want to paint. You can't blame me for being curious about why you've abandoned your creative life?"

The words hit me like a punch in the chest. "Abandoned my creative life? Are you serious? *You* want to talk to me about abandonment?"

He swallowed. "The Charlotte I knew was happiest when she had a paintbrush in her hand, that's all."

"Neither of us is the person we once knew." My words came out sharp.

Cole's face froze, as if my words had stung. I hadn't meant them. Not today, of all days. Today was the first day since he'd come back into my life that it felt like we were *exactly* the people we'd once known. This was Cole's fault. He shouldn't have kept pecking at a bruise I tried to ignore.

He took my hand, his fingers warm and reassuring against mine. He raised my hand to his lips and pressed a kiss to the back of it. "I'm sorry. I went too far."

Our eyes locked and held. Surprise at his sudden display of affection made my words come out hoarse.

"Yes, you did."

He nodded. His warm fingers entwined with mine. I should have pulled my hand away, but I didn't.

"I know why you're pushing me on it. Art was a big part of my life. Whenever I was painting, I had this sense of satisfaction, like the world was moving through me. It felt like being . . . plugged in. Connected. I miss that." A knot rose in my chest. "But things are different now. Everybody grows up."

He stepped closer, towering over me, blocking out the sun. He let go of my hand, and a part of me wanted to reach out and grab him again.

"I didn't mean to make you upset. I'm sure you could get it all back if you wanted to," he said.

"Maybe," I murmured. "One thing is for certain. I'm getting Renata back as my guide tomorrow." I gave him a playful shoulder bump. Anything to smooth the tension and get us onto a different subject. "She gives me way less drama than you."

He flashed a sardonic smile. "Right, but I bet you'd have more trouble convincing her to catch a bus with you into the middle of nowhere."

"There is that."

He glanced at his fancy watch and his eyebrow hitched. "Fuck."

"What is it?"

"The bus is about to leave."

"Then we'd better run for it. Last one there pays for dinner tonight."

Amusement flickered in his eyes. "I always pay for dinner."

"Then I'd better make sure I beat you." I set off at a sprint.

Chapter 35

Cole

We walked from the bus stop back to the hotel. The sun sank low, painting the narrow cobbled streets in gold. I couldn't get what Charlotte had shared out of my head. Art school hadn't been what she'd hoped. It must have been awful to learn of Roy's condition and come home. I'd abandoned her. I'd had no choice, but it was still a terrible thing. While I'd been in New York selling my soul to the devil, Charlotte had been single-handedly holding up the heavens.

"Wait," Charlotte said, grabbing my hand. "Let's sit for a minute and drink it in."

I let her pull me up the crowded Spanish Steps to perch midway up. Charlotte balanced a pizza box on her knees. She tore a slice off and handed it to me. "Nothing can top street pizza. Not even that posh restaurant at the hotel."

I took a bite. The artichoke melted against my tongue, and the crisp base cracked perfectly against my teeth. "I agree. Ten out of ten pizza. No notes."

"This city is alive." She put her hand on her chest. "It makes my heart beat so hard. Does it do the same for you? It's another world. I feel like I've sailed away in a tiny boat and left everything behind. It's as though there's a filter on the world and everything is brighter."

My heart was beating hard, but it wasn't Rome. I'd traveled all over the world and never felt like this. It was Charlotte. She'd described how being back with her felt. Today was like we'd both been sixteen again. Charlotte was my eternal city. The only place my heart wanted to dwell.

We ate in silence, knees touching, watching a street performer at the bottom of the steps who was imitating the walks of unsuspecting tourists. Children chased pigeons. The scent of warm tomatoes and herbs hung in the air.

She took another bite of her pizza. "You know one of the worst things about you leaving the way you did?"

I turned to face her. "Tell me."

"I swear you took my *Buffy* DVD box set. All these years, and I could never find it."

"DVD box set? Why would I take that? Nobody has owned a DVD player since the Dark Ages."

She narrowed her eyes in exaggerated suspicion, but her voice was teasing. "It vanished around the same time as you. It's the only explanation."

"Not guilty. I don't even like *Buffy*."

She gasped, feigning shock. "Lies! Take that back. You loved *Buffy*."

"I only remember you forcing me to watch them all."

Her eyebrows flew up in outrage. "Forced you? Whatever. You knew all the words in the musical episode. Your eyes were always bugging out of your head whenever Cordelia Chase was on screen. You cried when Xander brought Dark Willow back. Don't tell me you weren't a fan."

I shrugged, but I couldn't help the smile pulling at my lips. *Fine.* Maybe I had enjoyed watching it, even if it had just been a way to spend time with Charlotte.

"Who did you ship? Spuffy or Bangel?"

"I'm sorry?"

She tore off another slice of pizza and handed it to me. "Who did you want to be together in the end? Spike and Buffy or Buffy and Angel?"

"I think Spike understood Buffy's darkness in a way that Angel didn't."

She flashed a triumphant grin. "Ha! That's insightful analysis from a non-fan. Don't tell me you haven't been on the forums. I'm sorry that you're wrong."

"Oh?"

"Buffy and Angel were endgame. He was her first love. They were meant to be together. You can't convince me otherwise."

"Spike and Buffy literally banged a house down."

She munched her pizza. "That's good sex. That's nice, but it's not what matters."

"What matters?"

"Finding the person who will put you first. Someone you can be yourself with and makes you feel safe. Someone you can depend on." Her eyes slipped away. "They won't ever hurt you or leave you."

Like me. I hurt you, I know. My gaze lingered too long on her mouth. I knew every one of her smiles. I missed the easy smile she'd worn when we were kids. Now every smile was guarded. Had I done that to her? I'd been trying to convince myself that I could ignore these feelings, but I'd never be able to. The truth was, I'd loved Charlotte since I was eleven and I'd first laid eyes on her at Roy's house. All these years, and it had only ever been her. No one could ever compare. Nothing had ever felt more right than being with her last night, even if it had been a game.

Charlotte had talked about finding a blank page. I'd played along, knowing I was kidding myself. We were too deeply connected. We had too much history. This woman hadn't been a side character in my first act; she was written on every page. This was just another chapter in a complicated story.

The moment I saw her at Roy's funeral, I'd known I could never leave her behind again. I'd only ever wanted to protect her from my father, and at some point that had morphed into protecting her from me. My father had probably loved my mother at the start, but he'd destroyed her. I couldn't do that to Charlotte.

She took another bite of pizza. The gooey cheese stretched between her mouth and the slice. She laughed. "Oh God. Don't watch me eat. It's hard to eat pizza elegantly."

Could she ever forgive me? Would she let me try to win her back? It should have been the easiest thing to ask her, but my throat felt too thick and my chest too tight. It wasn't in either of our best interests for this to be real. Charlotte would be better off without me and the world I moved in. She could take the money, walk away, and start the new life she deserved. One about her and what she wanted.

The one thing I remembered from watching that show with Charlotte was that Angel was putting Buffy first when he left. He knew she would have a better life without him. He didn't leave because he'd stopped loving her, but because it was impossible to stay. A human and a vampire could never work in the real world.

Charlotte offered me the last slice of pizza from the box, but I waved it away. Of course she couldn't forgive me. Not when I couldn't offer her a reasonable explanation. It was impossible. Too many years. Too much damage.

Tomato sauce streaked her cheek. I brushed it away with my thumb. Her laugh was self-effacing. "I'm getting this all over myself, aren't I?"

My heart was as heavy as a stone. "I'm just glad to see you enjoying yourself."

Chapter 36

COLE

The next morning, a server set up breakfast on the balcony. Sunlight glittered on the plates and silver lids. The heat yesterday had worn us both out. I'd gone to make tea after dinner and come back to find Charlotte asleep on the couch. She hadn't even stirred when I'd carried her to bed. I grabbed my phone and made a call.

Theo's growl reached my ear. "Why the fuck are you calling me this early?"

"I need your help." I spoke quietly so as not to wake Charlotte.

"I'm hanging up."

"Wait. I need information. An old art teacher of Charlotte's. It was a long time ago, but I'm going to send you the details, and you're going to dig up dirt."

Theo sighed. "What the fuck is wrong with you?"

"Morning." Charlotte tightened her dressing gown and stepped out onto the balcony. Her eyes fell on the food laid out. "What's all this? It looks amazing."

"Await further instructions and then get the fuck on with it," I said into the phone and hung up.

Charlotte gave me a disapproving look. "You're so charming on your work calls. I'm glad you don't talk to me like that, or we'd have a big problem."

I pocketed my phone. "I don't need to talk to you like that. It's not my fault I'm surrounded by incompetence."

She laughed. "You're the boss from hell. You know you catch more flies with honey?"

"Why would I catch them when I can swat them?" I grabbed a couple of cups. "Coffee?"

"Please." She grabbed a pastry and dropped to sit in the chair next to me. "Back to the grindstone today? I suppose someone's got to do it. Your employees aren't going to shout at themselves, are they?"

Church bells rang in the distance. Charlotte put her bare legs up onto a chair and crossed her feet at the ankles. The sun gilded her chestnut hair. I tried to drag my gaze away from her. I had work to do, but fuck it. Yesterday had been the best day I could remember. I wanted more, and I'd arranged a treat for her. I had to be there to see her face.

"No work, but I'm not letting you hijack my tour this time."

Her eyebrows shot up as she buttered a piece of toast. "You're coming out with me again?" Her face lit. "Good for you. All work and no play makes Mr. Ackroyd a dull boy. What are we doing?"

I dragged my gaze from her lips and sipped my espresso. "Patience, Mrs. Ackroyd. It's a surprise. You'll have to wait and see."

I knocked on the door of the address my PA had messaged. A slim woman with dramatic streaks of white in her black hair opened the door. She wore an apron covered in clay stains.

"Signor Ackroyd? I'm Rosa." She inclined her head and flashed a polite smile. "We've been expecting you."

Charlotte flashed me a confused look. Rosa led us into a bright art studio. Light poured in through tall windows, illuminating a row of potters' wheels. The musty scent of clay clung to everything. The mess made my skin crawl. Cool air hit my face, and it was a welcome relief after the sweltering heat outside.

Charlotte surveyed the studio and a smile touched her lips. "Pottery?" Charlotte took the apron that Rosa handed to her. "Please tell me you're doing it too?"

Rosa offered me an apron, but I waved it away. "It's not about me."

Charlotte took the apron and pulled it down over my head. "No way, signore. You're not getting out of it. If we're here, we're both doing it. I want to see you getting your hands dirty."

"I booked this for you."

Her eyes glinted with chiding. "I'm not doing it on my own. Don't be boring."

"I'm thirty years old, Charlotte. You can't peer-pressure me into doing pottery."

She laughed. "Then I'll guilt-trip you. I don't want to do it on my own. Just try something different. It'll be fun, and it will make me happy."

I sighed. Fine. It wasn't my preference, but if it made her happy. There probably wasn't anything I wouldn't do for that. I held my arms up and let her tie the apron around my middle.

"You've shaped on a wheel before?" Rosa asked.

Charlotte nodded and took a deep inhale. "That smell. I've missed it."

The room reeked of wet dirt, but from the look on Charlotte's face, you'd think she was smelling a bouquet. Charlotte's gaze traveled over me, and she smothered a laugh.

"Something funny, Mrs. Ackroyd?"

"Just you in an apron. I never thought I'd see the day."

You and me both. I rolled my eyes. "Stop laughing, or you're on your own."

She zipped a finger across her lips. "I'll stop."

Charlotte drifted to the sink and admired the shelves crammed with pots of different shapes and sizes. Rosa hovered around, watching us. Three would be a crowd. I wanted Charlotte all to myself.

I kept my voice low so Charlotte wouldn't hear. "My wife knows how to do this. You can leave us."

Rosa's eyebrow hitched a fraction. "You booked a private lesson."

"Right, and I'll pay double if it's even more private."

She shot me a disapproving sidelong glance. "I'm afraid I can't leave you unsupervised."

"Did I say double? I meant to say triple."

A small knowing smile curved her lips. "Very good, signore. I'll leave you in peace."

We sat on rickety wooden stools next to each other. Charlotte shaped a tall, smooth cylinder beneath her palms. I had a rotating heap of mud, wet clay all over myself, and absolutely no idea what I was doing. Clay clung to my palms and hid under my fingernails. I flexed my hands, wishing they weren't so filthy, frustrated that I couldn't just relax and go with it.

"How does yours look like that? This is impossible," I said.

She glanced at my gray lump of shame and smiled like a benevolent primary school teacher admiring a dried pasta creation. "You're doing great. It just takes practice."

Her fingers glided inside the spinning cylinder on her wheel, shaping. The gentle rotation hummed around us.

She lifted her gaze from the pot to me. "Tell me about your mother."

Jesus. Now? Where had that come from? My throat tightened. Those weren't memories I wanted to dredge up. Not here. This was supposed to be a fun day.

Her eyes were on me, patient and expectant. "You don't have to talk about her. Not if you don't want to."

I shifted on the stool and it creaked on the stone floor. An ache pierced my ribs. I never talked about these things, but opening up to Charlotte about my family had felt like a relief before. I'd kept so much from her when we were kids. She deserved more.

I cleared my throat. "She was a musician. A flutist. My father said he fell in love with her when he saw her in an orchestra in Prague. He brought her to London. I think she must have been happy at some point, because I remember her singing in the kitchen."

Charlotte's smile was charmed. "A musician? How lovely. That must be where you get your love of music from."

"Maybe. She was many wonderful things until my father destroyed her with his criticism, his neglect, and his womanizing. When she lost Penny, it sent her into a spiral. Rather than take care of her, my father left her alone with three kids. She was working hard in rehab. She would have been able to turn things around."

Charlotte's voice was soft. She stopped her wheel and reached for me. Her clay-covered hand hovered over my arm. "I'm so sorry."

Bitterness twisted like barbed wire inside of me. "Don't feel sorry for me. Pity my father. I'm going to make him pay."

"You know the best way to get revenge? Find your peace. Your father's punishment is that he has to be him. You can make a choice to be nothing like him."

"I'm not a good person like you."

"You can be anything you want to be. You can let all of this anger inside go if you want to."

"It's not that easy."

"No, it's definitely not easy." She threw another glance at my pile of mud and gave me a faint smile. "Don't stop your wheel. Here. Let me help you." She got up, grabbed her stool, and sat behind me. Wrapping her arms around my middle, she took my hands and put them on the clay.

"Like this."

She interlaced her fingers with mine, smooth and wet. "Think of it like a negotiation. You must learn when to apply pressure and when to ease off. Let the clay lead you. If it goes wrong, you start again. It doesn't matter. At this stage, it's nothing but potential. Just like you."

"Me?"

She chuckled, soft and warm. "Yes. You."

You're a Thorner. Men like us don't change. I was set. Brittle and unmalleable. Full of cracks and imperfections.

As the wheel spun, her hands were firm, guiding my palms over the clay. "We're always unfinished. There is always an opportunity to reshape."

Her breath was warm on the back of my neck. God. I couldn't get this woman out of my mind. Did she feel this way about me? This incredible yearning, like a sickness?

"Look how well you're doing," she whispered.

I twisted to capture her lips with mine. It was an instant collapse and death for the pot taking shape between our fingers, but fuck it. Our mouths met in a passionate kiss. We were both splattered with wet clay, but I couldn't care less. I just needed her. I lifted her into my arms, carried her to a table, and deposited her with a soft thud.

"We can't do this in here," she said, wrapping her legs around my hips.

"Then why have you opened your legs for me?"

She wrinkled her nose. "Don't be an arsehole."

I kept kissing her as I fumbled to drag a condom packet out of my back pocket. My sticky fingers trembled, trying to get it open. We were both too messy and frantic.

"Fuck it," she cried. "I'm on the Pill. Just pull out."

No, I didn't have sex without a condom. This woman drove me crazy, but I had to keep some scrap of control.

"Don't you dare move," I growled.

I dashed to the sink, rinsed the clay off my hands, and sheathed myself.

"You're killing the vibe," she cried.

I strode back to her and hiked her apron and sundress around her hips. "Where were we?"

She gave me an amused look as she lifted off the table enough for me to pull her underwear down. "You were about to fuck me, but you got freaked out about the condom."

"Ah, yes. I remember now. Lie back."

She glanced behind her and did as I instructed. I lifted her legs and propped her feet on my shoulders. Lining myself up, I slid my cock through her wetness. All this sass. She wouldn't be sassing me when I fucked her senseless.

"Remember when you told me sex was off the table?" I took her weight in my hands. "This is me filing a motion to put it back on."

With one hard stroke, I penetrated her without mercy.

She gasped and arched her back. "Stop being so smug about it and file harder."

I slipped a finger between us to work her clit. "Keep sassing me and I'll file you so hard you won't be able to walk straight tomorrow."

I circled her slick flesh with my finger. God. It felt so good to be so deep inside her. Another moan escaped her, and her eyes rolled back. This was all I wanted. To study how to make her breath hitch and her knees shake. To worship her. To be a fucking servant to her pleasure.

Her hips bucked as I pounded her. "Someone could walk in."

"So what? Let them see who you belong to. You're mine, Charlotte. You know that, don't you? My wife."

"Fake wife. I don't belong to you or anyone."

I slowed my pace to lazy, shallow thrusts. Teasing her with just the tip of my cock. Trying to drive her as fucking wild as she made me. I looked down and watched myself moving so painfully slowly inside of her.

"Please." Her voice was a breathy moan.

I held still. Her perfect pussy made my cock throb with the need to slide home. "Please what?"

She ground against me and clawed at the table. "You said I never had to beg you for anything."

"Orgasms are the exception." I stilled with my thumb on her clit, pressing lightly. "Admit that you're mine."

"Fuck! You're a maniac. Just get on with it. Anyone could walk in here."

"That just makes it more exciting, doesn't it?" I pushed into her again in one long, slow stroke, getting off on her squirming. "Tell me you're mine. Tell me you're not faking."

She slipped her fingers down to her clit, but I held her wrist by her side. "You don't get to come yet."

Her eyes widened in shock, and her whole body shook. "You're not serious?"

"Deadly. Tell me. Say the fucking words," I instructed.

She frowned. "That's not what we agreed."

Her defiance only made me want to pound her into submission. I grabbed her ass, lifting and holding her wide open for me, and drove my cock deep. I punctuated each word with a merciless thrust. "Tell" thrust "me" thrust "you're" thrust "mine."

"Oh God," she moaned.

"God's not going to help you, Charlotte. Only you can help yourself by saying the words."

A red flush climbed her neck. She ground against me desperately. The feeling of her tight, hot pussy throbbing around me was going to fucking destroy me. She was giving herself to me, whimpering and shaking. But it wasn't enough unless I heard her say it. *I don't care about control. I don't care about anything but you. What will it take to bring you back to me?*

"This doesn't feel fake to me." I was going to come any second, but I needed the answer. "Does it feel fake to you? Please. Don't make me fucking beg. Just put me out of my misery and tell me. What is it going to take for you to forgive me, Charlotte?"

She writhed on her back on the paint-stained table, her fingernails digging into the wood. She spoke between desperate gasps of air. "It's not fair to conduct negotiations with your cock inside me."

I thrust into her in sharp, rapid strokes, looking down to take in the view as I pounded her. I fucked her like we could fuck the building to the ground around us, like I could fuck her hard enough to make up for all the ways I'd hurt her, and forget everything that had come before.

I rubbed her clit firmly with the pad of my thumb. A series of agonized cries left her lips. Her orgasm face tipped me over the edge with her. We came together, breathing hard and panting. I pulled out and lifted her to face me, perched on the edge of the table. My lips found hers and we kissed in a clash of tongue and desperation. I rested my forehead against hers and tried to slow my breathing. None of it was fake. Not to me. Every moment with her felt like the only thing in my life that truly wasn't.

Chapter 37

Charlotte

"I hope you're happy. I'm never going to get this clay out of my hair," I called through the bathroom door.

I sank deeper into the enormous tub, letting the hot water soothe the ache between my thighs. Cole popped his head around the door. His eyes raked over me, and I covered myself with my hands.

"What are you doing? Get out."

Slowly, he rolled the sleeves of his pale-blue shirt to the elbows. "Relax. It's nothing I haven't seen before."

I threw a sponge at him. "You can't just come in here when I'm in the bath. Get out. Shut the door behind you."

He dodged the sponge, walked to the gigantic tub, and kneeled down at the side of it. "Come here." He grabbed a jug from the cabinet underneath the sink. "I'll help you. Sit up."

I didn't have the energy to argue after what had happened between us in the pottery studio. Also, I genuinely needed the help, or I'd be picking dried clay out of my hair for days. I did as he commanded and sat upright in the water, covering my breasts.

Lathering his hands with shampoo, he began washing my hair.

"You don't have to cover yourself." Carefully, he massaged the shampoo in with perfect pressure. Yes, I did. I'd lost my mind in the pottery studio. Now, I had to scrape back some control. The lush coconut scent filled my nose. Closing my eyes, I surrendered to his touch. The tension left my body, like the hot steam curling from the tub. I couldn't help my sigh of pleasure.

"Feels good?" His voice was a velvet murmur.

Like you have to ask. He had to know I was wrapped around his little finger. I'd just thrown every one of my inhibitions away and let him have me in such a compromising position. Anyone could have walked in and seen us. That had been the wildest thing I'd ever done, but I'd been powerless to resist. "So good."

"I've been thinking about what you said before."

I opened one eye. "What did I say?"

His fingers raked through my hair, carefully picking out clay, like I was something fragile. He rinsed off the shampoo. Hot water cascaded down my neck.

"You met my nephews at the wedding, right? Oliver, the youngest, had a birthday party a couple of years ago. Thirty small children running around in a soft play. It was one of the worst afternoons of my life."

A laugh burst out of me at his earnest expression. "I'm sure it wasn't that bad."

He mock-shuddered. "No. It was. Intolerable. Believe me. I bet there have been less chaotic war zones. I had to lie in a dark room afterward. It took days to recover."

"Your nephews must have been thrilled to have you there."

He scooped more water into the jug and tenderly rinsed the ends of my hair. "Oliver loves to build towers. He made this enormous creation out of blocks while the rest of the children were running wild. But do you know what happened to it? Just as he was putting on the last block, some kid came running across and kicked it over. Oliver didn't even cry. He just looked confused. That's the part that really fucked me off."

"This one next." I passed him a bottle of conditioner. "Kids can be mean sometimes."

He squeezed the conditioner into a white blob in his hands. "The kid who did it ran off with this look of glee. I helped Oliver rebuild the tower, and if any kid got so much as within a sniff of us, I gave them my death glare."

"Your death glare? You know you're going to have to show me now."

He tilted his chin and stared me down with his icy eyes. It was probably intimidating to anyone else, but it only made me chuckle.

"So, this is basically a story about you terrorizing small children at a party? What does it have to do with me?"

He combed the conditioner through the length of my hair with his fingers. My scalp thrummed with pleasure at his touch.

"The point is, some kids build the towers and some kids kick them over. History is divided into creators and destroyers. Deep down, everyone would prefer to build the tower because that's where the satisfaction comes from. The joy is in the creating. You were born a creator. My mother was the same. My father said her solos were so affecting, she could make a grown man weep."

I closed my eyes again, surrendering to the heat and pleasure at his hands. "Anyone can learn to paint if they want to. Anyone can make music. Creativity is within all of us. It's not some mysterious spark. I wasn't born a creator. I think artists are made through practice and hard work."

"But in that moment, for whatever reason, that kid wanted to destroy something someone else had built. Maybe he got a rush from punching down, or maybe he was just jealous because he wanted to build his own tower, but didn't know how."

He leaned forward to rinse away the last of the conditioner from my hair. "My father is a destroyer. I have no doubt he was born that way. It's all he's capable of. He has spent a lifetime kicking over other people's towers. It shames me to say, I've kicked over a few myself. It sounds like your old tutor was the same kind of man.

"You can't allow someone like that to get inside your head. Destroyers spread hate because that's what they have inside. They don't know how to do anything else. Never let people like that stop you from building your towers, because then you deprive the world of your gifts, and everyone loses."

A pang pulled at my heart. *If only it were that simple.* "And if someone kicks the tower over again? You get hurt twice. It's easier not to try."

He fixed his gaze on my breasts. "You think I'm ever going to let anyone get near one of your towers?" He reached out and gently circled my nipple with his thumb. "If anyone tries to kick down anything you build, you tell them to go fuck themselves, and you start again. They don't matter. Kids don't build towers to impress art tutors. They do it because they enjoy it."

"Did you tell a five-year-old to go fuck themselves?"

His hand plunged under the water and explored between my thighs. "No comment."

Heat surged through my body as his finger slid over my entrance. "There can't just be creators and destroyers, because which category are you going to put yourself into?"

"I'm a destroyer," he said without hesitation, his finger circling my clit lightly.

My breath hitched, and I tried to keep rational thought in my head, despite his touch making me senseless. "No. You said yourself you sat there and warded all these other kids away with your death glare. You're not a creator or a destroyer."

"Then what am I?"

"A protector. You wouldn't let anyone get near that tower. I think you're the favorite uncle for a reason, and not just because you bring gifts. Your nephews see the real Cole. The one you don't show other people. The one I see."

His finger slipped inside me at the same time as his mouth covered mine. He kissed me until we were both breathless. My hips jerked against his hand, willing him to work faster. *I shouldn't want this. I can't not want it.*

Breaking the kiss, his eyes locked with mine. "A protector?"

"You're not full of hate. At least, you didn't used to be. You don't have to be now if you don't want to be. No one is born a creator or a destroyer. You can choose who you want to be."

He slipped another finger inside me and rubbed my clit just the way I liked. My head fell back, and my fingers gripped the tub painfully. *If I let him close, he'll hurt me again. I can't fall like this.*

"Please." My breath escaped me in sharp snatches.

He chuckled darkly. "So needy, Mrs. Ackroyd." Smoothing my wet hair back from my face, he whispered low in my ear. "I won't make you wait. You're so fucking beautiful when you come. I want to see you let go with me, Charlotte. Please. That's all I want. I'm the one who needs to beg."

He rubbed my clit relentlessly while pumping his fingers in and out of me. My hips writhed at his mercy, sloshing water over the sides of the tub. Pleasure sparked at the base of my spine, and a cry left my lips. I came hard, my pussy clenching around his fingers buried deep. He bit his lip and groaned. Maybe it was weakness that had made me break the contract, maybe it was forgiveness. Hard to tell the difference anymore.

He kissed the tip of my nose, stood, and grabbed a towel from the rail. We were due to fly home in two days. The water held me as I caught my breath, but my stomach dropped. How had the time gone so quickly? What would it be like when we got home? Back to normal? How could it go back to normal after all of this?

Cole held the towel out and beckoned for me to stand. I got out of the bath, and he wrapped the towel around me, drying me tenderly. I couldn't put it off any longer. There were still a few places I hadn't been.

"I need to see the Sistine Chapel. Then on our last day, I want to go to the Trevi Fountain together. We'll throw a coin in, and that means we'll come back again."

He wrapped a towel turban around my head. His eyes clung to mine. "You think we'll come back again? Together?"

My heart took a leap. "I hope so."

He took my hand, and despite every reason not to, I let him lead me to the bedroom.

Chapter 38

We entered the Sistine Chapel with a throng of tourists through the labyrinthine Vatican Museums. I took a breath as I stepped over the threshold into the cool air of the sacred space. Vibrant frescoes covered every inch. A faint odor hung in the air—something musty like the most treasured books in Dad's library.

A backpack brushed against my shoulder, and a tall woman elbowed me as she shuffled past. I tried to edge forward, but I could barely move against the crowd. Everyone stood staring up at the famous ceiling, transfixed. I craned my head to look. I'd seen this place in textbooks, and built it up as something in my head, and now, here I stood.

Someone pushed past me again, and Cole gave them a fearsome look. "Watch where you're going."

I touched his arm. "It's fine. It's busy."

A guard's voice sliced through the chaos. "Shh. Quiet, please."

Cole threw a disdainful look at the entrance. "The guard's the one making all the noise."

I turned as best I could, scanning the intricate biblical scenes. Hard to see anything above the sea of heads.

A body pressed against me, forcing me to step closer to Cole. I whispered in his ear, "Michelangelo painted all of this alone. He couldn't find an assistant he was satisfied with so he did it all by himself. If you want to get a job done, do it yourself, right?"

He raised an amused eyebrow. "I've never found the sixteenth century more relatable."

Another elbow landed in my back, and I was moving forward even though I didn't want to. I reached for Cole's hand, but he slipped out of sight. He found me again a moment later. Too busy. Too many people.

"We should go," I said. "Maybe come back later."

Cole peered down at me. "Are you OK? You don't look happy."

This wasn't how I wanted it to be. I shouldn't have come. It was better in my imagination. "I don't like how crowded it is."

The guard's annoying voice sliced the air again. "Shh. Quiet, please. Stop talking."

"This is ridiculous." Cole wrinkled his nose. He took me by the shoulders. "Wait here."

"Where are you . . . ?"

He was gone before I could finish, cutting his way through the horde of tourists back the way we'd come. I craned my neck to the ceiling again, only to get shuffled forward. Never mind. Sometimes things just didn't live up to your expectations. Maybe I'd known it never could. That's why I hadn't come here on the first day. Cole returned. He cupped my face and stroked my cheeks with his thumbs.

"It's OK. It's going to be better in a minute," he said.

The guard's voice reverberated through the space again. "Everybody move out, please. Keep moving forward."

I shot Cole a look. "Time to go?"

He glanced at his watch. "Not us. We've got five minutes."

Bodies filtered around us to the exit. "What do you mean?"

"We've got five minutes in here after the crowd clears out before the guard lets anyone else in. Needless to say, I also asked the guard if he'd be so kind as to shut the fuck up."

The realization dawned on me. It was too crazy to be true. "How much?"

He ran his thumb around his lips, but said nothing.

"You bribed the guard. How much? How is that even possible?"

"'Bribe' is an ugly word." Cole glanced at his watch again. "We struck a deal on favorable terms. Don't think about it. Just enjoy it while it lasts. I'm only sorry I couldn't get you longer, but then I'd have to bribe the pope, and I imagine he's a more upstanding kind of bloke. At least, that's what it claims on Wikipedia."

I watched the last person leave and turned back to Cole in shock. "I can't believe you pulled this off."

He pressed a kiss on my temple. "Savor it. It's all yours."

With no people, the space was vast and soaring. The tight feeling of compression around my lungs eased off. Ditching my backpack on the floor, I dropped to my knees and lay on my back. Cold marble kissed the length of my spine, and I pressed my palms flat at my sides, drinking in the images I'd been obsessed with as a child. My heart pounded in the stillness. There was so much life in the frescoes. Everything was in motion. A fizzy energy buzzed inside of me. The beauty hit me like a freight train.

I was a little girl in the woods. Cole sat on a mossy rock next to our bikes, cross-legged, watching me. Sunlight pierced the canopy and splayed light over my easel. A carpet of bluebells sprang from the earth, and the colors and shapes held me transfixed. My paintbrush moved across the white page in confident violet strokes. And I had the deepest sense that I was exactly where I was supposed to be, doing exactly what I'd been born to do.

Cole's finger touched mine, sparking me to life, bringing me back to myself. A lightness and warmth like I'd never known filled me. My face was wet with tears. I couldn't speak. I could barely breathe. He turned his face toward me. I couldn't judge his expression, because I couldn't tear my gaze away from the ceiling. I stared up at the almost-touching fingertips of God and Adam. The moment before creation.

A quiet revelation wrapped around my heart. In among the duty and responsibility of caring so deeply for someone else, my life had become small. I didn't begrudge that. I'd wanted to be with my dad when he needed me. It had mattered. But I had to figure out what came next. I missed Dad so terribly, but that didn't mean I couldn't try and open my arms to the world, to create, to laugh, to travel, to have adventures. To work on making my life . . . bigger.

Another tear slipped down my cheek. "It's amazing . . ." I opened my mouth and closed it again. "I hoped it would be."

Cole wrapped his fingers around my hand. His whisper was low in my ear. "Is it wrong that you're probably lying here having a profound experience, and I'm thinking about all the dirty things I'd like to do to you in here? I don't know how much I'd have to pay the guard to turn the other way."

I whacked him lightly on the arm. My laughter echoed around the cavernous space. "Yes. It's very wrong. You're a sex maniac. It's a chapel. Look at the ceiling. Behold the enduring greatness. Stop thinking with your dick. There's no way we're fucking in here."

"Spoilsport." He squeezed my hand. "The problem is it doesn't matter what's in a room, all I ever want to look at is you."

I turned my head to gaze at him. His eyes locked with mine, and I couldn't tear myself away, not even to the ceiling. *Behold the enduring greatness. Stop thinking with your heart. Your poor, stupid heart.* Footsteps and chatter brought me back to my senses. Tourists began to swarm in again.

The guard's voice rang out. "Shh. Quiet, please."

Cole sighed. "Looks like our five minutes is up."

"I can't believe you did that for me."

He stood and offered me his hand. Pulling me to my feet, he gave me a relaxed smile. "I told you, Mrs. Ackroyd. You marry me, I make your life better."

Chapter 39

I dragged the heavy white train behind me and stepped out of the bedroom in my wedding dress. Cole was sitting on the couch, dressed in a smart suit for dinner. His dark hair was still damp from the shower. I held out my arms, feeling self-conscious. Maybe this had been a silly idea. "You said you wanted me in the wedding dress."

Pocketing his phone, Cole swallowed and sat upright. His gaze raked over me boldly. "Jesus. Look at you."

Heat seared my cheeks as I fumbled with the seam at the back of the dress. "I can't reach the buttons at the back. It's not on properly."

"I wouldn't worry. It's not staying on for long." He stood and beckoned me with a finger. His voice was rough. "Come here."

I dragged the train behind me and planted myself in front of him.

"The most beautiful bride in the world," he said, lifting the veil away from my face.

My hair was still wet at the ends, and my face scrubbed after a bath. "I looked better on the wedding day with the makeup."

"No, you've never looked more perfect." He caught my hands and held them in his. "Just as you are."

With one hand around my waist, he pulled me to his hard chest. He kissed me as if he'd never stop. Worshipfully, he undressed me, stroking my body, whispering his praise against my thighs as he tugged my stockings down.

"Do you know how addicted I am to your body?" Dropping to his knees, he swirled his tongue around my belly button. "I love it." He planted kisses on my stomach. "Every inch. I can't get enough. Spread your legs for me."

I stood bare and vulnerable. He hadn't taken off a single layer of clothing, but that only made it hotter. I did as he commanded. "I'm sure you've seen better?"

"Never. Not possible."

Pleasure jerked through me when he buried his face between my thighs. His hot licking and probing made me senseless. I rocked against him, raking my hands through his soft hair, savoring every minute. He rose and pushed my breasts together, taking both nipples into his mouth.

With trembling hands, I unbuttoned his shirt. He helped me to pull it off, along with his trousers and boxers. Then we were all over each other. He touched me like he didn't want to leave any part of me unexplored. Electricity sparked with every stroke of his hands. Lifting me into his arms, he laid me gently on the bed. He covered me with his body, his erection pressing hard against my thigh.

"Condom. Don't move," he whispered against my ear.

No, I wanted to feel every hot, hard inch of him. "Or not?"

He raised an eyebrow.

"I'm on the Pill. It's to help my migraines. Hormones are a trigger."

He bit his lower lip. "I've never had sex without a condom."

I stroked the firm planes of his back. "I trust you. If you trust me?"

He gazed into my eyes with a serious expression and nodded. I reached between us, grabbed his thick cock, and guided him to the aching heat between my thighs. We both moaned as he seated himself slowly.

"Fuck." He buried his face in my neck. "Fuck!"

I pushed my hips against his, encouraging him to move, but he held perfectly still. "Something wrong?"

He spoke through gritted teeth. "Feels too good."

"Stop?"

He groaned and dropped his head onto my chest. "Give me a moment."

My core ached with the fullness. I clenched around his cock, squeezing him. He'd teased me so mercilessly before. Fun to get my own back for all the times he'd made me beg for him.

"Please," he whimpered. "Don't do that."

A chuckle escaped me. "You're going to have to move at some point."

He drew back and pushed into me slowly. His elbows trembled next to my head, and his shaking hand gripped the sheet. I ground my hips underneath him, rocking against him.

"Fuck." He sucked in a harsh breath. "Please. This isn't going to last long if you move like that."

I wrapped my legs up high and hooked my ankles around his back. "It makes a change to hear you begging me. I have you at my mercy for once."

"That's not a change. You've always had me at your mercy."

He pressed his forehead to mine, and his warm breath fanned my face. I squeezed him and rolled my hips. He fought for control, before his face scrunched and he moaned. I felt him pulsing and spurting as he found his release deep inside of me.

"You're wicked." He collapsed and pressed a kiss to my temple. "I'll make it up to you."

"No one's keeping score. We already have a serious orgasm deficit. I owe you."

His brooding gaze met mine, and he pulled me protectively into his arms. We held each other, breathing heavily.

"You owe me nothing. I love giving you orgasms. It's my favorite pastime," he said.

"I thought work was your only pastime. Mr. Big Shot CEO has a hobby?"

"Yes, it's making you scream my name." His expert fingers slipped between my thighs, and he pushed his wetness leaking from me back up inside. "Mine," he whispered against my throat.

His fingers found my swollen clit, and pleasure sparked at my core as he rubbed. I pressed my face into the damp hollow of his neck, smothering my moans against his cool skin. My harsh gasps punctuated the stillness.

"I always dreamed about this. I dreamed about the two of us together. Me and you," he whispered.

His soft kisses on my cheeks were enough to undo me. Pleasure sparked at my core, and my spine arched off the bed. I was already so high today. High on the beauty and the quiet revelations in my heart, but Cole pushed me higher. All that mattered was this moment together. No past. No future. I fell apart, chanting his name as he kissed every scrap of skin on my throat, my shoulders, and my breasts. When he'd wrung every drop of pleasure from me, I rested my head on his chest, listening to his heartbeat.

I always dreamed of this, too.

Chapter 40

Cole

"Tell me about your previous boyfriends." I took Charlotte's hand as we walked down the stairs to dinner.

Her eyes widened. "Why do you want to know? Jealous?"

"Extremely. It's helpful if I can put some names to the imaginary men I'm kicking the shit out of in my head."

"There's only been a couple. None of them were ever serious. You don't have to be jealous." She swung her hand in mine as we stepped into the lobby and flashed me a dry smile. "For a start, none of them ever made me sign a confidentiality clause or asked me to fake marry them."

I met her teasing eyes. "Slackers."

We walked together, our joined hands swinging between us, through the cool hotel foyer. A familiar cold voice drifted to my ears, and my heart stopped beating. A tall silver-haired man stood at the reception desk. He pointed a berating finger and spat out impatient words at another recognizable face. Reuben stood quiet and still at my father's side, eyes on his flashy tennis shoes, his shoulders hunched with mortification.

For a moment it was me. My father was screaming and shouting at me for some perceived slight. *Spit it out, you stuttering fool.* Panic curdled in my stomach. Words clogged my mouth, but I couldn't speak. My father had told me over and over again that I was nothing. His vicious words had become a backing track on a loop in my head. He'd made me believe that he was right. That he knew me in a way that others didn't and those cruel eyes of his saw everything lacking in me.

Shame dripped down my spine, and I was a powerless boy again. Coming across him when I was unprepared made me feel like I was sinking, like I'd landed on a snake in a game of snakes and ladders and slid right back to the beginning of the board. He'd made my life a living hell as a child, but that hadn't been enough for him. He'd still had to trap me by his side as a teenager. Just when I'd had my whole life ahead of me.

A wave of sympathy washed over me for Reuben. I knew how it was to be on the receiving end of my father's anger. Reuben wasn't my favorite person in the world. He was annoying as fuck, and I swear he was trying to get in my wife's pants. But who could blame him? Who wouldn't want to fuck my wife? It was hard to see Reuben with fear glittering in his eyes when he was usually bouncy and carefree like a big overgrown Labrador.

The next couple of seconds happened too fast. My father raised his hand, ready to slap Reuben. But I intercepted, grabbing his arm and holding him still. I shouldn't have stepped in. The last thing I wanted was to attract Philip's attention. My father's mean gaze drifted from me to Charlotte. A fire ignited under my skin. *Don't look at her. Don't you fucking dare.*

My father ripped his arm from my grip. My mind reeled, but I stood tall. *Get it together. You have to, for Charlotte.* I wasn't a powerless kid anymore. I was a man. A husband with a wife to protect.

My father didn't get to make me tremble. He got to behold the strength I'd forged to survive him.

"You." He looked me up and down with a cold appraisal. "I knew you'd be here."

I believed him. He'd probably found out I was here from a listening device in one of my offices. Theo's moral compass might lead us away from corporate espionage, but this man's moral compass was set to "relentlessly awful" mode.

My father's lips thinned. "Meeting with Gabe?"

I fought to maintain some stillness and composure. "Wouldn't you like to know?"

My father's eyes flicked to Charlotte. Realization dawned on her pretty face as she understood who this was. My stomach dropped. *Shit.*

"Hi," Reuben mouthed at her awkwardly.

She gave him a strained smile and a quiet "Hello."

"Don't you have better things to do?" My father straightened his tie. "Stay out of my affairs. You're pathetic."

Charlotte stiffened at my side. "Now wait a minute, you can't—"

"It's fine. Don't get involved. Please." I squeezed her hand. *I can't stop him. Please, just don't listen to him.*

My father inclined his head in Charlotte's direction. His voice was ice. "You're not going to introduce us?"

"No." I gave Charlotte a meaningful glance and tugged her hand. "Let's go."

My dad held his hand out. "You must be the new Mrs. Thorner."

No. Charlotte would never suffer the burden of being Mrs. Thorner. Not like my mother. Memories of her brushed my mind. *All those times I'd found her passed out alone in her penthouse suite and I'd been the one to clean her up and take her to the hospital. Her head resting on my shoulder while I'd played the piano for her, trying to ease a sorrow that was heavier than either of us could bear. She'd looked so tired and frail at the end, like a bird with broken wings.*

The pain was like a grinding ball inside that I'd never be able to remove. I'd failed her. I wouldn't fail Charlotte. I had to destroy Philip Thorner before he destroyed us. Whatever it took. He had to be punished. That was the only way to right such a terrible wrong. I couldn't allow him to prosper.

I managed to keep my voice calm. "No. She's not. I'm the new Mr. Ackroyd."

Philip's eyebrows rose so far they almost touched his receding hairline. If my heart hadn't been pounding out of my chest, I might have been able to enjoy his shock and horror. But all that mattered was getting Charlotte away from him.

Don't talk to him. You don't have to talk to him. If he hurt Charlotte, I'd kill him. He didn't even deserve to share air with her.

"Charmed." He fixed his gaze on Charlotte, although his words were for me. "And does your wife know you brought her on honeymoon here so you could attempt to swipe a deal from under your father's nose?"

Charlotte stiffened again but said nothing. A hollow ache spread in the pit of my stomach.

"It's not very romantic, is it, dear? Your husband doing business on your honeymoon? The two of you should be enjoying your time as newly-weds." His gaze drifted back to me. "No idea how to separate business from pleasure."

His sharp voice gave me that old feeling, like I wanted to shrink into the carpet and disappear. Anything to not be the subject of his attention. I rolled my shoulders back and kept any hint of unease from my voice. "Is there any pleasure in your world?"

A haughty smile touched his lips. "Plenty. When I sign the contract on this hotel, it will give me immense pleasure. You'll never outbid me. I heard Gabe won't even take your calls. It's pathetic that you're persisting. Shame you're such a sore loser, when you've spent so much of your life . . . not winning."

My jaw clenched. Charlotte rolled her shoulders back and met my father's unflinching gaze with one of her own. "Of course I knew about the offer. It makes perfect sense to come here on honeymoon. Better to kill two birds with one stone." She glanced at me. "Isn't that right?"

I should have told her. Guilt made my jaw tighter. "Right."

"Well, I'd like to say it was nice to meet you, but I've never been a good liar." Charlotte wrinkled her nose. "Don't you dare speak to my husband like that again. You're a disgrace."

Philip raised an amused eyebrow, but didn't reply. With a gentle tug on my hand, Charlotte led me away.

"Goodbye! Enjoy your honeymoon," Reuben called.

He gave an awkward wave, trying his best to be polite despite the tension. An unexpected pang pulled at my chest. I'd been him once. Trailing around after my father, getting shouted at in hotel lobbies. It was no life. Being Philip Thorner's son was a hard burden to bear. Nobody deserved it. I couldn't help but wonder what my father had over Reuben. I'd stayed for so long to protect the people I'd cared about. What trapped Reuben? If it was a desire to win Philip Thorner's approval, then he was hopelessly deluded.

I stopped midway to the stairs and called back. "We'll be going for a drink in the bar shortly. You can join us if you want, Reuben."

A look of surprise and delight lit Reuben's face. "Really?"

My father's stern gaze made him shrink back, a faint flush in his cheeks. After a moment, he straightened and pasted on a bright smile. "No. I'm fine. But thanks for the invite."

◆　◆　◆

Charlotte pressed the button to call the elevator. I fucking hated elevators, but I'd have to do it. There was a time and place to share my opinions on the obesogenic environment. This wasn't it. The doors opened and Charlotte stepped inside. She pressed herself back against the mirrored side.

Her face was pale. "What did he mean? You're trying to swipe a deal?"

The elevator doors shut, and my heart pounded at being trapped in a confined space. My father made me feel like a cornered animal. I needed open skies, not tight walls. "I want to buy this hotel."

"And so does your father?"

"Yes."

"Two billionaires squabbling over a luxury hotel?" Her voice was loaded with sarcasm. "How delightfully petty."

This was more than a squabble. It was justice. I'd told her what he'd done to my mother. What he'd done to my family. Panic still bubbled inside, sharp and raw. It was stupid. I was a grown man, not a kid. *Why did I let him make me feel like this? I have to be better.*

Her voice softened, and she rested a gentle hand on my arm. "Look at you. You're shaking. You're arguing with an old man in a lobby. It's not a good look. You're lucky there were no photographers around. Don't you think you need to let this one go?"

"If I let it go, he wins."

"No." She gave me a sad smile. "If you let it go, *you* win. How can you not see that?"

A shivery feeling spread through me. She didn't get it. She didn't understand what he was capable of. He'd never back down. I had to make him pay, and I couldn't show the slightest weakness. He'd only come down harder.

The words left my mouth before I could stop them. "You're a fine one to talk about letting go. You cling to that old house. It's crumbling. No one's living in it. Tiffany's right. You should sell. Give yourself some peace."

A shadow crossed her face. "Dad loved that house."

"He wanted you to sell it. Tiffany told me. He wanted it to be a family home. It's just bricks and mortar. It won't bring him back, clinging on to the past."

Her lips twisted in anger. "That house means way more to me than bricks and mortar, and you know it."

"I do know, because this hotel means way more than bricks and mortar to *me*." *And you should know it.* "This is all bullshit. He's going to win. I can't even get a meeting with the guy selling it. He bought into all this bad press about me being an arsehole. I don't know how to convince him I'm not."

She threw her hands in the air in exasperation. "I don't know, Cole. Have you considered being less of an arsehole?"

Softly piped elevator music drifted in the silence. A surge of defensiveness flooded me, but she met my glare with her own unwavering defiance and determination. Her words cut like blades because they were true. My reflection hit me from every angle in the mirrored lift, like something tormenting, like something that I couldn't escape. Staring back at me was a fucking arsehole. Online and IRL. I had no fucks to give about what other people thought, but Charlotte was my exception. If Charlotte thought badly about me, then I cared.

She pinched the bridge of her nose. "I knew this wasn't a real honeymoon, but I at least thought you'd brought me here because you knew I'd always wanted to visit. I thought you'd brought me here because of Dad."

I wish with all my heart that that was the only reason. "Can't it be both?"

"No. You brought me here because it was convenient to shaft your father. I was an afterthought."

"I did what was best for my business. That's what we agreed this was. You signed a contract."

I regretted the words as soon as I'd spoken them. It never went well when I brought up the contract. This was all pretend. But the kisses felt real, and when I held her in my arms, it felt real. The truth was it could never be real, because she was right about me. I was squabbling in a hotel lobby with an old man. I was petty and vindictive and mean. Damaged goods. The armor I'd forged to survive my father had shaped me into something ugly. Everyone knew it.

He'd done this. This fucking bastard of a man. Ruined everything. I could never let go. He'd fucked me over too much. Charlotte was wrong about me. I wasn't unfinished clay. I wasn't even a vase with cracks and dents. I was broken pieces scattered all over the floor. A blade fired in the flames by Philip Thorner. Charlotte deserved better than my grievances and my pettiness.

She shook her head woodenly. "The contract. Right. How could I forget the contract? You know what your problem is. You say your father ruined you, but instead of rejecting him, you choose to be like him. Every day we get to decide how we show up in the world. You don't have to be like him. You could be like your mother. She's within you, too."

I balled my shaking hands into fists at my sides. "This was her favorite place. The one place she was truly happy. I won't let him take it. He's taken too much from me already. He ruined my life. I don't give a fuck what it costs me. I don't care what the shareholders think. It's my fucking company. I gave everything to build it. They can't control me. They can't take it away from me. I'll fucking destroy them, too."

She cupped my face, her hands warm and soothing on my cheeks. I didn't deserve the gentle tone of her voice. "Breathe. It's OK. Just breathe."

Irritation made my teeth grind. "I don't want to breathe."

A small smile touched her lips. "We all need to breathe, Cole. You loved your mum. I get it. You're angry. I'm sure you had good intentions when you went after this place, but look at what it's doing to you. You can't go to war over it. This isn't helping anything. It's good to be strong, but not to be mean. There is strength in forgiveness and in gentleness. That's what my father taught me. I'm sorry that yours taught you so many other things."

My hands felt heavy by my sides. A sudden exhaustion washed over me. "Then why won't you forgive me, Charlotte?"

She shook her head and chewed on her thumbnail. "That's different."

"Is it?"

She folded her arms across her chest. "You hurt me. I need to protect myself."

I swept my arm around. "And what do you think I'm doing? I'm protecting what my mother loved."

"No. You're hurting what your mother loved. She loved *you*. She wouldn't want this for you. Be honest with yourself, Cole. You're not doing it for her."

Her words fixed me to the spot. The elevator doors opened, and relief flooded me to be away from all these iterations of myself in the silver glass.

Charlotte raked a hand over her face and stepped into the corridor. She moved close, but didn't touch me. "This has been one of the most incredible days of my life. The most incredible fortnight. I can't do this tonight. Not on our last night."

All those years ago, I'd broken her heart. I hadn't meant to. It had broken mine too, but what did it matter now? Easier not to have a heart at all.

She stepped closer and tilted her chin up to me. "I'm exhausted. Let's get some sleep and talk tomorrow."

She swiped the keycard against the door to the suite. It had been so intense between us earlier. The first time I'd ever felt like she let me make love to her and not just fuck her senseless, and now I could feel her slipping away from me. I should have kissed her for longer, made her sigh with pleasure more, begged her to dig her nails into my back harder.

I stopped her with a hand on her arm. "Do you still want to go to the Trevi Fountain with me tomorrow?"

She drew her arms tight across her chest and nodded. When she spoke, her voice was quiet and sad, which was much worse than anger. She shrugged. "Let's see how we feel in the morning. Goodnight, Cole."

Chapter 41

Cole

Charlotte sat cross-legged on a patch of grass outside, her head bowed to a book in her lap. I watched her from the window in Roy's office. Lavender dungarees wrapped around her shapely body, and her dark hair fell in two loose ponytails. She was studying a patch of daffodils. A frown furrowed her brow and she tapped her lips with her pencil. My heart was full of everything. Hope that one day she'd want me the way I wanted her. Fear that she never would. An ache that I'd never be worthy of her.

"This looks bad, son." Roy moved closer, studying my swollen eye in the dim light of his study.

Usually, my father didn't leave a mark. He'd been so frustrated with me, he'd got sloppy. He was more skilled with words as weapons than fists. I dragged my gaze from the window.

"It's nothing."

The sentence left my mouth fluidly. No tricky sounds. It was f and s that gave me the most problems. Sometimes q. If I could avoid words that began with those letters then the stammer was undetectable these days.

Roy watched me and cleared his throat. "Life is a storm, my young friend. You will bask in the sunlight one moment, be shattered on the rocks the next. What makes you a man is what you do when the storm comes." He gestured to the open book on the desk in front of me. "The Count of Monte Cristo. It's one of my favorites." His eyes roved over me again. "If you give me a name, I can help you."

No. He couldn't, but I loved him for wanting to. No one could. I could only help myself. And I would. My father would pay for the misery he'd inflicted on all of us. It wouldn't always be like this. Some of us were playing the long game. I'd have power, too. One day. "I walked into a door. No need to worry." I sat at the desk and grabbed my Latin textbook. "Shall we carry on?"

The sheets were cold next to me when I woke up. I grabbed my phone to check the time. It was already 9 a.m. I took a quick shower, threw on a robe and found Charlotte sipping coffee on the balcony. She wore a white sundress with a sunflower print. Tinted-pink sunglasses perched on her chestnut hair, which was still damp from the shower. *Beautiful.*

"Good morning."

Her eyes slipped to me and drifted away. "Morning."

I sat tentatively next to her. The sounds of the awakening city filtered on a welcome breeze. Tension crackled between us, and I had a feeling like I'd sat an exam I hadn't studied for and got all the answers wrong. It was always so natural when we were pretending to be other people. I had to fix this. Her words from last night resounded in my head. *You brought me here because it was convenient to shaft your father. I was an afterthought.* No. Charlotte had never been an afterthought for me. She was every thought. She was also right about everything she'd said last night. I'd lost this hotel anyway.

Somewhere along the line I'd lost perspective. It wasn't doing either of us any good, chasing this so relentlessly. It had to end. I had to change things. I couldn't lose Charlotte. I'd choose her over anything every time. I couldn't allow her to think she was an afterthought. But what did it matter if she wouldn't forgive me? What if I couldn't change? What if I could never be the kind of man that deserved her?

She avoided my gaze. "Are you working today?"

"No."

I want to spend the day in bed with you. Let me make love to you. Let me make you happy. For reasons beyond me, I couldn't speak the words out loud. She'd say no. I should have kept to the contract, except after this time together, the contract felt ridiculous. This was real for me. The contract was easy and safe, but I didn't want that anymore. What did I have to do to make her mine for real?

"I'll get ready. I just need to do my makeup."

She got up, and I grabbed her hand, holding her still. "You don't need to do anything. You look beautiful like this."

She gave me a faint smile. "I appreciate it, but I definitely need makeup."

No. She didn't need to do a thing. The goodness inside of her shone through her eyes and her smile. It was natural and radiant. Effortless. "No. I mean it. You're beautiful, Charlotte. Exactly as you are."

Our eyes locked and lingered for too long. The most natural thing in the world would be to pull her down onto my lap and kiss her, but it was also the hardest thing after last night. Did she even want that from me? She was set on *enduring me* and *protecting herself* from me. Who could blame her? I had to do better. Whatever it took. I'd make it up to her today. There had to be a way. With a slight frown, she released my hand and disappeared to the bathroom.

My phone buzzed in the pocket of my robe as I returned to the suite. Theo's grumpy image flashed on the screen. This photo always gave me a wave of amusement. Even in a candid moment at a wedding, his facial expression was "I'm over all of this shit."

"Gabe's on his way." Theo's voice was rough.

My body became suddenly alert. "Now?"

"He'll be landing soon. He was supposed to be here yesterday, but he stood Philip up."

"You're kidding?"

I had no idea if my father was still here. If I got down to that lobby, then I could speak to Gabe first. Maybe it wasn't too late to get the hotel after all. This was too good an opportunity. I couldn't miss a chance to speak to him alone. "Thanks. I thought you didn't want to help me?"

"I don't," Theo grunted.

"I'm going to send you the details about the art tutor later." I hung up.

Charlotte emerged from the bathroom. Her eyebrows shot up in surprise.

"What's going on? I've never seen you move so fast."

"Something's come up." I scrambled to find clothes and yank them on. "I have to go."

"Go?"

"I need to get ready. Gabe's on his way."

Her face dropped. "What about the Trevi Fountain?"

"This is about the hotel. It won't take me long. I'll come back after I've spoken to him."

"The hotel. Right." She nodded woodenly. "So everything else gets dropped?"

No. It's not like that. I just had to act on this now. "I've been waiting for Gabe to get here. I have to jump on this."

I scoured the dressing table, looking for my cuff links. There was too much crap on here. Jewelry. Perfume. Loose change. This was what happened when you let someone else into your space. Total fucking chaos.

Charlotte watched me warily. She folded her arms. "I suppose I'll just do my own thing this morning then."

I finally located the cuff links under one of Charlotte's bras, and I could have kissed them. "No. Look, I'm sorry. I'll be back later. We can still go." I dashed toward the bathroom to brush my teeth. "Call Renata if you don't want to wait. See if she'll go with you." My shin slammed into the sharp edge of the coffee table in my haste. A jolt of pain shot up my leg. "Fuck!"

"You want me to go to the Trevi Fountain with Renata?"

The chill in her voice held me at the bathroom door. I sighed and pressed my forehead to the cool doorframe. My leg throbbed from where I'd bashed it. There was nothing I wanted to do more than spend a morning with Charlotte, but this opportunity had just dropped into my lap. It was too good to miss. If I played this right, I could have it all. I could get this hotel in the bag and go with Charlotte to the Trevi Fountain afterward.

"I have to speak to Gabe before my father does. We can catch up later."

"There is no later. We're flying home this afternoon. I told Tiff I'd be back for her birthday."

"Then we'll come back to Rome another time. It will be fine."

Her eyes narrowed. "Who were you on the phone to just then? Why were you talking about my art tutor?"

Really? Now? I gave my teeth a hurried brush, using the opportunity to stall my reply. "He can't get away with fucking you over like that. That's not how things work. Theo's going to help us."

She blinked, disbelieving. "Theo?"

I dashed past Charlotte into the bedroom and fiddled with my tie in the mirror. The knot was too tight and small. I'd have to do it again. "Theo's good at finding dirt on people. There'll be something."

Her lips pressed flat. "It was years ago."

"It doesn't matter how long ago it was. He can't get away with it."

Her mouth dropped open. "I don't want that. I didn't ask you to meddle."

I tied another lousy knot in my tie. My father could already be down there with Gabe and I couldn't even get my fucking tie straight. "If it's a problem, I'll call Theo and tell him to drop it. I just won't allow someone to get away with treating you—"

"It was years ago. You're butting your nose into something that doesn't concern you."

Fine. As soon as I'd spoken to Gabe, I'd call Theo. I'd only been trying to help. A growl of exasperation left my lips. "I don't have time for this. Can you help me with this tie?"

"No." Her voice was brittle. "I hope your meeting is worth it."

She snatched her purse and slammed the door on her way out.

The lobby was chaotic and crowded. A lively group of women in matching pale-blue sweatshirts dominated the small space. In the middle, with a huge blue duffle bag slung over his shoulder, was the man himself, Gabe Rivers. I bided my time, watching him smile and make jokes with the staff. I intercepted him before he made it to the elevator.

"Gabe? Hello."

He stilled, and astonishment flashed in his green eyes. "Cole? What are you doing here? Are you stalking me?"

I held my gaze level. *Yes. That's exactly what I'm doing.* I forced a smooth smile. "Stalking? No. Of course not. I'm here on honeymoon with my wife. Charlotte's always wanted to visit Rome. It's her first time."

A blonde woman with a ponytail joined us at the elevator.

"Honeymoon?" The blonde smiled. "Congratulations."

"Thanks. We've had a wonderful time. Shame it has to end." I kept my expression relaxed and my tone casual. *Nothing unusual here. Just a happy coincidence. Completely innocent.* "Actually, I was hoping to bump into you again. Do you have time for a quick coffee?"

Gabe's football team filtered into the small space. Their excited chatter bounced off the walls. He hoisted his duffle bag higher onto his shoulder.

"We're about to start a training camp out here. I don't have time to put my business hat on. And I wouldn't want to deprive you of time with your wife on honeymoon."

A bead of sweat ran down my neck despite the air conditioning. "Just a quick chat over coffee. My wife's popped out this morning. She won't mind."

Gabe's gaze drifted to the blonde at his side. Was that a hint of skepticism? *Shit.*

She gave him a friendly nod. "Fine with me. You can't disappoint a man on his honeymoon."

Gabe blew out a breath and glanced at his Rolex. "Fine. Let me unpack, and then I need to be on it with the team."

My father could be lurking anywhere. I had to get in first. "No. Now. It has to be now."

His eyebrows shot up.

Too pushy. Dial it down. I forced a chuckle that I could only hope was disarming and didn't make me look too much like a sociopath. "It's just that I have to be somewhere. I'm supposed to be meeting my wife later for lunch."

"Then let's do it another time. When we're back in England. We both have places to be."

The elevator doors opened. He got in. *Fuck it.* I squeezed in after him, and so did half his football team. My heart pounded in the cramped space.

"My team has been trying to schedule a meeting for a while now. We can't seem to get hold of you," I said.

He flashed a faint smile. "I'm a busy man."

An elbow nudged my hip. Bodies pressed too close in the elevator. My chest felt tight. I couldn't let him leave here without pinning him down. "What he's offering you? I can beat it."

"Not everything is about money."

Gabe's wife lifted her eyebrows and gave him an amused look, as though sharing some private joke.

The mirrored walls were closing in around me. My arsehole-ish face everywhere. I had a sick, exposed feeling, like the horrible words on my Wikipedia page were painted above on the ceiling for everyone to read. "It's business. I want this hotel. You can't let him have it. Whatever my father has told you about me is a lie."

A tense silence descended. The elevator music grew loud. Gabe flattened his lips and scanned the crowded space. "You want to do this here?"

My breath came hot and sharp. This fucking elevator was giving me vertigo. "You can't trust him."

"And I can trust you? I've heard how you do business. One of my HR managers used to work for your company. She said it was an unpleasant working environment."

"I have high standards."

"She said you threatened to sack everyone because they threw you a birthday party."

I loosened my tie. The bloody thing was tighter than a noose. I was sweating now. Shaking. "Not everyone. Just the people at the party. And it's because I hate surprises. Any normal person should.

And if you think I'm a problem, then you're going to be in trouble with my father."

The blonde at Gabe's side shot him a worried look. "What's wrong with Philip?"

"Don't worry about it. I've got it under control," he murmured.

"No. You haven't. He might want you to think that, but you haven't. Philip will always have the upper hand. He lies. Constantly. He'll tell you anything you want to hear."

The doors slid open. The team filtered out. Some of them shot me curious looks. Most went out of their way not to look at me at all. I was embarrassing myself. This was humiliating, but I couldn't let him win. I just couldn't.

Gabe gave me a dark, layered look. "I don't appreciate being ambushed. If you want to talk, do it in office hours."

A snap of irritation sharpened my voice. "Then answer your fucking phone. I can't get hold of you in office hours. You're screening my calls."

He pressed his lips together. "So you turn up at my hotel on your honeymoon?"

"I don't see what choice I have if you won't take my calls. You can't sell this hotel to Philip Thorner." My voice cracked, low and raw. "Are you fucking crazy?"

My outburst rattled in the stillness. Gabe's expression shifted to unease, and he took a step back. I couldn't blame him. This wasn't me. I'd completely lost control.

"You're too late. I've already made up my mind. It's not for sale. Not to you, anyway. Please don't bother me about this again." He grabbed the blonde woman's hand and shielded her protectively as he stepped past me. Discomfort flared in his gaze, but also something much worse: pity. He patted me lightly on the shoulder. "If I were you, I'd forget about whatever is going on here and move on. It's not worth this. I hope you enjoy the rest of your honeymoon."

Chapter 42

CHARLOTTE

I didn't even know why I picked up the art supplies. It was a stupid, impulsive thing. The little art shop had looked so inviting. Now, the sketch pad weighed heavy under my arm and made me feel ridiculous. I should have pitched it in a bin somewhere. I also should have gone to the Trevi Fountain at sunrise, before the streets were crowded and stifling. Tourists with their phones held high crammed every inch of the low stone ledge around the fountain's base. I studied the intricate carving and turquoise pool, glittering with coins. Trickling water and conversations in a host of different languages filled my ears.

A couple got up and I darted to sit in the gap they left behind. Water cascaded in sheets behind me and the spray caught the bare skin of my arms. Balancing the sketch pad on my knee, I took a pencil from my bag, and the blank page stared back at me. *Who do you think you are? It will be terrible whatever you do.* People were probably looking at me. I knew what they'd be thinking: *she thinks she's some kind of artist.* At my side, two lovers kissed. My face felt hot and tense. I shifted position, turning my body away. *Just make a start. It doesn't have to be good. Rebuild your fucking tower.*

Cole had blown me off for a meeting. We should have been here together. It shouldn't have bothered me this much, because I knew exactly what I'd signed up for. A contractual arrangement. Cole had wanted a wife he could pick up and put down whenever he liked. Someone he could ditch and walk away from without consequences.

It didn't matter how real it felt. When it was a choice between me and his own agenda, I didn't factor in. He'd made me think he was bringing me to Rome because it mattered to me, but really it had just been to shaft his father. He'd tried to dig up dirt about my art tutor just because I'd mentioned it once. It was all so petty and vindictive. I wasn't a wife. I was an employee. Somehow, this place had made me forget that he'd made me sign a contract. Cole fucked all his employees one way or another, he was just a lot nicer about it with me.

I held my pencil poised over the page, but I couldn't do it. Not in this crush of tourists. I found a quiet curb at the corner of the piazza and sat with my legs crossed and the sketch pad in my lap. I studied the carved sea horses and water nymphs. *Where to start?* The pencil felt awkward and alien in my hands. It had been too long. *Why was I even bothering?*

Cole drifted back to the forefront of my mind. On paper, the arrangement with him was worth it, but the reality was something different. The reality was too painful. I'd done a lousy job of protecting my heart. I'd jumped into bed with him, knowing I'd never be able to park my emotions. I'd let myself fall for him all over again, despite what he'd done to me in the past. He'd broken my heart without any remorse or excuse. There was no reason to think he wouldn't break it again. I would never be Cole's priority.

I glanced down at the page to see that I'd been doodling without even realizing. Two hands reaching for each other, their fingertips almost touching. It was a crude effort. Not good. Not even a shadow of the hands in the Sistine Chapel. But they were there. I'd drawn them. The first step. A realization settled in my heart. Michelangelo could have drawn the fingers touching, but he hadn't, because the tension was in the gap. My spark of life was so close, but I had to reach out and touch it.

I'd put everything on hold to care for Dad, and I didn't regret a moment of that. For years, I'd been surviving what life had handed me. Dutiful daughter. Compliant sister. Always going through the motions to keep myself and Dad afloat. Now it was time to start living again. To figure out what my life should look like. To put myself in the driver's seat.

Cole would never prioritize me, but I had to prioritize myself. No matter how much money he was offering, if I couldn't commit to this agreement without feeling like my heart was breaking, it wouldn't work. No amount of money was worth feeling stuck and heartbroken. As much as I'd fooled myself that I wouldn't fall for him again, I had. Despite every misgiving, I cared about him so deeply. I couldn't be with him every day pretending to be his wife when it felt like this.

Cole had offered me a lifeline, but the price was too steep. Maybe there was a way out of the contract. If I sold the house, I could pay him back the money I owed. Yes, it would be painful. But it was still the healthier option. I needed a clean break. A new chapter. One where I would be my own lifeline. I pulled my phone out of my bag and texted Tiff. This would affect her, too.

I'm leaving Cole. Is there somewhere else you can stay?

Her reply pinged back instantly. *What? Why? What about the money?*

It's a long story. You can go back to the house.

My heart sank. Good that I wasn't making things difficult for Tiff with her accommodation, but I'd hoped she was done with Paul.

We can sell the house. It has to be the right people.

She replied. *Why the change of heart?*

Because it's not worth it. I'm over billionaire dick.

I walked to the fountain and threw a coin over my shoulder. Rome had my heart. I'd be back here again one day. Alone.

I dragged my case through the lobby to the exit. It was about to cost me a fortune to fly home, but I'd take the hit. Better that than spend any more time with Cole.

"Charlotte?"

Reuben strolled across the lobby. He flashed a broad smile and rocked back on his Air Jordans. "Sorry about all that awkward business last night with my dad." He took off his neon-orange baseball cap and fanned his face with it. "He can be like that."

"Don't you get tired of him?"

His smile dimmed a little. "Sometimes. He's not always that bad." He scanned the lobby. "Are you checking out? Where's Cole?"

"I don't know, and I don't care."

He frowned. "You're leaving alone?"

"Yes. Excuse me. I don't want the taxi to leave."

He propped his cap back on his head and offered an amiable smile. "Do you want a lift?"

"It's fine. I booked a car to the airport."

"No. I meant a lift back to England. I'm just about to fly home. The jet is waiting."

Absolutely no way did I want an awkward trip on a private jet with the fake father-in-law from hell. "No. Thanks. I'll make my own way."

"Dad's not coming, if that's what you were worried about. He's staying on. It's just me. Come on. Avoid all those awful queues at check-in."

"You don't mind?"

"Of course not, Sis." He beamed. "We're family."

He tried to take my case, but I gripped the handle. "I've got it. Thanks."

In the cool, air-conditioned interior of Reuben's limo, I sent Cole a text.

I want a divorce.

Then, with a sigh, I sent a follow-up message because I couldn't help myself. *Don't forget to pack your laptop charger. It's on the bedside table.*

Chapter 43

Cole

"Checked out? You're sure?"

The man behind the reception desk, wearing a suit and tie in the blistering heat of Rome, clicked his mouse over the screen again. "Yes. Just over two hours ago."

What the fuck? Charlotte had gone? "But where was she going?"

"I don't know, signore. All I know is that she returned her room card."

The piped music pouring out of the speaker made my blood boil. Charlotte had taken a leaf out of Gabe's book and wasn't replying to my messages or answering my calls. Just a text. *I want a divorce.* My jaw tightened. Why would she forgo five million pounds? Surely life with me wasn't that bad.

My teeth gritted. "Where the fuck is my wife? Did you call a car for her? Did she book a flight? I want to know. She can't have just vanished from the lobby. Someone must have seen her leave."

The man behind the desk shrugged. "I'm sorry. I don't know."

"Do you have a problem, Cole?"

My father's imperious voice grated my ears. I turned to see him with Gabe Rivers at his side. *Great.* Why didn't they just get their contract out here and sign it right in front of me? They were probably about to ask me to be a fucking witness to the signatures.

"If you're looking for your wife, she left here with Reuben." Philip's face dripped smug superiority.

Oh, he fucking loved that. The golden boy. Now Charlotte's choosing him, too.

"Reuben?"

"He was flying home today, so he offered her a lift."

Of course. This just kept getting worse.

"Maybe you should have spent more time with your new wife, and less with your nose in my business."

Don't react. Don't show your hand. I'd always prided myself on my composure, but a taut wire snapped inside of me. My anger spilled over and I barked the words out.

"Oh, fuck off, will you, Philip? Give it a rest."

Gabe raised an unimpressed eyebrow. My father stared back at me with a glint of amusement in his eye. I'd lost control. He'd won. This was over. It had been over for so long, and I'd kept going, trying to force a meeting with a man who wouldn't even take my calls. It was humiliating.

I moved in the other direction, back to my room, away from my father's smug grin, but some reckless impulse made me swing back to him. He glared at me, and for the first time I noticed how old he looked. Gray, sallow skin. Age spots dotting his forehead. A slight tremor around his lips. Once, he'd been the most powerful man in my world, and now he was tired and fading. Was this what lay in store for me? A vengeful shell of a man. Petty and tragic.

"You call me pathetic, but look at you. I saw you with Reuben last night. The only son you have who can stand to be around you, and you talk to him like that. Let the poor kid go. He doesn't deserve it."

Gabe coughed awkwardly and averted his gaze. Charlotte had told me arguing with an old man in a hotel lobby wasn't a good look, but fuck it. *Chalk it up.* Another couple of hateful lines for my Wikipedia page.

My father shook his head, feigning embarrassment. "I apologize, Gabe. Ignore my son. He's never learned how to be gracious in defeat."

Behind Philip, against the wall, stood a vast stone Roman urn with fluted sides. Green foliage with flat, broad leaves poked out of the top. The Romans had cremated their dead. Roy had taught me that. That urn would once have held the ashes of someone's parent or sibling or child. Now it was a planter in a hotel lobby. I had the strangest urge to kick it over. To watch it smash all over the marble floor. The urge made me recoil. I didn't want to be a destroyer. I hadn't always been that way. Charlotte had known me before. She saw the boy I'd once been.

A sharp lump rose in my throat. "This hotel means something to me. It was always personal. But you know that, Philip. Good luck to both of you. I hope you'll be happy doing business together." I swung to look at Gabe. "You can kiss goodbye to La Dolce Vita. My father will turn this place into a faceless piece-of-shit motel, like he always does. He has a chronic lack of style. It can't be helped. Apparently, good taste is the one thing money can't buy."

Gabe's lips pressed flat. He raked a hand over his hair uneasily.

My father narrowed his eyes. "It's over. You lost. Now you're just embarrassing yourself."

The piped music grew louder, grating my brain. "He'll destroy it. Smash it to smithereens. He destroys everything. His staff. His wife. His kids. He breaks us all. It's a damn shame, because this is the most beautiful place I've ever stayed. Although, you need to sort out your Wi-Fi. How can you have perfect reception in an underground crypt and not in a penthouse suite? That's a fucking shambles, but the rest? The food is the best I've ever had. The risotto was so good, we were wondering if you'd put drugs in it.

"Your gold-plated toilet seats are excessive. Tacky, actually. But everything else is worth it. The art. The sculptures. You can't put a price on beauty. It should be cared for with the respect it deserves."

A sudden ache speared my chest. *I want a divorce.* Charlotte had gone. I hadn't given her the respect she deserved. The most beautiful person in my life. We should have been at the Trevi Fountain right now, but I'd chosen this. She'd walked out of here alone.

I drew a sharp breath. "But most importantly of all, my mother was happy here. That's what mattered to me. I would have paid anything for this hotel, and I wouldn't have changed a fucking thing. My father is a destroyer of beautiful things. I choose not to be. I would have protected every inch of it."

Gabe frowned and eyed my father warily. "You've committed to keeping the staff. Preserving the building and the tunnels."

My father inclined his head in a nod.

I couldn't help my bitter laugh. "He's lying. Just look at his previous purchases. Look at the Luxe in Milan or the Hotel Fernando in Granada. Look at what he did to them."

A tense silence wrapped around us. People were looking. My heart pounded. I'd failed. My father had won. And Charlotte had left me. *A divorce? Why?* Was I really so fucking bad? She'd rather be broke? With me, she could travel the world, but she'd rather choose Ecclesdale?

We'd had the most amazing time together. The sex had been incredible, but that was nothing compared to how it had felt having my best friend back and just hanging out, talking, laughing, holding hands, watching her have new experiences, making her nose scrunch when she smiled. She was gone. It was a knife in my back and I was bleeding out all over this fucking lobby.

The loss of this hotel paled in significance to the panic flooding me. Charlotte didn't want me anymore. Even five million pounds wasn't a tempting enough proposition to endure me. Because that's how she'd always seen this. I loved every moment in her company, and to her, I was something to be *endured*.

My father glared at me with disdain. He made everyone around him miserable, and I'd done the same to Charlotte. The truth was so blindingly obvious. It hit me like a punch in the gut. My voice came out a whisper.

"You destroy everything, Philip. You made me leave the only place I've ever felt happy. You've already cost me too much. I can't do this with you anymore. You only have all this power over me because I give it to you."

A muscle worked in his jaw, but he said nothing. There was nothing he could say anymore that mattered to me. I'd fallen in line when I was a kid, but I'd got away from him, and now I could make my own choices. *Enough. This can't go on.*

Charlotte had looked so sad this morning, and I'd chosen my vendetta over her. So many times over these past two weeks, I could have been with her, but I'd pulled out my laptop instead. I'd wasted so much of our time here when we could have been together.

My eyes drifted back to the urn. To the detail in the stone that had been so lovingly crafted. Time moves on. Empires rise and fall in the blink of an eye. Life is short and precious. My father was an absolute bastard, but he was right about one thing. I should have kept my nose out of his business and paid attention to my wife. My beautiful, smart, incredible wife.

Yes, my mother had been happy here, but would she be happy to see me like this? To read my Wikipedia page? To know that I'd taken on my father's cruelty and pettiness instead of her kindness? Whatever it took, I needed Charlotte to know that this was real. That I loved her. That this had always been real. That I should have stopped being a coward and come back for her so much sooner. I'd just never had the balls. Love wasn't a weakness, but putting your heart at the mercy of someone else took strength. I could be strong. I had to be, because Charlotte was written on every page of my first act, and she was the rest of my story. It could be a happy story. A love story. I'd fucked this up. I had to rectify it.

I inclined my head to Gabe. "I don't care if you don't sell to me. I shouldn't buy it, anyway. My shareholders are going to have me by the balls if I do. But this place is too special. You don't like me, and I get it. I don't like myself much at the moment, either. But do yourself a favor and sell it to anyone else but him."

I headed for the door. My stuff was in the suite, but it didn't matter. Someone would handle it. Everything in that room was replaceable. Charlotte wasn't.

"Wait." Frowning, Gabe looked up from scrolling his phone. "Are you still interested in making an offer?"

"Not right now. My wife is my priority."

The doors slid open, and the heat and bustle of the city hit me full in the face—the crazy whine of mopeds, exhaust fumes, sightseers, history. I breathed in the chaos. It was fucking glorious.

Chapter 44

CHARLOTTE

"You didn't have to drop me all the way back here."

Reuben smiled good-naturedly. "It's no problem. I don't get up north much. Any excuse to go for a ride in the chopper."

It had been my first time in a helicopter and, now that I was divorcing Cole, probably my last. "Do you want to come in?"

"Thanks."

A musty smell hit me in Dad's hallway. Tiffany wasn't exaggerating about things falling into disrepair.

"Any idea how to get rid of mold?" I peered at the black stains splattered all over the hallway.

Reuben shrugged. "Paint over it?"

A smile crept onto my lips. "I'm pretty sure you have to do more than that. I'm just hoping it's not the kind that infects your brain. Although, that would explain a lot about Tiff's behavior."

And mine too. Marrying a man I hadn't seen in over a decade had hardly been my finest hour.

Reuben chuckled. "Sounds like hard work."

"Right, but most things that are worthwhile are."

"If you say so." Reuben looked around the small kitchen and smiled. He'd probably never set foot in a poor person's house before.

"So cute, like a little toy kitchen."

I snorted. Had it seemed like a toy kitchen to Cole? When we were young, I'd never thought much about his life outside of Ecclesdale or how different our backgrounds were. It had never mattered. We'd just connected.

Reuben's smile was huge. "I love it, honestly. It's all perfect."

Dad would have been endlessly amused by Reuben. He had a boyish exuberance about him that was impossible not to like. Dad had been similar. He'd had a great interest in people. So many people had come to his funeral because he'd been so well loved. My gaze fell on his slippers sitting by the back door. I'd never moved them. Not even when he was bedbound at the end and had no use for them.

"My dad would have loved you."

He brightened. "Yeah?"

"Yeah. Do you want a cup of tea?"

"I'd better get off. I suspect Dad might call me back to Rome."

"You don't have to let him bully you, you know."

"I can handle him." He shrugged.

"You shouldn't have to. You *don't* have to."

He frowned and rubbed the back of his neck. "No. I suppose not."

He peered into the living room. "It's so cute in here, too." He rocked back on his heels. "You know, it's really something up here. I love how . . . green it all is."

"It's not bad. We've got a retail park now with a Nando's."

He pulled a confused face. "Nando's?"

"Portuguese? Peri-peri chicken? Don't tell me you've never had Nando's?"

He shook his head. "I don't eat fast food. Dad says it takes years off your life."

"He's not wrong, but I don't know if I want to live a long life if I'm deprived of halloumi fries. We need to rectify this. Let's get dinner."

He flashed a small smile. "You're taking this well. Leaving Cole. I thought you'd be devastated, but you're talking up peri-peri chicken."

Because I'd moved past devastation to depressing reality. I'd spent too much of my life feeling sad over Cole leaving me. I couldn't do it again. Now, I was just grateful to be moving on from him. At least now I knew things would never change. He'd made his choice. This felt like closure. Something he'd denied me the first time. Now, I'd be the one to walk away.

He flashed a look at his watch. "I should get back."

"Screw your dad. He can wait."

He let out a thoughtful sigh and flashed a lopsided grin. "Right. Screw him. Let's go and take years off our lives."

Chapter 45

COLE

I flew straight from Rome to an airfield in Yorkshire. When I knocked on Charlotte's door, Reuben answered.

His face lit in a beaming smile. "Boss-man! We were just talking about you. Lottie took me to Nando's. Have you ever had it? I'm very into the rainbow slaw—"

"What can I do for you, Cole?" Charlotte joined Reuben at the door. She folded her arms and looked right through me.

"Can we talk?" I flashed a meaningful look at Reuben.

Miraculously, Reuben actually took the hint and jumped into action.

"I'd better leave you to it."

Charlotte frowned. "You don't have to go just because he says so."

"It's fine. I need to get back. Fist bump?" He bumped her fist with his.

"Fist bump, Bro?"

He held out his fist to me with a hopeful expression. I was beginning to wonder whether I'd got him wrong. Maybe he really was just a puppy looking for friends. Maybe I'd been wrong about a lot of things.

I bumped his fist with mine. "You get one of these. Never ask me to fist-bump again. Thank you for escorting my wife home safely."

Reuben flashed his un-Thorner-like friendly grin. "No problem."

He headed up the drive and turned back. "Golf again soon?"

He looked so hopeful I couldn't say no. "Fine."

"Bring Lucas and Theo?"

"I can ask Lucas. Theo is a long shot."

"I'm sure we'll get him out." He beamed and rubbed his hands together. "I have a good feeling about it."

Charlotte sighed and headed back into the house. "Come in then. I'm giving you formal permission to cross the threshold."

◆　◆　◆

We both avoided the armchairs. Charlotte sat on the sofa, and I stood at the window, giving her space.

"I understand why you left."

She studied the ornaments on the mantelpiece. "You do?"

"This situation with my father has gone on for too long. I've spent most of my adult life trying to get back at him. It's made me petty and vindictive, and the hotel pushed me to the edge. It's done, I promise. I don't want a divorce. I want the opposite. We could have been spending the day together. I made a mistake. Why don't we go back now? The jet is waiting. Let's finish the honeymoon."

"I don't want to go back to Rome," she said quietly.

"Then let's go somewhere else. Anywhere. Somewhere less hectic. We can relax on a beach together."

She walked to the glass doors and peered out at the back garden. "What happened with the hotel?"

"Gabe is selling to my father."

"So you lost?" She nodded her head slowly. "You lost out on the hotel, and now you're coming to me as your second choice?"

"No, I knew as soon as you left how badly I'd fucked up. I don't care about the hotel. You're right. I've spent all this time being like my father. I don't want to be."

She wouldn't turn around. She pressed her fingertips to the glass doors. "I'll give you the money back that you gave Tiff for this house. But it may take a while for the sale to go through. I'll pay you back for all of it: the clothes and the jewelry."

"I don't care about any of that. I just want you."

I watched her reflection in the glass. Her expression was calm, composed, and emotionless. No tears or anger. This was something much worse. Indifference.

"I'm sorry, but it's over. For good. I want out. I should never have agreed in the first place."

Over? She couldn't mean that. She had to give me a chance to put this right. A blackbird landed on the overgrown lawn and pecked at the grass, plucking out a worm. My chest ached so much, it may as well have been pecking out my heart.

"Give me another chance. Let me be your husband for real. Let me take this seriously. You were right. People aren't born to create or destroy. They just make choices. Let me choose to put this right. I'll make it up to you. I want to be the husband you deserve. Anything you ask of me, I'll do it."

Her eyes flickered to a stack of fading board games on the sideboard. "Do you remember that time when we were playing Scrabble, and I was winning? When you got up to go for a drink, you *accidentally* knocked the board onto the floor. You've never liked to lose. This is no different." Her voice was flat. "For all I know, you'd say anything to save face. You just want me so you have another shot at your deal."

Frustration made my voice terse. "No. That's not what this is. I don't care about the deal or what anyone thinks. I don't want you as my wife because it makes me look good. I want you as my wife because life feels meaningless without you. Nothing else matters. I've never loved anyone else, and I never will for as long as I live. Only you. It was always you. You are everything to me, Charlotte."

She squeezed her eyes shut. "Always me, huh? Then why didn't you ever call me when you left here? Why didn't you reply to my emails? You kissed me and said all those things to me. Do you know how much it hurt me? To be ignored. I felt like you hated me, and I didn't even know what I'd done wrong."

One of Roy's photos stared down at me from the wall. I'd loved him. He'd been a father to me. I couldn't betray his memory. It wasn't right. "Because I was young and selfish. I'm sorry I hurt you."

She drew a breath and turned to face me. "You did. Then and now. It has to end. I'll never tell anyone about the contract. But please don't make this divorce harder than it needs to be. Let's get it done swiftly so we can both move on. It's just an admin task. At least this time it's one without an audience."

"Divorce? You don't really want that. I can't leave you here. Come back with me."

"Why? So you can dump me in the middle of nowhere again with your housekeeper to babysit me?"

My fingers itched to reach for her, but I didn't dare. Instead, I placed my fingertips lightly next to hers on the glass. "No. So that I can look after you. To love and to cherish. From this day forward."

"This was a farce from day one. You've never wanted a wife. You wanted an employee."

"I was a fool."

She shook her head and let her hand drop to her side. "If you care about me as much as you claim, then you'll leave me alone. Let me move on. Please. This has to end."

She was so cold and composed. So strong. Something was cracking inside of me. A hairline fracture splitting wide open and she didn't even care.

"This has been a terrible couple of years. I want to heal, Cole."

"That's what I've been trying to help you with. I want to bring you joy."

She held herself rigid and composed. "I have to bring myself joy, too. I have to protect myself."

Because I'm something to be endured. "From me?"

She wrapped her arms around herself. "You hurt me. You're going to keep hurting me if I allow it. It's better for both of us if we don't see each other again. I won't cause you any bother with the divorce. Let's just get it done quickly."

The words landed in my chest like fists. She was looking at me like I was a stranger. The way she'd looked at me when I saw her again at Roy's funeral. A huge surge of anxiety stole my breath. She meant it. This was over. Deals went in my favor, but this was collapsing, and I had no idea how to salvage it. I could tell her the truth about Roy, but it would only hurt her more, and it might not even be enough. He wasn't around to explain himself or defend his corner. It wasn't right. A promise was a promise. I only wanted to make her life better.

"I don't want to hurt you. I'm sorry." I sank to my knees. My hands were trembling as I took both of her hands in mine. "Please."

I didn't know what I was begging for. *Forgive me. Please know how much I want to make this right. Please say you love me, too.*

Her voice was quiet and strained. "Get up. Please, don't make it worse."

Unsteadily, I stood.

She withdrew her hands and her eyes slipped away. Her sigh was the most final sound I'd ever heard. "I'm sorry. I really need you to leave now."

Chapter 46

CHARLOTTE

Numbness crept over me as I watched Cole's driver ferry him away. It was over. My legs felt heavy, but I dragged myself up to Dad's study.

"Hi, Dad," I said to the air. "I've been to Rome. It was amazing. I bet we saw some of the same stuff."

My pointless words lingered in the silence. So much silence. The desk sat exactly as Dad had left it when he'd stopped coming in here. Books piled high on his walnut desk, gathering dust. The chalk had long since faded from the blackboard on the wall. A dank smell clung to everything. I pulled open a desk drawer. There were decades' worth of my dad's treasures: old letters, fossil fragments, photographs of people I didn't recognize, rusted toffee hammers, yellowing maps. It would all have to go. How?

At the back of a tall cabinet, I found a faded shoebox stuffed with leather-bound notebooks. I selected one at random. Dad's neat, methodical handwriting filled the page.

I had a plan of activities to keep the girls entertained. Today was scrap-modeling. Much to Lottie's distress,

*Tiffany decided that we should build a robot. With some
coaxing, Lottie was persuaded, but alas things took a turn
for the worse.*

My heart pounded, and I slammed the book shut. This was a
diary. It was a terrible invasion of privacy, but this was Dad's voice
leaping off the page. His intelligence, his wit, and his sparkling
eyes. These were his private thoughts and experiences that I hadn't
been privy to. It wasn't my business. But I couldn't stop my eyes
from drifting back.

*I couldn't get the tape off the roll quick enough, which
caused Tiffany to have a tantrum. Not one to be out-
done, Lottie soon joined her. In the end, both girls became
locked in a battle to see who could cry the loudest. I finished the robot myself, using margarine tubs for feet and
a silver foil antenna. In all honesty, it was magnificent.
I have multiple degrees, but this robot will still stand as
one of my greatest achievements.*

I scanned another notebook, and another. With each flip of
the page, my stomach fluttered with guilt. There were some gaps,
but the diaries spanned the years from when Tiffany and I were
young to when we were teenagers. I'd need to text Tiff. I couldn't
sit here and read this without her. But I couldn't tear myself away
either. Instead, I curled up in the corner of Dad's office and read
his thoughts on the weather, on teaching, on his pupils, on me and
Tiff (and how naughty we'd been as toddlers). Some entries were
so funny, I couldn't stop laughing. These diaries were so precious.
He was here with me in these words.

I closed my eyes and I could almost feel how it had been before,
when this house had thrummed with life. When the curtains were

open and the carpets hadn't faded. When everything smelled of the hot beer that Dad had brewed in the bathtub, and Cole was by my side, building a tire swing with me in the woods, introducing me to some obscure indie band, eating popcorn on the couch. Life had felt like nothing but opportunity. It was all gone. There was just echoing silence, and a crumbling house full of memories.

An unbearable ache inside made my chest hurt. I had too much feeling—sorrow, regret, disappointment, remorse. Too much of all of it, like burning inside. I had to get it out, any way possible. I stumbled through the house, past the stair lift, through the musty hall, and to the garage outside, where I found my old art supplies. I'd thrown so much of it away, but not all of it. There were still some blank canvases. Art hadn't just given me meaning, it had been the way to get my feelings out. To understand myself. Some part of me must have known how precious it all was. Some part of me must have known that one day I'd come back to rebuild my tower. With trembling hands, I salvaged whatever I could, and I began to paint.

Chapter 47

COLE

The rain battered me. It soaked through the wooden bench beneath me, and pitted circles in the greasy puddles at my feet. A stiff wind made me shiver. *Hello, British Summer Time. How I've missed you.* I'd intended to go straight to the office this morning, but somehow I hadn't made it. Instead, I was sitting in a park opposite the office, trying to figure out why I was sitting in a fucking park opposite the office when I had work to do.

"Are you sure you don't want the umbrella, sir?" my valet asked politely.

I glanced up at him. The rain was steady now. A relentless gray assault that had soaked through my coat, through my shirt, to the skin. I made no effort to move. I deserved this kind of punishment, but my valet didn't. The poor man was as soaked as me. I'd told him to leave several times. From his stoic expression, you'd think sitting in the rain like this was completely normal.

"It's fine, thank you, Dave. I told you. Take the car. I don't need you anymore."

He glanced around the park, his eyes drifting from the over-flowing bin to the run-down playground where a group of rowdy teenagers larked around under a graffiti-covered shelter.

"I don't want to leave you here on your own, sir."

"What do you mean?"

He cleared his throat and adjusted his wet cap. "You don't look . . . You don't seem yourself."

Right. I wasn't my fucking self. I hadn't slept in a week. My gut wouldn't stop churning. Every time I closed my eyes to sleep, my brain wouldn't give me a minute's peace. I tore off the crusts of my sandwich and threw them to the pigeons. Not like I was going to eat it, anyway. My appetite had disappeared. The birds flocked in a loud, squabbling chaos that grated on me.

"Why don't you let me take you back home, sir? You can dry off."

"I'm supposed to be in the office."

He held his face perfectly expressionless, despite the large raindrops running down his nose. "Shall I accompany you to the office now?"

I hunched in my drenched peacoat. A great shiver ran through me. No. I couldn't face it. It was all so pointless. I couldn't sit through another meeting when none of it mattered. All that mattered was Charlotte.

"No. Please, just go. No point us both getting wet."

"Sorry to bother you, Mr. Thorner." A tentative voice drifted to my ears.

Thorner. I'd have to go back to it. Not yet. Not until the divorce was finalized. I looked up to see a vaguely familiar blonde woman in a smart suit.

"What is it?"

She swallowed. "We were just wondering if you're coming inside. You have a solid calendar of meetings today."

"Cancel them."

She exchanged an uneasy look with Dave. "All of them?"

"Yes."

She bit her lip. "Also, it's Alice's last day. We've organized a fuddle in the conference room."

I couldn't keep the irritation rolling under my skin from my voice. "I don't know what that word means."

"A buffet. Everybody brings something to eat." She cleared her throat. "I thought I should make you aware in case you see people enjoying themselves and get mad about it. I promise it will only be during lunch break."

I cut her a sharp glance. She clasped her hands tightly in front of herself. She looked frightened. The way people looked around my father. Charlotte's words rang in my head. *Have you considered being less of an arsehole?*

"What's your name?"

The rain bore down heavier. She held her hands protectively over her blonde curls.

"Olive."

I motioned to Dave. "I think Olive might appreciate the umbrella."

Dave opened out the sleek black umbrella, holding it over Olive's head. She stepped under the arc of shelter and nodded her thanks.

"How long have you worked for me?"

"A year."

This woman had worked for me a year, and I couldn't have picked her out of an identity parade. The turnover of my assistants was usually so high, it wasn't worth learning their names. But maybe if I wasn't such a prick, I'd get to keep an assistant, or a wife for that matter, longer. At least Lucas would be pleased. He'd won the bet. My marriage had lasted less than six months. Amazing that Theo had been the optimist of the two of them.

I stared over the wet grass to the jutting steel and glass offices beyond. It reminded me of New York. Philip Thorner had always made me feel small, but standing in Times Square after the quiet pace of Ecclesdale had made me realize that I wasn't just small, I was infinitesimal. That moment changed me. I understood that if I was ever going to escape my father's clutches and make my mark on the world, it would take supreme effort and relentlessness. It would take every fiber of my fucking being. But I'd been a boy. It was the logic of a child. Now, I was a man. I wouldn't be terrorized, and I would do everything within my power to be better.

"Your wife called and left a message."

A flicker of hope lit my chest. I sat straighter. "Oh? Did she like the handbags? What about the flowers? Did you organize the villa in the Seychelles?"

She avoided eye contact. Not nervous. Afraid. "She said she wants you to stop sending things to the house."

"Did she say anything else?"

"No."

I ran a hand through my soaking hair. The hammering rain and the squawking of the pigeons at my feet as they fought each other viciously for the last crumbs filled my ears. I'd lost her. None of this mattered anymore. Not my father. Not the business. Only her.

Olive took a step back. "Was there anything else, Mr. Thorner?"

"What are the names of my other assistants?"

"Fiona and Seth."

Olive, Fiona, and Seth. I could remember that.

"Apparently, a member of staff left, and they said this isn't a pleasant working environment. What can I do to make it better?"

"Better?"

"Yes. How can I be a better boss?"

Rain machine-gunned off the umbrella over her head. She blinked. "I don't know, Mr. Thorner. Everything is great as it is."

"I know that's not true. You can be honest. You won't get into trouble. What would make you want to stay? What do I need to do? A more sophisticated coffee machine? Donuts?"

She frowned. "That would be nice. Maybe, if it was a little less . . . intense. If you were a little more . . . approachable." Her smile was tense. "Some flexibility in working hours would be good. More work–life balance."

Fine. I'd have HR do a staff survey. I could find out what people wanted and accommodate it.

She brightened. "Casual Fridays?"

If I didn't feel so depressed, I might have had it in me to laugh. I managed an eyebrow raise. "Don't push it, Olive."

She smothered a smile. "Right."

"Why don't you get some more things for your fuddle? Whatever you like. Put it on expenses. Other people having a party doesn't make me mad. I just don't like surprises."

"Thank you. Was there anything else?"

She glanced back at the offices, as though desperate to escape me.

"There is one thing. Do you believe a person can change, Olive?"

She swallowed and swiped her hands down her pencil skirt. This poor woman looked unnerved by me. This was the legacy I'd built for myself. It wouldn't do.

"It doesn't matter. I don't suppose I'm paying you enough to answer questions like that."

"No. It's fine." She took a step forward and straightened her shoulders. Dave shuffled with her, holding the umbrella over her head. "Yes. I believe people can change, but they must want to, and they must do the work."

"What work?"

"It depends how you want to change? I had a fear of driving a few years ago, and I went to therapy. It helped a lot."

"I'm not the type to go to therapy."

She fiddled with a chain around her neck. "Maybe you'd surprise yourself."

They say what doesn't kill you strengthens you. I used to believe that, but it was a lie. Sometimes, things just diminished us. They broke our hearts. Made us weak. Cracked us open. Sometimes life molded us into men slumped on benches with coffee stains on soaked shirts and staff tiptoeing around us like we were unexploded bombs. But maybe this was the point you had to get to. Raw. Repentant. Lost. What if I wasn't broken? What if I was just a mound of wet clay, ready to be reshaped? Why couldn't I change? Didn't I get to make that choice?

One thing was for damn sure, I wouldn't give up. I had to find a way in. A way to show Charlotte that I could be the man she deserved. Obviously, flowers and diamonds wouldn't cut it. Charlotte had never cared for those things. I needed some advice. Someone who knew Charlotte. "One last thing. Could you set up a round of golf with my brother?"

"Which brother?"

The one who, for some unfathomable reason, Charlotte seemed to like. "Reuben."

◆ ◆ ◆

"No one else could join us?" Reuben held his tongue between his teeth as he lined up his shot with an excessive amount of wiggling.

"Lucas couldn't get childcare, and Theo's got some new bodyguard gig."

Reuben looked up from the ball. "I didn't think he did private security anymore?"

"He doesn't. It's a favor for a friend."

Hard to decide what was more surprising about that situation. The idea that Theo would do anyone a favor, or that he had a friend who would dare ask for one. Reuben struck his ball and it flew off down the fairway.

I lined up my shot. "I'm glad it's just the two of us. I wanted to talk to you about something. Have you seen Charlotte at all since Rome?"

Reuben kept his gaze on the flag in the distance. "We've texted. I haven't seen her."

"How is she?"

"She says she's OK. I think she's very sad. I've been trying to get her to go out of the house, but she doesn't want to do anything." He shot me a worried glance. "As friends, obviously. Just friends. I think that's what she needs the most right now."

Friends. My heart hurt. That was the worst part of all of this. I missed my best friend.

"Lucas told me you all had a sweepstake about how long my marriage would last. You were the only one who thought we'd go the distance. Why did you think that?"

He lifted his neon baseball cap and arranged his floppy hair. "That's an easy one. I see the way you look at each other. You're meant to be together."

"You think so?"

He gave an earnest nod. "I know so. You're soulmates. It's obvious."

Opening up to Reuben was weird, but I needed someone to hear me. Sure, he was annoyingly cheerful, and his nose was too straight, but he wasn't the villain I'd thought he was.

"She's adamant that it's over. I can't keep trying to fix it because it's making it worse. She doesn't want any of the gifts I send. Charlotte is a kind and decent person, the best kind of person, and

I hurt her because my focus has been all wrong. I wanted her to know that I'm ready to change. But it's too late. She wants me to leave her alone, and I'm trying to respect that, but the worst part is that she's alone. I don't want her to feel alone. She needs friends around her."

Reuben nodded, thoughtfully. "You could still be friends."

"I love her. Deeply. I can't just be her friend."

"But loving someone means putting their needs first. Maybe that's all it can be right now as far as she's concerned."

Friends wasn't enough. Still, it was better than nothing. Why couldn't it be easy? Wouldn't it be lovely if I could just show up at her house with an orchestra or something and ask her to love me? I supposed that was marriage for you. The point of all that admin. The only way to show her that I'd changed was consistency. Time and effort. Marriage wasn't for the faint-hearted. But I'd never been more determined to make mine work.

I'd do whatever it took. I'd find a way to show her that I'd changed. Clearly, my words were meaningless. I'd show up even if I was just a friend, cheering her on from the sidelines. At least I'd be in her life. At least I could be in the same room with her.

"How mad is she? Too mad to speak to me yet?"

"It wouldn't hurt to see if she's open to a chat about being friends. If she says no, then you have to respect it. You'll also have to accept that it might never be more."

My heart ached. How could I accept the unacceptable? But if that was Charlotte's choice, then I would always respect her boundaries. I could still be there for her, in whatever capacity she'd have me.

I took a breath, mulling it over. "That feels like pretty solid advice from you, Reuben."

He flashed a proud smile. "You think?"

"Yes."

I held still and lowered my voice so my words wouldn't reach the prying ears of the caddies. "I'll help you, you know. If you ever need it."

His eyebrows lifted in confusion. "Help me?"

With a solid swing, I sent my ball into the air. I watched the ball land, and turned to see Reuben looking at me with an uneasy expression.

"I know what Philip's like. I know how he manipulates people and controls the purse strings. Whatever he has on you, I can get you out. Whatever you need. A job. Money. A place to stay. All of it . . ."

Fear flashed in his eyes. He chewed his lip. "I don't understand."

"It's OK to be scared. I was scared of him for a long time."

"*You* were scared?"

"Yes. He told me he'd destroy everything I loved. I didn't doubt it."

"But you're not scared anymore?"

"No. Not anymore. He's a weak old man. I won't give him any power over me. I won't be investing a scrap of my energy in him."

Maybe it was too soon. Philip ground people down. He'd probably destroyed Reuben's confidence and made him feel like he wouldn't be able to stand on his own two feet. I could plant the seeds until he was ready.

We set off walking together. "You won't be alone. Just come to me. I'll get you sorted."

His voice filled with disbelief. "He wouldn't like it."

"We'll handle it. Together."

He swallowed. "Thanks, but I'm fine. You don't need to worry about me."

Right. I'd been fine once too, until I wasn't. "I am worried, because I used to be you. He blackmailed me into falling in line.

If you do want to get out from under his thumb, just know, you have us."

"Us?"

"Me, Lucas, and Theo. We don't always see eye to eye, but we're brothers. You're one of us."

His cheeks pinked and he sniffed as though he was about to burst into tears. "Thanks, Bro."

"No problem." I'd better stop, or he'd try and hug me or ask me to pose for another selfie.

We continued to the hole. Reuben's ball had landed neatly ahead of mine on the grass. *This fucker.* Was he some fucking golf prodigy?

He flashed me a curious glance. "What kind of job?"

"I'm sorry?"

"You said you could help me with a job."

I shrugged. "Whatever you like. If you want to keep racing, I'll help find you a new team, or I could bring you on board at Vexo. Get you trained up with a mentor."

A smile touched his lips. "Yeah? You can see me behind a desk?"

Nope. I kept my face neutral. "We'll figure something out."

He slammed his cap back on his head. "I'll think about it."

"You do that."

He stopped suddenly, and opened his arms wide. "This is some heavy stuff, Bro. Hug it out?"

I sighed. "Always just assume that I never want to hug it out."

He snorted and dropped his hands to his sides. Then he putted his ball and flashed a shit-eating grin. "Is it still beginner's luck if I beat you twice?"

Very funny. I raised an unimpressed eyebrow. "I'm starting to rethink this job offer."

He unleashed a beaming smile and threw his arm around my shoulder. "Don't. I'm up for it. If I get to keep thrashing the boss-man at golf, I'm coming round to the idea."

Chapter 48

CHARLOTTE

I stopped and peered at my handiwork. When I'd run out of paper, I'd had to find another surface. Cypress trees and ancient stones under a rich blue sky covered the expanse of wall in the lounge. Paint dripped from my brush onto the sheets I'd laid over the carpet. If Tiff came in here now, she'd assume I was having a breakdown. Maybe I was. But it didn't feel like that. All the tension in my shoulders had gone. My heart beat a calm rhythm in my chest, and I was filled with a deep sense of peace. All I knew was that it felt good. What did it matter? These walls were due to be painted over anyway.

A commotion sounded on the drive, and I moved to the window to look outside. My car was being hoisted high and onto the back of a tow truck. A different car sat on the driveway where mine had been—a silver tank-like monstrosity with a prominent grille glinting in the sun. What on earth? Ditching my paintbrush, I ran outside to the burly man in a plaid shirt who was securing my car to the truck.

"Wait. No! What are you doing? That's my car."

He gave me an unconcerned glance and pulled out a scrap of paper from his back pocket. "Fourteen Manor Road? Charlotte Ackroyd?"

I wiped my paint-covered hands down my overalls. "Yes. This is my car. I don't want you to take it away."

He shrugged and readjusted his baseball cap on his thick mop of red hair. "I just go where I'm told."

"Wait. No. You can't take it." I took a deep breath, trying to steady myself. "There's been some kind of mistake. Where has this car come from? That car isn't mine."

That's when I noticed the number plate: *LOT 11E.*

"It's yours. Congratulations," he said flatly, putting a set of keys on the bonnet. "Shouldn't be any problems, but my number is in the glove compartment if you need anything."

"I don't know what's going on here, but I'm begging you. Please don't take my car." My voice pitched an octave higher in desperation. "This is a misunderstanding."

He squinted at the scrap of paper again and moved to the cab of his truck. "Vexo Inc. Call them if you've got a problem."

Vexo? That was Cole's company. Was this Cole's doing? Who else? He was the only person I knew capable of affording a car like this. The tow-truck guy climbed up into the driver's seat and slammed his door. The truck rumbled to life. Frozen on my front doorstep, I watched as my car disappeared from view.

"I didn't order a rental car," I cried after him.

"It's not a rental car. It's your car." The crisp voice almost made me jump out of my skin.

I spun and met Cole's familiar pale-blue eyes, but nothing else about him was familiar. He was dressed as a laborer in heavy-duty navy overalls. A mop rested over one shoulder and a couple of bags over the other. It was the most incongruous thing I'd ever seen, like a kid had raided a dress-up box.

A strange laugh spluttered out of me. "Why are you doing cosplay as a blue-collar worker? Is this how billionaires have to blow off steam? Pretend to be normal people for the day?"

He hitched an amused eyebrow. "How are you, Charlotte? It's good to see you."

I'd never wanted to see him again, but a wave of relief washed over me to have him close. My hands were shaking. I slipped the car key into the pocket of my filthy jeans and gripped my hands behind my back.

"I was fine until you came and stole my car in broad daylight. I should call the police."

He surveyed the drive. "Not stolen. Replaced. I can organize something different if you don't like it."

"This is . . . I didn't ask for this." I peered at the car. It was ridiculously huge. "You can't just go around buying people cars. This look like it belongs to a Russian oligarch."

He tapped the bonnet. "I'd say more premier league footballer than oligarch, but I didn't think you'd appreciate a supercar."

"You know I can't accept this from you."

"Why not? It's an apology for my shitty behavior."

"Because you can't just buy your way back into my good graces."

He nodded solemnly. "I know that. And I accept it. Truly. This is my last gift. I'm here because I want to be your friend." He frowned. "Actually, there is one more gift, if you'll allow it."

He slid a bag from his shoulder and opened it just enough to show the contents. I peered inside to see a slim DVD player and a bunch of box sets.

"*Buffy?*"

"Every season. I thought you could do with a replacement since you accused me of stealing yours."

"Is this your admission of guilt? You did take it?"

His level gaze met mine, but his brow lifted with humor. "I admit nothing." I made no move to take the offered bag. "Thank you, but you know I can just stream them."

"Take them, anyway." He put the bag at my feet with a wry smile. "It's always good to have a backup."

He brought the mop down from over his shoulder and planted it at his side like a wizard's staff. "My boss sent me here, actually. He said you have a house in need of a clear-out. I've come to help you with that. I've got all the gear." He thumbed at a white van across the street. "I thought we could take it step by step. One room at a time. Patch up the roof. Sort out the plumbing. Clear out the furniture. Strip the walls. Give it a new lick of paint."

The spreading ache behind my eyes was back. Cole wanted to help me paint and decorate? It was ludicrous. Cole had probably never got his hands dirty his whole life.

"Do you even know how to do any of those things?"

He inclined his head. "Of course. I'm a handyman. Anything I don't know, I'll learn on the job."

I blew out a breath. We were done with this. Sexy role-play had been fun in Rome, but not now. "I appreciate the gesture, but I told you this was over. I want to move on from you. How can I do that if you're here?"

He studied my face. His voice was low and earnest. "I understand. I promise that this is not a romantic proposition. You don't even need to talk to me if you don't want to. Just let me do my work. No funny business. You put your feet up and let me take care of it. This is just me helping you because I know that hell is going to freeze over before you ask for help."

I folded my arms. "But why?"

"Because you've been doing everything on your own for so long, and this isn't a job that anyone should do alone. I want to be here for you. No strings attached. Just friends. You're doing me a favor, anyway. Making you happy gives me a lot of pleasure."

"It does?"

His eyes locked with mine. "It always has."

All I wanted was to collapse into his arms. I'd missed him so much. Despite all of it. Even though this relationship was confusing and he'd hurt me, I missed him. I couldn't forget how he'd hurt me. I already had closure.

My usual misgivings clamored to the surface. *You're too late. I've coped on my own for years. I don't need help.* But the weariness inside wouldn't let me say them out loud. Because the truth was louder. *I do need help. This is too much. I don't want to be alone anymore.* If he wanted to help, then who was I to stop him? It didn't mean I had to jump into bed with him again. I wouldn't. Not now. He'd let me down too many times. It was different back home. Being in Ecclesdale kept the past at the forefront of my mind.

I folded my arms. "I still want a divorce. You can help if you want, but I'm serious about that."

"I understand. I still want to help. Please. Let me do this."

I toed his work boot. "Who designed your outfit? Valentino? Those must be the cleanest overalls I've ever seen."

His eyes sparkled with humor. "Are you going to invite me in or not? I'm on the clock. My boss won't be happy with all this slacking."

"I'm sure he won't. I've heard he's difficult." I opened my front door and gestured for him to come inside. "You don't know how to deal with mold, do you?"

"As it happens, I do. You can't just paint over it. You have to strip the room back. Find the source of the damp. Tackle that first." He offered a faint smile. "It's going to take a lot of hard work, but I'll give it everything I've got."

Chapter 49

CHARLOTTE

Cole followed me into the kitchen. Sunlight streaked my half-finished mural on the wall. I'd filled the lounge with Hadrian's Villa and this room was going to be a sunset over the rooftops of Rome.

Cole stood completely still, awe rippling over his expression. "This is incredible."

My face felt warm, but I shrugged. "I thought I may as well. It's going to get painted over, anyway."

"No. Seriously, I mean it. It's amazing." He traced a finger lightly over the brushstrokes. His voice was soft. "You brought Rome to Ecclesdale."

"I'm thinking of doing some frescoes in the hallway. I just need plaster."

He nodded as though it wasn't an absurd suggestion. "Then we'll get you plaster."

The air was thick with the smell of paint. Heat crept up my neck as I caught a glimpse of myself in the kitchen window. Paint caked my overalls and streaked my face and hair. What must he have thought? Not that it mattered. I hadn't invited him here.

He'd just turned up on my doorstep. He seemed to be making a habit of that.

Cole smiled in invitation and lifted his mop. "Are you going to put me to work?"

He couldn't be serious, could he? What did it matter to me? He'd probably get bored after a couple of hours and give up. I passed him a bucket and a bottle of disinfectant. "The cupboards need to be emptied and scrubbed inside. How have you got time for this? Don't you have a huge empire to run?"

He took the equipment from me. "I'm taking a sabbatical."

"For how long?"

"For as long as it takes to get this house in order."

"You can cope with missing work?"

His eyes locked with mine. "I can cope. You just carry on painting. Let me handle everything else."

"You don't have to do this. You've got better things to do."

He moved to the sink and filled the bucket with soapy water. "This is the only place I want to be. I cared about Roy, too. If I can help, then I want to." He transferred the bucket to the floor and knelt down by one of the cupboards. "I'll make a start. We'll get it done."

"You really don't have to."

He smiled, small and genuine. "I know. I want to. Let me help you, Charlotte. That's all I want to do."

"Thank you." I met his eyes for the first time since he'd turned up on the drive. "I appreciate the help."

◆　◆　◆

I took the last of the bubble-wrapped heavy octagonal plates and put them in the box destined for the charity shop. We'd never even eaten from these. Dad had kept all the fancy stuff on the top shelves, and we'd forgotten about it.

"Christmas stuff?" Cole presented a faded tin full of Christmas-tree-shaped cookie cutters and little snowman cake toppers.

"Keep," I said.

He smiled. "I remember Tiff's Christmas cakes. I've never had better."

"I'm sure she'll give you the recipe."

"Great. I'll have to give it to Marco."

He put the tin in the box to go into storage and glanced at the clock. "I'm going to take these boxes before the charity shop closes." He gestured to the fridge. "Make sure you eat one of Marco's meals. There are a couple of risottos."

The first thing Cole had done when he arrived was unload a host of Tupperware boxes from a cooler bag into the fridge.

"Thanks."

He scanned the kitchen and dusted his hands together. "We've made a great start."

I dumped my brush into a jar of turpentine. "You're tidying up. I'm just making a mess."

His eyes landed on the outline of the Colosseum that I'd added to the mural. "It's not a mess. It's important."

"It is." I couldn't quite articulate why, but I knew it was. I needed to do it. Warmth radiated in my chest. It felt so much less overwhelming when I didn't have to be in this house alone. He loaded his powerful arms full of boxes, and I tried not to gawk. Cole always looked gorgeous in his smart suits, but his handyman getup was like a fantasy made real. Part of me wanted to ask him to stay for dinner, but I bit the words back. That was too familiar. Maybe one day we could do that in a friendly way. But not at the moment. The feelings were too raw. I had to treat this like a professional cleanup operation.

He hitched an eyebrow. "Same time again tomorrow?"

"You really don't have to do this."

"I know." His voice was gentle. "But I want to. Goodbye, Charlotte. Have a good night."

Chapter 50

Charlotte

We worked methodically, dusty room by dusty room, finding a routine. Cole arrived at 8 a.m. sharp every morning, and he cleared out the mess, while I covered the walls in paint. On the third day, Cole broke apart the furniture that wasn't in a fit state to donate. Despite the pain lodged in my chest, there was a spark of satisfaction in creating order from chaos. And in among the tearful moments were pockets of joy, like when I found my old school photos and reports to laugh at.

On the fifth day, Cole found me on the floor of Dad's study, sobbing. He brought me a cup of tea and sat next to me until I'd recovered enough to keep going. After a week, when the company had come to take away the stair lift, we were ready to strip the wallpaper on the landing. Cole steamed, and I worked with my scraper, chipping away the most stubborn bits of faded paper to reveal the blank wall underneath.

Sometimes I felt like this house was crying, but today, among the light and clouds of hot steam, it felt like it was breathing. The steamer hissed as Cole ran it up the wall, soaking the paper. He shot me a casual glance. "I had a meeting with a therapist."

I looked at him in astonishment. "What?"

"It's online. I have this critical voice in my head sometimes. It's my father's voice. The therapist said I have to imagine it like a parrot, and when it pipes up, I tell it to shut up. I enjoy that part. Very satisfying." A faint smile crossed his face. "I'll keep going. I have a lot of stuff to unpack about my time in New York. But I want to do it."

It was unbelievable to think of Cole opening up to anyone, but it could only be a good thing. "I'm glad you're doing some work on that. Well done."

He nodded. "I ripped up the contract. When the divorce goes through, you're entitled to half of everything. It shouldn't be too long now."

My paint scraper fell out of my hand. I sucked in a gasp of air. The dank smell of wet wallpaper filled my nose.

"You can't do that."

Clouds of steam billowed from the device as he worked. "It's your legal entitlement as my wife."

His voice was matter-of-fact, as though we were talking about divvying up loose change he'd found down the sofa and not a multi-billion-pound empire.

"You're not serious. I don't want it. I don't want a penny from you. It's not been earned. It doesn't belong to me."

"Take it up with the lawyers. Give it away if you don't want it. It's yours." He peeled a strip of wallpaper away in one long piece. A satisfied smile lit his lips. "Don't you just love it when that happens? You got the whole piece in one go?"

I stared at him, dumbstruck. The lawyers could say whatever they wanted. There was no way I'd take that money. I'd point-blank refuse. I couldn't help my laugh. "You're crazy."

"No. I'm your husband. This wasn't fake for me, Charlotte. It might have started out that way, but only because I didn't have the sense to realize or the courage to be truthful about my feelings. You've always been the one for me. I've never stopped loving you. The moment I saw you again, I knew I couldn't leave this place without you. I'm trying to be a better man. Not to win you back. I know you don't want me. But because it's the right thing to do, and I don't want that Wikipedia page to be my legacy. Take the money. I want you to live a wonderful life, full of love and adventure."

"You left me. If it was always me, why didn't you keep in touch?"

He kept his eyes fixed on the wall. "Because I was young, and I was an idiot. I just have to hope that one day you'll be able to forgive me, and we can be friends again."

Friends was safe. Friends was nice. Cole had helped me accomplish the impossible with this house. I couldn't have done it without him. I wouldn't have wanted to. A devilish impulse grabbed me and I dipped my brush into a pot of white paint. With a swift flick, I splattered his blue overalls.

His eyes widened and humor danced in his expression. "Really?"

I shrugged. "Yup. Pretty much. It's about time you got your designer overalls dirty."

He stared down at the paint mess with laughter in his eyes. A hint of mischief under all that controlled elegance. "You're in trouble now. You know I'm a terrible loser."

"I know." I raised a wry eyebrow. "But I still fancy my chances. You're done for."

"Oh, yeah?" He dipped a brush into a pot and retaliated, flicking me with paint.

"Yeah."

I splattered him again and took off, squealing. We raced around the house splattering each other, playing like kids until we were breathless from laughing and covered in paint. I collapsed against a wall, sucking in deep breaths. The house breathed with me. And the walls rang with laughter, the way they'd done for so many years.

I held my hands up in the hallway. "Enough. We need a truce."

He wiped paint from his hair and flicked it away. "Fine. We'll call it even."

I held out my wet hand. "Friends?"

His eyes locked with mine. He smiled and shook my hand firmly. "Always."

Chapter 51

Charlotte

The last remnants of summer slipped away and the overgrown trees at the bottom of the garden began to let go of their leaves. It felt like everything around me was exhaling in one deep, long sigh. Still we worked. We worked until there was nothing left to tackle but the untouched room at the end of the landing.

Dad's study was the hardest, but I couldn't put it off forever. From the window, I watched Cole hacking the hedges back. He'd hired a professional to replace the cracked paving stones and skim the pond. I pulled out the box of Dad's notebooks. Tiff was due over later to look through them with me, but I couldn't resist another quick scan.

The first time I'd opened these pages, it had been so painful, but the ache had dimmed a little. It was a comfort to see Dad's beautiful handwriting. To hear his words. This was a new side of him that I hadn't known. These books were a gift.

The girls took the news as well as could be expected. It is a comfort to me that they have each other. I have been blessed with the most wonderful family. Lived a wonderful life. It is enough. I am grateful for all of it. I hope my girls will remember me well.

We'd lost Dad in pieces. But I'd picked those pieces up and tucked them away inside. I'd been carrying parts of him with me even before his final breath. This cruel disease had stolen his memories, robbed him of his personhood, but I kept those pieces inside of me. He was always with me.

He'd walked with me down the aisle. He'd stood at my side marveling at St. Peter's Basilica. He was in the laughter of the children chasing the pigeons on the Spanish Steps. He was the sky—blue and limitless. He'd thrown a coin over his shoulder into the Trevi Fountain when he was a young man, and once again with me. I would always carry him inside. The way he'd carried us.

I scanned through the notebooks, remembering all the silly, mundane things we'd done together as a family: endless summer holidays, school misdemeanors, seaside trips. Dad's illness had been hard, but we'd still laughed when we could, and we'd once all been so happy together in this house. Then one entry made my heart stop.

A terrible thing this evening. This poor boy. Cole. I feel for him. He's a good lad, smart and kind, but I have to think of Charlotte. He was in tears, begging for my help, but what can I do? Philip Thorner isn't a man who anyone would want to get on the wrong side of. He said he'd destroy everything Cole loves, and I don't think that boy loves anyone as much as my daughter. I can't risk her. She has a bright future ahead of her, and she's besotted with him. She'd try to follow him to New York, and that could only end in disaster.

I'm forgetting all the time. It is a curse. I will have to tell them soon. I don't know how. It's no time to be distracted by puppy love. It's for the best if he goes. I've grown so fond of him. It's a terrible thing. But Charlotte needs to focus on getting into art school, not a teenage love affair.

If he truly loves her, as he says he does, he must leave her alone. Let her go and not drag her into this mess with his father. He seemed to understand. He begged for one of her sketch pads to take with him. I could hardly say no.

◆　◆　◆

I reread the words over and over again, but they still said the same thing. It wasn't my brain tricking me. My dad would never have done anything to hurt me. It couldn't be. But he had. Whether or not it was to protect me, his decision to send Cole away with no explanation had cut me so deep. It had hurt Cole too. My father had been one of the few adults that Cole could trust in his hour of need. He'd been let down.

My father had sent Cole away.

Cole hadn't told me the truth. I crawled on my hands and knees to the window, because my legs felt too shaky to walk. Cole was mowing the lawn, walking slowly in straight lines. It was such a mundane scene. But the shift in my heart was seismic. Cole had said he'd always loved me. For the first time, I actually believed him.

Chapter 52

Cole

Charlotte sprinted out onto the lawn. She was waving a notebook in the air. I turned off the lawn mower and pulled off my ear protectors. She thrust the notebook into my hand. "Please. You need to read this. I found it in Dad's study."

She smoothed her hair and fiddled with the buttons on her plaid shirt.

I scanned the page, reading Roy's take on the night I'd asked for help. My heart sank. I'd have happily taken it to my grave if it protected Roy's memory in her mind.

I looked up to find her watching me. "He told you to cut off contact."

I sighed. "You have to understand what I was asking of him. You mustn't think anything bad about him because of this. He was trying to protect you. My father is a tyrant. He's petty and deranged. He could have taken away your dad's job. Shut the school down. Ruined your chance at going to art school. He was capable of anything to get his own way. Roy couldn't fight him. We only wanted to protect you."

"I would have managed. I could have taken care of myself."

"You spent years taking care of your father. Maybe you could see this as his way of taking care of you."

"Why didn't you tell me the truth?"

"Because I hated the idea of you thinking anything bad about Roy."

"I get it. I do," she whispered. "I love my dad. It's easy to put someone on a pedestal after they're gone, but we're all just human. We all make human choices. These diaries are full of how much joy he took in being a father. It's on every page."

"I wasn't pleasant company for the years I was in New York. I don't like the man I became, and I wouldn't want to have dragged you into it all. Roy made a good decision. We were just kids."

Her eyes glimmered with tears. "We were kids, but we were the real thing. Don't you think? I loved you so much."

"I'm sorry I hurt you." I hardly dared move. "I never really cared much for Latin. It was just a way to be here and close to you. If I came over to the house, I might see you."

Her eyes softened. "Learning a dead language to see your crush is quite the flex."

"Right?"

She stepped closer. "I'm sorry for what you went through alone. It must have been such a difficult time. All these years." She chewed her lip and frowned. "I need some time to process this. I have to let it sink in. Tiff's coming round later. We're going to go through the diaries together." She took a deep breath, as though trying to steady herself. Hope and vulnerability flickered in her eyes. "You can join us. Would you like to stay for dinner?"

A glow lit inside my chest. "Yes. I'd like that. I'd like that very much. Thank you."

"Maybe we could watch one of those DVDs together after?" She toed the ground and shot me a bashful look. "You don't have to if you think it's silly—"

"It's not silly. I'd like that, too." *There's nothing I'd like more.*

Chapter 53

CHARLOTTE

On warm Friday nights, the village came together to watch the kids playing cricket. Cole and I sat at the edge of the green, drinking tea from polystyrene cups. Tiff and I had played on the junior cricket team for years. Dad had watched every practice session and match. I sat with my back against a tall oak and my sketch pad in my lap.

Cole tipped his face down and his eyes locked with mine. "Are you sure this is my good side?"

"Both sides are equally lovely. I just need you to keep still and hold back on the death glare."

The lines at the corner of his eyes crinkled with amusement, and I sketched them in. I'd been learning every new line in his perfect face since he'd come back into my life. Tiff was coming round later to read some more of the journals with me. Reading them together was a new way of getting to know Dad. I could forgive my father for sending Cole away because I understood his intentions were good. If things had been different, maybe Cole and I would have never parted. Maybe we would have. Who knew? History was important, but never a good place to dwell for too long. We had to live forward.

I took a deep breath. It felt good to get out of the house, away from the paint fumes, and breathe. We'd glossed the skirting boards today. That was the last big task. The house was almost ready. Cole must have been thinking about leaving here soon.

"I bet you're itching to get back to work," I said.

"No." He ran his hand absently over the grass. "I haven't missed it at all. The reasons I set up the company don't interest me anymore."

"You haven't heard anything from your father?"

"No. I don't care to bother him. I spoke to Gabe yesterday, and he's going to hold on to the hotel. The meeting with my father made up his mind. He said it's a good location for the squad to stay during training camps."

On the cricket pitch, a little girl thwacked the ball. A fielder jumped in the air to catch it, but it slipped through her fingers.

"Have you decided what you're going to do with the house yet?" he asked.

"I'm going to sell it. It's a family home. Too big for me. It needs a family. Dad would have wanted that."

Cole shot me a casual glance. "I'm thinking of extending my sabbatical. I'm actually considering early retirement."

A warm rush ran through me. "You are? What will you do?"

His eyes clung to mine and shifted away. "I don't know. I thought I might stay around here for a while."

"In Ecclesdale?"

"It stands to reason. Big things are happening around here. I heard you have a Londis now." He looked in the direction of the fields above the village where he'd kissed me all those years ago. "Also, it makes me feel . . . free. I was happy here when I was younger. It still feels like home. I'd love to have a little retreat around here." His voice was as soft as a kiss. "How would you feel if I stayed?"

I didn't dare believe it. Cole couldn't seriously leave London behind for the middle of nowhere. "I can't make that decision for you."

He tilted his head to mine. "You told me you wanted to move on. If you still want that, I respect it. I always want to be your friend. But I have to tell you that I am desperately and hopelessly in love with you, and there's nothing I want more than for you to be my wife. My real wife. I want to spend my life loving and cherishing you.

"I will never put anything before you. Not work. Not my grievances. Nothing. Making up for lost time with you is my only priority. I never want to go back to being a Thorner. I hope you will accept me as an Ackroyd." He raised a wry eyebrow. "Of course, you could just walk away with half my fortune, and I wouldn't blame you."

I laughed. "I mean, it's tempting. But I don't want you for your money. You can't put a price on me and you."

His eyes dropped to my lips. "No. You can't."

"I've decided I'm going to edit your Wikipedia page."

"Yeah?"

"Cole Ackroyd né Thorner is much less arsehole-ish these days."

"Arsehole-ish is still not a word." He trailed his thumb over his cheekbone. "But, you know, Roy would have said language is evolving all the time, so there's no point being pedantic."

I abandoned my sketch pad and crawled across the grass onto his lap.

I covered his mouth with mine and kissed him slow and deep.

"You should keep the house if you want," he said. "You're right. It needs a family. It would be ideal for ours."

"Our family? What do you mean? Kids?"

He nodded. "If that's what we want. Kids. All those dogs you wanted. They'll be less inclined to eat you if we're all there together."

It wasn't something I'd had much chance to think about, but with Cole, I could see it.

I gave him a playful punch on the arm. "You'd trade the big city for Ecclesdale?"

His eyes locked with mine. "No. I'd trade it for you. Everything I have. All of it. You're all I want. All I've ever wanted."

The sincerity in his voice made my heart melt. I kissed him again.

"*Quos amor verus tenuit, tenebit*," he whispered against my lips.

"What?"

"The tattoo on my chest. 'Those whom true love has held, it will go on holding.' I got it when I first moved to New York. It gave me hope that one day we would find our way back to each other. I know it's soppy—"

"It's not." I pressed my forehead to his. "It's perfect."

He glanced over my shoulder at the half-finished portrait in my sketch pad. "I hope you're leaving enough room for my nose."

"I love your nose. I love everything about you, Mr. Ackroyd."

"You do?"

"I always have." I rested my head on his shoulder. "I hope this means we get to go on another honeymoon?"

"Yes, Mrs. Ackroyd. Let's never stop going on honeymoons. I want to take you everywhere. I've been thinking we should start with a safari."

"Great idea." I nudged him playfully in the side. "The rhinos get to thank their patron saint in person."

THANKS FOR READING!

Not ready to say goodbye to sexy billionaires yet? Stick around to see which Thorner brother is up next, or if you're curious about Gabe Rivers, his story (PLAYING THE GAME) is the first in my sports romance series. PLAYING THE FIELD comprises five interconnected stand-alone books set in the world of women's football.

For updates on future releases, please feel free to subscribe to my newsletter via my website: www.sashalacebooks.com

I send newsletters once a month with personal and book updates. No spam, I promise!

LET'S HANG OUT!

All I've ever wanted from life is a crew to hang around with so that we can all wear sunglasses, look cool, and click our fingers in an intimidating fashion at rival crews. We can chat all things romance and occasionally you might be called upon to become involved in a choreographed dance fight. I will also be your best friend forever. NB: Dance fighting skills not mandatory (but encouraged).

Join my reader group: https://www.facebook.com/groups/979907003370581/

Follow my author page: https://www.facebook.com/profile.php?id=61553872688253

Sasha Lace Author (@sasha_lace_author) | TikTok

https://www.instagram.com/sasha_lace_author/

Psst! Hang on! I'd love a review if you've got a sec? If you enjoyed this book, please consider leaving a review wherever you like to leave them. Amazon, Goodreads, or BookBub. Reviews are the lifeblood of authors, and are very much appreciated! Thanks so much.

ACKNOWLEDGEMENTS

Thank you to the Montlake Romance team, who are so wonderful to work with. I appreciate everyone's hard work on this manuscript and all of my previous works. Thank you to my editor, Hannah Shaw. We haven't worked together that long, but I'm so excited for the opportunity to work together on this new series. Thank you so much for the love and enthusiasm you've brought to it.

To Lindsey Faber, I don't know how you manage to figure out exactly what is going on in my head and pull those threads together, but you are amazing. Working with you is a gift and a joy. I am always grateful. Thank you so much to Jenni Davis for your wonderfully thorough work and polishing this story to a shine.

Thank you to my agent, Clare Coombes, and Liverpool Lit.

Thank you to my lovely friends Angela, Heather, Helen, and Tammyanne, for the support, laughs, and for propping me back up whenever I topple over.

Thank you to all the readers who have supported me, whether it was taking the time to message with words of encouragement, leaving a thoughtful review, or telling people about my books. A special thank you to my lovely readers in my reader group. Many of you have been with me since you ARC-read my first indie book. I cannot tell you how grateful I am for your support. It means the world, truly.

Thank you to my mum for all your support and for passing on to me your love of romance and fantasy.

To James, your support makes my writing possible. Your support makes everything possible. You've made me laugh every day for the past twenty years. I'm sorry we haven't had any football scenes to choreograph this time, but being married to you is like living my own billionaire romance fantasy, without the funds. Instead of hiring out the Sistine Chapel, you sanction the heating being turned up at the start of November. From a Yorkshireman, this is a truly grand gesture that I cherish with all my heart.

Last, thank you to my kind, beautiful, bright, funny, smart, wonderful boys. I became a writer when I became a mother. You gave me the will to be the best version of myself. Please know that you are the greatest joy in my life, and I love you more than anyone has ever loved anyone EVER. But please allow me to repeat my disclaimer. Do not under any circumstances read these books. Not even when you're grown-ups. I cannot afford the therapy you will need from reading your mother's sweary, spicy books. I have given you fair warning.

ABOUT THE AUTHOR

Sasha Lace used to be a very serious scientist before she ditched the lab coat and started writing kissing books. Sasha worked in the NHS before completing a PhD in nutritional epidemiology and working as a postdoctoral researcher. She lives in the North of England and is a mom of two young boys and a Labrador. As a scientist and mom, her hobbies include: mulling over the complexities of the universe, treading barefoot on Lego, chipping dried Play-Doh from fabric surfaces, and dried-flower arranging (because you can't kill something twice).

Follow the Author on Amazon

If you enjoyed this book, follow Sasha Lace on Amazon to be notified when the author releases a new book!
To do this, please follow these instructions:

Desktop:

1) Search for the author's name on Amazon or in the Amazon App.
2) Click on the author's name to arrive on their Amazon page.
3) Click the "Follow" button.

Mobile and Tablet:

1) Search for the author's name on Amazon or in the Amazon App.
2) Click on one of the author's books.
3) Click on the author's name to arrive on their Amazon page.
4) Click the "Follow" button.

Kindle eReader and Kindle App:

If you enjoyed this book on a Kindle eReader or in the Kindle App, you will find the author "Follow" button after the last page.